“BOAT PASSAGE”

by

Bob Curtis

R&I
Publication.
Brixham. Devon.

Dedication

This book is dedicated to my lady: who held my hand through the storms, smiled when things went right and comforted me when things went wrong.

***

Acknowledgments:

Neighbour Kevin: whose graphic skills steered me around the middleman.
Bookshop owner, Matthew Clark: for charting my way clear of the commercial sharks.
To the Talented Texan, Verna Bice: for permitting the use of her lovely photograph as a cover.
And, not least, true friends, Mary and Roy, for believing in my story.

“Boat Passage”

Bob Curtis.

ISBN Number 0-9546226-0-X

Author:

Devon born, Bob Curtis, equipped with only a so-so education, left home in Brixham at 16, travelling to Liverpool to become a merchant seaman. Beginning in the Irish Sea coastal trade, a few years later he experienced deep-sea voyages to different parts of the world, South America, India, Italy and the Persian Gulf ... mostly in tankers.

Eventually returning to his first love, coasting, he became a master mariner at 26, gaining command of his first ship in that same year. After ten years as captain, married with a son, he was appointed Trinity House pilot for Torbay, servicing ships for 25 years.

In retirement, writing became the new challenger and from that endeavour ... this story evolved.

Boat Passage

Prologue

May 1992 ...
...The spirits wait

In the darkened sky, skimming above the sea, a lone seabird slowly heads towards where its life had begun. In beginning light, shadows became coastline as cresting waves tumbled across the back of each passing swell.

Closer to the land the bird altered its flight-path towards limestone cliffs protecting a cornfield that wandered up a hill towards the ruins of a broken church. In the centre of the sloping field, a dead elm, in line with the church, drew the flight-weary traveller towards a sheltered creek. The seabird was home.

Viewed from the church, grey cliffs land-locked a gully curved between tall trees on the land side, leading towards a deserted stretch of sandy beach. The deep water within the sheltered creek appeared a darker shade than the ocean outside.

At the seaward end of the cove the seabird glided onto a small hollow churned with mud and ageing guano. Stamping its wide feet to gain purchase, adjusting tail feathers, the bird settled, peering into the misty shadows below.

About ten feet from the base of the cliffs, half buried in the sand, its flukes pointed down like a crude crucifix stood an old stock anchor. Sitting, legs outstretch against the anchor's shank, a coloured soldier sipped coffee from a multi-purpose army mug.

Brooklyn born, G.I. Sergeant Jo-Jo Christmas, a member of the Allied U-force, separated from wife and home by a war and the Atlantic Ocean, silently watched the approaching dawn.

From its vantage point, the bird scanning the cove, studied the bear-like figure of an old man leaving footprints in the wet sand as he slowly tracked along the shadowed beach. Thigh-boots turned at the knee, Walter Francis, fisherman, limped towards a barnicle-

covered reef dividing the cove from the creek. Under grey eyebrows resembling breaking surf, Walter staring into the gloom, mumbling, " Nearly time, Mayo ... nearly time."

The gull's attention moved towards a small fire in the shadows of the southern ridge, about twenty paces from the anchor. A bulky man, younger than the fisherman, older than the soldier, broad shoulders covered by a weathered leather coat, sat huddled on a damaged crab pot. Skipper James Francis, elbows on knees, hair and beard glowing white in the firelight, poked a stick at an iron kettle resting on a flat stone in the embers. Without shifting his gaze from the fire, James Francis' right hand closed around a cognac bottle jammed into the sand. Flipping the cork free with his thumb, he drank, head well back.

Stretched out within range of the fire's warmth, paws dug into the dry sand, a scruffy Jack Russell slept. The dog's black body appeared to have been stabbed over one eye by a white stencil brush. As James lowered the bottle, without warning the terrier sprung upright, scattering dry sand into the fire before scampering down the beach until the tide reached neck high, barking in the direction of a black hole in the facing cliff. Frantically wagging a stumpy tail, the dog growled, backing from the water. Just beyond the ripples, yelping twice, the dog listened and then suddenly dashed up the sand, swerving around the American soldier, before skidding to a halt beside the fire, panting. Replacing the bottle into the sand, James Francis growled, "Mister ... you bugger!"

Finishing his coffee, the coloured G.I dipped the army mug deep into the sand, cleaning it and raising one knee, trickled damp sand between his legs, forming the letter M.

Glancing up at the southern ridge, Jo-Jo studied the patterns of half-light beginning to exaggerate the higher contours. Along pencil-sharp peaks, he watched the remains of night unfold into pinkish-grey lines. Sitting there in the damp sand, the soldier realised that nothing in Uncle Sam's training had prepared his mind to deal with the fear that three thousand miles across the ocean, Maria was about to give birth to a child he might never see, maybe never touch. Perhaps never hear the baby's laughter or *wipe away the tears.*

From upstream, in the shadows just beyond the curve, an almost inaudible sound disturbed the changing pulse of daybreak. The faint splutter of a four-stroke engine turned the seabird's head a nanosecond before the dog twisted its ears and only slightly ahead of the old fisherman. Halting, just beyond the tide, holding his breath, Walter focused beyond where the old schooner was moored. Still too early to pierce the shapeless trees welded together against the calm black water, he listened as the stuttering echo of a boat's engine grew louder.

The long wait was nearly over ...

****

Chapter One

... London: June 1990.

For what seemed like an age, seven thousand people hesitated and then, from seats in the high curving roof, the rumble began. Foot stamping, whistling, wild applause, gathered volume surging towards the single spotlight in the centre of the stage.

With the final note from the lst song still lingering, Maria Jo-Jo lowered her head. Taking a deep breath she could taste the warmth from the unseen faces in the magnificent auditorium. Emotion closed around her like a protective cloak.

She acknowledged that the tour had been exhaustive but on this last night her voice was in great shape. Between each number they'd yelled her name, clapping, stomping and whistling. They loved her. Maria Jo-Jo Christmas was 'back'… and yet she felt empty.

The Musical Director's grin, together with his appreciative nod confirmed that the black lady's programme on this final night had been special. Each high note, soaring, sweet, long and clear. The lower sounds had purred, soft, delicate, straight from the soul. But, now that it was nearly over, the need to get away raced through her thoughts.

Gifting a smile to the orchestra the beautiful forty-six year old woman moved front stage. Running long fingers through ink-black hair, she waited for the standing ovation to end. As people began to resume their seats, the signal Maria Jo-Jo gave to the MD was clear and final. "And now, dear friend, we'll say goodnight to these wonderful folks."

Leaning against the dressing-room door, eyes closed, she sighed, allowing the silence to calm her. When she looked up, Max was smiling. Bubbling foam from a magnum's excessive gases trickled down over his wrist. "Magnificent, Honey. You were sensational out there …fucking sensational."

Passing the champagne, Max reached up, kissing her forehead

before pouring another glass. "Now! Drink. Grab a shower. Pour your hot ass into the Carboni dress and we'll rattle London city to its bones." Raising his glass, toasting, "So'long Royal Albert Hall …|Hello Vegas."

In the shower's semi-darkness, powerful jets, preset to range from hot down to ice-cold and back to warm, drummed a steady beat on the singer's body. Above the hiss of the water, Maria Jo-Jo formulated her argument.

So far, Max seemed to have followed her instructions to the letter. Traditionally, after a final performance, her dressing room would be overflowing with wall-to-wall celebrities. Some genuine A-list personalities but mostly freeloaders sucking onto the singer's renewed success. Instruction number one had been clear: Ruby, Frankie and Max only. No others. Leastways not until she was ready.

From outside, the light in the shower was suddenly switched on. Opening the glass door, Ruby eased the younger woman's steaming wet body into large warm towels. "Cum girl. That's long enough in the dark."

As the powerful arms of the large Negro woman began massaging her dry, Maria Jo-Jo surrendered her adrenaline-drained body to the comforting pressure. Smiling, she reflected on the number of times the sixty-year-old dresser/companion/ roadie and best friend had treated her like an adolescent child.

Ruby had materialised one night following a disastrous spot at a second-rate nightclub in Philadelphia. An all-gone-wrong gig when the young singer learned that Jack Daniels is no cure for bronchitis and a drunken crowd will not tolerate an even drunker performer.

After knocking on the broken door of the filthy dressing room, the black woman had gathered the sobbing girl, lifting and stepping, both fully clothed, into the shower space. Twisting the cold-water jet full on, over both their bodies, Ruby calmly said, "You gonna be a star, lady, but you ain't worth shit without Ruby in your corner. We work out the details later." That was over twenty years ago and they still hadn't talked contracts.

Alone in the dressing room, Maria Jo-Jo stood before the full-length mirror, naked. Leaning closer, inspecting the reflection in the tinted glass, she searched for ware and tare around the eyes, mouth and neck. There were none. The years had been kind. High structured cheekbones gave the appearance of feminine strength. Wide full lips and skin the colour of mahogany colour evolved from a Mexican mother and an Afro-American father.

Stretching on tiptoes, eyes closed, she completed a short yoga exercise before slowly beginning an examination of each breast.

Discovering nothing abnormal, eyes open, she followed slender fingers cupping the fullness her left breast. As if acting independently, a long index finger traced a birthmark just above the jutting nipple. About an inch in circumference, its paler pigmentation contrasting against brown skin, the discolouration appeared almost white. It resembled a seabird in flight.

When Ruby returned, Maria Jo-Jo was dressed. "Did you make the arrangements?"

Fussing around, gathering damp towels and discarded underwear, Ruby mumbled, "Uh-huh"

Moving towards the door, Maria Jo-Jo spoke softly, "Well, let's pull the trigger." Reaching the door, she halted, asking, "What you told Frankie?"

"Told him zilch! The little guy will offer one of his silent looks but he'll fall into line, believe it."

Max and Frankie looked up as Maria Jo-Jo and Ruby entered the room. Frankie's slight frame moved around the room collecting cups, discarded make-up and good-luck messages. Green eyes displayed the true score of years and his face was lined beneath the slicked-back grey hair but he moved with the quiet easy of a man untroubled by arthritis or back problems. Frankie smiled a greeting to the singer. "Great show, Maria Jo-Jo."

Max's mouth dropped open. Without looking he placed his glass down onto the small table. Toe-to-toe he was the same height as Maria Jo-Jo, maybe six inches shorter that Ruby. Most times a slight stoop gave the impression he was checking the points of his handmade Italian shoes. Standing, he appeared somewhat shorter than five foot seven. Perhaps because of a large head and a round, almost pink face. Thinning dark hair was pulled hard back in a ponytail. The black silk suit covering a slightly overweight frame was expensive, Jewish New-York. Smart, rimless spectacles, purchased in uptown L.A had set him back ten dollars more than his first automobile. At fifty-seven, Max Stone was the complete manipulator. Skilled in the art of exploiting other people's talents, he possessed the ability to trade contracts and agency agreements with high-flyers and wheeler-dealers of recording companies. Hollywood, Vegas, Carnegy Hall, battlegrounds, where, over the last decade wars had been won.

For almost fifteen years, Max Stone had acted as Maria Jo-Jo's Agent, Manager, financial advisor and during that period, on two separate confused occasions had shared her bed. "Sweet Jesus, lady, are you sick? People are waitin' … at the Royal Savoy Hotel … as I speak! A reception, settin' the record company back twenty-five K –plus taxes. British blue-blooded-shit-nose Lords and Ladies … Elton promised to be there … a Duke or two even…" His voice dropped, "You sure as hell ain't out to impress nobility dressed in jeans and cowboy boots." He hissed, "Lady, where the fuck are you at?"

Staring at the singer, he nervously undid and then refastened a button on his jacket. Without looking, he lifted the magnum to refill his glass, spilling Champaign over the table. "Song-lady, take another Christ-almighty-question, what's this baggage doing here?" Almost overbalancing, he lifted one foot in the direction of two items of luggage sat in the centre of the room.

Looking at him straight, she replied, "One is mine. The other, should you decide to accompany me, yours. Sorry, Max, tonight this girl don't party. The tour worked fine. Maria Jo-Jo Christmas is back … makin' a dollar an' change. But I need time to figure the future before signing five years to Vegas … even for the top spot." Lowering her voice, almost to a whisper, she added, "Right now, I'm headin' for a place called South Hams. My daddy died there, same night I was born, forty-six years ago. When I've figured out some answers, paid my respects, done a little thinkin' … well, we'll see."

Taking one step forward and raising his arms, Max gripped her lightly by the shoulders. "Listen, madam, life is only so many roads. Five years back you were up there with the greats. Streisand, Bassey, Whitney Houston … Diva-fuckin' Ross hated your lungs. You blew it all …tossed it down the can."His voiced dropped, "Okay! Not 100% your call. The 'trade' could've been more supportive," his hands were almost caressing her arms now, "Honey, you came to terms with reality. After the spell in 'that place', contracts died. Life hit a deep-low. Broke, confidence kicked in the ass, what was bottom-line? I-tell-you-what-was bottom-line", he was yelling again, a vain in his temple pulsating in time with his words, "The ol' ranch, out in the valley; a Manhatten apartment, which fer'instance needs off-loading to clear taxes on the ranch. Some dribbling royalties that might just keep Rastafarian Ruby and Fly-weight Frankie here in doughnuts …"

In spite of his seventy years, Frankie made a sudden leap towards Max. "Leave her be … bastard!"

Lifting a hand, Maria Jo-Jo said, "No, Frankie, hear him out. He ain't done … close but not quite."

Max ignored the smaller man. "So! Is this pay-back time, Lady? My reward for draggin' you screamin' an' kicking from shitsville? On my knees, kissin' ass to small-time promoters, begging them to give you one more chance." The sweat was spreading across his face. "You might own the talent, girl, but my graft drew Vegas men to your door. These amigos don't construct a multi-million dollar casino for some darkie-has-been who wants to go diggin' fuckin' war graves …"

He began slowing, anger almost spent. "It's-make-up-your-mind-time, Maria Jo-Jo Christmas. In seven days, you sign the papers, we become super-rich. The daddy you never knew has been dead forty-six years, another five or so don't mean …" He stretched his arms wide for an answer.

Her voice, low and determined, cut the silence. "I need to do this, Max. Maybe after visiting the last place he walked on this earth, well maybe I can find some meaning to my life. You can come or you can walk away … whatever! She moved towards the door. "Frankie will drive. I'll send him back Monday. That's it, Max."

Not taking his eyes from Max, the little man moved across the room, picked up Maria Jo-Jo's bag and started for the door.

Reaching it, he placed the luggage down,walked back to the magnum and poured two glasses of Champagne. Handing one to Maria Jo-Jo the other to Ruby, before filling another glass. Smiling, he toasted, "Ladies, your health." Taking a sip he tossed the remaining contents into Max's face. Pulling the bigger man forwards, Frankie rammed the champagne flute, upside down, between Max's vest and shirt. As Max opened his mouth to yell, Frankie palmed him in the chest. There was the faintest sound of splintering glass, followed by a scream from Max. Without another word, Frankie turned, picked up the bag and left, closing the door behind him with just the faintest of clicks.

Max leapt, frantically pulling at buttons. "Help me, Maria Jo-Jo, I'm bleeding here. That Sicilian midget is crazy. Get rid … before somebody is killed." Withdrawing his hand from beneath his shirt, two fingers showed a slight trace of blood. Turning to Ruby, he pleaded, "For God's sake woman, call a doctor. I'd draining blood here."

Towering over him, Ruby calmly opened the remaining shirt buttons, "heck, it's nothin' but a scratch. Best get to the john an' shake the splinters before a sliver drops south, snippin' your main event. You surely ain't gonna' die, least ways, not to night, Max."

With one hand holding his shirt open, the other pressed close against his waistband, preventing any glass from falling, Max stumbled, bow-legged towards the inner bathroom.Reaching the door, he burst through, shouting over his shoulder, "Maria Jo-Jo, I need help… "

Ruby cupped the singer's face in her large hands. "You sure about this, girl? Say the word … we can be on a plane tonight."

Maria Jo-Jo smiled, "I'm certain. Flying back to the States, I'd carry a thousand maybe's for the rest of my days. This is something I gotta do."

The big woman handed Maria Jo-Jo a package. "Here's the instructions how to reach the hotel. I spoke to the owner-folks, seem like nice people, discreet. Not a soul will know you're there. Don't heed Max. Once he's stalled the Vegas suits he'll bull the media about where you're at." She hugged the singer. "Take care.

Send Frankie back when you're ready. I'll take-in the London sights till you call."

Maria Jo-Jo slipped the small package into her handbag, from which she drew a folder. "Now, here's what you do. When Frankie gets back … say, Monday, take some free-time. The apartment's booked for another week. Stay longer if you've a mind. When you're both ready, go home, to the ranch."Indicating the folder, she said, "There's the papers for the ranch. It's yours, yours and Frankie's. I want you to have it. You love the valley. Go. Make your garden grow. Take the little man to your bed. And, Max is wrong. The rented pastures cover taxes and the fishing rights bring in substantial income."She pushed the papers into Ruby's hands. "No buts, Ruby… allow me to do this. You hate the desert … you'd never be happy there in Vegas. After twenty years of you givin,' let me give somethin' back … please!"

Ruby stared at the papers, trembling, "Lady, the ranch gotta' be worth a million dollars, I … we couldn't"

"One point five is closer but it's only money. I've watched you, up to your ass in roses … do this for me, Ruby. If I pass on Vegas, I'll return to New York, sell the apartment and … fuck! Who knows? Now, a big hug, I'll call in a couple days."

At the door the singer turned. Ruby stood in the middle of the room, clutching the folder to her chest, quietly weeping.

Catching sight of herself in the in the mirror, Maria Jo-Jo reached up, removed the long black hairpiece and tossed it onto the dressing table. Blowing Ruby a kiss, she glanced again at her reflection. Looking back was a tall beautiful woman, hair clipped to a quarter inch. The hair was pure white.

Sitting in the passenger seat of the Rolls Royce, she handed Frankie the directions. After fumbling for his glasses the little man began studying the route with the aid of the map-lamp. Maria Jo-Jo gazed at his lined face, warming to the gentleness of this tiny Bronx-Italian, to whom she owed her sanity.

For the first few weeks in 'that place' they'd kept her deeply sedated. As the mental fog slowly began to clear there'd been long nights when tormented nerves begged for chemical assistance. Screaming produced shadowy figures, injecting something that quickly dragged her down into troubled oblivion.

It was a long time before she realised the change of pattern. Clouded confused areas before working out that on some nights, pressure on the call-button resulted in the arrival of an attendant who didn't mutter, curse or jab the spike sending her into the twilight zone. When she swore, struggled or spat and on occasions pleaded for release, he'd quietly settled her arms back inside the blankets, tucking the bedclothes so tight she found it difficult to move.

The silent figure gently washed the sweat, wiped the foam from her lips, cleared the dribble around her chin. Switching on the small bedside lamp the man would read aloud poems by Robert Frost, Keats, William Wordsworth.

And, after a while, against the fury raging inside, her disturbed mind began to listen to the soothing rhythm. Not only to listen but slowly to want more. It took her over a month to work out that the 'readers' roster came around every four nights. Another month to wait before pressing the 'help' button. By which time she knew his name was Frankie Luzo; sixty four, born in Catania, Sicily and from the age of ten he'd grown up in the Bronx, New York.

Requesting that Frankie be appointed her permanent night-attendant she was informed that it was against the rules.

"Fuck your rules" Maria Jo-Jo had yelled, "I'm paying top-dollar. Change the rules. Charge it to my account … but do it."

They did it.

Six months later, Maria Jo-Jo had improved. It was time for home convalescence. Frankie came to say goodbye. "Seems like we're on the same bus outta' here. You on the mending road, me down the road to retirement. I'm sixty-five. House rules."

Taking him back to the ranch. Frankie became driver, cook and her friend. During bad moments of depression, when her mind retraced ugly passages, he was there. They'd sit quietly on the wide porch, watching the sun trace a golden trail down the distant hills towards night. He would read to them and the troubles would melt.

Between Ruby and Frankie a tolerant acceptance existed that amused Maria Jo-Jo. Confronted about the relationship, the big black woman shuffled her feet. "Okay … okay! If the Wop was twenty years younger, a foot taller, maybe … just maybe I wouldn't bolt my door come lay-down time. God! Did I really speak those words?"

When Maria Jo-Jo asked Frankie, he'd thought for a while. "In truth, she's the only dame scared the crap outta' me. You know, Maria Jo-Jo, I lost the need for sex some five years back. But I tell you this, at night, if I'm in the same house as this woman, I grow's an erection."

Watching him carefully fold away his reading glasses before slipping the route instructions into the glove compartment, the singer reached out to touch his hand, "Don't worry. You'll do just fine."

As Frankie started the powerful engine, there was a loud knocking on the window…

****

Chapter Two

Outside, rattling the glass with his knuckles, Max mouthed, "lower-the-god-damn-window, mutt-head"

After pressing the down-button, Frankie and Maria Jo-Jo stared at the flushed face. "Okay, put my bag in the trunk, Ass-hole, I'm driving. Get your butt back inside with Dark-invader."

When the little man looked at Maria Jo-Jo, she reached across, touching his hand. "It's alright, Frankie. Take care of |Ruby. I'll be in touch in a couple of days." She kissed his cheek.

Settling himself in, Max adjusted the driving seat, mirrors and flicked switches. "That crazy bastard don't do justice to this class of motor. And, I say this for nothing, lady I'm pissed-off with his pasta cookin'. "

"Can we go, Max? It's about four hours, M4/M5. At a place called Exeter, we head for the coast. I'd like to arrive come daylight."Her voice was without warmth.

Speeding the big car into Queen's Gate towards Cromwell Road, Max drifted easily in and out of the night traffic, blending a natural driving skill with arrogant contempt for the congestion travelling on the 'wrong' side of the highway.

Maria Jo-Jo fingered the switch that reclined her seat. She felt relaxed and confident. Whatever Max's faults and there were plenty, behind the wheel, even in a foreign country, he was mister cool.

Slowing in the heavy night traffic entering Hammersmith, Max drummed impatiently against the padded wheel. Flicking the music button, the soul-sound of Roberta Flack's 'Angelitos Negros' echoed through the car from the seven speakers. Glancing across, he noticed that his passenger was snuggled back into her seat, eyes closed, a soft blanket tucked under her chin. "That's one hell of a song," she murmured.

Accelerating hard, swishing past a high-sided transport carrier, Max muttered, "She plays good piano, but your voice is from another place, lady."

When illuminated signs indicating the approaching M4 came

into view, Max glanced to his left. She was asleep. On the motorway, changing into lower gear curved the Rolls out into the fast lane. As the powerful engine increased to a deeper purr. Max stole another look at the sleeping singer. In the dim light, the crop of white hair covered her head with a radiant glow.

Allowing his eyes, plus instinct, to deal with the mechanics of steering, Max recalled their first meeting. It had begun about day-three into a serious bender. A fog, caused mainly by the financial burden of a divorce settlement - his third - and further clouded by two long-term clients cancelling management contracts. Sitting at his usual table in the Middle Room of the Oxford Hotel, Max acknowledged that his career as an agent was running about two blocks behind his ability to sustain a lasting relationship with a woman.

The Oxford Hotel's Middle Room was *the* place. Agents, Producers, Managers and recording company's hot-shots gathered there after midnight. Following dinner for the hotel residents, which ended about ten, the room died until the first minutes of the new day. Then, the dimly lit lounge came to life, buzzing with music men, smoking, doing deals, drinking in huddled groups or sitting quietly at tables, unwinding from the turmoil of yesterday's madness.

Between midnight and three the hotel's owners encouraged selective artists, for minimum fees, a fifteen-minute spot to present their talent to the makers and breakers of the show business industry, who might or maybe not listening with no more than half an ear. Would-be artist, struggling for a break, would sometimes sign away a percentage of future earnings, just for the opportunity to show what they could do to music vultures perched out there in the darkness.

In a half-light haze, Max Stone - *Agent to the Stars* - had watched the tall black woman glide across the marble floor, making her way towards the small stage offset to one side. She moved with an assured grace, unhurried, composed. Walking slowly, without appearing to be nervous, looking strangely detached from the heavy smog of indifference hanging over an area.

She was dressed in a tight pale green trouser suit and cheap green plastic shoes with heels that set the heightened Afro hair almost six feet above the floor. 'Lady, you're so wrong,' thought Max but his eyes followed each step the girl took crossing the room.

Sitting at the piano, Maria Jo-Jo Christmas took longer than was clever to arrange her music while various clouded eyes from different table that had followed her progress across the floor, floated back to other interests. Without introduction or apparent acknowledgment of the power assembled in the darkness, the singer quietly hit her first low note … and Max Stone felt the soft hairs on his legs begin to rise.

His jumbled mind struggled to clear a thinking space. Her piano was weak, almost dragging, bordering on the ordinary. Yet closing his eyes the musician in him shuddering as the primitive phrasing and her naive ignoring of the audience almost made him wince but, deep down, something moved him, something that on one else in the smoke-filled buzz appeared to have caught. He gripped his half empty glass almost to breaking.

Even without looking, Max knew that experienced, hard-assed people were present in the room. EMI's McCann was in his usual seat; Joe Dorn from Atlantic Records, Billy Bonds, in company with an exaggerated chesty blonde, tucking into a blood-filled steak. None of them gave the girl at the piano a second glance. Running his eyes swiftly around the lounge, Max knew that most of the men in the semi-dark outgunned him in the business … and yet, every last bastard appeared to have missed it.

When her set was over, no one applauded. Watching her gather her music and walk, calm and serenely from the room, Max wanted to scream, 'Geroni-fuckin-mo'. Counting to four from an intended ten he followed her out. Back in the darkness deals were being struck, contracts agreed, sweaty hands shaken over refilled glasses and yet, 'they' had passed. Every last motherfucker had missed it.

In the empty foyer, Max had presented his card. Black, with italic letters in gold."Max Stone" *Agent to Stars.* Plaza 123123. Maria Jo-Jo glanced at the card, looked into his eyes and handing it back, turned towards the revolving door, without a single word. As she placed a hand on the glass door, Max quietly said, "Song-lady, I can change your life … believe it."

About to push, she paused and then turned back to where he stood. After what felt like an age she spoke. "I'm listening, Mister..." Taking the card from his hand, she read, "Max Stone."

From that moment, Max took control. First he introduced her to 'Uncle' Marco, who in his day had been a fine opera singer but was now an even better teacher. Over the following months her range extended by several octaves. Controlled breathing became second nature. The Afro hair was replaced by tight wigs that softened her face, displaying to greater effect her magnificent cheekbones.

Max encouraged her to study the styles of Johnny Mathis, Nat 'King' Cole, Sinatra. She'd spend hours watching TV and movies to gain knowledge regarding fashion, composure and presentation. He fixed support gigs in small venues; a five-second spot as a club-singer in a television commercial. The music scene didn't catch fire. In the early days he tried to persuade her to dump Ruby. Maria Jo-Jo wouldn't even discuss the option. Max backed off knowing when he was beaten.

Repaying a favour, Nelson Riddle allowed Maria Jo-o to sit with his band during a short Mid-west tour. Over the phone she'd shouted, "... they won't let me to a number. I'm dirt-cheap vocal backing."

Max had yelled back, "Of course they won't let you out front, you're not ready, lady. Don't stand there pushin' your tits out ... listen to the arrangements, absorb the brass sections. Watch and study their breathing techniques. Most important, learn to read the crowd ...take-every-fucking-thing-in. Your turn will come, soon. Trust me, I'm an honest New York Jewish entrepreneur person."

Six months after first hearing her sing, Max and Uncle Marco considered she was ready. Calling in another favour, Max acquired the use of a top recording studio, for one hour only. Midnight to one, with some good session musicians they cut four tracts.

A month later Max had secured a recording contract for his singer. The contract terms, undisclosed to Maria Jo-Jo, entitled the company to five percent of gross earnings for the next ten years. When he'd outlined most of the details of the agreement, the understandable excitement, mixed with jubilant anticipation, plus a certain flush of gratitude, led Maria Jo-Jo, for the first time to share her bed with her agent/manager.

Max fully expected this physical arrangement to roll-over. Not only had he recently split from Mrs Stone, number four, he figured it would save on hotel expenses. Not to mention the sexual benefits.

Having gained nothing approaching enjoyment or an orgasm from the frantic sweaty encounter, Maria Jo-Jo refused to play ball, firmly slamming shut the sexual door. It was to be nearly a year before time number two.

Following some rave reviews after a Hollywood Benefit concert they'd been invited to a party at the Beverley Hills house of a gay movie star. Because it appeared to be expected, Maria Jo-Jo sniffed her first -and last- line of coke. Waking, hours later, naked in a strange pink, King-size waterbed, she was partially relieved to discover that the groaning lump on top and inside of her was Max.

Two days later, Mr Max Stone was 'invited' to the penthouse office of a major TV station. The Vice President offered Maria Jo-Jo a leading role in a television musical production that, under normal circumstances most agents would have willingly traded their mothers. For reasons he couldn't explain, Max had declined. As he rose to leave a large folder was eased across the eight-foot leather topped oak desk. The grey haired executive, wearing an expensive European suit, rimless glasses, smiled without any warmth. "Come-come, Mr Stone. This deal is in both our interests. We have certain other in-house projects that will make your girl a world-class star. To establish sincerity-of-intent, we shall require only 15% futures…"

Studying Max's reaction, he indicated the folder. "Perhaps, while you reconsider, you might care to examine the contents. They could of course be delivered to your home but I'm sure we won't find that necessary. Can you afford another costly divorce settlement at this time?" His smile was sickly.

A contract was stuck for 12.5% of Maria Jo-Jo's gross earnings for the next ten years, plus a package of negatives in which Max recognized the Beverley Hills bedroom and was shocked to discover that the sensitive photographs showed an increase in the area of his balding crown.

The English suit offered his bony hand. “Mr Stone, my company will project your, sorry, our singer into an international star. My management people will be in touch within the next few days.” Smiling, he added, “As a point of interest, the lady appears to have an unsightly tattoo over her left nipple. There might be a call for some plastic surgery at a later date. G’day to you Mr Stone.

****

Chapter Three

After overtaking three different types of German cars, an illuminated sign informed Max they were about to pass Junction 11, on the M4 motorway, south of a town called Reading.

Following the Hollywood meeting, not only did Max fail to disclose to Maria Jo-Jo that a tenth of her gross income, for the next ten years, had been signed away but he omitted to explain that she might also be forced into cosmetic alterations to remove a 'tattoo' birthmark .

Protecting their investment, the TV Company researched into Maria Jo-Jo's past. When the investigation was completed a copy was faxed to Max. He'd known she was born in New York in '44. Knew that her Mexican mother had died in 1960 and was aware that the singer's father, an Afro-American GI serving with the Allied services in England, was reported killed on the same day she was born.

The report outlined her career. The teenager had become a member of the church choir where her mother worked as Housekeeper to the priest. Winning a spot on local radio led to several singing jobs in the Harlem club circuit. After the death of her mother, the sixteen year old boarded a Greyhound bus, spending two years travelling around the country. Sometimes singing, often waiting tables but always waiting to be discovered.

The statement contained details about her Social Security.Medical treatment she's received during the past five years; appendix, glandular fever, broken arm from a bus accident. There was no evidence of alcohol abuse, hard drugs or STD. Most of the information came as no great surprise to Max, who'd done some digging into her background. Snorting at the news that her credit account contained only 433 dollars 54 cents he was amazed to read personal details about the loss of her virginity, Dallas, Texas, Friday November 22nd. '63. While the report pinpointed time and place of Maria Jo-Jo's first sexual encounter, it said nothing about the how and why.

Howard T Bell was the drummer in, 'Lightning', a small Country band the young singer had joined forces with in Houston. To cut expenses, the group shared motel rooms and Maria Jo-Jo drew Howard T. After a collage gig, around three in the morning, the drummer-man had climbed from the second bed to make coffee. Maria Jo-Jo was never sure what he'd added to her drink but, whatever, it worked.

After downing his coffee, Howard T had scrambled across into her bed and lay across her. Holding both of her arms above her head with one hand, he pushed up her T-shirt with the other. Words from her brain, "No-No. Fuck off, Howard" never made it to her mouth. She'd tried kicking but her legs wouldn't work. Neither would her arms, nor, for some unfathomable reason, could she even close her eyes.

While a part of her mind pleaded that the 'first time' shouldn't happen like this, she discovered that other sections of her brain had ceased sending terminal nerve signals to any of her limbs.'Shit-shit-shit!'

Rational accepting that what was happening was beyond her control the young singer struggled to experience some degree of pleasure as the frantic drummer increased his beat … but apart from his bad breath she felt nothing. In less than sixty seconds, Howard T shuddered, yelled "Wah-hoo" and bit Maria Jo-Jo's lip, hard. Crawling back on all fours towards his own bed, he'd mumbled, "You struck lucky, Maggie Jo, I surely am great cock."

An hour later, as the effect of the drug wore off, rolling into a ball, quietly weeping, she listened to the deep-throated snoring from the other bed. "Shit-shit-shit!"

During the course of that earth-shattering, unforgettable, black Friday, when three shots from a Texas bookstore changed the political structure of the western world, the band's next gig was cancelled. Maria Jo-Jo's virginity had been taken by force, Mrs Jacqueline Kennedy's husband had been shot dead and the people of the United States of America had lost their President.

Two days later, with most of the confused world in emotional shock, 'Lightening's concert in Fort Worth had been a bummer.

After payout, the Bass player, Billy, a skinny, pot-smoking

odd-ball informed Maria Jo-Jo they'd be sharing a room that night. In the small hours, when he'd stumbled from the other bed, muttering, "I gotta piss. Coffee, doll?" she'd tossed him into the hall, double locking the door before throwing his boots and jeans through the window.

Next morning, seven months beyond her 19th birthday, Maria Jo-Jo journeyed north, alone. Crossing the State line on a crowded bus, severe irritation caused her to seek help from a pharmacist at a service station. The singer's world became fragmented by having to rub an evil smelling ointment into her pubic area to combat an invasion of Phthirus pubis.

Eighteen years would pass before she sang again in the Lone Star State. She never again caught crabs.

***

Passing Junction 14, Max checked the clock on the dash. It read seven minutes after one. At the next service area he planned pulling in for coffee and doughnuts. Stretching his legs, max realised how much he was enjoying the night drive. The pulse of his mind became tuned with the steady hum of the powerful engine cruising along the British motorway at ninety miles an hour, the comforting atmosphere inside the motor broken only by the occasional swish of passing traffic.

Smiling, Max reflected on how successful the period with the TV people had been. A 'Tony' award, followed by a zipper tour of Japan and the Far East. In the same year, Maria Jo-Jo wrote her first song. 'White Wings' made number two in the US charts. Royalties from the follow-up album, 'Believe', which held number one spot for five weeks, purchased a five hundred acre ranch out in the valley.

The sprawling single-storey building, open-plan, had five bedrooms four bathrooms and was constructed of local timber and stone. Maria Jo-Jo replaced most of the west wall in the massive living room with floor to ceiling glass. Outside, on the veranda, a large swing seat was positioned to capture the setting sun rolling slowly down the higher tips of the Crowfoot Mountains.

The 'Double D' spread consisted of the house, stables, two barns and five hundred acres situated in the wooded valley beyond Fresno. The name came from the way the San Joaquim river doubled back on itself, twice, before flowing through pinewood meadows separating the three mile stretch of deep water between Borock and the small town of Bonding (pop. 651). On a slightly raised plateau the main house, facing south and west overlooked the second bend of passing river.

Designed in the fifties by a Hollywood scriptwriter, whose ambition to breed Quarter horses for film work collapsed after Senator McCarthy accused the Jewish homosexual of being un-American. The man, whose life was the written word, strung himself from a post on the back porch. Leaving an undignified but simple note that said, 'Fuck ya!

The estate lay empty and neglected until Maria Jo-Jo considered purchasing the package from the bank. When she'd taken Max to the ranch for a look-see, he'd rambled on about tax advantages, real-estate investment benefits, State development grants and shooed aside the downer of residing in someone's grave. Watching magic colour changes taking place as the last of day's sunlight disappeared into the western horizon, Maria Jo-Jo wasn't listening. She'd already fallen in love with the tranquillity of the curving river, the tree-lined drive from the road up to the house and the peace from the peaks of the far-off mountain range. Ignoring Max's request to negotiate a better price, she phoned the bank. All she said was, "yes" and wrote the cheque.

***

Drifting in and out of sleep as the miles fell behind in the darkness, Maria Jo-Jo Christmas relived certain memories. A year after purchasing the land she'd been sitting, watching the hazy orange ball, roll, like a slow magnet, between two shadowed peaks. A whispery nor-westerly breeze rustled through the avenue of the drive's timbered posts, causing the tall grass to weave changing patterns.

Picking up a book, see could see Ruby, on her knees beside the low hedge of young roses. Her friend's generous backside pointing skywards as her hands probed the soil, tetchily scolding the growing flowers, "Cum-on, you beauties, grow some for momma."

Placing a finger on the page, Maria Jo-Jo looked over half-rimmed reading glasses, watching the slow-moving figure of a man walking up he drive.

Stopping at the base of the porch steps, he removed a weather-beaten hat. She saw a gangling persona, maybe in his early forties, with an open square face, more office than outdoors. He was dressed in faded but clean jeans, a grey shirt and wore strong, dust-covered shoes. Lowering a canvas grip from his right hand, he placed it at his feet before dropping a small plastic bag from his left hand beside the grip. Hat in hand, a yard beyond the first step, he gave his name. "Evening, Ma'm, Hazelwood Boyde."

Hazelwood Boyde had been Financial Consultant for a major organisation in Stockton, when, five years back, an addiction to heroin blew the corners of his mind. Pleading guilty to embezzlement to feed a thousand dollar a week need, the thirty-eight year old was sentenced to three years in the State Penitentiary.

Directing his eyes at the singer, he quietly explained that ten days ago, released from prison, cured of drug dependency, he needed to reshape his motivation. High on his agenda was the determination never again to return to prison.

Out of the corner of her eye, Maria Jo-Jo observed Ruby, still on her knees, listening to what was being said. The black lady had ceased cajoling the roses.

"Inside", Hazelwood went on, "to preserve what remained of my sanity, I studied organic farming. The plan is to grow vegetables, maybe some fruit, without chemical additives." He paused, " It is surely no business of mine, M'a'm but, do you own this land?"

Maria Jo-Jo studied his face. Closing her book, she replied, "Yes. From that pasture where the river first bends to a little beyond the third twist south. So, Mr Hazelwood Boyde, make your pitch." Her voice was clear, non-committal, slightly mocking. Ruby, still on her knees, looking down at the soil, slowly shook her head.

His gaze fixed on the woman above him, Hazelwood went on,"A little-ways upstream, under the low hill, there's a five acre meadow that would surely suit my purpose." Taking a breath he said, "my request is you rent that small meadow to me. I've studied market forecasts. In my bag is a production plan and a contract agreement I'm guessing your legal people might live with."

Maria Jo-Jo waited for him to continue but that was it. He'd made his pitch. Now it was her call. Rising from the swinging seat she'd looked at him for a moment before turning towards the house. "Hang there a moment, Hazelwood Boyde."

Returning with a glass of cold orange juice, Maria Jo-Jo walked down the wide steps, handed him the drink and walked back to her seat. "Three questions. One, what capital you have? Two; the nearest town is ten miles, where'd you live? And three, why should I trust you, mister?"

Sipping the drink, he wiped a trickle of perspiration from his forehead before replying, "Capital? Exactly forty-two dollars and fifty-eight cents, lady." Tapping the canvas bag at his feet, he continued, "There's a small tent and come cookin' pots. It will do till I'm settled. Trust?" A tired grin drifted across his face, "There's no good reason in the world why you should trust me. I doubt any bank or finance house in the State of California would allow my ass inside the main door but ..." he reached down for his bags. "I'm indebted for the drink, ma'm."

As he turned, she asked, "Do you drive?"

Behind the stretching shadow of the man, Ruby, knees in the soil, smiled. Looking direct at Maria Jo-Jo, she again shook her head before resuming attention to her roses.

Hazelwood nodded, "I'm three years rusty but yes, I can drive."

Coming down the steps, she handed him a set of keys. "Left, at the main gate is a stone barn. Inside you'll find a motor-trailer. Consider it a loan. Take care, those wheels were home and sanctuary for long years when we were on the road."

When he'd accepted the keys she offered a slip of paper. "There's a cheque, made out for one thousand dollars, cash. We'll give contracts and legal stuff a miss ... " Stretching out a hand,

Maria Jo-Jo added, softly, "Don't fuck with me, Mr Hazelwood Boyde!"

Without glancing at the cheque, tucking it into shirt pocket, he fixed deep blue eyes on the singer. His handshake was firm.

Replacing his hat, picking up the bags, he turned and started down the drive. When he passed Ruby, without lifting her eyes from the roses, she murmured, "Bull…shit!"

Halting his stride, Hazelwood dropped the smaller grip. Loosening the neck of a plastic bag, he walked along the rose bushes sprinkling brown powder at their base. "No, sweet-lady, it's horseshit actually.Sun dried. Your roses look fine but water that in … it will add an extra edge."

That was ten years ago. Away on tour for the first few months they'd heard nothing from him. Later, Ruby mentioned she'd seen him working the meadow. "He'd kind of waved …"

Seven months later, returning from a concert in Phoenix, they'd discovered a box of carrots and some onions on the porch steps.

On the first anniversary of the handshake, Hazelwood Boyde walked up the drive and handed Maria Jo-Jo a cheque for one thousand one hundred dollars. They invited him to stay for diner.

Halfway through the second year Maria Jo-Jo and Ruby were introduced to Lillian, a smiling, ex-nurse he'd met at a 'drugs aware' rally in Monterey and married. For a wedding present the singer gave them the deeds to the five-acre meadow, adding an extra slice of the riverbank so they might build a house. She talked Max into brokering a loan for the couple and six months on Hazelwood and Lillian moved into a small timber-built they'd helped design. The motor-trailer was returned, looking smarter than new.

During year three the singer and Ruby became Godparents to the twins, Beth and Joanne. On the forth anniversary of their meeting, Hazelwood, Lillian and the girls arrived at the ranch in a smart pick-up. Painted on the doors were the words, H. Boyde: Family Business: Organic Produce. Inc.

That same evening, sitting with Maria Jo-Jo on the porch, watching twilight fade over the Crowfoot Mountains, Hazelwood handed her an envelope. "Sorry, Maria Jo-Jo, put it down to years of legal training. I couldn't sleep nights if you didn't accept this."

Inside was a document stating that she owned a third share in the Boyde family business. Without telling Hazelwood or Lillian she arranged for Max to transfer the stock holding into a trust fund for the twins.

****

Chapter Four

...The journey west

As the Rolls drew into the service area, Maria Jo-Jo stirred.Max parked and turned off the engine. "I'll do a pee-pee, collect coffee-to-go and we'll roll west." Glancing at the clock, he'd added, "It's a quarter before one. Stretch your legs, Maria Jo-Jo."

When he returned minutes later with coffee and two large doughnuts, Maria Jo-Jo was sitting in the driving seat. She took a single bite from a doughnut, handed the sugary bun back to Max and sipped at her coffee. "Catch a break, Max. I'll drive till we hit the town of Exeter. According to Ruby's details, it gets a little complicated west of that." Taking another sip, she remarked, "Hey! This is half-decent coffee. Climb in the back, you'll rest better."

Settled in the rear, Max pulled a travel rug around his legs.

Gulping the last drains of coffee he munched into the second doughnut. Maria Jo-Jo asked, "Just one question, Max, where the hell are we on the map?"

"Some spot named Gordeno Services. New Mexico, it ain't. In an hour or so we hit Exeter by-pass. There's a service stop there. I'll resume command ...okay?"

Tossing the empty plastic cup through the open window he pressed the button raising the glass and snuggled down pulling the rug over his head. From beneath the rug came a mumbled, "G'night."

The singer sat quietly for a moment observing the steady flow of transport into and around the service area. Truck drivers, crowded coaches with people stretching and yawning. Young couples. Lone travellers, one or two family groups, coming from or heading towards the brightly illuminated cafeteria. Finishing the last of her drink she climbed from the car, picked up Max's discarded cup' depositing both into the waste bin against the wall. By the time she'd returned to the driving position, Max was snoring, four beats to the bar. Jabbing the switch closing the screen between driver and the rear section silenced the sound of Max's rattle. Flicking the lights on she smoothly eased the large motor back into the night traffic of the English motorway.

Passing Junction 20, Maria Jo-Jo turned switched the air-conditioning off and pressed the button lowering the window on her right. Salt-laden air from the dark Bristol Channel beyond Clevedon replaced the mechanically produced coolness from the engine.

At Junction 21, distant twinkling lights from Weston-Super-Mare cast an orange glow into the night sky. The sea-air was fainter now, but she kept the window down, breathing the cool clean night, her eyes ticking-off romantic names from the passing signs. To her left, Glastonbury; Wells, Shepton Mallet. And to the right, Bridgewater; Wellington, Bickley Castle.

At Junction 27, the signs warned, Exeter 14 miles. As she opened the dividing glass behind her, a white Range-Rover silently overtook her in the middle lane. Looking across she smiled, 'Hi' to the youthful police officer, who returned the pleasure before doing a double take. Its not every night he overtook a Rolls being driven by a beautiful black woman. Certainly not one where the slight glow from the dashboard gave an almost halo-like appearance to her skin-tight white hair. Touching his cap, the young traffic-cop grinned before speeding on into the night, faster than was legal. 'Surely that was the American singer … No!'

Max had ceased snoring but his steady breathing told Maria Jo-Jo he was still asleep. The singer's mind drifted back over the years of their association. At thirty-one, earning 'bread-dollars' on the road, she'd become resigned that 'stardom', 'big-time' whatever, had passed by on the other side of the street. Since teaming with Ruby she'd obtained steady engagements in different States. Nightclubs. Radio-work. Occasionally, a local TV spot doing one song. She'd appeared, 'first-on' in various Benefit concerts for a couple of major stars and toured South America with Neil Diamond's Band, as opening act, for a month. The South American adventure earned enough bucks to purchase the motor-trailer, which she and Ruby used as both base-camp and travelling home.

Meeting Max Stone changed the singer's life. A moderately successful agent, Max had steered several good singers along a road that never quiet arrived any place special. Hungering to manage a top-of-the bill star, when his performers didn't make the grade, Max dumped them, sometimes 'after' they'd already left his agency. From their first encounter he was convinced, to the point of spending his own money, that this lady was destined to transport them into the international arena. Maria Jo-Jo Christmas was his track towards being megga-dollar rich.

During the first year, Maria Jo-Jo almost walked away. Time after time, Ruby talked her into staying. While streetwise maturity warned her against Max's sincerity, Ruby admitted that he knew the marketplace. Knew how and when to take the next leap towards a higher rung on the show business ladder. "Don't get deep with this Jewish mother's-son, Lady. Mister Stone sits down to shit with wolves but I gotta' say he can surely open doors. Watch yer back girl. Rule one; don't sign no blank papers."

Into year two, Max secured a recording contract and obtained several guest-spots on major TV shows. By the end of that year Maria Jo-Jo Christmas albums were grossing the million-sale mark and even after expenses and taxes, she was flying. In year three, she filled Carnegie Hall, toured forty different States and played most of America's famous concert halls.

On her return to the Lone Star State for the first time since '63, the Maria Jo-Jo Christmas Show sold out the Austin Bowl. Twenty thousand fans screamed for more. Driving back across the Texas border in the early hours she made Ruby stop the trailer. Standing at the side of the Freeway, in the clear crisp desert air, last night's stage clothes were heaped, sprayed with lighter fuel and a match tossed. Climbing back into the trailer she motioned for Ruby to drive on. In the rear mirror the two women watched the embers glowing off the roadside. The ugly memories of Texas became as dust.

Gazing at the bright stars in the English sky, she acknowledged that sleeping with Max, both times, had been a mistake. An error of judgement... made in moments of different emotions. Sexually they were not compatible. After the first flurry of Max's wet kisses, with his fumbling hands reaching for breasts, her brain sent scrambled messages to different parts of her body, commanding the erogenous departments to 'enjoy'. There was no one at home. During the one minute twenty-eight seconds (she'd counted) it took Max to achieve a noisy climax, Maria Jo-Jo had strung together the first refrains of the melody and most of the lyrics of 'The Roar Of Distant Seas.' The song made number three in the winter charts.

Their second sexual encounter (over quicker than the first) was recalled with deep regret. Resulting from a stupid attempt to ride with the Beverly Hill's party-people, she'd discovered that in the cold light of morning, the folks-on-the-hill weren't really worth a sad fuck.

There'd been others besides Max, of course. Men from within the business and guys from the broader spectrum of life. Twice the singer had been convinced 'true-love' had fired the arrow, hitting the right spot but somehow it never lasted beyond the morning after. A costly New York therapist informed her, after pocketing great lumps of dollars, that at thirty-eight, her music had drained any ability to relate to any sexual relationship in what might be considered a 'normal' way.

Maria Jo-Jo wasn't sure what men expected from her, or indeed what she expected from sexual contact. Certainly nothing physically triggered a reading on her personal Richter scale like the composing of a new melody.

Years later, preparing to leave 'that place' she'd listened to yet another expensive psychiatrist attempt to button-down what he considered to be her emotional complications. The theory ran along the lines that, because she'd never known her father, the subconscious searched every relationship for a father- figure.

Further more, compounded and complicated by her moral and religious upbringing, the end result was emotional blockage.

"So, you're saying, mister, that I don't cum 'cause my mind feels guilty, believing I'm doin' it with a phantom daddy? Like symbolic incest? Am I reading this correct?"

Confused and angry at the indecency of the diagnosis, Maria Jo-Jo had stormed from the lavish consulting room. Her lasting memory was the pained look on the therapist's face, sitting at his desk, red faced, snapping a black pencil between chubby fingers. She took delight in slamming his door.

Outside Exeter, in the glow of the lights illuminating Granada Service Station, Maria Jo-Jo switched off the engine. In the rear mirror she could see that Max was still sleeping. Inside, walking along the counter she purchased coffee, a packet of chocolate biscuits and some red apples. Thanking the girl at the pay-desk she made her way towards the exit collecting a deep whistle of appreciation from a table where three young truckers sat smoking. Presenting them with a 'why-thank-you-gentlemen' type smile, she returned to the car. Max slept on. In the passenger seat she tasted the steaming coffee before switching on the dash light to study Ruby's instructions for the onward journey.

"I smell coffee. What time is it? Where we at, Maria Jo-Jo?"

"3AM… on the button. Un-knot your bones, Max, while I check the route. The coffee's plenty hot."

Returning to the car, Max clambered into the driver's position and drank noisily at the coffee. "Ah, chocolate cookies, great."

After quickly eating two, still crunching, he muttered, "Okay, lady, I'm fired up. Point the way. We'll head west into the green valleys of Devon-shire."

Taking a small bite from one of the apples, Maria Jo-Jo began, "There's about 45 miles Freeway, before we hit the A380 highway. That's about 12 miles on to a market town, Newton Abbot. We circle there, joining the A381 … Abbotskerswell, Ipplepen. Don't you feel the history in these ancient names, Max?"

Quietly, Max inquired, "Any more cookies?"

Tossing him the packet, Maria Jo-Jo continued, her voice buzzing with anticipation, "we go through Totnes Town. According to the book it's one of the oldest seaports in this country. Back before Francis Drake even."

"I'll have an apply now, Maria Jo-Jo."

"On the A381, after Churstow village, it gets a bit fluffy. You drive, Max, I'll do the readin' an' pointin' stuff. I guess we got about an hour before first light. If you've done with the coffee, let's go. There's an ache in my bones that ...." her voice trailed off into inner thoughts and dreams not for the sharing.

Dawn had not quiet begun spreading its marks across the sky when the Rolls eased to a halt in the wide Square at Kingsbridge. The odd street light, mingled with a few dimly-lit shop windows, cast ranging shadows across the high tide lapping at the silent deserted quayside. Glancing at the map, Maria Jo-Jo remarked, "My guess is we caught a wrong-one back some ways, Max."

Bumping his head impatiently against the padded steering wheel, Max moaned, "If this ain't a one horse crap excuse for a town I'll ..." Looking through the window, he added, "Wait on. Over there in that doorway, something moved".

Easing the car into gear he moved silently across the empty square. A big policeman stepped from the dark doorway, his right hand supporting a bicycle. Standing beside the driver's door, he waited while max lowered the window. "G'morning, Sir. Lost are we?"

"Lost?"Max hissed. Listen, Amego, before midnight we hit out from the Royal Albert Hall in London town. We're headed, you understand, for our apartment in Knightsbridge. Right now, after what feels like three days, we hit this crusty asshole called ... " he glanced at the signpost, ... "Kings-bridge. Lost? Believe it, buddy, believe it". When Maria Jo-Jo placed a restraining hand on his thigh, he added, softer ... "officer."

The policeman stooped down, looking into the car. In a deep red-brown accent, he asked, "Are you the owner of this vehicle, sir? May I see some form of identification ... please?"

Leaning across Max, Maria Jo-Jo said, "Actually the car's mine. This person, is my driver, Mr Policeman. He's tired, pissed off and yes you hit the button, lost. If you'd be kind enough to direct us towards the Quarry House Hotel, we'd be eternally grateful". She beamed her best smile.

Walking slowly around the front of the car, both hands on the bicycle, the policeman paused to glance down at the registration number before placing a large hand on the window Maria Jo-Jo had lowered. "Morning, M'a'm. Welcome to the South Hams. Quarry House Hotel, you say. Let me see ... yes, you go back as far as Churstowe, after that 'tis a left, then left again ... or, straight up the hill over there, through West Alvington an' when you come to the old church turn off behind 'er … down the tracks. Mind you, in dimpsy light,with your driver chap 'ere, it might be a bit of a challenge."

"Thank you, kind sir. It will be daylight soon. We'll take the pretty route. Head towards yonder hill, Max. We're on our way."

The policeman had not moved his hand from the door ridge. "I was wondering if … perhaps, a favour, your autograph … please? Not fer' me, for the missis. She's a great fan." He handed Maria Jo-Jo his notebook through the open window.

She signed her name, adding…'without you, we were lost. Thanks.' Handing back the notebook, she gripped his large hand. "Were you catching a quiet smoke in that doorway?"

Pushing the book into his jacket pocket with his free hand, he nodded. Slowly turning his hand, Maria Jo-Jo placed a red apple in his palm. "Take this, it's so much healthier. G'bye Mr Policeman … have a nice day."

As the Rolls made its way across the Square towards the roundabout leading to the hill, in the rear mirror, Max watched the policeman standing in the middle of the road, bicycle in one hand, apple in the other. "Maria Jo-Jo Christmas, you are one hell of a woman."

Climbing the long curving incline from the sleeping town, Maria Jo-Jo's thoughts drifted back six years, almost to the day. Returning from South Africa's Sun City, following a successful six weeks engagement, she'd flown to the ranch, emotionally drained. A rasping throat produced tears each time she tried to swallow.

After three days in the cool valley, sleeping, sipping orange juice and catching up on her reading, she felt relaxed. A week on most of the pain had faded but her lungs felt sticky and dry.

She experienced difficulty reach and sustaining high notes without a tight ache in her chest. Concerned, Ruby drove her to a throat specialist in San Francisco. The doctor shone a small light down her throat, took blood for testing, asked a hundred questions and requested she spit, twice, into a plastic tube. Helping remove her bra, the specialist lifted the singer's full breasts, prodding, probing and at times almost caressing. With eyes shut tight, Maria Jo-Jo felt the right nipple being taken between thumb and forefinger and squeezed … "Does that hurt?"

Opening her eyes, Maria Jo-Jo observed the medical hand moving towards the birthmark over her left areola. Their eyes locked as the specialist's tongue flicked involuntarily across her top lip. Maria Jo-Jo's right hand flashed out striking a sharp blow across the woman's flushed face. "No more than that did, honey."

Recovering her composure, the specialist walked back to her desk, stammering, "Th …th…there was no need for that reaction." Beginning to write, not looking at the singer, she said, "I'll have the results in a week. In the mean time I'll prescribed medication. One capsule, three times a day. No alcohol, no hard drugs and no singing … for at least a month."

Handing the prescription to Maria Jo-Jo, she'd extended her hand, which the singer ignored. "Please leave the room while I get dressed."

Phoning the results of the test seven days later, the doctor coldly informed Maria Jo-Jo that she appeared to have picked up a virus in South Africa that had attacked her lungs. "I'll draft another 'script for stronger antibiotics which should clear the problem in about ten days. I also suspect a slight iron deficiency in your blood. This can be adjusted with drugs. Perhaps we can arrange another appointment, to monitor progress …say in three weeks? "

Maria Jo-Jo's reply had been ice. "Send your account to my manager. He'll deal with it. Goodbye!"

After a month in the valley she felt better. Not 100%, because her appetite and energy levels had fallen away. In creasing the dosage of tablets helped but only for a few days and when she tried to manage without medication she became bad tempered and dizzy. Within three months the singer was doing ten tablets a day, consuming a bottle of vodka between sunrise and dusk and sleeping ten hours at a stretch. Ruby's concern travelled from gentle persuasion to full-blown yelling and screaming.

Her next album took four months to record and never made the top 50.

Two days after Max flew too Europe to finalize a seven city

tour, Ruby discovered Maria Jo-Jo wandering, naked, a mile down stream from the ranch. Gathering her friend gently in her arms, she had delivered the singer to, 'That Place'.

For seven days she was kept deeply sedated in a darkened room.

Ruby kept Maria Jo-Jo's whereabouts hidden from Max for ten days. When she relented, he cleverly sheltered the singer's problems from the media for two months.

Returning to hazy consciousness during the second week, Maria Jo-Jo had been aware that someone was holding her hand. A distant shadowy outline sitting beside the bed quietly said, "Hello, Maria Jo-Jo, I'm Dr. Sam. Here's the truth. Your tests indicate an addiction to prescribed drugs. Sadly, its most likely you never required them in the first place. Plus –and you don't my word on this –you've developed an alcoholic dependency almost as severe as the medication."

"She'd croaked, "Can you help me, Dr Sam?"

"The short answer is no, little lady. The only person who can help is you. We can offer support, but mostly it's your fight. You can surely kick this but don't place a time limit on walking through the exit. When we both agree you're ready we'll do more tests and then … there are plenty manyanas. For now, get some rest. We'll talk again." He squeezed her hand.

Five months, seven days later, she'd sat in the pale blue consulting room, watching the tall pine tree standing guard through the window behind Dr Sam's desk. The young doctor had smiled. "So, Maria Jo-Jo, how do your feel?"

"Better … no, I feel great. I'm ready to go home, sit in the sun for a while and let what's around the bend take its course."

Her smile matched his, "I want to thank you for …"

He'd stopped her gratitude. "If only the world had no place for people like me, Maria Jo-Jo … but then I'd never get to meet wonderful folks like you." Shuffling her notes he added, "I understand you're taking Frankie Luzo home with you. He's a unique kind of guy. I hate to see him go but we have some pretty sharp State employment rules." He passed her an envelope, "This is a letter to a friend of mine at St. David's Hospital in Sacramento. I'd like you to see him for some extra blood tests. I'm certain it's nothing to do with the medication or the Russian-vinegar but there appears to be something in your red cells that I'm not qualified to identify." Grinning, he went on, "Don't look so concerned. After this place, St David's will seem like the Hilton."

A week later the hospital consultant informed Maria Jo-Jo that she had a rare type of leukemia that, thankfully, they'd caught in the early stages. She suffered six months of excruciating chemotherapy as the St David's medical team struggled to control her bone marrow from producing too many leucocytes.

One month into chemo' her voice faded to a croak and during the second month her weight shot up forty pounds. By month four of the treatment her hair, eyebrows and lashed had gone. Taking a shower one morning she watched the last of her pubic hair slipping away through the drain hole.

It would be seven months before the radium treatment ended. Her eyebrows began to grow. In month eight, her hair showed signs of recovering, only now it was straight and almost pure white. Ruby and Frankie tried to keep her away from mirrors but on a visit back to St David's hospital, in a cloakroom, stealing a glance at her reflection … she wept.

One year on from the day Ruby had delivered her to 'that place', she climbed from her bed before the sun rose and walked down beyond the first bend in the slow moving river. Sitting on a broken tree trunk, she watched a multi-coloured Kingfisher dip for his breakfast in the clear water. As the first streams of sunlight splintered a cluster of tall cedars on the far bank, she could make out a lone pre-dawn fisherman casting a silent line into a shimmering eddy. A hundred feet from where she sat, on a shallow gravel-covered bank, an old heron waded, contemplating breakfast. Reaching down, Maria Jo-Jo had lifted a small twig, tossing it high into the air. The gentle splash in mid-stream caused the heron to turn before resuming its concentrated vigil with a small trout.

Disappearing for a moment the twig reappeared, twisting and bobbing downstream, gathering speed on a new purpose. With the sun's rays shafting bright colours along the western curve of the river, Maria Jo-Jo walked slowly back towards the ranch house. It was time to arrange some new order in the plan of things.

"Max, I require a full assessment of assists. Stocks, property, mortgage commitments. IRS statements, cash in bank … the whole works."

They hadn't spoken for nearly eight months. Fanatically obsessed about any type of sickness, Max had, on occasion phoned Ruby for updates but hadn't come within three hundred miles of the ranch or the hospital during the singer's recovery.

As they spoke, he was in New York closing final production details for a TV documentary , 'Maria Jo-Jo. Yesterday's Singer.' And to settle terms over divorce number five.

"Hey, Maria Jo-Jo, Baby. Only this afternoon I'm talkin' to some people about a TV Special … by the way, how ya' doin'?"

Without waiting, he charged on, "Papers? Why would you want financial reports? Let 'ol Max take care of that headache material … like always."

"Send down the books, Max." Her voice was tired but the tone rang warning bells in his head.

"Listen, Honey, I understand how you're feelin'. Okay! So you ain't worked in nearly a year and maybe, just maybe, the income has slowed some but your records are still hot and investments are … tell ya' what I'm gonna' do, I'll dispatch a short appriz for after dinner readin' out there on the porch." He laughed, "Books? Hell, Song-lady, everything's on floppy-disc these days. It's the age of computers …"

She cut him short, "Max, even I know that computers have print-out's. Press the buttons, right up to date and courier it down to the ranch … like today. G'bye, Max."

Two nights later she'd tossed an inch-thick folder aside. The mumble-jumble of complicated statements, balance sheets, gross returns, reserved taxation, profits on ordinary activity stock and tangible assets dazed and confused her.

"Hazelwood, my friend, how you an' Lillian doin'? Joanne and Beth keepin' fine? Great! Listen, I know you don't care for the hassle but I'd appreciate you casting an eye over some papers for me. You will? I'll send Frankie down with the folder." They chatted for a while. "Why don't both come to dinner,Friday? Bring the twins, it's been so long. That's if you folk don't mind breakin' bread with yesterday's voice?" She listened while Hazelwood talked and then said, "Honest, I feel fine. It will do me a power of good to laugh with the girls again. See you Friday and Hazelwood … thanks!"

That Friday evening she'd enjoyed seeing Hazelwood, Lillian and the girls again. The twins, warned about 'best behaviour' held back for all of twenty seconds. While Frankie took charge of the kitchen and Ruby fussed around drinks, Maria Jo-Jo watched the two beautiful children, in bright party dresses, standing, hands behind backs, heads slightly lowered. With tears beginning to flow, Maria Jo-Jo dropped to her knees and opened her arms, "Well look at the wonder of you two."

The girls ran to her. "Maria Jo-Jo, we missed you heaps … Just luv' your new hair."

Later, while Frankie, Ruby, Lillian and the twins went to inspect the fishpond, Maria Jo-Jo sat with Hazelwood on the porch. They remained silent for a few moments, watching the late sun kiss the tops of the far mountains, brushing gold,orange and grey light towards the deeper pocket of coming night.

"I'm sorry, Maria Jo-Jo, it's not good news. Your income during the past year or so has dipped. The accounts are a mess."

Sipping her coffee, she smiled, "Make it easy to read, friend."

Hazelwood watched the group around the fishpond. It was easy to tell there was much laughter even at that distance. The twins were flinging fish-food across the clear water and he could imagine the red carp leaping to take their offer. "Well, until last year you were grossing top-side of three million per annum. Max took 25%, from the top. 10% went to the record company and another 15% was sidetracked to the TV people. Although I suspect Max creamed an extra ten there. Your share of the total juice was 50% gross. Then comes expenses: Living costs, travel, Ruby, Frankie, the ranch, your New York apartment. Then, taxes!"

She tasted her coffee, "Am I broke?"

"Lordy, no! If you - if you stopped work, royalties from albums will supply income. But, you do really need to make certain management adjustments…"

Maria Jo-Jo could see Ruby lift one twin across her hip and walk slowly with Lillian towards the main gate. Frankie carried the other girl on his shoulders, walking a few steps behind. She thought the far scene whispered peace and tranquillity.

"Do I own this place?"

"Yes. The ranch, land, river are apart of your personal estate, as is the Manhatten apartment. The vultures can't touch them. Because I can find no trace of your Boyde stock I can only assume you've done something wonderfully stupid with that."

They both smiled.

"Now is a good time to put your house in order, Maria Jo-Jo.

You require expert help." Handing back the folder he went on,"I'm too far removed from such matters but I can recommend some able folk to assist. "

They both noticed that the others had turned and were now heading back towards the main house. Frankie and the girls were singing but were too far off for the sound to reach the porch. "To summarize, I've drafted four, do-now's. Sit Max down and define your contract of association. Make him get shot of the bloodsuckers, Maria Jo-Jo. Take control of all future projects. If Mr Stone hits the wall, go see the people I've marked on the folder."

Beth and Joanne rushed excitedly across the wide porch, "Daddy-daddy, Maria Jo-Jo, we fed the fish … they jumped to the sky."

During the following days she read Hazelwood's report over and over again until his recommendations were stamped clear in her head. Then, she sent for Max.

Before his arrival she rode out to the far end of the land. Down stream, towards the third bend in the river, allowing the mare to wander at her own pace through the shaded woods of the lower valley. When the horse stopped, grazing in the lush grass, Maria Jo-Jo dismounted. She looked down the hill at the outline of the Boyde's house sheltered by tall pines from the highway. When the animal had eaten its fill, they backtracked slowly along the high ridge, easing into a canter as the ranch house came into sight. She was ready for Mr Max Stone.

At first he'd listened in silence, staring at the horizon. Then he began growling. " How you think his business is conducted, lady? It became necessary to trade off parts of the deal … just to make bread-dollars ... to fuckin' survive. That's how the god-damn game is played." He ranted on, gathering fuel and fury.

Eventually he crumbled, muttering, shifting the blame from record producers to cable TV, Nixon, the Las Vegas mafia, Hollywood fagots and the exorbitant costs of international tours.

His voice dropped, he looked at his shoes, "We have to face the ball here, song-lady. You sure as hell ain't been reading from the script during this past year. Am I right?"

"The only reason you're not a complete prick, Max is because you lack a foreskin. Now listen, listen hard. Here's the deal. Get-me-out-of-the-recording-contract. Pay off the TV people. Basket the agreement between you and me, from this very moment. Do it, Max no matter the cost. I want to be free from those shits. Do you read me, max?"

As he opened his mouth to reply, she spoke again. "I'm not sure if I'll perform again, not even clear I want to but if there's to be any tomorrow … and you want a part of it, here's the bottom line. You manage me, alone. Your cut is 25%, after expenses."

Max shut his mouth.His eyes glazed over.

"Here's the game-plan, Max. Appoint a respectable accountant to handle the financial package and the IRS. Give it a year, two tops and you sure as hell don't support wife number six on my back."Maria Jo-Jo stretched out her hand, "Do we have a workable deal here, Max?"

Early in '87 they started again. TV channels, Recording Companies, people running the top shows, ignored her.

Max arranged for 'second-on' spots in tiny concert halls in small towns. Late night cabaret in un-syndicated hotels across different States. She returned to Uncle Marco, who assured her the voice was only 'resting' not broken. At first, slowly, over the months, the warm embers began to glow, beating like a pulse in her mind, humming across her lips until the old fire burned. The bewildering magic returned, sending her music out over the air like the curving flight of a lone seabird.

Max spent hours on the phone seeking engagements, calling in forgotten favours, often working for break-even fees, or less. Frankie drove the trailer hundreds of miles over roads leading in or out of various States on different gigs. And, as always, Ruby was there by her side. A chance meeting with an old Hollywood friend resulted in Maria Jo-Jo recording the title song for a low budget film that won a French award. The soundtrack from the movie sneaked, without help from the 'trade' into the top ten … and Joe Public began requesting more. Record producers and TV folk came calling, waving olive branches wrapped in uncountable bundles of dollar bills. Only this time, on her ascending flight, Maria Jo-Jo Christmas became the navigator.

****

Chapter Five

... arrival

An intrusive sound disturbed the sleeping seabird. Opening one eye, its prime concern centred on a bundles of speckled feathers snuggled down in the collection of twigs wedged into the base of the angled steeple. Satisfied that her young were safe, the gull stretched before waddling along the narrow parapet to peer into the grey haze.

Further up the hill headlights dipped and then disappeared for a moment before reappearing to gleam skywards, as the unseen motor moved slowly along the winding road leading down towards the church.

Establishing the cause of the noise, mother bird shuffled back over the guano-covered stonework, halting to listen as yet another, duller beat, further away, invaded the quiet approaching dawn.

Below the stones of the broken church, beyond the unseen meadow, lower even than a lone elm tree and past the black shapes of the copse, another motor throbbed. A deeper tone than the car, creating a different echo that carried a constant putt-putt sound up from the hidden creek towards the damaged masonry of the silent building.

Ready to begin her search for the first intake of food, the gull checked the progress of the approaching headlights, deciding to wait until the intruder had passed before flying southwest towards the open sea.

The Rolls Royce seemed to be crawling along the lane's twisting hedgerows tightly packed with tangled wild hawthorn, immature elm and prickly blackberry brambles. At each bend, Max slowed, gripping tighter on the wheel, knuckles white and extended.

Whimpering, he prayed that no other driver would be so insane as to venture up this crazy English, no fucking-passing-place, dirt track. A frantic glance in the rear mirror confirmed there wasn't a dog-in-hells chance of reversing back along the ten-foot gap of overgrown green darkness.

"Is this the god-forsaken church ahead? Ah fuck, lady, it's only a bunch of busted stones … a ruin. Look, Maria Jo-Jo, there's no road beyond the gates. That cop was a lyin' bastard."

"Just pull in, Max. Stop the engine. We'll take a look-see. It will be full daylight soon."

Easing the big car onto the grass verge alongside a low Devon wall protecting the gateway from the road, Max switched off the engine. Resting his head onto the leather steering wheel, shoulders heaving, a relieved sob escaped from somewhere deep inside. Climbing out, he looked around, thankful that any crazy early-rising farmer now had some passing space … 'not that the son-of-bitch had any place to go!'

What remained of the church stood fifty feet back from a limestone archway cut in the low wall on the perimeter. An iron gate, half open, led a straight path towards the black-timbered door at the main entrance. The undisturbed pathway, pitted with weathered pebbles was splashed with small clumps of moss and minute pink flowers. No feet had trod along the path into the church for some considerable time. The vestibule sheltering the main door was constructed from slate and shaped like the up-ended bow of a small boat. Clinging to each side, its main trunk hanging like forgotten oars, a climbing wisteria in full bloom sparkled in the soft light of a new day. Magical colours blended into the faded stonework.

Only three sides of the building remained intact. The eastern wall lay in a jumbled heap of moss-covered stones. In the southern gable, where there'd once been a window, thick strands of ivy climbed, cobweb-like, shielding daylight from the holy place.

The overgrown graveyard surrounding the church resembled a forsaken battlefield. Scattered untidy gravestones, whole and broken, some partly hidden under brambles, listed at various angles like fallen soldiers in the quiet act of prayer.

Family names, Dates. Lines from poignant poems chiselled in granite, fading towards obscurity by the passage of winter storms. The ancient ground and those buried beneath the dark red soil appeared to have been abandoned by indifferent generations of passing congregations.

Max yawned.Spreading his arms above his head, muttering,

"Need a pee, Maria Jo-Jo." He climbed from the car, ignoring the half-open gate and scrambled awkwardly over the low wall to disappear behind the side of the building.

Maria Jo-Jo watched him out of sight before slowly emerging from the passenger side. Standing in the gateway she read the letters carved over the support beam, "St Mary's – 1888." Glancing up at the ragged parapet she saw the herring gull, head cocked to one side, peering down at her. "G'mornin', sea-bird. Maybe you can point out the right direction?"

Scanning the panoramic view beyond the tall spire, the singer could see wispy pink clouds painting a fine line between sea and sky. A low hedge divided the scattered gravestones from a wide field that dipped gently towards uneven cliffs. Young corn stood waiting for the first morning breeze to commence its early dance to the sun. Looking down the slope, she watched distant squalls swirl upwards from the sea, causing the golden-eared strands to sway in changing patterns.

Almost in the centre of the cornfield, about fifty feet lower, a giant elm stood in splendid isolation. At first glance the tree appeared stark black against the skyline. The main body formed a circumference, like the twisted ribs of a broken umbrella. Its lower branches arched back towards the soil while other limbs spread horizontally. The tips of the tree's uppermost branches reached skywards. A close inspection showed that the elm's main trunk was blanketed with dark ivy. The mighty elm tree was forever dead.

Climbing onto the low wall to the right of the heavy gate, the singer's eyes followed shafts of daylight searching into the lower valley. About two miles to the northwest, huddled between three small hills, she could make out the shadowy lines of a village. Scattered lights dotted yellow amongst rooftop shapes that nestled like a grey irregular blanket over the sleeping inhabitants. Perhaps half a mile below the church, in the depths of the valley, dawn had begun exposing the edges of a large excavated hollow. A semicircular amphitheatre, quarried into a Q, almost a hundred yards in diameter, lead towards a tiny quay overlooking a wide creek. Uneven stone steps dropped from the quayside down into the water. In the centre of the man-carved clearing the glistening roof of a building rose like two overlapping circles. Maria Jo-Jo had discovered the Quarry House Hotel.

Even from distance, in the confused light, she could make out level walkways, climbing in six-foot high stages around the chiselled crater. The outer quarry walls were softened by gradients. Tight dry-stone walls ringed the edges of the quarry, creating plateaus about twelve feet across. Each terrace was carpeted with evergreen shrubs and dwarf trees.

A small spring, cascading from the top ridge, splashed onto the different levels, falling towards a pond that overflowed into the creek. From the moss-covered quay, dividing the camomile lawn, a gravel drive curved against dark granite steps lifting towards the hotel's wide entrance.

From the high vantage point of the church gate, what lay below appeared as a circle within a circle. Large picture windows on the southeastern side of the hotel reflected the first rays of sunlight. Dew-wet roof slates sparkled different shades of purple and grey.

In the soft expanding light, Maria Jo-Jo could make out the shape of a gravel drive meandering from the hotel down past the stone quay towards the creek head, before easing into a narrow tarmac lane that veered northwards up a winding hill.

At the junction where the lane wandered to the left, faint tracks led into a thick hedgerow of spindly hawthorn and young ash. Following the bushy cluster to where the creek widened in a slight curve she observed that the hedge altered direction, skimming the rim of the dipping meadow. It appeared to head upwards in the direction of the church. Maria Jo-Jo had discovered the way down into the valley.

Rushing from around the broken wall, tugging at his zipper, Max yelled, "Maria Jo-Jo, you ain't gonna' believe this. There's a guy lying back there, dead, okay! Recovered from a shipwreck back in 1890 … and, are you ready for this? His name's Maximillian Stone. 57 years old. My age. Hold your horses, lady, 'cause … he was laid to rest, June 3rd. Today! Exactly one hundred years ago. Now! Is that destiny or is that destiny?"

"Sweet Jesus, Max, your family name was never Stone ... Steinman, maybe. And, I've long had doubts about you being only 57." She smiled at the excitement in his face.

"Sure-sure! But, just suppose the poor sailor-man suffered the same racial kicks as my folks? Could be he was smart enough to change his name! There's gotta' be records someplace... perhaps we can find a priest? Say ... he could be kin!"

"Did it say how he died?"She asked.

"Some kind of pox thing but ..."

"Ah!" Maria Jo-Jo laughed, "Now it's beginning to make sense. He could well be kin. Did you find a way down into the valley back there?"

"Believe me, Song-lady, fields an' ferns back there ... not even a dirt track."

Grabbing his outstretched hand she helped him clamber up onto the low wall. "Down there, Max. Whadya' you see?"

Shielding his eyes against the light, Max could make out the creek stretching just inside the sheltered gully of cliffs. About a hundred feet wide it extended from what looked like an enclosed basin back along a narrow beach before curving inland through thick woods. From the outer cliffs, back through the trees and on towards the stone quay and the hotel, Max guessed the distance to be close to a mile.

From the church wall, looking down, it seemed that nature had carved a lagoon between the sea and the land for no other reason than to be different. On the inside of the seaward ridge a narrow strip of white sand rose towards a plateau covered with bright yellow gorse. Above the gorse, sandstone rocks, acting like a barrier, separated the channel from the heaving swell of the outside ocean.

Standing beside Max, Maria Jo-Jo watched a small fishing boat emerge from the shadow of the trees at the darkened bend. Listening, she could just make out the muffled throb of the boat's engine rising in the still air. The craft moved steadily towards the high cliffs of the basin at the southern end of the lagoon, its wash splitting the green water in perfect diagonal lines, fanning constant ripples astern onto the sand.

As she watched, as if by some clever illusion, the boat disappeared into the cliffs. Blinking, not believing what she'd witnessed, Maria Jo-Jo waited for her mind to make sense of what had happened. Her eyes were drawn to the different texture of motion and colour between the sea outside and the calm inside the creek. Outside, a ground swell slowly heaved, pulsing latent energy, rolling towards the shore before falling back on itself, reforming, to surge against the rugged coastline.

Almost hypnotized by the scene below, the singer observed the tiny fishing boat mysteriously reappear, perhaps a hundred yards beyond the rocks. It climbed sluggishly up the back of each swell, heading south, slightly to the right of the rising sun.

Maria Jo-Jo took a deep breath. Aware, as surely as the orange ball lifting above the horizon was about to warm the sleeping world, that she had arrived at the correct place. The moving craft, fast becoming a speck in the deeper troughs must have passed through the boat passage.

G.I Sergeant Jo-Jo Christmas had described this strange place in his last letter home, written on the day of his death … the very same day that Maria Jo-Jo Christmas had been born.

"Back to the car, Max. Drive beyond the church. Believe me on this one, there's a way down."

Slipping the Rolls into low gear, sighing, Max eased away from the low wall. Bumping over the grass verge, he stabbed at the brakes. Facing the vehicle, clumps of young brambles and tall nettles formed a screen. "You're crazy, Maria Jo-Jo, there ain't no way through this …"

"The ground, Max, what do you see?"

Almost hidden in the tufted grass, rusty small-gauge tracks disappeared into the tangled darkness ahead. Staring first at the ground, then at the greenery ahead, Max muttered, "Okay, lady, so one time a toy locomotive came up this bush-trail. What makes you think this baby can make it down the mountain? A four-wheel drive it surely ain't."

Climbing out, Max found a broken stick and began slashing wildly at the nettles. Advancing into the brambles he quickly became hidden from sight. Returning after a few moments he tossed aside the stick. Without speaking, he scrambled behind the wheel and eased the car slowly forward into the bushes.

After the high bonnet parted the brambles and elm, once through the outer foliage, an old lane opened, just wide enough for the motor to descend. Proceeding at crawling pace, headlights full on, they travelled gingerly downwards through a dark green cavern. Occasionally a break in the overhead foliage cast a shaft of daylight onto the rusted tracks ahead. Max sweated and cursed, loudly.

At one point, bringing the car to a halt, he leant forward, banging his head against the steering wheel. "For Christ's sake, Maria Jo-Jo, this is like falling off the end of the fuckin' world." He screamed, as something furry dropped from an overhanging branch, rose on its hind legs and peered intensively through the windscreen. "Sweet Jesus. Hell! It's a rat … make it go away … please!"

Maria Jo-Jo laughed, "Max, for pity's sake, it's a baby squirrel. Do you have any spare nuts?" She chuckled again, pressing the water-wash switch on the dashboard. The squirrel ran to the edge of the bonnet and leapt, four legs extended in different directions, into the hedge.

Max lifted his foot from the brake and they moved on, slowly, downwards. "Shit and four hurricanes."

***

There'd been a time, about four months into the chemotherapy, when it seemed as if she'd reached the lowest ebb of life. Deep depression filled most of the waking and many of her sleeping hours. Ruby and Frankie took turns sleeping in the main bedroom, while Maria Jo-Jo slumped on a bare mattress in the adjoining windowless dressing room.

Medical advisors suggested that to overcome melancholy periods, she'd benefit from the removal of all materialistic comforts. Their theory was based on the belief that if nothing of value exists, the will to recover becomes stronger.

Sometimes, in hours before dawn, when sleep would not come,

she'd paced the length of the room, fighting against the terrible rages within her mind. Moving from corner to corner, stopping, she'd curl into a tight ball, hugging herself against the agony. Biting her lip until the blood flowed.

On one such morning, reaching under the mattress, she drew out a silver framed photograph that had been concealed from Ruby and Frankie. Holding the cold glass to her steaming face, she'd whimpered, "Help me, Mamma. Ease the pain. I don't want to die this way …please!"

The photograph showed her mother and a father she'd never known, smelt or touched. Taken when Maria Christmas was six months pregnant and soldier Jo-Jo was preparing to depart for Europe to begin training for invasion. After her mother died it was the one treasure Maria Jo-Jo held on to, carrying the photo near or close to her bedside along every road travelled.

Rolling into a tight sweating mass, Maria Jo-Jo had waited for the next surge of twisting pain, stabbing nerve cells, jerking every bone and joint of her body, scraping away what trace of dignity remained. The quick physical jabs attacked in waves. The first, hurting almost beyond endurance. A secondary pain followed close behind, before the first shock cleared, zooming from another direction, fiercer, more intent, violent and raw. She'd tensed, taking slow breaths, struggling to arm against the next assault.

As the second wave ebbed to a dull ache, the singer gasped as a third, excruciating jolt dragged her moaning to her knees. While damaged nerves fought to transmit cries of help back to her numbed brain, the need to scream outpaced the savage message. She screamed.

The singer's pitiful sobbing woke Ruby in the next room. Quickly scrambling from the bed, the black woman stood at the door for a second before dropping to her knees on the mattress and gathering her friend into her arms. "There, there, girl, Ruby's here. This bad time is surely bottom spot. From here you can only get better."Without looking up, Ruby knew that Frankie stood behind her in the doorway. In a voice a little above a whisper, she said, "Fetch a pan an' brush. She's broke her picture. An' careful 'bout the glass, little man."

Two hours later, still rocking the singer quietly in her arms, Ruby said, “Maria Jo-Jo, behind the photo Frankie found a letter your daddy wrote your momma …you best read it, girl.”

***

The leaf-splattered Roll Royce, headlights full on, emerged slowly from the covered lane onto the dew-wet grass bordering the creek. Daylight was gently beginning its first yawning stretch into a new day. They had arrived.

Quarry House Hotel looked even more impressive from ground level. It spoke quietly of a gentleman’s house … with nautical influence. Shafts of irregular sunlight touched the first floor windows, ricocheting bright colours onto different sections of the circled garden terraces. Max stuttered the car to an untidy halt on the small quayside, facing downstream. The creek cut like a small river between thick trees on the inshore bank while mossy limestone cliffs protected the outside bank from the sea.

Climbing from the car, Maria Jo-Jo gazed into the hazy light expanding upstream like a silk sheen. It was one of the most beautiful settings she had ever seen. Walking, almost on tip- toes, towards the narrow set of stone steps leading down to the flowing water, she watched spiralling whispers of white mist distort the distance to the first bend some four hundred yards to the south. “I can feel you were here, my father.”

****

Chapter Six

... Felicissima & Invincible
Most fortunate & Invincible: September 1588

As the Atlantic storm began to ease, two ships slowly beat their way down the west coast of Ireland. Battered by the sea, battle scared, they were the remains of King Philip 11, of Spain's mighty Armada. They were trying to make it home to Spain.

Five months before, the fleet had assembled at the port of Lisbon. Sixty thousand tons of total fighting power, from towering galleons to three-masted pataches with tiny dispatch boat and sloop-rigged zebras dotted between the larger vessels at anchor. An Armada, preparing for war.

By early May, the main force had grouped outside the port of Belam on the River Tagus. Crewed by over eight thousands conscripted seafarers, the fleet's fighting force numbered more than 20,000 troops, mustered from different parts of the Catholic world. Sailing masters waited for favourable winds to begin the first stage of the voyage across Biscay.

On May 29th vessels began to weigh anchor. Ship after ship turned on the ebb tide, mains and foresails dropping from high yards, as they gathered steerage-way towards the open sea. The larger flagships under the command of Philip's senior Admirals began forming into line, forging west before heading north.

The passage plan was to sail to within sight of the Scilly Islands and then northeast towards the English headland known as the Lizard.

West of the Channel Islands Dutch allies would supply charts to the fleet for navigating through the English Channel. Stage two of the plan was to anchor off Calais and embark the Duke of Parma's army. From that position the magnificent Armada would proceed north to invade and overthrow the throne of Elizabeth 1 of England.

And now, four months on, those who'd survived the ravaging from the Englishmen, were attempting to drag battle broken ships down the outside coast of Ireland before making a course towards Spain and home. Disgraced, dishonoured, scattered and broken in spirit ... but, still alive.

The once splendid galleons, masts splintered, yards broken and sails torn, they struggled to weather the inhospitable coastline of Ireland. The sun had not been sighted for three days. At night, no recognisable stars appeared between the low clouds that scurried in from the western ocean. Heavy rain reduced visibility to little more than the distance between the two vessels.

In the crow's nest of the leading man-of-war, farmhand-turned-seaman, Juan Miguel Cortez strained tired eyes against driving, rain-filled spray shutting out everything beyond breaking crests surging against the pitching vessel.

Seventeen years old, Juan Miguel shuddered, cold to the marrow of his bones. He wore most of the clothes he owned, including fine leather boots that had belonged to his older brother, Don Pedro, killed in battle off Calais. A victim of the Englishman, Lord Howard's ferocious fire-ships.

Bracing himself against the mast as the great ship rolled and pitched in the darkness, scanning the seas ahead, his mind dreaming of warm sunshine and the farmlands of his home in Granada.

Closing his eyes for a moment, Juan pictured his mother's face, glowing from the joy of cooking a meal for her menfolk when the day's work was done. He could almost taste the sweet roasted meats and the red wine from the sheltered valley.

As the vessel lifted on a large wave, jerking the foremast, the youngster searched his memory, trying to recall the last time he'd sat down to a hot meal.

Far below him, in a deep-green trough, a big black-backed gull suddenly appeared, swimming between the dipping hull and the next wave beating across and in opposite direction of the main swell. Confused by the sight of the lone seabird and the changing motion of the seas, Juan Miguel strained to penetrate the spray filled horizon. His ears struggled to accept a slow rumbling beyond his scope of visibility. Wet, fighting seasickness caused by the height of the lookout position, the boy-sailor prayed for his relief to climb the rigging and end his misery.

What he did not know, could not see, was that the battered vessel and the other, close astern, were less than half a mile from the outer ridge of Inishtooskert, black jagged rocks, just seaward of the Blasket Islands. Additional information, unknown to the young Spaniard was that with the combination of a southerly tidal set and the near gale-force westerly winds, neither of the beleaguered ships could weather the dangerous reefs ahead.

On the poop deck, standing beside two seaman wrestling to control the large kicking wheel, an exhausted Sailing-Master suddenly jerked awake at a scream from aloft ... "Finisterre."

He could only stare, his open mouth showing broken teeth, as the next swell heaved, twisted and flung the barnacled timbers of the great ship onto the waiting stones of death.

As misty autumn light crept along Inner Sound, the Bay of Dunmore's strands filled with the splintered timbers of the galleons. A massive upturned keel lay marooned in deep sand like a washed reef. Strips of decking, broken masts and tattered sails twisted around spars had quietly tumbled ashore on the swells of the rising tide, to lie criss-crossed in a tangled mess.

Over six hundred mariners, took their last breaths, on this foreign shore, drowing, less than six days sailing from their original port of departure.

Local inhabitants, frightened by the enormity of such destruction, hauled the dead and nearly dead from the beach. They stripped the wet bodies of rings, earrings, weapons, boots and wearable clothes. In the scramble to recover items of any value from the wreckage, dying men were abandoned to the mercy of the next tide. Other inhabitants scavenging the beach, with little humanity, dug collective graves into which they tossed both the lost and the still living.

Without ceremony or common prayer, these things happened along the southwest coast of Ireland ... on days following the nineteenth of September 1588.

***

Thomas Power farmed three good fields under the lower shadow of Mount Eagle, on the road between Slea Head and Ventry.

Thomas Power didn't own the land outright but paid taxes on the barley, oats and wheat that he harvested. He did however own a mountain pony, a lame cow and two pigs, together with a foul tempered goat and several chickens. As a young man, he'd helped his father build a windowless stone croft against the side of a dry hill, covering the low roof with great sods of earth.

Slightly lower down the same hill they'd constructed a rough stone shelter where their animals huddled from winter gales that screamed in from the Atlantic Ocean. Diverting a small mountain stream, they fashioned a well that served both men and animals with most of their needs.

After the death of his father, Thomas Power, into his fortieth year, travelled to Milltown. There, from a Kerry tinker, he purchased a mountain cart to suit the mountain pony. Next he journeyed to Dingle, a market town, from where he obtained for his comfort, a young wife.

***

On the second day following the sinking of the Spanish warships, with the storm passed, a gentle breeze from the southwest teased along the flat sands towards Parkmore Point.

Thomas Power harnessed the pony to the cart and set off for the wide stretch of strand. Experience told the mountain farmer that the storm would have washed bundles of fresh seaweed high onto the shore. With his fifteen- year old daughter, Magda, Power would spend the next few days gathering, storing and then spreading the iron-rich seaweed over the three sloping fields.

The deserted stretch of sand between Dunbeg and Parkmore lay smooth as a lake for nearly a mile. The old pony splashed contentedly along the tidemark while Thomas Power sat on the cart's rim, puffing an old clay pipe. Further long the beach, Magda raked dark-green seaweed into manageable heaps and with the energy of youth, hurried on. As the cart drew level with the piled seaweed, without command the pony would halt while Power clambered down and scooped the wet bundles up onto the cart.

Father and daughter saw the wreckage at the same time. Magda, ten steps ahead, stopped and, shielding her eyes, took in the stub of mast with the shattered crow's nest lapping in the shallow waters, a hundred steps from where she worked. The varnished timbers of the topmast and the yardarm shone in the early sunshine like a fallen crucifix.

Never having seen anything of this nature, Magda raced over the wet sand, eager to establish if what was hanging from the twisted ropes was really the body of a man. Hurrying the loaded pony, father and daughter reached the wreckage at the same time. "Magda, wait ..." Thomas Power ordered.

Taking an axe from the cart he walked waist deep into the tide and with a single blow cut the body free. Thumping the sharp edge of the axe into the mast he dragged the man clear of the water and began wrenching off the leather boots.

As the first boot came free Power, struggling to match the boot against his own feet, called to his daughter, "Look for gold ... rings, earrings, teeth. Pull away his jacket and vest ... they will dry so. Quick now, girl, he's dead ... can't hurt. God's curse on these boots, they were build for a Cork dwarf fella'".

Crossing herself, Magda knelt on the warm sand and began to gently ease off the seaman's wet jacket. Glancing at the pale youthful face she noticed the black curling hair reaching almost to his shoulders. She looked away.

"Earrings, girl?" She could only shake her head as her father dropped beside her, tugging at the silver buckled belt around the boy's waist, before tossing it with the boots up into the cart.

When Magda's slim fingers fumbled to undo the laces holding the shirt-neck in place, Power's roared, "Stand away." Grabbing hold of the hem he dragged the canvas shirt from the cold body. Beneath the rough shirt the sailor's chest was clad in a silk smock- intended as a present for his mother, if ever they'd reached home. Thomas Power's eyes blazed, "Ah, 'twill do better on your mother's back, so it will. Hold him still, daughter, while I pull."

As Magda gripped the boy around the hips and her father

reached down to remove the delicate garment, the body heaved, coughing seawater, bile and blood over the girl's hands. She screamed, tightening her grip on the lean hips. The young man's eyes rolled, flickered and then opened wide for a second. She saw that his bloodshot eyes were coloured deep blue with splashes of speckled sea green.

Shocked by his daughter's scream, Power had sat back on his haunches in the retreating tide. He stared, mouth wide as convulsive spasms raked the young body. Leaping to his feet he rushed towards the stranded mast pulled free the axe and splashed back onto the beach. Raising the great blade above his head, he aimed at the base of the boy's skull.

"No, Dadda, no ... look, so". Magda pointed at a mark over the boy's heart. It resembled a white seabird and against the tanned skin it appeared to have a luminous glow. Her fingers reached out with slow dilation, touching the birthmark. "It's a sign. If we harm this man, we'll be surely cursed."

Her eyes pleaded, searching from her father's face to the axe lofted over his head. "He can work the land ...your slave."

Thomas Power slowly lowered the axe.

Juan Miguel was lifted onto the cart and covered with the drying seaweed. When they returned to the hill, his body was dumped, with the cart's contents, against the animal shelter. Thomas Power collected the boots, the belt with the silver buckle and the other clothes and walked further up the hill for his meat.

Magda dragged the boy into the barn, shaped a bed from the straw and fetching a bucket of water washed the salt and seaweed from him. Covering his near naked form with dry straw she gently touched the birthmark once more with her finger. Then she removed the pony from the cart before following her father up the hill towards the living croft.

Later, after she'd eaten, when sleeping sounds came from the place where her parents slept close to the turf fire, she returned to the lower barn. He was still unconscious.

Feeling under the straw, she found he was shivering. Crawling beneath the straw she pressed her young body tightly to his ...and slept.

Within a week he was walking. Slow, weak, resting every few steps. After one month the boy was put to work. Following the passing of another storm he collected seaweed from the long strand and in the calm helped Thomas Power cut up the remains of the beached mast. His clothes and boots were returned, minus the leather tops, which Power had severed from the knees up, utilising the supple leather for leggings. Also missing was the silk smock.

Power worked him from daylight until dark, every passing day. He slept with the animals in the lower shelter, eating alone from scraps thrown out by the family. When garrison soldiers came, the young mariner was hidden from sight.

He spoke to no one and understood not one word of their strange language. After another gale had hurried on beyond distant mountains, he discovered a sack of potatoes washed high onto the beach and took great delight in showing Power's wife how to prepare and cook them. Clearing a small track of soil behind the shelter, he planted what remained, explaining with signs that when the flowers died, the vegetables would be ready to harvest.

When six months passed, on a night when a deep depression raged from the northwest, Juan Miguel huddled in the cold barn, craving for home, wondering what thoughts and fears burned away in the minds of his parents back in the sun-filled pastures of Granada.

He recalled the day, almost a year since, when with his older brother he'd walked to the port of Almeria to watch the majestic ships assembling for their voyage to a distant war. Caught up in the hypnotic splendour of the grand adventure they'd made their marks on paper. With only fleeting thoughts of home, the two boys found themselves passing through the Straits of Gibraltar, on passage first to Lisbon and then northwards, in the service of King Philip 11, of Spain.

Juan Miguel had no idea where on the face of the earth he had journeyed or where he now lay. He had watched his only brother burn to death, been shipwrecked, beaten and starved by people whose language he couldn't understand. When he sometimes gazed out across the sea he knew not in what direction the shores of his birth lay.

In the shelter of the stone barn, with only the steady breathing of the animals for company, listening to the driving rain, the young mariner lowered his head onto his knees and tumbled, quietly weeping, into a restless sleep.

Magda's small warm hand, brushing tenderly through his hair, woke him. "The storm frightens me," she whispered. "Sometimes it feels the mountain will fall. We shall all die. Are you afraid, so?"

Not fully understanding, yet sensing her fear, he held her hand as a brilliant flash of lightning lit up the darkness. In the split second of light, Juan Miguel observed the animals herded together in the far corner, waiting for the deep rumble of thunder that would follow.

As the low thunder growled, echoing from the higher mountainside, he felt the girl tense. Reaching out he gathered her closer. Magda trembled, pulling dry straw over them, clinging to him until her bones ached. Within the next flash her wide eyes stared at his naked chest and when the thunder began she touched his birthmark with her finger- tips, caressing it gently.

As the noise faded, drifting southwards towards the sea, she reached forward, softly kissing the mark of the white bird on his skin. Without fully understanding why, Juan Miguel's hand tenderly cupped the girl's small breast.

During that long rain-filled night, while nature raged assault across Eagle Mountain, screaming on into Dingle Bay and towards Valencia Island ... the children surrendered their innocence. Without guilt, with no wild urgency, almost without the aid of verbal communication, they touched ... boy and girl.

By the time the first grey streaks of morning began stretching into the lower barn they had experienced, more than once, breathtaking emotions over which they possessed little control or understanding.

***

When the soldiers came, Magda, three months pregnant, sat milking the lame cow in the lower barn. Two men grabbed her, holding her down on the straw. The officer stood over her lean body, shouting in her face, "Where's the Spanish fish-boy? You bastards can hang for harbouring enemies of the crown. Speak, girl." He kicked her.

Magda's scream carried to the higher croft where her mother knelt preparing turf for the fire. The cry echoed on, further up the hill where Thomas Power worked the plough alongside Juan Miguel. Leaving the pony they ran down across the freshly turned furrows towards the lower barn. Before man and boy reached the croft a single musket shot split the mountain air.

Passing his home, without halting his stride, Thomas Power grabbed the axe from its resting place.

Juan Miguel entered the dark barn just ahead of the farmer. He saw Magda struggling on the scattered straw, two soldiers squatting on her arms. The white-faced officer was slumped against the far wall, blood poured from a gash in his torn sleeve. Beside him on the ground, Magda's mother, blood oozing from a hole in her back, sobbed. In her hand she grasped a scythe, red with the officers blood.

From somewhere deep, Juan Miguel uttered a strangled roar of anger ...and then blackness as a musket butt smashed against the back of his head. His unconscious body lay with his right hand just touching the scythe, while the fingertips of his right hand rested on Magda's foot.

After the fourth soldier used her, the girl's mind mercifully closed against reality and when number five lurched forward, fumbling with his buttons, she drifted into a coma of stunned silence ... from which she would never return.

Thomas Power had been forced onto his knees to witness the rape of his daughter and then, they hung him in his own barn, in full view of his watching beasts. They took the lame cow, the pigs and would have taken the pony except that it remained standing at the plough in the higher field. One man tried to capture the ill-tempered goat but it ran off. While one soldier kicked straw over Magda's naked body, another raised his musket to end the life of Juan Miguel.

The wounded officer mumbled, "No! If he's alive, he can be sold. Take him."

The Spanish boy-sailor was transported to the port of Cobh, and sold, for one guinea, to the master of a British slave-trader.

A year later, nineteen years into his life, sickened by the inhuman treatment of 'living cargos' transported from the rivers of West Africa to the New World settlements of America, Juan Miguel, together with an old Negro slave jumped ship.

They made their way slowly across the vast new continent to a country called Mexico.

***

Under the shelter of the dry hill, in the croft Thomas Power had helped his father to build, Magda laid her parents to rest.

With the aid of the mountain pony she formed a lasting tomb by pulling the turf roof down over the bodies. Loading the chickens onto the cart, tethering the bad-tempered goat behind, she drove away from her mountain home without once looking back.

Six months later, living with a small band of tinkers who had taken the silent soul into their keeping, Magda lay down roots in the County of Mayo, within sight of the Nephin Beg Mountains, at a place called Srahmore. She gave birth to a daughter she named Tee.

Baby Tee had a tiny birthmark over her heart that resembled ...

****

Chapter Seven

... Jo-Jo's Christmas

Sister Brenda's face formed an almost perfect circle. Perched on a button nose, at falling-off angle, tiny spectacles covered sea-green eyes, radiating calmness. Her vocation was to gather damaged children, sheltering them in a cloak of warm protection. Unofficial 'mother' to seven other dedicated nuns, Sister Brenda administrated the smooth running of the Harlem Orphanage on West/23rd Street.

The orphanage activity began at five o'clock each morning, three hundred and sixty five days throughout the year. Following meditation the task of caring for 46 children of different colour, race, greed and earthly needs would begin. By seven o'clock, kids of various shapes and sizes would have scrambled from beds, washed behind the ears, dressed and seated in the dining hall, hungrily awaiting the first chatter-filled meal of the day.

The building was owned by the City and managed by the church. On high-days and holidays it was traditional for local residents and shopkeepers to leave tokens of gratitude, on the clean wide steps.

On Christmas morning, 1923, while the other housemothers prepared breakfast, Sister Brenda took delight in gathering gifts and offerings from the front steps. Already, before first light that morning, she'd collected a box of woollen scarves, two crates of fresh fruit, an envelope containing seventy-nine dollars and three large jars of candy … it was still only six-thirty, when standing in the main hall, she heard the knocker rattle yet again.

Sister Brenda observed a cardboard box sitting in the first wisps of new snow. A trail of smudged footprints on the steps leading down towards the sidewalk brought a smile to the nun's face. Even though she'd left her specs on the hall table she could read the large writing … Jo-Jo (Apples).

Lifting the crate and closing the heavy main door with a heave of her ample bottom, she'd almost reached the kitchen when she heard the first faint whimper. Placing the box on the hall table, Sister Brenda carefully raised the cover. Snuggled into a clean blanket, glowing pinkie-brown, a baby, no more than a day old, struggled to free tiny arms, reaching for contact with another human being.

The unshakable Bride of Christ could see, scrawled on the inside of the lid the words, 'God Bless my baby.' Reaching down, she lifted the warm bundle, touching her lips to the tiny tears, "Hello, little fella, welcome to the world … and by the way, Merry Christmas."

The authorities attempted, half-heartedly and unsuccessfully, to trace the natural mother. By mid January, the Sisters had registered the tiny mite, baptised him Jo-Jo (from the apples) and Christmas (from the day).

Slightly undersized by the age of six, Jo-Jo nevertheless enjoyed school, even though occasionally bullied by bigger kids. Reaching twelve, along with four other boys from the home, he joined a boxing club three blocks away. Within a month, the other lads, bored, moved on to other attractions such as girls, smoking and gangs. Jo-Jo stayed, intrigued by the skills, co-ordination and the disciplined energy of the pugilistic art.

Within nine months the youngster had become the club's Junior Flyweight, winning three cups. Travelling up-town to Queens where he out pointed a thirteen-year old, his name - wrongly spelt - appeared in the sports section of the New York Times. At school the bullying ceased.

Aged eighteen, with academic levels below college entry requirements, Jo-Jo's instructor advised trying for a sports scholarship. He refused, stubbornly seeking independence by obtaining employment as a rookie longshoreman on the Brooklyn Docks.

Renting a Spartan one-room apartment in the Bronx and working a shift system on the waterfront, Jo-Jo boxed semi-pro, under the management of a Russian-Jew. Mr Pollisky matched him, before he was ready, against a Cuban Golden-gloves contender. He took a beating.

Walking home in the rain, bruised, one eye already closed, the other puffed, feeling very sorry for himself, he stumbled into a dark alley behind a drinking club and found four thugs attacking a girl. Dragging one youth away, Jo-Jo ducked inside a knife thrust and broke the assailant's knee with a vicious kick. While one man wrestled with the struggling girl, the other two jumped the boxer from different sides.

His equipment bag cushioned a blow from a short lead pipe but he wasn't fast enough to avoid the kick that took his legs from under him. Rolling back to his feet, another slash from the flaying pipe broke two of the boxer's fingers. Stepping neatly inside he delivered a one-hand combination shot to the stomach, followed by the sweetest of uppercuts that lifted the man clear off the ground.

Straddled by thug number four, the girl, screaming in Mexican, lashed out at the youth thumping her head against the wet tarmac. Jo-Jo aimed both feet at the man kneeling on the girl, sending him sprawling into the gutter. Cursing, the girl scrambled to her feet and began beating the man on the ground across the head with her bag.

Pain ripped across Jo-Jo's head … somewhere from behind … blinding … falling … warm blood … no power in legs or arms. And far off, drifting in fog, a New York voice pleaded, "Help me, Mick. Da' fuckin' nigger broke my leg…"

The night became total darkness.

***

The blurred figure in a nurse's uniform gently informed him he'd been unconscious for three days. Two fingers of his left hand were in plaster. Slipping in and out of troubled sleep every bone groaned. Later, a kindly voice explained that the bandages now covering his eyes were protection for the wound behind the right ear.

Next day, an elderly doctor with a slight stutter, pointed out that he would recover, but it would take time. Some hours later, he felt warm fingers take hold of his good hand. "ello … is Maria. You brave. For your help I thank you."

She told him about the arrival of the police after he'd been knocked down. About the arrest of the kid with the busted-knee, together with the unconscious yob in the wet alley and how the others had fled as the police car arrived.

Most evenings, Maria sat by his bed, chatting, or quietly holding his hand. Occasionally she'd hum strange music or read the newspaper to him in a fractured Mexican/Bronx accent. She described her life as live-in housekeeper to a freethinking Brooklyn priest. She was twenty. Her name was Maria Lomas.

Long before the bandages were removed from his eyes Jo-Jo was in love. From the first moment her brown eyes and radiant smile came to his view, Jo-Jo Christmas was committed. This would be his woman.

Maria related that her family bible traced ancestors back to the 'Alamo'. Told how a three-times-removed grandmother, had been chosen by Colonel Travis to escape just before the Mexican Army made a final onslaught on the stockade. During fierce fighting, together with an army scout named, 'Spanish-fish', whom she later married, great-great-great Grandma was smuggled through enemy lines to carry important documents to the Texas Senate.

Released from hospital, Jo-Jo discovered his apartment trashed and employment at the docks terminated. To add to his problems, the broken bones in his fingers meant that his boxing career was over. Maria introduced him to her employer, Father Brian Mullan, who offered the young Negro work as driver/handyman. Within one month the same holy man conducted the service making Maria Lomas and Jo-Jo Christmas, man and wife.

In the early spring of '43, Uncle Sam waved a Stars & Stripes Banner and pointed a patriotic finger at America's brave sons, requesting that they take arms against Japan and Germany in a global struggle for civilisation and man's right to freedom. Uncle Sam, it seemed was even prepared to take coloured boys onboard his war-wagon.

Twenty-year old Jo-Jo Christmas stood in line with other young men rallying to their country's call. After a medical, consisting mainly of a cough and a count, six weeks basic training led to two months specialist work and almost before he'd had time to discover the exact location of Berlin on a map of Europe, PFC Christmas, together with thousands of men as confused as himself, found themselves lining the upper decks of an ocean liner, it's name painted out, watching the New York's waterfront drift slowly astern in the blue-orange haze of the setting sun.

Guided by a river pilot, the ageing vessel slipped by the mist-shrouded Statue of Liberty, slowly weaving along the buoy-marked channel of the Hudson River. Standing near the stern the young Negro gazed back at the long twisting wake. A giant of a man in a sergeant's uniform rested his elbows on the varnished rail beside the young G.I. Tossing a cigar butt over the stern, he asked, "First time overseas, soldier?"

Jo-Jo's reply began, "I never once been outside New York State in my born days, Sarge. Now, here we go, headin' for Europe, to fight a war against some guy who don't even know my name." Nodding in the direction of the fading skyline, he added, "Back there, I've a steady job for a preacher, a wife more beautiful than I deserve and, five months from now, I'll become a daddy."

The bigger man sighed, "Dem politicians better have good reason to drag coloured boys to fight a white fella's war … and that's a fact."

The majestic vessel, capable of speeds over thirty knots, was at stage one of a voyage transporting three thousand un-blooded, raw troops across the Atlantic Ocean. Proceeding eastwards at an economical 25 knots, it began a great circle course from departure point Latitude 40' 45" North, Longitude 74' 00" West.

During the second day, zigzagging at full sea speed to outrun reported U-boat positions, the ocean lady passed two slow moving Allied convoys before skirting clear of a deep depression south of the coast of Ireland. Five days after departure, in total darkness, the great grey/black hull docked at Southampton, England. Latitude 50' 54" North, Longitude 01' 23" West.

With the rest of his unit, Jo-Jo's initial fumbled steps onto foreign soil lacked any spirit of adventure. Tired, cramped from the voyage, heavily laden with equipment, he and his comrades shuffled down the steep gangway onto berth 102. MP's, cigar butts glowing, yelled directions to cross unlit cobbled streets towards a blacked out railway station. Shuffling in each other's footsteps, they boarded the dust-covered coaches of a steam-hissing train. A smiling rounded woman in a Salvation Army bonnet offered cups of warm sweet tea, "God goes with you son …"

Seven hours later, following unexplained stops of varying time spans, the old locomotive hissed to a stuttering halt in a small station lit by only a single oil lamp. As shrill whistles split the cold air, shouts of command rattled along the platform. "Okay. Get yer tired asses off d'train."

From inside the dark building a loud hailer spluttered … a slow Kansas drawl, "Y'all's in Merry ol' England. Move it. Smart time, outside where d'trucks is waitin.' Short-ways along you'll be tuckin' into hot chow. Keep movin', ya' hear?"

Pressed shoulder-tight within a cluster of crumpled uniforms, most of whom he'd never set eyes on before, Jo-Jo edged his boots slowly towards the station entrance. Passing a large board, crudely painted out, he could just decipher, 'The historic town of Totnes.'

Outside, in the frosty dimness, rattling trucks cluttering the small square crawled slowly towards the station's main doors and the rows of waiting men. As each truck's back-rail thumped down, silent men clambered onboard, until a faceless glowing cigar yelled 'Yoh!' before its owner hooked up the rail and banged the truck into motion. For thousands of travel-weary Americans, their early impression of England was cold, fog, and the damp unwelcoming darkness.

Five minutes away from the station square a truck slowed to a crawl at the base of a steep hill. Sitting shivering in the crowded semi-darkness, Jo-Jo watched as the gnarled fingers of a hand reach in, gripping onto the rim of the boarded side. The curved knuckles were worn, exaggerated by years of toil, each fingernail on the hand discoloured by dark soil. Easing back the canvas the young G.I. looked down at the bent figure of a man sitting astride an ancient bicycle. Glancing up at the soldier the red-brown face smiled, exposing a two-inch gap where front teeth had once grown. Sprigs of tufted white hair poked from under a battered cap covering the old man's head. While one bony hand steadied the handlebars the other gripped the truck's sideboard, dragging cycle and man slowly up the hill.

When the truck's engine revved into a deeper growl, gathering pace up the gradient, the man glanced up at the black face of the American, "Do'e naw where'e be gwain, bay?"

Puzzled, Jo-Jo shook his head. Not because he didn't know the answer but because he'd no real conception of the question … or indeed if the strange language had been a question.

Above the steady rumble of the truck the cyclist said, "You'm in Gawd's own country, me 'andsome. A word of 'eed, keep off the Ruff cider. Scrumpy will drive 'e maize as a breesh." and after a quick glance at the road,"Cum drekly you'd grab a 'and-full of sprats off our maids … an' a'fore 'e nawze what, they'm up the shoot, proper."

Staring out at the dark hedges of the hill, Jo-Jo could feel the truck increase speed as the gradient eased. Below him, the bike's wheels began humming a faster tune, sending misty spray into the air. Just as the soldier opened his mouth to shout a warning the old man let go, his voice trailing away behind the departing truck, "Mind 'ow e' go's, soldier boy,"

The G.I squatting beside Jo-Jo mumbled, "What did the Limey say?"

Jo-Jo shook his head, "Beats the hell out of me. 't'wasn't Ronald Coleman, is fer sure."

When the line of trucks reached sea level, scrambling down across the tailboard, Jo-Jo gazed along the full stretch of Slapton Sands. First light was beginning to blend different shades of grey and blue along the shadowed horizon. The strong flood tide rushed almost parallel along the beach, clattering and clinking small shingle. In the distance he could just make out the shape of Start Point Lighthouse where the land dipped towards the sea. Away to his right, wispy smoke from a cluster of cottages bordering a freshwater lake drifted straight up into the morning sky. In even formation, three swans glided silently in from the sea, skidding, almost in slow motion down onto the lake's calm water, coming to rest among a family of ducks searching in the muddy shallows for breakfast.

In the early stages of the German conflict, brass-laden Military Commanders, together with power-bellied politicians from various sections of the Allied Alliance had designated this stretch of tranquil coastline to be transferred into a battle school, to prepare for the eventual invasion of Europe.

Without proper consultation, over three thousand residents were uprooted from their homes, shops, village pubs and farms. The boundaries of enforced evacuation covered nearly twenty-five square miles of traditional Devonshire coastline and countryside.

Quiet country folk, old men who'd spent most of their lives working the warm red soil, women of different ages living in untroubled harmony, grandparents, grandchildren, farmers and farm labourers, traders, builders, fishermen ... all received notice to vacate the area immediately.

Under government instructions, the people of South Hams were ordered to pack treasured belongings, depart their homes and seek accommodation outside an area stretching from the low-water mark at Blackpool Sands, north to Blackawton, across to East Allington and curving back towards the lapping waves at Torcross.

The doors of ancient places of worship, which had remained open for centuries, became sealed.Historical trappings and religious valuables were stored for the duration in deep cellars and bank vaults, away from temptation and possible destructive hands of the 'invited invaders'.

Priceless stained-glass windows and age-creaking timbers were protected from modern armoury by rows of sandbags stacked high against ages old walls. Help, in the form of land-girls, was offered to assist gathering the last of the harvest and find shelter for animals before farmers walked from land that had been their homes for generations.

South Hams natives were assured that when the last of the gathering forces had sailed for France, farms, cottages, shops and pubs would be refurbished and returned to rightful owners.

Because they were |British, because they feared change and because there were those who'd never ventured far from the villages in which they'd been born, there were moans, groans and complaints galore. It was reported that one old lady refused to budge from her cottage until a home had been found for her six cats. An eighty-five year old dairy farmer negotiated, long and hard, with suited authoritarians over the purchase of his entire reserve stock of home-brewed rough cider. 90 gallons, stored in a large vat marked, tractor fuel.

Excited children took delight in stripping the contents of classrooms and loading books, desks, pens and blackboards onto lorries, transporting the education equipment to different schools outside the area of evacuation. It was rumoured that one couple, fifty years married under one roof, took to their beds and just silently faded away in the night.

For all the stories, fact and fiction, publicans, preachers, poachers, farmers and fishermen, together with shopkeepers and bank-workers, mucked in and did what had to be done … all in the quiet order of the English.

Ministers of His Majesty's government, pushed by Allied Warlords, shepherded bewildered residents away from a section of the coast that was to become a 'secret' American Army Battle school.

The ultimate purpose of the exodus was so that men and machinery might begin preparation for the greatest invasion in the endless history of wars. A frightening period in man's evolution that would be written in tomorrow's history books as 'Exercise Overlord.'

During that chill autumn of '43, G.I Jo-Jo Christmas lived, ate, breathed and dreamed the stern lessons of war. In the first month he became an expert at field camouflage, even hiding his Lieutenant's jeep for three days (it stood ten feet from the office, disguised as a bank of oil drums.) For this initiative he won his first stripe.

Because of the stevedore experience he was appointed squad leader, responsible for loading, discharging and stowage onboard

LST's (Landing Ship Tank.) which had begun arriving from the United States.

These strangely shaped craft had bow ramps that could be lowered onto a beach and wide-open spaces for deck cargo. The engine and crew quarters were positioned right aft. Under peacetime trading rules they would never have been granted seaworthy certificates to operate more than a mile from any coast, let alone cross the Atlantic Ocean. In the main, these cumbersome vessels were commanded by enlisted men, taken from various trades and rushed through navigation colleges to become known as '90-day-wonders'.

LST's, affectionately called, 'Lumpy-standing-targets', originated from a British naval design, in the early days of the war. Refined and modified by American shipyards, they were transported across the ocean to become a major contribution in the preparation for the invasion of Europe.

Displacing about 5,000 tons, measuring some 320 feet from bow to stern and shallow drafted, the box-shaped vessel was constructed in welded steel. Designed to transport tanks, lorries or other trappings of war, including men, the boats could venture right up onto a beachhead.

Self-respecting naval architects shuddered at the thoughts of these craft floating upright, let alone fighting. There were no deep keels, frames or reinforced bulkheads to establish a decent stability curve. The theory behind political thinking was that cheaply constructed and easy to replace, the LST was a dispensable means for transporting factors of war from one shore to another... with death as the common denominator.

From the first LST's sideways launching, without ceremony or official send-off, the hardest working member of the ship's company was the Chief Welder. As the grey-painted hulls gathered trial speed (12 knots flat out, down river) cracks appeared in the welded seams on the deck, bow ramps, the sides, stern and the after accommodation block. No one ever recognized the welding man during rare off-duty moments, for the simple reason he was mostly on his knees, a welding mask obscuring his face, whilst resealing the latest split in the new steel.

Each LST was armed but more for fright than fight. Most had twelve 20mm cannon, with larger 40mm guns positioned at bow and stern. Rumour was that one brave Commander requested heavier armament when sailing without escort. A short memo from the Navy's top brass informed him that the extra weight might well result in exaggerated rolling, which could cause stress fractures in the welded seams. There are unconfirmed reports that the Commander's next request was a transfer to submarines.

Jo-Jo Christmas was freezing. This was a different cold from dry New York winters. Wrapped in a greatcoat, a woolly hat pulled over his ears, with a scarf covering what remained of his exposed face, he also wore two pairs of army issue gloves and still his bones ached.

Flicking the bulldozer into gear he turned the cumbersome machine in a tight circle and begun skimming the frost covered top surface expertly from the side of the low hill. Through small gaps in the thorn hedge he caught glimpses of a speeding jeep, at least a mile down the beach, heading in his direction.

It was February. A three-day halt had been called in the landing practice programme. South easterly gales roaring along the English Channel, tossing spray-filled breakers across the tide, depositing boulders, gravel and sand high up onto the Slapton Sands Road.

Jo-Jo's squad had been detailed to bury thirty days accumulated garbage into unmarked ground in one of the meadows, inland from the beach. After selecting a site, the black soldier had trimmed away the turfs, setting them to one side, before gouging a trench with the 'dozer, along the slope.

When the hole was ready, trucks from various camps delivered rotten food, broken machinery parts, out of date rations, along with discarded mail, comics and work-fatigues past repair. The trash was tipped into the deep hole and the trucks rumbled away for more. When the trench became full, the 'dozer compressed the contents before a layer of lime dust was scattered. When the space was level, Jo-Jo would replace the cut top-grass. To the passing eye, nothing had changed.

The jeep came through the narrow gateway at frantic speed.

As it braked hard, all four wheels locked, sending mud, grass and small stones high into the breeze. It skidded to a halt alongside the throbbing 'dozer and two young officers leapt out, laughing.

Lieutenant Joe C. Brown, a 22 year-old law student, who'd interrupted college to do personal battle with Adolf Hitler, grinned at the dirt-covered 'dozer driver. "Hey, Jo-Jo, shut down the machine, man. Take a coffee break."

Clambering into the covered back of the jeep, Jo-Jo accepted the hot coffee poured from the flask held by his pink-faced Company officer. "Jo-Jo Christmas, this mad sucker," he nodded at the young man sitting in the passenger seat, "is Lootenant Paul Carter. We were at college together. Paul's a walking example of what the navy produces after only 90 days training." Slurping his coffee, he went on, "He's Exec-officer on an LST at … shit! He can tell ya."

Switching the mug to his left hand, 21 year-old, First Executive Officer Paul Carter reached back to shake the coloured man's hand. "Hi, delighted to make your acquaintance, Jo-Jo."

They shook hands, smiling, neither man removing his gloves.

"Here, let me doctor the coffee some." Lifting a hipflask from the jeep's map-pocket, he poured a generous amount into each of the steaming mugs. The aroma of good whisky filled the jeep.

"Joe C. tells me you're top-beach man." Sipping, he carried on, "Ah! That's more like it. My boat's holed up in a small fishing cove, Brixham, up the coast a ways. Leastways till the weather lets up. Locals do say that when this easterly sets in she forgets to change direction. Whatever. My skipper figures that once it moderates, we're down for some night-run landings on these sands. Cap'n reckons it's a must-do, before the 'major exercise' no one's talkin' about but we all know is brewin', begins. Now, here's the problem, Jo-Jo. I don't need to tell you that there's one bitch of a cross-tide buzzes along Slapton Sands on the flood. Durin' daylight we can work transits for … "

Lt. Brown laughed and interrupted him, "Steady there, Paul. We army boys have trouble keeping abreast of navy jargon.Slow it a pace. More coffee?"

The three men sat quietly, hands wrapped around steaming mugs, listening, as outside heavy seas rumbled onto the beach.

Sliding slowly back, each retreating wave sucked the moving shingle clean before folding over on itself, going in, pressed by wind and tide screaming, over the Skerries Bank.

Lt. Carter spoke again. "Right! Where the hell was I? Night landings. Our skipper figures to hit the sand bang-to-rights, off-load tanks, trucks and personnel and be away for load number two. He surely don't wanna be dragged, ass-up, along the shore by unpredictable cross-currents. No sir. The question, Mr Top Beach-man, is this, would you be willin' to operate a shit-light?"

Jo-Jo took another sip, feeling the contents stir warmth in his belly. "Hit me with that again, Lieutenant. Shit-light?"

"Sure. Here's how she works … the ol' man used it on the Italian landing. We approach the shore in darkness to about a mile off the landing spot. On the beach, you have two jeeps in transit, say about a quarter mile apart, backs to the sea. Our signalman flashes a quick S, three short dots. Your guy in the first jeep returns, H … four shorts. We get a bearing on this and about a half-mile out we give you an, I … two blips. Both jeeps send T, one long flash. The T-dash lasts five seconds to give a fix, off for ten seconds and then flash for another five. That way, keeping the two jeeps in line we keep going till we hit the sand. That, my friend, is the principle of a S.H.I.T light. Well, whaddya say?"

Jo-Jo smiled. "You sell a decent cuppa coffee, Mr Sailorman. You understand, if the beach commander sees this light, I'm one dead nigger?"

As the mud splattered jeep zipped out from the field, missing the gatepost by inches, Lt. Carter muttered, "Thanks for the help back there, Joe C. Permit me to offer some kindly advice. Don't return to this place when the war's done. In twenty years from now, that trash you're burying will have created a pocket of methane gas. Some poor farmer-man, stopping to light his pipe might well get blown into the next county."

A week later, close to 0400 hours, on an ink-black February morning, with spring tides ripping across the gap between the Skerries and Slapton shingle, six loaded LST's attempted to hit appointed spots along the beach.

Two boats ran aground nearly a mile from charted co-ordinates. Two others collided, damaging superstructures to the extent that their landings were cancelled. One commander tried twice, chickened out and remained offshore until daylight. Only one LST beached within a few yards of the intended position. Tanks and trucks were swiftly offloaded and one hundred and fifty men scrambled onto the wet shingle before the vessel backed off, moving stern first out into the shadows.

"Soldier, seems like it's my duty to award ya' a third stripe". Sitting at his desk, Major Willard Harris Jr. addressing a space below and to the left of Jo-Jo's head, hissed, "Boy, I tell ya', it surely cuts me but, according to these reports, you're one smart-ass beach-man."

Raised in Birmingham, Alabama, twenty-years regular army, officer-in-charge of the beach, Willard's piggy-eyes blazed. Under the desk his boots shuffled in anger. "Let me say, here and now that I truly believe army-niggers should only be doin' mess-work and haulin' trash." Knocking together some papers with thick fingers, he added, "Information is, three nights back, yours was the only LST to make it onto the sands. Your squad, it says here, off-loaded the boat in quick time and just before daylight the same boat made it back on a second run...."

The Major cleared his throat, spitting into a bucket beside his chair, "So ... you've made sergeant. "His voice dropped further, "But, hard up, you listen well, Mr Christmas. If I ever discover a 'shit-light' was used, I'll surely take delight in personally drawin' my colt 45 and blowin' your black fuckin' head away. You got me?" Tossing two sets of sergeant's stripes across the desk, he growled, "Sign there, boy."

Jo-Jo stepped forward, gathered up the stripes, signed the paper and took a smart pace back. Both men saluted.

That evening, everyone in the Sergeant's Mess acknowledged the promotion. After six beers, ready to settle for an early night, the new sergeant was about to make his excuses when Lt. Brown joined the table. "Congratulations, soldier. I'm buying - before you guys head for Union Street to get laid."

A colour-sergeant, downing a beer, laughed, "Jo-Jo's the only guy on the beach who couldn't find a pussy-parade if he was handed a map, Lieutenant. I wonder sometimes if maybe he's lost the need for a little lovin'. Don't ya' get horny, Christmas?"

Jo-Jo grinned finishing his drink, "Sure I get horny. At times I've even gazed thro' the window but it never got so bad I wanted to enter the store."

Slightly unsteady, the promoted G.I got to his feet and began heading for the exit. "What's waitin' at home … well, it will keep me warm till we're done over here. Right now, I got a letter to write. G'night, gentlemen. Thanks for the beer, Lieutenant."

With just a little stagger, blinking to adjust his eyes to the crisp air of the English South Hams, Jo-Jo began walking towards the sound of the surf breaking on the beach. He'd found it difficult to write letters home. Maria's mail would arrive every ten days, on the button. Her words bubbled with news about New York, the church, neighbours and the growing baby swelling her belly. 'When he/she kicks me awake in the dark, I lay there in the warm, thinking about you, darlin'. I pray God keeps you safe. Father Brian, he says, "hello" An' your job is here, whenever. Hey! My chest is sure grown big, soldier boy …'

In return, trying to transfer thoughts into words, he blanked, unable to convert any emotion onto paper. Standing at the water's edge, listening to waves rattle across the pebble bank, Jo-Jo wanted to yell. Angry that personal correspondence was subjected to army censorship. It sure didn't make it any easier.

There were times tossing aside the note-pad, he'd reach for a flat stone, flicking it hard across the tide, watching it skip five times …M-A-R-I-A … each extra leap becoming a kiss.

"Hi Honey, Guess what happened? I made Sergeant …don't ask how. Christmas in (censored out) was cold, wet and with no seasonal festivities. A gang of us went into (censored) city to watch Joe Louis fight an exhibition.I got to shake the great man's hand. He remembered me fighting Carlos Poni for Mr Pollosky, at the Gardens. Can you beat that?

We're still training hard, army stuff …not boxing. The camp's chow is so-so, but getting better. Only five cooks bumped-off last month (joke, honey).

Tell Father Brian, thanks for the 'hello' and return my best wishes. I sure want to come back to work … maybe a better class of automobile? (That's not a joke!)

Remind me, honey, when I get home, to tell you about the beautiful birds flying hereabouts.

Your loving husband,

Jo-Jo. (Big kisses.)

P.S. Give our soon-to-be-born daughter (I know) a warm hug from her soldier daddy."

****

Chapter Eight

... Mayo: 1990

Some distance from the land, the groundswell eased. Over the stern, Mayo could make out the spire of the old church silhouetted against the skyline, standing in transit with the dead elm lower down the meadow.

Checking that the magnetic compass pointed due south, he glanced at his watch. A sun-flash, high on the hill beside the broken church caught his attention. "Tourist. Gucci sunglasses or a discarded bottle, " he muttered, flicking the auto-pilot switch. "Ten-after-five. An hour, twenty to run."

Settling into a trip, he often spoke aloud. Perched on the low rail, lifting bait, cutting and flipping the dead fish from one basket to another, his body moved in rhythm with the boat's steady rise and fallover the glassy swells.

Every now and again a severed head or tail was tossed over his shoulder and as the discarded fish arched through the air, a lone gull traling in the boat's wake, swooped, catching and swallowing in one action. After the fourth catch, the bird wheeled, turning back towards the shore, gliding just above the glassy sea laden with food for hungry young waiting in the shelter of the old church wall. Without watching the retreating gull, Mayo called, "See you later, bird. Now! Time for a mug of tea."

There was no embarrassment felt by his audible words. Years working alone had cured the need for a two-sided conversation. The normal morning routine would begin with talking aloud until the land dipped below the horizon astern. From then on, his thoughts remained silent, transmitting necessary instructions into occupational actions. Later, homeward bound, sighting the distant coast, Mayo would start his one-sided conversation again - "There's the land, boat. Time for another cuppa."

Mayo Francis had been born in the small cottage behind the

Quarry Hotel, twenty-four years ago. After learning to walk, much of his life was spent off-shore, helping his father haul pots from various banks and sandy ledges ten miles or so south-west of Bolt Tail.

Mayo's father, James Francis, at one time a 'Don' trawler skipper, out of Plymouth had returned to Cove and crabbing in 1966, after his Kathy had died giving birth to Mayo.

The old boat, 'Receiver' was thirty-five feet overall. Blunt bowed, with a generous beam. Constructed by Mayo's grandfather, Walter Francis, in 1917, the crabber's timbers were of Burmese teak on English oak. Twenty years after construction, a protective whaleback was added, together with a forward cuddy. The wheelhouse, positioned aft, was spacious enough for two fishermen. Below, a 40hp four-cylinder Lister engine (the third engine in the craft's life) chugged the old boat along at eight knots … in all but the worst of weathers.

Catching sight of the orange marker buoy bobbing in the slow swell, Mayo lifted a weatherproof apron from the hook behind the wheelhouse door and slung the canvas loop over his head. Easing the throttle before switching off the auto steering, he knocked the engine out of gear and walked slowly along the starboard rail as the old craft drifted towards the limp flag.

Although the sun had not yet broken through the blanket of haze the drop-line of the first string was clearly visible thirty feet into its journey to the seabed, twenty fathoms below.

Under the boat's keel, another swell yawned in from the west, like a pulse of invisible energy, only slightly disturbing the glassy surface of the ocean. Leaning over the rail, dragging the first dan-marker onboard, the fisherman walked aft, leading the top rope back towards the spinning capstan …

***

Captain Albert George Mitchell:

On the first day of January 1910, Captain Albert George Mitchell reached his fortieth birthday. He'd been in command of the S.S 'Sassandra', a single-decked 6,000 ton steamer, for a little over five years. Loaded to Winter North Atlantic marks with almost nine thousand tons of general cargo, including a deck cargo of West African logs, the 400ft. vessel ploughed north towards a position, ten miles outside the lighthouse on the Ile. d'Ouessent, west of Brest.

With a clean bottom, in moderate weather, the Clyde built quadruple-expansion engine propelled the ship through the water at twelve knots. Each 24 hours the six stokehold fires feeding two boilers, consumed sixty tons of Welsh steam coal.

Double-checking the bearing and distance from the flashing light, the captain studied the Admiralty Chart of The Western Approaches. The new course plotted the vessel towards a position south of Start Point Lighthouse, one hundred and twenty miles to the northeast.

Walking onto the bridge wing, Captain Albert gazed at the dark horizon for a moment before turning to look astern at fluorescent sparks spreading from the wash. Sniffing the cold air told him there'd be fog by dawn around the Channel Islands before a breeze settled in from the south. Returning to the wheelhouse, with tired eyes adjusting to the soft glow from the compass binnacle, he wished the deck officers and quartermaster a Happy New Year before moving to the door leading to his night cabin.

Below, removing a heavy Bridge-coat, he poured a tumbler of dark rum and taking a sip, Albert silently toasted the beginning of another year. Emptying his bladder, he washed, finished the rum, undressed in the dark and climbed into his bunk. Curling into his sleep position, he began mentally plotting the different markers through the Channel. Start Point, Portland Bill, St Catherines, Owers light vessel, Beachy Head, Royal Sovereign and on … feeling old beyond his years he slipped into slumber.

At the age of fourteen, straight from boarding school, his father, a North Yorkshire boat builder, had apprenticed the youngster to a four-masted barque, trading between British east-coast ports and West Africa's festering hellholes. Seasoned by Atlantic voyages, at the age of twenty, ambitiously he'd signed articles with the new

Anglo-African Steamship Company and by his twenty-fifth birthday had gained a foreign-going Master's Certificate of Competency.

By four bells on the first watch of the New Year, Captain Albert's vessel passed clear of the Channel Islands on a voyage that had begun in the high humidity of West Africa's port of Lagos and would end in Middlesborough on the cold east coast of England.

Master Mariner, Albert G. Mitchell slept soundly, accepting he was a dying man. Recurrent malaria, caught while a young third officer in infested places such as life-draining Warri and Takoradi, aided by winter nights on the open bridge, searching spray-filled horizons for different lighthouses, had taken its toll.

The company doctor had been unyielding. This was to be Albert George's last voyage. In less than a week, when the ship docked on the Tees, he would unceremoniously be cast onto the maritime scrap heap.

A shrill blast from the bridge voice-pipe burst into Albert George's dreamless slumber. Reaching for the toggle, eyes blinking, he focused on the dimly lit gimballed compass over the bunk. The needle pointed NNE.

"Sorry, Captain, lookout reports a red flare on the starboard bow … 'bout a couple of miles he reckons …"

Albert was already climbing into his trousers, "What time is it? What's our position? Have you called all hands?"

The reply echoed down the brass pipe, "Ten after six, sir. DR position puts us about nine or ten miles south of Bolt Tail. It's raining, mucky visibility, freshening … the cadet's rousing the crew at this moment."

On the bridge-wing it was bitterly cold. Grey-black clouds scurried across the sky. Wearing a uniform greatcoat over two sweaters, with thick woollen gloves protecting his hands, Albert sipped at a mug of scalding sweet tea. His uniform cap was pulled forward, shielding eyes from the driving rain. "There's another one, Mister Mate. 'Bout half a mile, I'd guess. Port your helm, quartermaster." Taking another sip he muttered, 'Happy birthday, Albert George.'

In the gloom of the unfolding day, the British freighter drew close alongside a deep-laden German vessel. In the glow from the stern light he could just make out her name, “Stadt Essen.” Hamburg.

Signals passed between the two ships established that the German was on passage from Bremerhaven to New York, with a full cargo of copper ingots. Her master also advised they’d lost the propeller two hours into the New Year. The starboard anchor had parted one hour later and the port cable snapped just before the first distress flare had been fired into the night sky. Using coded flags, the German tried to negotiate a ‘contract-to-safe-anchorage’ agreement, which was firmly but politely refused by the British captain during his second mug of sweetened tea.

As daylight crept into the eastern sky, the two vessels, roughly the same tonnage, drifted closer, the British ship slightly astern, perhaps half a length inside. With the rain easing, the wind backed more to the south. The two freighters rolled almost in unison on the same swell as the dull loom of Bolt tail became visible, about three miles to the north.

Half an hour later, drifting sideways across a shallow ridge, two nautical miles from the shore, the master of the “Stadt Essen”, reluctantly, agreed salvage terms. Lloyds Open Form. No cure-no pay.

“We’re ready, sir.” The Chief officer yelled to his captain, on the bridge wing. “Do we go in now?”

“Not yet,” replied Albert George. “First we do a run inside her, spreading a few barrels of veggie oil. About a mile off the land there’ll be breakers, we need to flatten the sea. Have the heaving lines ready, Mister Mate.”

On the second turning circle, this time edging closer, S.S Sassandra manoeuvred tight under the port quarter of the German ship. The crew of the disabled craft had braved seas breaking over her foredeck to connect strong ropes to what remained of the port anchor cable, leading it aft to just below her bridge.

The blunt stem of the British ship passed by the wheelhouse of the German with hardly fifty feet sea-space between the hulls. A thin messenger line soared through the air and as anxious hands reached to grab it Captain Albert rang full astern on the ship's telegraph. Side by side the two vessels lumbered down the edge of the same swell, moving slowly towards the land.

In the freshening breeze, the British master could hear his chief officer frantically urging deckhands to connect the towline. When it was done, he yelled back to the bridge, "Done! She's fast. When you're ready, Captain.

On the weather side, Captain Mitchell peered across the gap at his German counterpart. For what seemed like a long moment each mariner studied the other's expression. The German's eyes were red rimmed, sunken, his wet beard tinged with grey streaks. Broad shoulders appeared to be slumped inside his oilskin coat. Giving a brief nod of acknowledgment to the Englishman, he turned, staring at the slack towrope.

"Dead-slow ahead, mid-ships the helm". The order was firm.

Softer, he requested, "Perhaps another mug of tea might be in order, Mr Steward."

Albert George Mitchell knew that the tiredness he felt now was nothing. The long struggle had only just begun. What had been achieved so far was the easy part. Keeping the towline intact, making any forward movement against the strong ebbing tide, clawing around Prawl Point and Start Point after that ... that would be the testing ground.

For over two hours the ships barely moved, except sideways, closer to the land. Through binoculars he could make out great seas pounding the foot of the cliffs, could hear the rumbling surf surging against black rocks. Searching for marks from which to obtain a compass bearing, Captain Albert caught sight of an old church spire on the brow of a hill and lower down, in a dipping meadow, a large elm tree, straining against the wind. The church and tree were in transit. That would do. Lowering the glasses, he gazed aft, studying the tow wire skip from the spray, stretch tight, twanging and singing, before falling back into the sea.

When four hours had passed the British mariner had not shifted from his position, huddled in the cold, on the leeward bridge wing.

At eight bells, the Glaswegian steward delivered a large mug of soup and a hunk of bread. "Are we winning, Captain?"

Albert George looked shoreward towards the church and elm tree ... they were still in line, only now, he didn't require the binoculars to pick them out. "Not so's you'd notice, McCloud. Still, the flood's started now. The next few hours will be the test. You might whisper a prayer or two."

Turning back towards the wheelhouse door, ducking low against the flying spray, the white-coated steward, replied, "Be assured that every last man onboard is prayin' for ye, Captain."

During the next two watches they struggled seven miles to the east. Six of those miles had been gained, courtesy of the eastbound tide. When the flood ended, the tow was gradually eased to a south easterly course. They only lost a mile. With the next surge of tide reaching up Channel, they'd drawn abeam of Torbay's Berry Head light, three miles off. The wind had increased but had veered towards the south west.

At three o'clock in the morning, slowly easing into the mouth of the open bay, the towline parted...but the main battle was won. There was no way they were about to give up the prize at that juncture. By daylight, secured again, they got underway and just after 0900 hours, "Sassandra" with "Stadt Essen" on a short tow, dropped both anchors one mile north of Brixham breakwater's occulting red light.

From the moment the first rope had passed from one ship to another, to the time the anchors took hold in the sheltered waters of Torbay, they had travelled only twenty-four nautical miles. The passage had taken one complete day ... two full circles of the clock ...plus, something indefinable from all their lives.

Captain Mitchell slept, without stirring or dreaming, for eight hours. That afternoon, the Brixham shipping agent informed him that both owners, being in agreement, had arranged for two salvage tugs to deliver the disabled freighter to dry dock in Southampton.

Next morning, both masters went ashore in the agent's boat to tender Notice of Protest with a Notary Public. Waiting on the damp quayside for the returning launch, the two men stood in embarrassed silence. It was the German who spoke first.

"Captain, one moment. Cum vis me."

They marched across the road to the Blue Anchor Inn. Entering the Lounge Bar the German placed an English five-pound note on the counter. "Cognac … flasche ..ah, bottle."

When the puzzled barmaid laid down the bottle and two glasses before the German captain, he pulled the cork with his teeth and poured two generous measures. Handing one glass to Albert George, he raised the other. "Danke vielen, Kapitan. Prosit!"

They drank. Draining his glass in one swallow the German waited for the Englishman to finish his before flinging the empty glass, hard, into the blazing fire. Captain Mitchell followed suit. The barmaid looked stunned. Thumping the cork back into the bottle the German tucked it into the overcoat of the British master. "Cum. Ve go ship now, ja?"

Five days later, 'S.S. Sassandra' arrived in the port of Middlesborough on the River Tees. After the ship closed articles, Captain Mitchell was taken to dinner by Anglo-African's Marine Superintendent. During coffee and cigars he was presented with a gold hunter watch inscribed, 'For Valiant Service', plus a cheque for three months wages.

The next morning a private car delivered Albert George to a seaman's hospital outside Hull, where he spent five months fighting severe bouts of malaria. Later, during convalescence in a nursing home, near Filey, which ate deep into his savings, he entered into extensive legal battles with maritime solicitors, barristers and representatives of insurance underwriters, in a drawn-out squabble to obtain settlement for services that he and his crew had administered to 'those-in-peril' on that cold January morning off the south coast of England.

One year and one day after the unforgettable act of seamanship, Captain Albert George Mitchell (Master Mariner Rt'd.) was awarded his share of the salvage money … £15,000. He was a rich man.

Early in the spring of 1922, on a whim, Albert George

undertook a train journey diagonally across the country from the Yorkshire coast to South Devon in the Westcountry.

Standing in the gateway of the old mariner's church he gazed down across the sloping meadow, past the long shadow of the single elm. For a long moment his tired eyes looked out over the creek to the calm sea, reliving the beginning of the tow. Turning to leave, he observed a small, disused quarry in the lower vein of the valley. Clambering through thick brambles, he stumbled down through a narrow pathway in which rusting steel tracks embedded showed through the soil.

In the quiet valley below, something unexplainable about the untidy circular excavation drew hope to his mind. 'Life is not over! Here is a place I could start again. This quarry can become my harbour … my home.'

The Kingsbridge Farmers Bank sold him the abandoned site for two thousand pounds, throwing in a hundred year lease on the creek and adjacent shoreline from quarry quay to the sea, via something known locally as the Boat Passage.

***

… looking up from the compass, Mayo could just make out the distant smudge of land. Thirty minutes later, shielding his eyes he picked out the dead elm slightly to the left of the church. He knew that the ebb would rectify the drift. Twenty minutes would see them passing through Passage, into the creek.

In the for'ard bin, seventeen 2lb. lobsters with banded claws, journeyed towards the shore. The seawater tank below decks held 50 or so fine hen crabs, also with thick elastic bands holding their main pincers closed, to prevent fighting. It had been a good day's fishing.

"There's the land, boat. Home soon."

****

Chapter Nine

... The Quarry House Hotel

The voice, a soft Devon burr, appeared to come from a hidden recess in the lower shrubs. Turning, Maria Jo-Jo could just make out a man's lower legs sitting on a wooden seat. Beside the seat, on a table clouded with age, lay a tray, teapot, cups, milk, sugar, several little covered jars and a heaped plate of toast.

Climbing to his feet, extending a hand, the man said, "Matthew Mitchell. You must be Miss Maria Jo-Jo Christmas. Welcome to the South Hams. Please … allow me to be mother."

While he poured, Maria Jo-Jo studied his face, guessing early sixties,with rusty coloured hair, growing without directional control. He was slightly taller than Max. She thought that his pale brown eyes were worldly and kind. Smiling, he asked, "Ah! What about your driver chap … Frankie?"

Sitting at the table sipping tea, amused at the surprise greeting, Maria Jo-Jo lifted a piece of toast, uncovered the honey and spread it over the crispy bread. She nodded towards the Rolls below on the quay, "No. Frankie stayed in London. That's Max. He'll be fast asleep. His body clock works in a different zone from normal folk. He'll be fine. If it's no trouble could you arrange an extra room?"

"Certainly, dear lady. That presents no problem. We trust you'll enjoy your stay here." Reaching for some toast he, too, began to eat.

In a silence, broken only by their munching, the New York singer watched a shaft of sunlight slowly unravel a path through the dense conifers at the creek's elbow. Expanding, it coloured the trees, the blue-green water and the gorse-covered ridge with a clarity she'd never before experienced. In a whisper she breathed, "Honest to God, I didn't know this kind of light existed."

For a while they sat in silence, drinking their tea, watching the changing patterns. "Sorry about our noisy entrance …"

Matthew laughed. "Your arrival didn't disturb me. I tend to rise early. But I did hear your vehicle coming down through the lane. That was extremely brave of you."

Maria Jo-Jo refilled their cups. "Max didn't find it the most rewarding ride of his life, that's a fact. Tell me, what's with the tracks in the … you call it a lane, right, Mr Mitchell?"

"Matthew, please. A hundred years ago there were shipwrecks a-plenty around this coast. Certain local dignitaries objected to 'Johnny-foreigner' being laid to rest on the same consecrated ground as good Devon folk so they purchased some land from the old workings. Limestone blocks were transported up the grade along those tracks by horse-drawn wagons, where the parish elders built a Sailor's Church. When the church was completed, any shipwrecked mariner was laid to rest in the churchyard."

"A Christian act…"

"Well, yes. But, politically motivated. And yet, when all's said an' done, the enterprise provided local employment. The businessmen who devised the plan just happened to own the land from which the stone was quarried. Another merchant ran the construction company awarded the contract to build the holy house and, would you believe it, the Mayor, who'd placed his seal of approval on the programme … well, it just so happens he was also the local undertaker! It all came to an end when the grade of stone didn't reach the same commercial standard being quarried at Berry Head, up Brixham way.

Anyways, the fog signal they later established at Start Point drastically reduced the number of shipwrecks."

Maria Jo-Jo gazed around the terraced gardens, fully lit by the advancing dawn. "It's so beautifully laid out … so much peace. I'm surprised plants survive in such salty conditions. You must have broken your back creating this tranquillity."

Laughing, Matthew held up both hands, "No credit this way, lovely lady. The quarry sits in it's own vacuum, devoid of strong breezes from any direction. Facing south, it becomes a suntrap. The spring from the top neutralizes any spray drifting over the cliffs during winter blows, so the plants flourish in almost perfect conditions. But, it was my father, a master mariner from Hull who began it all. He'd come here to die but during the five-year struggle to create this haven discovered that living's a better alternative."

Maria Jo-Jo eased the last of the tea from the pot, filling their cups. "Go on with the story …Matthew."

"Well, back in, oh 1912 or thereabouts, the old man saved a ship from running ashore, just outside the creek. He …"

Excitedly, she interrupted his flow, "Earlier, from the church wall, I watched a small boat vanish into the cliffs and then, moments later, there it was …out on the sea."

"Ah, that would be Mayo, passing out through 'Passage'. He supplies our hotel with crabs and lobsters. It was Mayo's grandfather, Walter Francis who befriended my father and helped construct what you see before you."

He halted, listening as a blackbird began it's beautiful song from somewhere on the higher ridge. They both listened, smiling.

"As a young fisherman, Walter'd lost a foot in a trawling accident and couldn't get a berth. After father purchased this hole from his salvage award, he and Walter sort of adopted each other. He became general factotum, advisor and drinking partner. Dad engaged a crazy Exeter architect to make sense of plans he'd sketched in the quarry dust. Together they designed a building that followed the same curve as the quarry area, apparently arguing for months over what was feasible and what was architecturally possible. No one's really sure who won the day but I'm pretty sure the old fella' wouldn't have given in."

They watched the sleek blackbird burst from a green hedge on the higher level, swooping towards the creek with a series of frantic wing action until it disappeared into the trees. Within seconds its captivating song echoed across the calm water.

"Father and Walter spent months manoeuvring giant limestone blocks, using A-frames, pulleys, horses and sometimes blasting great chunks of rock with dynamite. When the terraces fitted the plan, they hauled tons of red topsoil by horse and cart, distributing it along the ridges. Farm manure was mixed with seaweed to feed and establish the bones of a garden.

During the second summer, Walter 'acquired' the loan of a boat from Plymouth and they travelled to Tresco, in the Scilly Isles, to buy plants and shrubs that would survive these conditions. The story goes that they spent almost as much on rum as they did on rhododendrons but by autumn the backbone of the garden was set in stone, so to speak."

In a whisper, afraid of being hurt by his answer, Maria Jo-Jo asked, "Did you ever meet my daddy? He was an American GI Sergeant, stationed here back in'44. He … he wrote my mom about this place and some kindly folks he'd met, just before he was killed."

Reaching across the table, Matthew touched her hand. "I'm sorry to say I didn't. But Mayo's father, James talked about him. I understand Grandad Walter and Sergeant Jo-Jo became good friends. There are many stories … but no doubt Mayo can help. I wasn't here during the war."

His eyes focused on a kingfisher standing motionless on the edge of the lower pond, weighing up its breakfast. "In 1916, when the house was complete, father married. Mother was Margaret Downs, gentry from South Molton. There were times when the ol'man swore she only married him because of the stables he'd built behind the main house. She was a grand horsewoman. Rode with the Kingsbridge hunt for years. Strange but father both feared and hated horse. But they truly loved each other.

Just before the war, early in '39, someone connected with father's old shipping company came down with a representative from the Admiralty. They requested he go to Ireland to advise on enemy shipping that might seek shelter or trade along the neutral coastline of Eire. Typically British, there was no mention of salary or compensation. The deal was that the Ministry of Defence would lease Quarry House for the duration for discreet intelligence services.

While Dad pondered over their proposals, Mother took charge of the negotiations. She persuaded the government to settle me in a good boarding school at Taunton … at their expense. She also talked them into allowing her to accompany her husband to Ireland pointing out that with her knowledge they could pass as authentic horse-breeders."

"During the war, while Father reported enemy shipping movements along the Irish coast to the Admiralty, Mother gained a reputation among the horse-people of Galway and Connemara as a better than average breeder".

"When it was over, he'd developed an ulcer and angina, caused, most likely by the stress of patriotic duty. He would have really hated the lies and deceit. Mother meantime had acquired two champion stallions and four excellent brood mares. Yours truly had begun a half-decent education ... all at the expense of His Majesty's Government. "

Glancing at his watch, Matthew began collecting together the cups. "Twill soon be time to start breakfast. You'll perhaps want a bath and a sleep after the journey. Sit ... enjoy the morning and the garden. Welcome the sunrise. I'll call you."

As he turned to leave, loaded with the contents of the tray, she asked, "What made you turn the house into a hotel?"

Lowering the tray back onto the table, he looked down the creek, as if collecting his thoughts, "After the war my parents stayed on in the west of Ireland, in a town called Clifton. They purchased a small farm. She continued to breed horses, successfully. Thinking back, I'd guess Father longed for Devon but by this time he was eighty and had surrendered to Mother's way of life."

She followed his eyes down along the creek, watching the changing colours as the new day erased shadows along the banks.

"When they died, I was working in hotel management in London and married. Strangely, it was Mother who passed away first. A stroke. Dad was found a couple of days later, quietly looking at the ocean. Most likely watching the sun fall into the ocean that had been his life. Joanne and I went over to Ireland, buried Mother and sold the land and stock. That was Mother's wish. We brought Father's ashes home, scattering them in the creek on a falling tide...that was his wish.

We also discovered we'd inherited - if that's the correct word - Kathy, a strange gypsy-girl, who'd been with them for years. She'd become totally confused by their passing and just followed us around."

"When the dust had settled, my Joanne did some research. We employed an agent, borrowed some capital and set to work. The Quarry's off the beaten track, so to succeed, we needed to specialize."

"Bedrooms were added, the dinning room enlarged and the stables converted into classrooms. Joanne's an accomplished artist, with teaching experience. With carefully placed advertising we aimed at people seeking a different holiday. The offer was a week, in beautiful surroundings, with opportunity to improve artistic skills. It worked just fine. With time in France and Italy during hotel training I'd acquired certain culinary skills as a chef, so we began including 'cook-'n'-learn' weeks in the itinerary. That also, thankfully, was a success."

"The first few years were a struggle but, at present, touchwood, the art and cooking takes care of forty weeks each year. During the past two years, forward-thinking companies have used our facilities for management mini-conferences. We can accommodate twelve in comfort. Although it's unlikely we'll be quoted on the stock market, our bank manager has been known to smile."

"Maybe I was lucky to catch a room?"

Matthew grinned, "Fear not. Joanne has a class of only seven this week. An Art Club that books each year. Besides, the combination of my London agent, who's a great fan of yours, and pressure from your friend Ruby, there was no way we were about to say no."

He reached for the tray again. "Now, if I don't make a positive move, breakfast will be late. So, sit … enjoy and, once again, welcome to Quarry House."

Following his footsteps to the lower level, Maria Jo-Jo called after him, "Juice and coffee's fine for me. Max will appreciate the full works … perhaps without the bacon, if you understand me?"

Over his shoulder he said, "It will be my pleasure. Maybe I'll try tempting your friend to sample our famous hogs pudding."

She laughed at his joke, already enjoying her stay.

Maria Jo-Jo slept till noon in a room panelled in light English oak. The bed, a king-sized four-poster, had gathered around the singer like a warm cuddle. There was a small dressing room off from a sparkling modern bathroom. A large south-facing window presented the full stretching beauty of the creek as far down as the first curving bend.

Quietly opening his door, Maria Jo-Jo saw that Max was sleeping like a baby. His curtains were drawn, shutting out the brilliant daylight. Leaning over the bed she kissed his forehead.

Max twitched, rubbed his nose but didn't wake.

Leaving the hotel's driveway, she crossed the creek head, walking along a narrow path towards the woods. Bluebells and late primroses grew in abundance on either side. A lumpy toad hopped out from the grass ahead of her and leapt into the deep clear water lapping almost to the tall pines. Blackbirds, thrushes, a robin and birds she didn't recognize challenged each other using different songs.

Just over a quarter mile downstream the track swerved around the crowded trees, leading onto a curving semi-circle of white sand that carried to the sheer rock face. Tiny sand waves formed irregular patterns to the water's edge. It looked as if nature had taken a giant spoon, scooping a mini-bay between the trees and the ten-foot high ridge.

Moored against smooth stone, at right angles to the creek, in what appeared to be a deep-water inlet, sat the hull of an old schooner. A rusting cable extended from the bow towards an area beyond the sand where it was buried in the ground. Ropes at the stern led from the transom rail to steel rings positioned high up the rock. The schooner was without masts.

The fishing boat that she'd seen manifested through the cliffs earlier that morning bobbed quietly against the larger vessel. Onboard the smaller boat a young man was transferring crab pots up onto the schooner's deck.

Removing her shoes, Maria Jo-Jo could feel the warmth between her toes and yet an inch or so below the surface the sand felt cold and damp. Slowly she crossed towards the inlet, studying the rhythmic movements of young arms lifting tarred pots from one deck onto the other. If he'd seen her, he gave no sign. Reaching the gap between beach and boats, she stood watching perspiration zigzag from the dark curls at his neck down across the faded blue shirt. With only three pots remaining he stretched and from a distance of less than three feet they looked at each other.

'Jesus … this ain't happening. This kid's half my age. So, why the fuck am I burning up? How come I'm shakin' so bad my feet are melting in the sand? If he asked, right here and now, I'd go buck naked and …whatever-whatever!' Maria Jo-Jo's mind screamed for help from brain-cells stocked with a lifetime of street experience. For reasons she couldn't figure the lyrics of her first song became the only answer to distressed emotions.

…surely it would be enough
for one sad moment to linger,
reaching out as we pass down
different roads to touch, by only a finger,
… surely it would be enough?

Mayo had seen her from the first moment she'd broken cover from the trees. As she stopped to remove her shoes, he knew she was Maria Jo-Jo Christmas, International singer.

Lifting another pot, he'd smiled. By a strange coincidence, only a few minutes ago he'd been humming one of her early songs …'Different Roads.'

Close up, she was more striking than any of her album pictures or publicity photographs and, to his surprise, taller and more curvaceous. Her eyes, a deeper brown than her skin, sparkled in the afternoon sunlight. The crop of white hair came as no shock. Acknowledging that flowing tresses were mostly the 'added extras' of show business and having read about her medical problems, Mayo would have gambled that her own hair was this brilliant shade of white. It enhanced the full curve of her eyebrows, the cultured cheekbones and the full African mouth.

While their eyes exchanged questions, he cursed the deep breathing from the lifting, the panting and sweating. He regretted wearing his oldest jeans, a crumpled work shirt and not shaving for the past two days. While his mind registered that standing only three feet way, was one of the most beautiful mature women he'd ever come face to face with, a section of his reasoning believed she was looking at him like he was the village freak.

Her voice almost ghosted from her lips, "Are you Mayo?"

He nodded. "There's no need to ask who you are" and immediately regretting the presumption, added, "Can I help you?"

Maria Jo-Jo's brain panicked, 'I must touch him'. She managed to stammer, "I'm trying to discover information about my father, Sergeant Christmas. He was a GI stationed here in'43. I was told that …" Her voice faltered, faded and she wanted to scream,'Maria Jo-Jo girl, you actin' like a fuckin' teenager.'

Mayo said, "There's rain heading this way. Why not step onboard. I'll … do you need a hand?"

Reaching across the space, she stepped awkwardly onto the rail of the first boat and Mayo's hand shot out to steady her stumble. Turning with practiced ease, he swung up and over the schooner's rail before reaching down a hand to help her. "Use the crab pot, one step and up…"

On the wide deck of the old vessel she looked around, trying to take in the jumbled assortment of stacked pots, ropes and the large steering wheel, over which hung an oilskin coat, drying in the sun. "It's … different."

"Welcome aboard," Mayo smiled. "I guess as part-owner of this vessel, you hold certain rights."

"Pardon me?"

****

Chapter Ten

... E-Boats

By May 1944, two months before D-Day, the Allied Warlords had assembled over 1.5 million fighting men and women along the shores of Great Britain in preparation for battle against the awesome power of Hitler's fatherland.

The Master Plan was that by early June a mighty armada would assault the northern coast of France, from the Cherbourg peninsula eastwards to Ouistreham, the entrance to the port of Caen.

Their agenda was for the fight be carried into Belgium and Holland, across the Rhine, advancing to the streets of Berlin. It was to be a march of liberation that the history books would record as 'Operation Overlord'

For six months, General Dwight D. Eisenhower, Supreme Commander of the Allied Expeditionary Force, in close association with Chief-of-Staff, General George C. Marshall and General Omar Bradley (Commander US Army, North West Europe) plotted, planned and at times pacified various

British Field Marshals, Generals, Admirals and other senior members of His Majesty's war cabinet, in preparation to begin an invasion into Europe that was truly intended to become "the war that will end all wars".

Softly spoken folk from the South Hams in Devonshire, England, as requested by their government, walked from their homes, farms, shops, churches and warm country pubs. They moved out with understandable grumbles but no great argument. Country people departed from red-soiled valleys, hills and coastal shores in an orderly fashion, leaving their place of birth to units of the Allied fighting forces, so that preparation for the greatest conflict of their lives (or for many thousands of young men and women, their untimely deaths) might commence.

The evacuated area of Start Bay became known locally as, "the

Bloody Yankee Battle School" from which graduation by its members would mean crossing a stretch of water, displaying to the western world the final results of its teachings.

In the countdown leading towards the invasion of Europe, one of the tragic lessons to be learned was that of "Exercise Tiger".

Sergeant Christmas was informed that his squad's part in the exercise placed them on stand-by until beach engineers cleared defence obstacles in preparation for the second assault. In the hours that would follow daylight, 25,000 troops, loaded with equipment necessary to invade and hold a beachhead would scramble ashore onto Slapton Sands. To create authenticity, British naval vessels would bombard the beachhead, pretending to be the enemy, shooting live ammunition over the heads of the incoming 'invaders.'

When the first LST hit the sand, Jo-Jo's squad would supervise tank landings, dispatch artillery, offload the stores and equipment, moving them to designated areas to await the push inland towards the objective.

Leaving the operations tent after the briefing, Jo-Jo came face to face with Beach-master, Major Willard Harris, Jnr. Teeth set, Willard hissed, "I unda'stan' come mornin' you nigger boys will handle Convoy T-4 as they hit the sand. Know this, dark-man, Willard will be watchin' your action. You guys fuck-up in any way whatso' and ..." He patted the colt 45 on his hip before sauntering on.

Calmly, Jo-Jo saluted the Major's waddling rear disappearing into the officer's tent, retorting softly, "Yessir, Major." Dropping his hand, he added, "and up yours."

In the soft air, walking along the edge of the beach, Jo-Jo watched the distant silhouette of a tugboat on the eastern horizon, altering course to enter Dartmouth. In the failing light he could hear the strong ebb dislodge small pebbles from the sloping ridge, rattling over each other on the journey towards Torcross. Lifting a flat stone he flicked it out over the tide, watching it skip once (M) twice (A) three times (R) four (I) and five (A). And as the ripple from the last splash faded he spoke her name - "Maria"

After supper he'd drawn his men together, issued last minute instructions for the morning and thirty minutes later, with the cloudy night covering Start Bay like a blanket, Jo-Jo Christmas was tucked into his warm sleeping-roll.

Twelve hours previously, Convoy T-4's West section had departed from Plymouth Sound via the breakwater's Eastern gap. Outside, assembled into an orderly line, the lead LST 515 was followed by 496, 511, 531, with LST 58 towing two flat pontoons bringing up the rear.

As the small flotilla headed southeast, skirting the jagged Mew Stone Rocks about a mile inshore, the Flower-class corvette, HMS Azalea overhauled the first LST taking escort duties ahead. The LST captains assumed that HMS Scimitar, a 26 knot destroyer, earlier observed steaming back to Plymouth, would rejoin the convoy to ride 'shotgun', before the vessels joined up with the others at Torbay, forty miles to the east. They were wrong to assume.

The Exercise orders were straightforward. Make course toward Torbay. Rendezvous with LST's 499, 289, and 507 outside the fishing port of Brixham. From there to proceed eastwards, making several laps of Lyme bay, to simulate the sea-time required to voyage from Slapton to the Normandie coast.

On receiving the signal that the landing area was safe they would advance shoreward to offload men and equipment.

Their orders were to hold the beach and eventually force-march their way inland to 'liberate' Oakhampton. Such was the powerful plan…

A mile from the tiny village called, Frittiscombe, as the day slipped into its closing hour, Sergeant Jo-Jo Christmas slept soundly in his tent. Meanwhile, at sea, forty miles to the east, 8 American LST's fully loaded with anxious fighting men and the machinery of war, turned wide navigational circles ten miles south-west of the Bill of Portland.

***

Two hours before April 27 closed its account on the world, in the occupied port of Cherbourg, nine vessels of the 5th and 9th 'Schnessboote' fleet prepared for night patrol. Sleek, triple-skinned hulls, painted the colour of death, they were armed with twin torpedoes and two 20mm cannon. None of the boats was equipped with radar. Possessing a travel range of only 700 sea miles and almost invisible during darkness, their powerful engines were audible downwind for a distance of at least three miles.

On duty-operations, these 'fingers of destruction' would roar from occupied French harbours, fanning out across the Western Approaches, hounding allied convoys relieved to have voyaged the Atlantic in apparent safety.

The crack E-boats were manned by the wildest of Germany's young mariners. College students, studies placed on hold, waging war against the enemies of the Third Reich. Together with regular naval personnel, hot-blooded crew members enjoyed the buccaneering lifestyle onboard craft that screamed into action at forty knots. Driven by 6,000 horsepower diesel engines, the thirty meters long Schwarz-tod hulls hunted whatever targets the dark waters of 'der Kanal' might offer.

Each craft was commanded by young Ober-leutnants, with fire in their bellies, making their own crazy rules, respecting no authority … save those of Admiral Donitz.

After night operations, they'd roar, full throttle, back into port in tight formation, securing to moorings in the outer harbour. Before breakfast, damage checks were made and necessary repairs attended to without delay. Deck-ratings rearmed guns and torpedo tubes, while engine-room staff returned the throbbing machinery to pristine condition. Senior officers gathered aboard the leader's boat for the previous night's de-briefing. Only when these tasks were complete was it time to eat and sleep.

After the mid-day meal, off-duty crew heading ashore to sample different pleasures offered by French ports were honour-bound to report back at least two hours before sunset.

When dinner was finished, the night's plan-of-action was outlined and discussed. Every man was then expected to take three hours rest. By 2200 hours, they were ready for … whatever.

Fully aware that the Resistance transmitted departure times to England, on dark nights a small harbour tug would tow the fleet clear of the breakwater, prior to starting their massive engines.

When the outer harbour was floodlit by a full moon, powerful diesels ripped apart the night air as each craft charged seaward, turning east or west to confuse unfriendly observers, before striking northward towards the English coast.

During the first hours of April 28th 1944, while hunters from the 5th Pack prowled west of Alderney, the four boats from the 9th closed ranks and headed due north at twelve knots. Holding tight formation, their hulls within feet of each other would convince any scanning radar operator that the echo he observed was only one stray merchant craft (most likely friendly) on course towards the English coast.

More by chance than judgement, the pack fell upon the under-protected Convoy T-4 about twelve miles southwest of Portland. Breaking close formation and increasing speed, the E-boats delivered savage destruction with frightening velocity.

In the first attack two ships, LST's 507 and 531 received direct torpedo hits. Blown asunder and abandoned in panic, they drifted towards the mixture of mud and shale on the bottom of Lyme Bay.

Following the sounding of 'General Quarters' the remaining LST's scattered, zigzagging in confusion towards Chesil Beach, fifteen miles to the north.

Hours before the first panting breaths of the new day had been exhaled, uncounted numbers of American soldiers had perished, exercising for war, thousands of miles from the shelter of their homes.

The first area of initial attack was blotted with patches of burning oil. Flares, fired by unidentified ships, for whatever reason, illuminated overcrowded life rafts containing oil-covered men, shocked, clinging to bits of trailing rope or to each other.

Men, some silent, some sobbing, grasped frantically towards anything that floated ... anything that measured even half a chance between life and death. And of death there was plenty.

The cold choppy sea became littered with face-down, face-up uniformed bodies sleeping their final sleep. Many had died screaming for life, for a gun to hold, begging relief from the burning pains and some whimpered for the warm comfort of their mothers love.

Long before it was over, before LST's 507 and 531 had settled in 20 fathoms on the seabed of Lyme Bay … when hundreds of young bloods from the United States of America floated dead or alive on oil-stained patches of the English Channel, the enemy pack had turned, scampering back at full sea-speed towards the Cherbourg peninsula.

Ninety minutes later, between Barfleur and Cap Levi they regrouped, falling line-astern, roaring in close formation towards the protection of the Cherbourg breakwater.

In England, before first light began painting the sky, telephones began to ring …

Slumbering majors, generals, Commanders and Vice-Admirals scrambled hurriedly from comfortable beds. Transport was swiftly arranged and by 0530 hours, those concerned sat in glum silence around a table at Quarry House, poring over hurriedly typed or hand-scribbled reports. A large blue chart of Lyme Bay filled one wall of the room.

A British Naval Commander, freshly shaved, sipping at a cup of steaming tea, sighed. "Gentlemen, it would appear to be a bloody mess …"

Across the wide oak table a chubby faced American Major eased his hat onto the back of his head and lifted his papers, "Bloody mess? Jesus-H-Christ!!! We need some goddamn answers and we need 'em, like now!" Banging his large fist down, several of the cups rattled. "Here's a class-A Texas question. Where the fuck was your fast escort? Well, mister, I'm surely waiting."

A British Vice-Admiral lifted a dossier from his brief case. Clearing his throat, in a calm Dartmouth Royal Naval College trained voice, he began, "It appears that HMS Scimitar received certain hull damage that required urgent attention …" Consulting his papers, he resumed, with only the slightest of stammers, "We …we did not anticipate (A) repairs would delay her returning to Convoy T-4 by more than twelve hours and (B) it was assumed adequate protection existed in Torbay to cover emergencies …"

The angry, feather-spitting US Major started to speak but was stopped by a three-star General sitting to his left. "Excuse me!

Could you run that by me … just one more time … sir! You state that the fast escort put back to Plymouth, right? So! Did her skipper inform the convoy? Did he happen to mention to the Commander-in-Chief, where he was at?" Glancing quickly at his notes, he went on, "If so, we have no knowledge of any such message here."

The Vice-Admiral again cleared his throat. "Ahem! It seems there was a slight breakdown in communications regarding this advice. My most sincere apologies …"

A youthful-looking American Commander buried his head in his hands. "Sweet lord, are we on the same fuckin' side here or what?" Looking up he stared hard at the Senior British Naval Officer. "According to my info, Portland's radar observed an unidentified target as early as 0030 hrs. Okay! Maybe this is a stupid question but, WHY, in God's name didn't Port Control pass the warning to Convoy T-4? Am I makin' any sense here?"

A Major with a mid-west drawl burst in …"Buster, where I come from, if your horse drops a shoe, you gotta' replace it. But, heck, if you're a member of the possie, as sure as little apples, you tell the sheriff … Right?"

There followed a long silence. The British contingent glanced along the table. The Vice Admiral looked at the two and a half ringed Lieutenant Commander on his right, raising his eyes for an answer.

The young officer blushed before mumbling, "Ah yes, well, somehow the correct radio frequency wasn't passed on to the Convoy-Master. These things do happen. It's intrinsically why we practice such events, over and over again."

For thirty seconds there was total silence. In the wave of embarrassment flowing along the table, a red faced American General drained his coffee, lit a vile smelling cigar and puffed white smoke into the air. "For my money, you bastards might as well send invites to the Hun. 'Come across an' destroy our boys why don't ya' … they's all just sittin' here waitin' to get shot up.' Total crap, man"

Scrambling from his chair he made his way over to a smaller table in the corner and poured more coffee. Lifting a cookie, shielding his face from the others in the room, he quietly began to weep.

At the main table a British Vice-Admiral sipped his tea and replaced his cup onto the saucer, "Gentlemen, this bickering among ourselves will get us nowhere. It befalls our duty, ASAP, to inform the First Sea Lord regarding the events leading up to last night's unfortunate fracas. We shall, as a matter of course, require certain statistics regarding the incident to complete our report before he consults with your people …"

An American three-star General, sitting at the far end snapped upright in his seat. "Incident, what fucking incident? We're at war here, sailor. This weren't no 'incident' or even any accident. Last night was an error of judgement, big-time. One colossal fuck-up". Raw anger made him shake with rage. In an effort to control his trembling he lowered his voice, peering directly at the English naval officer. "Okay, okay, buddy. What godamn statistics do you need?"

Turning his notebook to a fresh page, the Vice-Admiral nodded. "Thank you, General. Now, first and foremost, how many dead?"

The Americans looked from one to the other down the long table. Some shuffled papers, a few gulped more coffee, while someone muttered, "It's too early to say ... but it will run into hundreds, for sure!"

"Dead, or just wounded?"

"Both. Right now we're still counting …"

The British officers glanced along their side of the table. The next question came almost in a whisper, "Well, can we start with the number of men reported safe?"

Silence. The questioner continued, "For the record, how many servicemen did you dispatch on the eight ships of Convoy T-4 …please?"

From the American side there was a hushed reply, "Until we receive clearance from the top, that information is classified."

The British, as one, rose from the table. The Vice-Admiral said, "General, naturally we have our own internal enquiries to complete before advising the Ministry."

Clicking his briefcase shut, he saluted, "In due course, no doubt historians will report to the unsuspecting world about tonight's fiasco. In the meantime, we'll leave you to bury your brave young men."

Glancing at his watch, he added, "This meeting ended at 0545 hours, April 28th. 1944. Gentlemen, I wish you good-day."

With the British gone, the Americans sat staring at the various patterned grain in the oak table. Someone pushed aside his coffee mug. Heavy cigar smoke hung like static fog on a low hill. A soft Montana voice muttered, "Them Limeys ... so cold. They wouldn't feel the heat if their ass-hole was on fire..."

No one replied. The shrill ringing of the telephone on the side desk clattered the silence. Slowly a three-star General rose, walked across the room and picked up the receiver, "Hi. Yes, this is Quarry House."

He listened for what seemed like a long moment before speaking, "Got it, yessir." He replaced the handset and walked back towards the coffee pot.

"That, my friends, was Ike. The Man arrives here in one hour and he surely sounded like he's about to kick ass ... and then some."

Almost filling his mug with coffee, he poured milk, spooned in three sugars and reached towards the last two cookies.

"Listen up, 'cause here's what we gonna' do ..."

****

Chapter Eleven

Following the tragic consequences of 'Exercise Tiger', secret graves were required for 600 slaughtered allied servicemen.

A torch shinning in Jo-Jo's eyes woke him. "Okay! I'm awake. Is it time?" Reaching for his pants, glancing at his watch he could see it read three minutes before 6am. "Ain't you a little early here, Lieutenant?"

Lt. Joe C. Brown sat on the end of Jo-Jo's bunk, not knowing where to start. "Change of plans, Sergeant. Seems like during the night a couple of LST's hit trouble near the Bill of Portland. T-4 landing is cancelled. In …in thirty minutes the bombardment will commence. That's still G for go."

Checking his watch he lit a cigarette, blew smoke and picked hard at a thumbnail. " Shelling stops 0700. At that time," his voice fell away and he cleared his throat, "at that time your squad will move out. Take two heavy trucks and two dozers. I'll ride point in the jeep."

Pulling on his boots, air from the coloured man's breath cast a cold mist in the tent. Lacing up he gazed at the youthful Lieutenant, noticing sweat trickling down the lean face of the officer. Quietly Jo-Jo asked, "What do I tell my boys, sir?"

Joe C. Brown leapt up and began pacing the tent. "Nothin' … nothing is what you fuckin' tell them, Sergeant. We're in this man's army and this army is at war, god-damn it. This`is not the day to start askin' fool questions, right, Sergeant?"

He moved towards the tent flap, not looking back. "Saddle-up at seven. On the button, okay, Jo-Jo?"

On his feet, Jo-Jo Christmas stamped his boots hard. "I'm your man, Lieutenant. One question…"

"Jo-Jo, for Christ-sake … "

"All I's about to ask was … how come you smokin', sir?"

In the grey morning, as the heavy guns offshore fell silent, a jeep and two trucks departed from Torcross, heading east. They moved without lights. Turning the bend almost at the brow of the hill, the sweeping stretch of beach lay behind them. In the half-light a panoramic picture began unfolding. Below, in the blue-black sea, bow waves from unlit landing craft swept in towards the indiscernible beach, leaving phosphorescent trails in their wake. The dull rumble of heavy machinery, grinding gears and men yelling orders echoed across the shingle, reaching even to the higher road. In the southern corner of the wide stretch of bay a low, unlit lighthouse stood sentry, as if watching the confused preparations for war.

Winding through country lanes, they drove for nearly an hour, at times, slowing almost to a halt as if unsure of direction. In the first truck, Jo-Jo could make out the figure of the young Lieutenant in the lead jeep, studying a map. On one narrow hill the jeep drew into a church gateway and stopped, engine throbbing in the crisp morning air.

While the officer ahead talked into his radio, Jo-Jo watched a lone gull take-off from the church's damaged roof, swooping gracefully towards the dipping valley. The bird circled a tall elm tree halfway down a ploughed field before beating it wings to chase a small fishing boat heading along a small creek that as far as the |Sergeant could work out, went no-place. Lifting field glasses from the map-pocket, Jo-Jo scanned the boat's wake. The gull caught up with the boat, drifting close under its transom … and then, fishing boat and seabird suddenly disappeared into the sheer face of cliff. "Christ! Did you see…?"

The man beside Jo-Jo spoke, "The Lieutenant's movin'-out, Sarge. Where you reckon we's headin' man?"

"Your guess is as good as mine, " Answered Jo-Jo, slamming the truck into gear. But be assured, soldier, come daylight, we're goin' find out. What gives now …?"

At the bend in the steep hill the jeep drew alongside an old man pushing a battered bicycle. The Lieutenant's head poked out from the window flap showing the old man a map. The cyclist bent, peered, removed his flat cap and scratched his head

Looking back the way they'd come he smiled a toothless grin and then turned to point up the hill. As Lt. Brown's head bobbed back into the jeep, the old man remounted and gripped onto the canvas roof. When the jeep restarted man and bike hung on and were pulled up the hill towards the brow. At the top of the hill, letting go, he smiled as Jo-Jo's truck rumbled by him, "Keep 'er goin', boy, keep 'er goin'.

Minutes before eight o'clock the small convoy turned down a muddy lane hardly wide enough for the trucks to pass. Thick copse bordered each side, filtering most of the daylight from the cloudy sky. About half a mile into the lane trees on the left gave way to an open field, separated from the track by a dry-stone wall about five feet high. The jeep halted at a wooden five bar gate. Climbing out, Lt. Brown swung the gate open indicating to the trucks to drive into the field. He walked a few yards further along the lane and spoke quietly into his radio, while the trucks parked.

Switching off the engine, Jo-Jo looked around the sheltered meadow measuring about a hundred yards by ninety. Completely surrounded by trees, there wasn't a house or farm building in sight. Nothing moved. Not a bird, rabbit or squirrel disturbed the eerie silence. Climbing down the young Sergeant kicked the truck's front tyre. He walked slowly along the low stonewall cutting the field from the lane. His experienced eyes measured the nature of the soil where the digging, for whatever reason, would be done. Below his feet, under the rich turfs, perhaps only inches down, they'd find clay.

Rounding the field he returned to the trucks parked away from the jeep. The lieutenant, turned away, mumbled into his handset. Jo-Jo's squad stood in a huddled group, close to the cooling motors. A large black private from Detroit began exaggerated trembles, "I's not takin' kindly to this hole, Boss-Sergeant. What say we head back to the beach and get on with that war-learning stuff?" Gazing quickly around, feeling the utter silence of the area, he trembled again. This time for real.

Seeing Lt. Brown, finished with his radio, was consulting drawings, Jo-Jo moved towards the jeep. He could see that the young officer's eyes were sunken, red-ringed. A cigarette in his hand shook, spiralling a thin line of smoke straight into the Devon air. "Lieutenant, do you mind me askin' where he hell we's at?"

When he answered, the Lieutenant's voice cracked, "Sergeant, I can't tell you what's goin' down here. It's more than my life's worth. Believe me … it's better you don't know the details. Do us both a big favour, act like the army trained you … get on with the job. Obey orders. That way, maybe, just maybe, tomorrow we can get back to the beachhead. Okay?"

For a long moment the two men locked eyes. And then, slowly, Sergeant Jo-Jo Christmas nodded acceptance. "You got it, sir. What's the plan? Where we dig? How deep?"

Dropping the jeep's tailboard the Lieutenant spread out the drawings. "Here's the field map. My guess is that close to that low wall is the best place to dig the first grav… trench."

He didn't look at the Sergeant. "Fifteen foot wide, eight foot deep, one hundred feet long-ways. When that's done, another pit, similar dimensions, maybe twenty feet lower down the meadow. And," his voice croaked, "a third hole, same size, lower again. Any questions … that I can answer?

Jo-Jo took a deep breath. "It surely ain't no ten minute operation, sir. A foot down we gonna' hit clay, so, we need one more digger. Whatever's gonna be buried in them holes will arrive in heavy trucks, so, we need tracks and supports. If we don't finish by dusk … lights; hot chow and some cookin' whiskey for the squad. We'll have …"

"I hear what you say, Jo-Jo. Leave the details to me. Just make it clear to your men … they were NEVER here. They're not to breathe about this operation to a livin' soul. Not to their priest, their God, the law, nor any woman they might ever screw. Not unless they hanker to be on the first boat hittin' French soil … their guns loaded with blanks. Do you get my meaning? Another point, the ETA for the transport is noon. Can you have one hole ready?"

Nodding his head, Jo-Jo turned to walk back to the trucks. Lt. Brown raised his voice. "Sergeant Christmas, one last thing. Take a real hard look. When this job is done, this field must appear, like we was NEVER here."

Gathering the men around the trucks, Jo-Jo calmly said, "This here's a no-question operation. Maybe the Lieutenant's not up to speed with the main-deal but for sure if he tells what he knows, he's dead. Most of you been with this officer long enough to figure out he's an ok sort of guy. For this job I'm askin' for your trust. Now, do I got it?"

To a man they nodded, not looking in the direction of the Lieutenant. "You de boss, sergeant," quipped the soldier for Detroit. "Anyway, as I see it, you's the only dude know's the way back to the beach. Just don't lay no heavy shovel on me. I'm a spade that like to sit in the shade."

Jo-Jo detailed five men into the woods to cut supports, while the others laid track-rails on the grass to assist the trucks, when they arrived. Off-loading a bulldozer, he began skillfully to skim the top turfs, running parallel with the low wall. Stacking the turfs lower down the field he began on the second area while the Detroit soldier on the other dozer started digging the first hole.

Within an hour the three trenches had been marked, the tops carefully placed to one side. When the depth of first hole was three feet, the men returned from the woods and began spreading supports leading to the hollow. During the second hour transport arrive with another dozer. Jo-Jo requested the extra truck to load dug clay and transport it … to wherever.

Just before noon when Lt. Brown's jeep zipped through the open gate the first trench was ready. Driving to the lower part of the field, parking next to a truck, he dropped the tailgate, yelling, "Sergeant… chow."

They ate in silence. Nine coloured soldiers, a black Sergeant and one white lieutenant. When the meal was over two men began clearing the mess-equipment, while the others smoked. As Lt. Brown went towards his jeep, Jo-Jo placed a bucket in the circle of men. "For the butts. Remember, we were never here."

Watching the officer lift a crate, carrying it to one of the trucks, Jo-Jo joined him. The crate was marked, 'Kentucky Bourbon' and below, in smaller print, 'Officer only'. "I'll be back about six, with more chow and anything else you might …" he patted the crate, "take charge of this, Jo-Jo."

Lifting out a bottle, Jo-Jo studied the picture of a fleeing horse as he undid the cap. He offered the bottle to the young officer who took a long swig before returning it. Without wiping the neck the sergeant drank, "Good health, sir, " he grinned.

As the lieutenant's vehicle moved towards the gateway, a ten-wheeler, its identification numbers painted out, slowly manoeuvred into the meadow. The Lieutenant's jeep stopped. Jo-Jo walked across to the driver's side . "Rejoin your men until I give the signal, Sergeant". The officer's face was drained of colour. Knuckles pink-red and pointed, gripped hard at the steering wheel.

The throbbing ten-wheeler backed towards the top trench. Two men in dark-brown fatigues jumped from the cab and directed the driver into the excavated hole. They wore woollen caps pulled low over their heads with shaded goggles covering their' eyes. When the truck was positioned in the opening, in silence the men donned mouth masks and gloves. Jo-Jo could see they were Negroes.

Taking two bottles from the crate, Jo-Jo offered one to the near-end of the semi-circle of his squad, tossing the other to a man at the far end. Without taking their eyes from what was happening within the first trench, they drank, passing the bottles along the line, man after man. They smoked. No one spoke.

When the truck emerged from the trench the upturned rear-end slammed down with a crash. One of the men in fatigues guided it towards the heap of clay. The other man climbed up and started the dozer. As Sergeant Christmas made a move towards the clay, a masked soldier, without looking in his direction held up a gloved hand. "Stay! Hold it here, buddy."

While the damp clay soil was being loaded into the big truck, another ten-wheeler rumbled into the meadow from the lane. It was directed, tail-first into the deep trench. Standing at least fifty paces from the action, Jo-Jo could taste the smell of burnt oil, salt-water, decay and death.

Four times during the afternoon, similar motors backed into the dug cavities and upended their contents. Once emptied, surplus earth and clay from the diggings were loaded and each laden truck chugged slowly away through the lane, their engines echoing from the dense woods. Later, a fifth vehicle drove in alongside the lower ridge of the first trench, unloading its cargo onto the grass. The stench of quick-lime drifted across the field. Emptied, the truck positioned itself in the gateway, engine beating, while a dozer was used to push the lime into the trench.

With the lime piled high, the masked soldier clambered from the digger and without a glance towards the squad, scrambled up into the truck, which set off back down the lane. The motor of the 'dozer was left running.

During the hours it had taken the transport to enter, off-load, reload with soil and move-out from the meadow, hardly a word had been spoken. The bourbon crossed along the line of confused drinkers, arriving at opposite ends of the semi-circle, to be tossed, discarded and empty into the trash bucket. Throughout the night Jo-Jo kept his men away from the lime-filed trenches while he bulldozed fresh earth from the second hole into the first, covering the lime before carefully replacing the top sods that he'd saved. Meanwhile his squad worked in stony silence on trench number three.

The transporters returned during darkness and again just before it began to get light. When Jo-Jo's squad heard the approaching rumble from the darkened lane they downed tools, retreating silently down the field to the shelter of their vehicles. Sitting in a semi-circle, facing away from what was happening higher up the meadow, the Kentucky Horse trotted quietly along the line until it was drained empty.

As daylight seeped above the treetops, Jo-Jo replaced the last cut sods in the third hole. His squad began removing tracks and supports. They worked aimlessly, without spoken orders. No man seeking eyeball contact with another. Close to eight o'clock, Lt.Bown returned with steaming coffee and hot bacon rolls. Not speaking, the men sipped the coffee but tossed the rolls, uneaten, into the trash bucket.

Looking at the officer standing beside him, Jo-Jo Christmas saw a man cloaked in the turmoil of his own particular conflict, from which he would probably never fully recover. A lonely war waged against the Lieutenant's soul. His eyes were sunken, lost in the deeply grooved lines of a youthful face. "I'll get the men back to base, Jo-Jo. Then I'll return for you. How long do you need to clear up?"

"Give me two hours, Lieutenant."

The Sergeant watched the exhausted soldiers climb wearily into the trucks, sprawling onto the floor space, as the motors slowly trundled through the gate into the lane. No one looked back at the field. When the sounds of the engines had died, Jo-Jo gathered the rake, broom, shovel and began to complete the job.

Two hours twenty minutes later, when the lone jeep came down the lane, Jo-Jo was leaning against the outside of the five-barred gate. Getting out, the Lieutenant rested his arms over the top bar, looking down across the meadow. The morning was bright. Crisp spring sunshine struggling to break through the surrounding trees. And yet, there was no sign of natural life. Not a rabbit, a stray fox, a farmer's dog or even a songbird appeared to draw breath for as far as the eye could see.

"You did a great job, Sergeant. We were never here."

Walking towards the jeep, it's engine still purring, Jo-Jo glanced back at the dry-stone wall. From the lane side the change wasn't visible. Earlier, inside, near the middle of the first trench, he'd removed some lighter coloured stones from the wall, replacing them with darker stones gathered from different parts of the weathered slate protection. Tucked behind a growing blackberry bush, he'd formed the darker stones into the crude shape of a cross.

Climbing into the driver's seat, Jo-Jo said, "I'll drive back, Lieutenant. You look kinda' beat."

By the time they reached the junction of the wooded lane and the road, Lt. Joe C. Brown's head had nodded gently onto his chest. Coming down a narrow green hill, Jo-Jo noticed the abandoned, 'Sailor's Church'. Easing the jeep into the set-back gateway, he killed the engine. The young lieutenant woke with a start, "What? What's goin' on? They can't ALL be dead?"

"Take her easy, Lieutenant. There's something I gotta' 'tend here." Climbing from the jeep he untied the spade and walked into the churchyard. Beyond the broken south wall, among the weather-beaten gravestones, he halted. Clearing aside the overgrown grass, he began to dig. Carved into the faded gravestone were the words, 'Maximillian Stone. Shipwrecked mariner. Laid to rest, May 1890. At peace from stormy seas.'

From his pocket, Jo-Jo drew a small chain. Behind him, the Lieutenant inquired, "What you have there, Sergeant?"

On his knees, not looking up, Jo-Jo replied, "Just before we left, back there … that place we was never at, I found this dog-tag. Seems only Christian to lay it alongside other folk far from home."

Dropping the chain into the small hole, he carefully replaced the soil. Glancing up at the gable-end of the church, he saw a white seabird peering down at them. Quietly, the officer asked, "Did you take the name and number?"

"No, sir, Lieutenant. I surely don't need to be haunted by no name and number."

They walked slowly back to the jeep. While Jo-Jo re-stowed the spade on the rear, Lt. Brown climbed into the passenger side. Before the engine started his head slumped and he was asleep. Before proceeding, Jo-Jo read the words carved in the wooden beam over the gateway … 'Hold thou thy cross before my closing eyes.' Glancing over he saw tears trickling down the young Lieutenant's face.

****

Chapter Twelve

... Welcome aboard

On the schooner's deck Maria Jo-Jo's first thought was that she'd stepped back into the age of pirates and treasure-trove. Looking aft, past the wheelhouse, she expected to see the skull and crossbones flag flying from the transom. Turning, taking in the full stretch of the ancient vessel her eyes locked onto the three-foot stump of foremast with the area to the bow stacked high with tar coated crab pots. The mainmast was also missing. In its place a slightly crooked cast iron chimney stood like some battered remains of an old sea battle.

As the first spots of rain dotted along the deck, Mayo said, "Shall we go below? It's a bit tricky. Better if you turn …watch, I'll lead."

Walking towards the curved hatch, just forward of the wheelhouse, he slid the half-doors open and eased himself down the companionway. Before his curly head disappeared below, Maria Jo-Jo grinned, "If Burt Lancaster jumps my bones down there, all teeth and cutlass, I'll hold you responsible, fisherman."

Thirteen steps down, his hand reached up, lightly touching her arm. In the semi-darkness she held onto his fingers … not caring what message it carried or what embarrassment she might be causing. Not pulling away, he said softly, "You'll get accustomed to the dimpsy in a moment. I'll open the inner door."

As her eyes adjusted Maria Jo-Jo could see they stood in a space about eight feet wide. Crumpled orange oilskins hung from a peg, with a pair of rubber boots tucked below. The area was panelled in varnished timber that glowed with age. Mayo opened a door and it was as if a light had been switched on. "Welcome to my humble home, Maria Jo-Jo Christmas."

She wanted to laugh, to cry and somehow freeze this moment in her mind. She couldn't remember, ever, anyone speaking her name with such warmth. Her mom perhaps, but that was a different emotion. Nothing, but nothing, resembled the feelings surging through her at this most precious of moments.

They entered into what she assumed must have been the schooner's cargo hold. Measuring about twenty feet by eighteen, it was windowless. Light came from a large overhead fiddley. The coloured glass scattered rainbow shades in different directions around the cabin like a kaleidoscope. The hull timbers were painted brilliant white, with the main frames, interspersed every six feet or so, deep brown. A wood-burning stove, topped by a black smokestack reaching through the upper deck sat in the centre of the cabin space. The flooring, once the hold's ceiling boards, was also varnished to a mirror glow. A battered settee, covered by a multi-coloured throw, faced the stove. The only other furniture was an old rocking chair, wide enough for two. Between the settee and the fire area an emerald green rug lay on which sat two big baskets of logs.

To the left a small kitchen had been fitted. Shelves housed plates, mugs and other attributes necessary to the basic requirement for a bachelor's existence.

Beyond the settee, on the right, there was a small TV and a music centre. Twenty or so LP's lay in an untidy heap on the floor. Ten feet past the stove a bulkhead separated the main hold from the forward space. Large irregular holes had been cut in the timbers and covered with coloured glass. There were two doors in the bulkhead. One led to a bathroom, the other opened into a bedroom. Both compartments were windowless but light came through the deck-head via skylights of frosted glass.

Maria Jo-Jo gazed slowly around the living area. It felt magical … like a film-set …pure Hollywood. Child-like she tried the rocking chair, sitting back, giggling, her eyes sweeping around the accommodation, savouring, measuring and recording the aura seeping into her mind.

While Mayo made coffee she moved from the rocking chair to the settee, easing off her shoes and tucking her lower legs under her body. Without shame or pretence she watched him pour the liquid into two mugs. With his back to her he said, "Sorry, I'm out of biscuits … cookies."

“No sweat…” It was too quick. She fired a warning message to an excited brain, ‘Cool it, slow down. You’re acting like a teenager with her pussy on fire.’ Thanking him for the coffee, she waited until he was sitting beside her on the settee. “Tell me, how come the name … Mayo?”

“Ireland. My mother’s family were west-coast travellers or so the story goes. Granddad Walter used to joke that our ancestors washed ashore in Kerry from what remained of the Spanish Armada, beaten by Drake and struggling to find a way home.”

She could see traces of Spanish in his face and skin. Black curls grew tight against his head. His eyes, which outside had appeared deep blue, in this light were almost black. His nose had a slight crook (rope accident at twelve) and an inch-long scar on his chin (lobster nip, thirteen) stopped him from being a drop-dead beauty. She guessed his age to be about 24 and she was correct almost to the month.

“Matthew and Joanne Mitchell, up at Quarry House, went over to Ireland to bury the old Captain and his wife. They kind of adopted my mother and brought her back with them to help run the hotel. She met father, who was a deep-water fisherman and, here I am … the end result.” He smiled.

“Are both your folks gone?”

“Yes. Mum died giving birth to me. Dad passed away … oh it must be eight years now. Yes, 1982.”

In a whisper she said, “My mom’s been gone thirty years, come this fall.

My father … he died close to this place, the day I was born, April 30th ’44.” Taking a deep breath she swallowed, “And that, Fisherman-Mayo is why I’m sitting here drinking your coffee. I need to know how and why? Maybe you could start by … how come I own part of your home?”

Mayo walked across to the coffee pot and poured refills. “Father was about 14. Granddad Walter, my dad and your father were hauling pots off the Skerries. They’d no business being there ‘cause it was a marked as a minefield. In the fog they came across this hulk. Half sunk, mainmast shot away, abandoned, most likely a battle-school target practice. It took a day and a half to get her in through Passage. Anyway, because of the work done by Sergeant Jo-Jo, Granddad Walter awarded him a quarter salvage rights."

Maria Jo-Jo's pulse raced into overdrive hearing someone talk about her father in matter of fact everyday conversation.

***

....Jo-Jo drove the Lieutenant through the camp gate and delivered him to his tent. He noticed that someone had parked a truck, with a 'dozer in the back, behind the officer's quarters. "Get some sleep, Lieutenant. If its okay I'll hold the jeep to make sure the squad's settled. Come later I'll return the truck an' 'dozer back to the pound. "

Watching the young officer stumble awkwardly towards the tent, head bent low onto his chin, Jo-Jo thought about checking that he made it to his cot but decided he'd better first check on his men.

Entering the large Bell-tent that housed his squad he discovered three men laying on their bunks, fully clothed. Two others sat on a bench, silently staring at the ground. Another soldier, holding a mud-covered sock gazed, eyes fixed, at his bare feet. The men lying on their beds, still plastered with the red soil from the meadow, had not even removed their boots.

The air within the canvas enclosure was thick with the smell of sweat, whiskey, fear and utter despair. The big private from Detroit stood with his head resting against the tent's centre post, mumbling incomprehensibly.

Jo-Jo began yelling at the crumpled squad. "What the holy fuck gives here? You sad-sad excuse for US soldiers. Not one bullet fired and you're hung low, like Custer's last stand."

He began pulling men to their feet, upturning beds, spilling limp bodies onto the ground, "Get your black ass into the shower. Clean up. Grab some shut-eye. Come mornin' ...well, let what happened be gone with the last taste of bourbon. Hear me ... you were never there, right?"

The man from Detroit was the first to move. "Okay, Sarge. Don't sound-off, man." He stumbled towards the opening, collecting a wash-bag from his locker en route. "Let's go scrub down, you guys."

In hushed silence, one by one the others started to shuffle towards the showers. The last man through the gap, still holding one sock, turned, "Don't suppose there's any more Kentucky juice, Sarge?"

Jo-Jo threw a boot in his direction.

***

Maria Jo-Jo watched, fascinated. Through the overhead skylight sunrays bounced different colours off the glistening smokestack. Bright streaks of light painted changing shades of purple, blue, green and red via the glass sections of the overhead fiddley.

"In his last letter home, dad wrote about meeting a friendly fisherman and his son. That must have been your father and granddaddy. He wasn't explicit as to how or under what circumstances they'd met. Do you know the full story?"

"According to my father, Granddad Walter and Sergeant Jo-Jo first met in the gents toilet in a Kingsbridge pub."

***

....next morning, before the bugler's first notes of reveille echoed across the camp, Sergeant Jo-Jo, dressed and shaved but still stinging from yesterday's Kentucky snake-juice, slipped into the jeep and headed for the Lieutenant's tent.

Quietly opening the flap, he tossed the jeep's keys onto a low table by the cot. "Keys, Lieutenant. I'll get the truck back to the compound before chow."

The young officer was curled in a tight ball, his back towards the centre of the tent, fully dressed from yesterday, except for his boots. A grey blanket was drawn over the lower part of his body. Jo-Jo could see that his eyes were open. He could also see a four-inch jagged hole in the back of the officer's skull. A pillow, bent double and covered with blood, was placed in front of the man's mouth. Gripped firmly in his right hand was an army-service automatic pistol.

"Oh! Sweet Jesus ... you poor bastard." Jo-Jo whispered, gently closing the Lieutenant's eyes. Removing the empty bourbon bottle from the bedside table, he found the officer's pocketbook and tore out the scribbled notes referring to yesterday's assignment. Searching the table drawer he found written orders together with reference maps concerning the unacceptable horror of the nightmare.

Tucking the documents into his tunic he quietly left. Climbing into the truck, Jo-Jo started the engine. He drove, unaware of speed, direction or destination. Sometime during the course of the morning, stopping on high ground, he looked back at the distant beach. Spread below him, minute figures and machinery buzzed along the shingle, in and out of the choppy sea, clattering and chugging deep inland to the dunes. Practising. Training for destructive acts of war. Man against man. Total insanity.

In the truck's map-locker the Sergeant discovered the last of the Kentucky bourbon. Restarting the engine, he raised the bottle towards the crowded beach. "May God carry your soul to a better place, Lieutenant." Drinking deeply, he roared the truck up the long winding hill away from the beach and the frantic Battle-school.

***

"...Mom tried to find out the details of his death here in England. But the army wouldn't play ball. Refused to show her any records. All she received was some personal stuff and a sick'o letter from the beach-Commander. 'Brave - patriotic - fine soldier - credit to his unit and other military crap."

She was silent for a moment. "After the war was done, a sailor by the name of Lieutenant Paul Carter, called on mom. Seems he'd met Sergeant Jo-Jo here in Southern England, with a Lieutenant Joe. C Brown, who died about the same time as dad. I was maybe six or so when the sailor called so it was nothin' to my young mind. Lookin' back I guess mom gave up about then and got on with her life as best she could."

Rising from the settee, she walked across to the music unit.

Skimming through the collection her grin sent his nerve-ends buzzing. "Hey! You're holdin' some of my stone-age albums here. Boy was I hot back then."

Picking up 'White Bird' she fingered down the titles on the reverse side. "This was my first. Recorded in New York City. There are some real deep tracks here …Oh my God, you'd have been in kindergarten when I laid this down."

"Drumbeat's my favourite …" He wanted to add, 'It's like a road seldom travelled' but it came out, "It's all great music …" and even then he fought to control his blushes.

"Thank-you, kind sir. I've never considered myself a great singer. Lucky maybe. Fortunately Max knows a commercial sound and has the marketing skills to sell it."

Finding his copy of 'Drumbeat' and studying the numbers, she murmured, "A whole heap of pain poured into this baby." Silently recalling the golden days and the five years turmoil that fired the making of the 'Listen people, I'm back' album.

Walking over to the wood-stove, looking up at the skylight, she stretched her arms into the air, reaching towards the coloured glass. The prismatic light displayed her tall figure like a spotlight. "These colours are amazing. I love it," she whispered …while her mind screamed, "Oh dear God, short of begging, how do I make this boy touch me?

Mayo followed the crimson shafts of light down from the high glass, draping the fullness of the singer's figure to excruciating perfection. His thoughts ranged from capturing the moment forever in his mind, to slowly drowning whoever this Max might be … or grabbing her hand and leading this beautiful woman into the bedroom. He blushed again, deeper this time.

Smiling, she said, "Before you tell me more, I need to use your john."

****

Chapter Thirteen

... Walter Francis. '44

Easing his considerable frame through the doorway of the Gents in the King's Arms Hotel, Walter began undoing his buttons. A farmer from Blackawton, whom he knew vaguely as 'Uncle', together with two young farm-workers, blocked his approach to the urinals. Behind them, backside against a washbasin was a slightly built Negro American soldier. From the stripes on his uniform, Walter could see he was a Sergeant and from the glazed expression in his eyes the darkie was well into drink.

'Uncle', barrel-chested, dark chinned, early forties, standing closest to the American, snapped, "Get out, fisherman. This be private like..."

"Unless you want me to piddle down your leg, mister, stand aside." And, without waiting Walter dipped his shoulder nudging one of the young farmhands across the room.

While he did his business, the only sound in the toilet came from the fisherman's flowing water. Turning, slowly fastening his buttons, Walter studied the face of the soldier. Although the Negro's eyes were blurred, Walter could see that the American's stance covered the probable line of attack.

As the big fisherman began to chuckle, one of the farmhands looked at him enquiringly, "What?"

"Think I'll hang about an' watch the fun. In Plymouth last week, I missed the best stuff."

The shorter, ruddier farmhand, directed his question to 'Uncle', "What's this daft bugger on about, Uncle Sam?" Turning to Walter he asked, "What gives here, Fisherman?"

"You sods don't know who this chap be, do 'ee? Last Saturday, in a Union Street car park, I watched an ambulance cart four Yankee marines to hospital. It seems, this fella", he nodded towards the Sergeant, "kicked the shite out of the four of 'em ... they do say one had a knife."

For a long moment the room was quiet. Walter said, "Allow me to do the introductions. This, me-beauties, is Sergeant Jimmy 'Sugar' Brown. Light-weight boxin' champion of the US army. Sergeant, these lads be Blackawton's bravest. Like I say, I'll watch. Now, get on with it … I've got a pint standing in the bar."

The two younger men took a slow step back. 'Uncle' looked at Walter, across to the farmhands and then towards the coloured American. He growled, "These bloody Yanks need to understand what us 'ave lost since they arrived over here. We British can take care of mister-soddin'- Hitler … without any fuckin' Texas 'elp. The sooner they bugger's off to froggie-land, the better …right?"

Roughly pushing aside the two farmhands, he walked towards the door. Before leaving, he paused, glaring back to Jo-Jo, "Consider yourself bloody lucky tonight, Mr Blackman."

The taller farmhand followed him out, shouting as he went, "Bugger" before slamming the toilet door.

In the silence that followed, Walter rinsed his hands. Smiling at Jo-Jo, he quietly remarked, "they don't mean no 'arm, Sergeant. Basically they'm 'ard workin' folk. Times 'ave bin rough …"

Scooping water over his face, the black sergeant said, "I'm obliged, sir. But I have to tell you I ain't never been to Union Street and never heard of no 'Sugar' Brown. But, thanks again."

Waiting by the door, Walter replied, "Neither 'ave I … on both counts. It might be better if we leave by the back door in case the farm boys have gone for reinforcements. If that's your truck outside, perhaps I can cadge a lift down the 'ill?"

***

Maria Jo-Jo sat back on the settee, long legs curled under her, gripping an ankle with her right hand. "You maybe heard I spent some time in rehab. Later, recovering …out in the valley, with help from Ruby, Frankie and the Boyde family, true friends, well …we came from the dark. In one truly low moment, I found a letter dad wrote to my mom … from here, in England. It kinda' gave a purpose to my life."

She remained silent for a while, staring as sunlight drifted a beam of pale green down from the outside. "A year ago I called in some favours from Capital Hill. The Chief of Staff at the Pentagon opened computer trails that many in Congress didn't know existed. We came up with zilch. Whatever happened during 'Exercise Tiger' in '44 was buried real deep." She sighed.

"I contacted a navy guy, a Captain Paul Carter. He was based in England during the preparations for the invasion. He wrote back saying that, sadly, he'd been at sea during those final weeks. But he gave me another lead. A Major Willard Harris Jr. who lived in Alabama. We paid this dumb-dumb a visit." She chuckled softly at the memory.

"The old buzzard must have been eighty, but his buttons still worked. On the porch, in the afternoon heat, when his wife went for some juice, I asked a question and he kidded he was deaf. 'Come close, honey, my hearin' ain't what she was…'

When I leaned over to speak the bastard slipped his hand up my skirt. He sure yelled when I dislocated his finger. As I walked away he yelled, 'what else you nigga' girls for anyway? I don't recall your kinfolk, missie but any black-boy in a white man's army can only mean trouble … capitol T, lady.'

***

"You in some kind of trouble, Sergeant?"

The truck had stopped at the top of the lane. Walter had opened the door, about to climb out but in the semi-darkness he sensed the American's reluctance to drive on.

"AWOL. Been on the run two days. I'm goin' crazy, fisherman."

Walter pulled the door shut. "You better cum 'ome with me, young fella'. Mother will make us some tea. Always feels better after a cuppa tea. Drive down the lane a bit."

At the quarry entrance there was a bold notice on the wire fence, 'Ministry of Defence. Keep out.'

Jo-Jo asked, "Ain't this place off-limits?"

Walter chuckled, "Don'ee fret. There's a cottage in the grounds, be'ind the big 'ouse. When the government leased Quarry House from Cap'n Mitchell they forgot about the cottage. He'd signed it over to me afore he left for Ireland. The Military people were right upset … till they began to appreciate the fresh fish. "

"Won't there be a guard on the gate?" asked Jo-Jo.

"Hold fast, mister soldier, we're not stupid, us British. Course there's a guard, but 'e goes 'ome to supper and won't be back 'til morning. Now, I'll jump down and open the gate …'er won't be locked."

***

" … My mother was the most beautiful woman that ever drew breath. Strong. Tempestuous. New York-Mexican. And a voice, like you never heard. She poured music into my bones. Opened all the gates."

Maria Jo-Jo spoke softly, with clarity, freedom and an ease that she'd certainly never experienced with the most expensive therapists. "In the church choir, being tall, they placed me way at the back. I'd close my eyes and momma's voice drifted over me. On good nights I hear her harmony … when I don't hear her, I sing shit."

"Long after she'd died, I found a poem she wrote, perhaps when her man didn't make it back from the war. It begins … 'if I could choose a place …' I've searched for the right melody to fit the lyrics. Maybe, if I do Vegas, I'll ask Mr Bacharach to write the music. Now, tell me about this lovely boat … do you call it a boat, ship, vessel? How long have you lived here? Did you hire a designer for the interior? It's really cool. Do you have a wife, a girl? Oh God, tell me to mind my own damn business, Mayo." Reaching over she touched his hand, apologetically. "Take no notice. Sometimes my mouth overlaps my brain."

Her brain, at that moment was pleading with her hand to hold on to his but fear of rejection drew it back. "Did your father ever talk about mine?"

***

"Sergeant Christmas, this is my son, James. When 'e's awake proper, he might grunt, 'mornin' … but don't hold your breath."

It was before daylight. The fishing boat chugged slowly along the dark shadows of the silent creek. Walter, at the tiny wheel, nursed a steaming mug of tea. The American was tucked in the corner of the narrow wheelhouse, sipping a similar mug watched the solid fourteen-year old, aft of the open door, perched on an upturned box. Between his feet lay a mug of tea and a two-inch thick bacon sandwich. Jo-Jo noticed that the lad's eyes remained closed as he cut a fish, tossing pieces into another basket, without taking aim. After gutting a couple of fish he gulped tea and bit into the bread without opening his eyes or cleaning his hands.

Fisherman Walter Francis and GI Jo-Jo Christmas had talked well into the early hours. Walter's wife, Annie, a round-faced lady, appeared to smile every twenty seconds. Her grey dancing eyes matched her hair and she'd produced a tray of tea and fruitcake almost while they were still shaking hands.

While the two men sat either side of the fire, drawn to the hypnotic changing patterns in the burning coal, Annie collected blankets and a fresh pillow from a chest in the corner of the comfortable room. "I'll leave you men to chatter a bit. 'Twas lovely to make your acquaintance, Sergeant Christmas. Now, mind you bank up the fire before you come up, Walter. We don't want the poor soul getting cold durin' the night."

Rubbing his eyes, Jo-Jo peered ahead over the bow. The faintest line of approaching dawn creeping above the high rocks emphasised the darkness stretching east and west. Up ahead there was no visible sign of any opening or exit. When deeper shadows loomed closer, like a dark cloud waiting to envelop the slow moving boat, Walter dropped the forward window and glanced once at the compass before switching off the binnacle light.

The army man gripped hard at the rim of timber below the corner window, biting back a yelp as a shape brushed past the side window, no more than three feet from the boat's rail. The steady putt-putt of the engine dramatically altered pitch to a higher echo as they entered a tunnel darker than any night. Hypnotized, Jo-Jo could hear Walter counting … "Five, six, seven … hard over. One, two, three … hard over t'other way … steady!"

Suddenly, they were out, clear. It wasn't daylight but neither the total darkness of wherever and whatever they'd journeyed through. And as the blunt stem lifted to a different motion on the first of the ground swell, Jo-Jo breathed a long sigh of relief. "Lordy-lordy! That was like comin' back from the grave, man."

The big fisherman laughed, "That was 'Passage', Jo-Jo. We nearly didn't make it that time. I need total darkness around me to catch the change of light ahead …there was so much white shinin' from your eyes, Sergeant, I almost blundered."

James' young voice from the stern offered, "With those gleamin' teeth you were bloody lucky 'e didn't smile, father. "

***

"… for years I carried my folks wedding picture. Dad's smile could light up a Billboard. Mom, well she was just Mom, alive, in love, beautiful. It wasn't 'til a couple of years ago I discovered a letter hidden behind the photo frame. Reading it triggered a need-to-know about what really happened here … this place, all those years in the past."

She fell silent, sighed and went on, "The Pentagon report stated that 'Sergeant Jo-Jo Christmas, N2456781 went AWOL, was captured, escaped and assumed dead. No body recovered.' Later, I spent maxi-dollars on investigators, trackin' army buddies and such like."

She pulled both knees up under her chin, angry at burdening this 'boy-man' with her troubles. "We found this one guy, in Detroit, recalled some special assignment, an officer's death and a sergeant goin' missin'. He mumbled about, Convoy T-4, diggin' and other stuff. But it was a mess, he was stoned out of his skull."

Mayo wanted to reach across and comfort her but was afraid to make a wrong move. She carried on, her voice becoming lower, "In '88 I received a call from a man in Utah. He'd watched a TV show I was in and traced my number through the studio. Turns out he was a censor-officer for the US post-office, here in Devonshire, in '43. Part of his duties was to collate personal effects of the dead or missing, before sending them to next-of-kin. You know, make sure there were no embarrassments."

"For reasons he couldn't explain, he broke army rules and posted dad's letter home uncensored, tucked behind a photo. He'd meant to contact mom after the war but was badly wounded in Germany … the TV show triggered his memory. Poor man, he was cut-up. I hadn't the heart to tell him she never read the letter." Her voice dropped even lower, "Nor that I'd only found it in a moment of crazy …."

She sat silent for a while and then began to tremble. Mayo eased her shoulders away from the back of the settee. Momentarily, she tensed, before her head fell forward onto his chest. Gently stroking the fine hair on her scalp, he quietly said, "It's okay, just let go …let go."

For what seemed ages there was almost no sound other than their breathing and then, she began to sob. Mayo's shirt became damp from her tears. Slowly stroking her head, his body welcomed the warmth of this lovely woman.

When the tears eventually passed, replaced by tiny hiccupping gulps, with her head buried into Mayo's chest, she breathed in the combined odour of fish, tar, his youth and something close to graphite. "In the censor-man's call he spoke about High Command Balls-up. He swore that in no-way was Sergeant Christmas responsible for the death of Lt. Brown."

***

…on the return journey towards the creek, concerned for his guest, Walter inquired, "Last evenin', when you parked the truck, did you make a good job of coverin' 'er up, Jo-Jo?"

The black Sergeant smiled, "I came top dog in the camouflage course. Even collected a badge. MP's wouldn't find that truck and 'dozer if they sat ass-down on the hood." Looking ahead he could make out the growing shape of the rugged coast. "Soon's we get back, I'll hit the road, Walter. Don't want trouble … not for your family."

"Mother'd be proper upset if you don't stay for Sunday lunch. There's no better roast dinner cooked in the whole of Devon. So there!"

“Heck, it’s only Friday …”

“Exactly. Now, take the ‘elm while I give the lad a hand on deck. Keep ‘er steady on those marks … the old church spire inline with the big elm lower down …see?”

About a hundred yards from the foaming kelp-covered rocks, Jo-Jo still hadn’t puzzled out the entrance. To a stranger’s eye, diagonal layers of speckled limestone, cross-blended, made the passage into the sheltered creek invisible. Lowering the wheelhouse window, Jo-Jo watched Walter and James separating cock from hen crabs, snipping their main claws before tossing them into different baskets. “We getting’ close inshore, Walter … I can’t make out the hole.”

His back to the land, without looking up, Walter asked, “Can you still see the tree?”

“Sure can but she’s about to fade…”

“When the tree’s gone, go left a ways, you’ll see the way in …”

****

Chapter Fourteen

... Joanne.

In her fiftieth year, Mrs Joanne Brady-Mitchell wore her light brown hair pulled back into a ponytail. A pretty pixie face complemented a slightly pear-shaped figure. Her eyes were blue, clear, honest and protected by smart rimless spectacles.

Joanne's father, a Dartmouth Bank Manager, had struggled to educate his only child at Dartington, a college specialising in the arts. A widower, John Brady became a proud man when at the age of twenty, Joanne was appointed Junior Art Teacher at the London School of Modern Art. Joanne was bright, independent and loved teaching with a passion.

In 1960, at an exhibition of African landscapes held in a smart London hotel, Joanne Brady stood before a large painting entitled, 'Daybreak.' Becoming aware of a tall young man with rust coloured hair, seemingly intrigued by the misty haze of African colours filling the wide canvas, she'd enquired, "What does it say to you?"

"It whispers, 'Exquisite!' It holds my breath," he said, "and, looking at the signature I'd say, 'JB, if you're a woman ... marry me'."

With a quiet smile, Joanne had murmured, "I accept."

By the end of that first day, Joanne knew that she'd met the one man in her life for whom, if necessary, she'd lay aside palette and brushes. A month later, without the wholehearted blessing from her father, Joanne married Matthew Mitchell, Manager of the London hotel and became Mrs Joanne Brady-Mitchell.

Straight from a South African honeymoon they'd travelled to the west of Ireland, where they'd laid Matthew's mother to rest. After selling the land and stock they'd carried the ashes of Captain Albert George Mitchell back to the seclusion of the Devon creek. They'd also brought with them, Kathy.

The very first sighting of Quarry House captured the artistic dreams of Joanne Brady-Mitchell. Arriving in the middle of the night they'd sat in the car watching a full silver moon roll down the hill beyond the broken church. Sliding silently past the old elm it fell towards the sea behind the dark cliffs at the southern end of the creek. Holding hands, Joanne and Matthew began mapping out their' dreams and ambitions to turn the house into a hotel. By the time the eastern horizon began to change colour they'd outlined a future that centred around the tranquillity of the boarded-up house, a future that included silent Kathy, sleeping soundly on the rear seat of the car.

While Matthew had stretched his legs, strolling into the woods beyond the stone quay, recalling boyhood years, Joanne had walked to the main doors of the darkened house and explained to the circular stone building that she was about to become its loving friend. "House, I am Joanne Brady-Mitchell. Myself, Matthew and Kathy will share all that we have with you. All that we ask is that your soul shelters us. And silently, the house answered, yes.

With Matthew attending to the legal and financial problems surrounding the project, Joanne set to work re-designing the interior of the grand house into a country hotel. Her plans included extra bedrooms and bathrooms, a larger kitchen, downstairs walls removed to create greater space. The outbuildings and stables were converted into classrooms. The fisherman's cottage, which they discovered wasn't part of the estate, remained untouched.

Handing her sketches and ideas over to a professional architect, Joanne obtained a part-time position as Art Teacher at a Plymouth college. When she wasn't shouting at or arguing with architects, planning officers and builders, she also did freelance work for a Cornish publisher, illustrating children's books.

Between them, Matthew and Joanne, patiently taught Kathy the basics of reading and writing and by the time the establishment was ready to open, a year on from its conception, the gentle Irish girl had gained sufficient confidence to act as the hotel's Housekeeper. Kathy rarely spoke and when she did, her sentences were short, direct and without emotion. Content in her own company, she preferred whistling to talking. Both Matthew and

Joanne often stopped what they were doing to listen, enchanted by the soft melodic Celtic tunes echoing from wherever the tiny girl went about her tasks ….

Joanne offered her hand, smiling. "Welcome to Quarry House, Miss Christmas. We sincerely trust that you enjoy your stay with us." Turning to Max, with the same warmth, she said, "Mr Stone, good-evening. Matthew may have explained, we're pretty informal here. At the moment I've a class of only seven students". She giggled, " Shame on me for calling them students. Many come back year after year, like old friends. For meals we use one large table. We'd be thrilled if you'd … well, just muck in." Hesitating, she added, "Naturally, if you wish to eat alone I'm sure we can arrange a private …"

The black singer gazed around the warm room. Most of the other guests were talking at the small bar. "Love it! On one condition, though. We're Maria Jo-Jo and Max, right?"

During the meal that seemed to go on and on, Maria Jo-Jo enjoyed the company of the two men sitting on either side. On her right a tall man confessed to being an Inland Revenue Inspector. He explained that this was his third visit to the hotel, returning each summer, partly to unwind from the tension of his occupation. Modestly, notwithstanding a little embarrassed fidgeting, he said that Joanne believed he'd become a half-decent seascape painter. Over the entree he whispered, "I'm delighted to say that last winter I sold three watercolours." Looking around, he added, "I'm also a little ashamed that the profits were not declared on my personal tax returns." He blushed, stabbing a pink prawn with his fork.

She laughed, "I won't breathe a word, Doc. There's been some 'pocket-dollar' payment for gigs that Max forgot to show on my IRS forms. Hell, life ain't much fun without breakin' a rule now and then."

The man on her left was quiet. He'd mumbled a friendly enough 'Hello' as they'd sat to eat but throughout the meal concentrated on his plate. She guessed he was late fifties, maybe early sixties, with thick grey hair that tended to curl. Reaching over to fill his wine glass, she asked, "Now, what do I call you, friend?"

Firmly fixing his eyes on the black-buttered wing of ray almost filling his plate, he replied, softly, "Milton. Royston, but mostly its Roy."

"There that wasn't so hard was it Roy? Is this your first visit?"

"Yes." Cleanly stripping the thick meat of the fish back to the bone and pausing before taking the first bite, he said, "Mary, my wife, gave me this week as a belated birthday present. It may seem strange but my trade was painting and decorating but since retirement watercolours have been my hobby. I'm still in the hopeless stage but," He was growing in confidence as the beautiful entertainer smiled at him, "I've learn't so much during the past few days. The others have been so helpful and Joanne … Mrs Brady-Mitchell, well, the lady's a treasure."

Taking another small bite, he went on, "When I get home, Mary will be green with envy. She's one of your greatest fans. We've weathered endless complaints from neighbours about your music blasting through the house."

Maria Jo-Jo laughed, "Well, you're one up on me, Roy. You know my work but I've yet to see yours. Perhaps …"

Joanne joined their conversation. "During coffee we normally spread the day's work out in the lounge. Sort of a group comment session … no holds barred. We'd be delighted if you and Mr Stone … Max, joined us.

Regarding Roy's pictures, all I can offer is a little brush-up advice. He's already an accomplished landscape painter. His trees and distant work are brilliant."

The quiet man bowed his head, blushing a deeper red.

Maria Jo-Jo touched the painter's hand, smiling. "Look forward to it."

Glancing across the table at Max, she saw his pink faced glowed with a 'New York Party-time expression.' Seated between two ladies of different proportions, he appeared in his element. The large, titian-haired woman on his right wore a bright purple smock over a black silk polo-necked sweater. She had the thickest fingers Maria Jo-Jo had ever seen on another woman. A heavy gold bracelet hung around her wrist and on the middle finger of her right hand, almost like a weapon, sat a man's signet ring. Now and again, her right hand dipped below the table and the tiny pale-faced woman, with sunken eyes, sitting on her right, blushed furiously.

On Max's left, wearing designer casuals, was an attractive blonde woman in her early thirties. From the conversation drifting across the table, Maria Jo-Jo understood that the lady's husband was in shipping. Apparently, the mutual understanding was that hubby spent a week in the Spanish sun chasing a golf ball, while she came to Devon for her annual art class.

During dessert, Butch-lady, deep into her second bottle of French red, suddenly dropped both hands below table level. Simultaneously, Max and Pale-face lady stiffened, turning bright red. The large woman turned her head right then left, winking at both of them.

During coffee in the curved lounge, flopping beside Maria Jo-Jo where she sat listening to Joanne's comments on her student's work, Max cried, "Maria Jo-Jo, don't leave me alone with the 300lb dike. Did ya' see the hand tricks durin' dinner? Jesus, I'm gonna' limp for a month."

"Be firm, Max," She smiled. "Most likely she's confused by New York friendliness … that, or she's looking for a good agent. Do you know any good agents, Max? Hell, if you can't handle a forceful chick, keep your door locked. By the way, we're fishin' in the morning. Early … 4a.m."

Glancing across the room, Max saw his table companion proudly showing her canvas. It consisted mainly of fragmented splashes of bright colours leaping from the picture. He found the subject flash, crude, yet strangely exciting.

Still looking at the painting he muttered, "Sure, sure … what time did you say? 4…A…M? For chrissake, lady, that's goin'-to-bed time in my blood group."

Seeing that Joanne had moved on to study pale-face woman's efforts, Max trembled. "Christ … there she blows. I'm away, Maria Jo-Jo. About the fishin' … I don't promise."

Dragging his eyes from the big woman, he glanced at his watch. "Okay, so what time is it in Vegas? Looking up as he moved towards the hall, he mumbled, "What the fuck are we doin' in this

Alec Guinness nightmare anyway?"

Towards midnight, Maria Jo-Jo sat with Joanne and Matthew, drinking coffee in the quiet conservatory. In the silence they looked down towards the darkened quay. Beams of moonlight played across the still water, casting long yellow strips towards the tall trees. "You guys come pretty close to havin' it perfect here. Right now, the world's troubles are …somewhere out there. Beyond. Other battlefields. Sorry! That's pure Rod McKuen …but maybe you appreciate where I'm comin' from?"

Matthew reached out, touching his wife's hand. They both smiled. Joanne said, "We understand you're fishing with Mayo tomorrow? You must have made some impression, it's rare for him to take passengers."

Refilling their cups, Matthew said, "Many years ago, before Mayo's grandfather died, I spent a day out here. I was 'Moby-dick'. Away from the land, I couldn't understand why men chose to work in such isolation. I recall feeling like a speck of dust … on the rim of the globe, fully expecting the slightest breeze to spin the tiny boat off into space."

Laughing, he added, "But please, don't let me put you off. I'm sure you'll enjoy the experience."

"Dad's letter mentioned a place called, 'Passage'. This afternoon, Mayo spoke about his granddad spending some days with my father. There's so much missing from the story. I need a complete picture …". There was pain in her voice.

Matthew rose from his seat, "May I offer you a nightcap, some cognac?"

Even as Joanne flashed a wifely glance of annoyance in his direction, he was attempting to make amends. "Ah! Sorry. You …you don't do you?"

Maria Jo-Jo giggled, "Matthew, I'd be delighted. My therapist is convinced that being a lush ain't cured by staying dry. He reckons, that's the easy way. If I feel like a glass of wine or a shot, I take it … sometimes a couple. The victory is being strong enough to hold it right there. So, a hit of your cognac sounds great. Thanks."

For a while they sat quietly, watching the moon turn slowly

outside the large south-facing window. "This Mayo, seems we both lost a parent on the day we were born, told me his mother died in childbirth." She paused, sipped her drink, "My father died … on the other side of the world, fighting for a kind of freedom he never experienced in his own country." She finished the cognac, "Sad … on both counts."

Joanne sniffed, removed her spectacles, rubbed them clean and replaced them. "Mayo's mother, Kathy was like a daughter. She'd come with us from Ireland, deeply shocked after the death of Matthews's parents. They'd looked after the gypsy girl for years. She hardly spoke, couldn't read or write and didn't care for strangers. It was two years before she trusted us with her thoughts and emotions,"

She looked at Matthew who nodded for her to continue, "We'd great difficulty accepting that she'd fallen for Mayo's father, James They were oceans apart. He was one hell of a wild man …"

Matthew took over the story, "When we decided to change the house into a hotel, Granddad Walter was living in the cottage Father had given him, back of the stables. He did a little fishing but mostly he took care of the gardens. A lovely man."

As he lifted the decanter to pour another drink, Maria Jo-Jo placed her hand over her glass. "Ol' Walter was missing a foot but you'd hardly notice. In the early days of Father and Walter's friendship, timber from a ship's deck-cargo washed ashore. Teak. They set about building the crabber, 'Receiver'. Mayo still uses the boat."

Replacing the cognac he looked again at the singer, she smiled, shaking her head. "Apparently construction took over a year because of arguments between them about design. Father accused Walter of wanting a craft that was only fit to put to sea in summer. Walter reckoned father wanted a vessel that would take ten men around Cape Horn, in winter. When 'Receiver' was eventually launched, Father commissioned a carpenter from Kingsbridge to make Walter an artificial foot from a lump of the remaining teak. He was so proud of that foot. When Anne, his wife, passed away, for reasons we never knew, Walter and son James had a blazing row. The youngster left to go deep-water trawling from Plymouth. James and I were born about the same time, even went to the same school up at Cove for a term or two. But we were never chums. When I went off to boarding school, well, that was it. Didn't see him again till 1962. He was a Don-skipper by then. Full of anger. A great barrel chest. His head was a cloud of black beard and wild curls. Sometimes he looked like an untamed bush ..."

Outside, the moon had rolled behind the distant trees but still reflected in patches along the calm water. ""He did return to bury Walter, who'd died quietly in his sleep. On the day of the funeral he was deeply drunk. Not falling-down or fighting drunk, you understand but anaesthetised from eyebrows to toes."

Joanne quickly said, "Fisherman Walter Francis was the last seafarer to be buried at the Sailor's Church. After the service, back here, James stood to one side, alone, staring through the window at the creek,"

Her eyes glanced to where a single ribbon of moonlight cut across the bend in the creek. Matthew touched her knee, before speaking, his voice low. "I stood beside him as the last of the day closed its moments behind Western Rocks. He heaved a great sigh. 'Thanks, Matthew for what you done … and Anne.' His voice was clear, only his eyes told the full story. 'Where do all the bloody years go, Matthew?'

"Then, he'd turned, walking towards the door. Just before leaving the room he caught sight of Kathy. Normally, ninety-nine times out of a hundred she'd have turned away from a stranger's direct gaze. Not this time. With a battered cap scrunched in his big hands, James appeared to search into her Celtic mind. Exchanging unspoken questions and finding no answers, he'd nodded once and was gone."

The creek had now disappeared. "We didn't see him for maybe two months. And then, one evening a Plymouth taxi arrived with Skipper James, juiced to the gills.

That week's group of students, from London, thought he was sensationally parochial. This great, bear-like fisherman doing a Dylan Thomas act, pickled out of his skull but still standing and talking. I was convinced we were in for trouble. He'd leaned against the bar, holding on, both arms outstretched. His eyes were fixed on Kathy, who was serving. When she placed a glass before him, he'd reached out, unsteadily. Reaching forward, she gently touched his massive hand with hers. Stretching, on tiptoes, she leaned over and whispered something in his ear. Leaving the drink untouched, he'd walked out … quiet as a lamb."

"Kathy didn't appear next morning. Late afternoon, when the Plymouth taxi returned to take the fisherman back to his trawler, she came back to work. We tried to warn her about the nature of the beast but it was wasted. She just smiled and worked twice as hard. Her whistling filled the high rooms with the sweetest music."

"There were times we didn't know he was back. Closing down for the night, Joanne would see the light on in his cottage and next morning Kathy would be absent. There were occasions when we worried ourselves frantic over her welfare but she was so obviously happy, it seemed wrong to meddle. So, we held our silence, knowing that when it ran its course we'd be there to pick up the pieces."

"One evening, the taxi driver asked to use the phone … some problem with his radio. In the office, over a cuppa, he explained the system. A three-week trip entailed dragging Liverpool Bay for sole, or scratching for skate off the Wolf Rock. Returning to Plymouth the crew off-loaded and then slept while the catch was auctioned on the market. Collecting settlement from the agent they'd gather in the Navy Inn on the Barbican, drinking each other's health until late afternoon. Eventually a taxi would collect those who didn't live locally, dropping men in different villages, which signalled another drink at yet another pub. By the time the transport arrived in Kingsbridge, where the engineer lived, he and the Skipper were the only remaining passengers.

"It seems that the accommodating hotel landlady was more of a temptation than the young Skipper could fight. Trip after trip, the taxi driver had listened to the ramblings …'just a couple with the Chief, Billy, then you can drive me down to Cove Creek … I'll make my peace with ol' Walter.

He'd wait for maybe an hour, before heading back to base. Thirty-six hours later he'd begin rounding up the crew, starting in Kingsbridge. Skipper James, the engineer and so on, picking up different crewmembers from villages until they all arrived back at the Barbican."

"Then, according to Taxi-Billy, the Skipper suddenly became a changed man. The crew still drank after landing, well into the afternoon and after setting-off they still called at several watering-holes but, pulling up outside the Kingsbridge hotel the Skipper would say, 'Wait Billy. One with the chief and, 'sure enough, in ten minutes they'd be on the road again, down to the cottage' … and Kathy."

Matthew continued, "They tumbled along like that for nearly three years. He rarely came to Quarry House. We'd know he was back because Kathy didn't come to work. One summer we noticed them down on the beach, painting the boat. Two months later, on the brightest of mornings they went through 'Passage', dredging for scallops. When he'd returned to sea, Kathy would come from the cottage …radiant, glowing."

"But there was a certain wildness about him, unreliable, prone to outbursts of savage anger. Sometimes he'd be away for months. Perhaps landing the boat's catch in Holland, Galway, Grimsby or Aberdeen. He was a maverick fisherman yet by all accounts a bloody good money earner. We also suspected that the Kingsbridge landlady had re-weaved her magic spell … but how could we know?"

"When it came time for his trips to be over, before locking up, Kathy would check through the window to see if the cottage light was on. Her expression never changed. The only tension felt was that with the passing months, her whistling ceased."

"She must have been seven months pregnant when he showed up again. Standing in the lounge doorway, swaying slowly backwards and forwards, as if his bulk was trying to decide which way to fall. There must have been about twelve people standing at the bar. They became silent, one by one, until the whole room was hushed. James held his battered cap in one hand and a bag of fish in the other. For what seemed ages they just stared. To Kathy's credit, without blinking or wavering in her gaze, she looked serene, Celtic, proud and truly beautiful."

"And in that haunting moment James broke first. Turning, he walked out, leaving cap and fish. When he'd gone the room suddenly hummed with chatter and the smell of fresh Turbot. Kathy finished serving a customer and then calmly walked across the room, picked up the cap and the bag of fish and tossed them both through the front door, before going to wash her hands. She returned to the bar … but next morning she was missing from her work."

"Two days later, after his taxi began the climb towards Kingsbridge, she sat us down and explained that after his next trip, they'd be married. They'd live in the cottage and … please, could she have our blessing?"

"We hugged, cried and cradled each other tightly. Tears of joy painting ribbons down over all our emotions."

While Matthew blew his nose and sipped a little cognac, Joanne resumed the story. "Twenty one days later, tides permitting, he should have been back. There was no word. Early one morning I discovered her slumped against the window, curled in agony, looking towards the road. We called the doctor and within an hour she was on her way to hospital."

"Complications in the baby's final development caused some concern. The consultant wanted Kathy to agree to a caesarean but she refused. Pleading for them to wait until James arrived."

Matthew took over again, "Phoning the harbour office and establishing that his boat had docked that morning, I drove to the Barbican to search for the bastard. I reckon I chased their taxi to half the pubs in the South Hams. Eventually found him in a Kingsbridge hotel, well plastered. A lady with an impossible chest was trying to hold him upright while directing his frame towards the back stairs… she was fighting a losing battle.

"James kept repeating, 'No-no-no, its over, Maggie. In two days …married. Let me sing you one more song … then I'm away.'

"In the car racing him towards the hospital he was silent. His great fists crunched against his knees, like he was fighting for control of the alcoholic energy raging through his brain. By the time we made it to the maternity ward, the child had been born. A son, complete with sets of fingers and toes, eyes, ears and a button nose. The sister assured us that he possessed dangly-bits necessary for manhood and strong lungs yelling notice that life is not measured in calculated justice, fairness or calm."

"Before they'd moved Kathy to Intensive Care, concerned by

the amount of blood loss and general weakness, the nurse had lain the naked baby across her chest. Kathy kissed the dark curls on his warm head."

"In the side-ward, James towered over the cot where his son cried for attention. Gingerly lowering one large finger, he traced the faintest touch between the boy's nose and lips. The boy stopped crying and appeared to sniff at the fisherman's skin before falling asleep."

"Inside the ICU, in a white bed, Kathy lay amidst the whirl of constant sounds of irregular bleeps and flashing digital numbers. Her face drained of colour, lips almost blue and her raven hair exaggerating the clinical whiteness of the ward. With slow awkward steps he'd approached and reaching down, touched her face. 'She's so cold.'

"Removing his knee-length coat that smelled of fish, tobacco and various aromas of countless public houses, he eased the battered leather over the top cover of the bed. Dragging a chair to the bedside he'd sat watching the almost indiscernible rise and fall of her breathing. With the same finger offered to the baby, tenderly moving it across her lips, he whispered, 'Macushla, macushla, Kathy…'

So quiet that Maria Jo-Jo leaned forward to hear the words, Matthew finished, "To the best of our knowledge, she never opened her eyes again. Yet I'm sure she knew he was there."

Joanne said, "It destroyed me … I had to leave. Outside, together with a young consultant we gazed through the glass at what for me was the most distressing scene of my life. Inside, this great lump of a man, hair and beard gleaming with rain, sweat and goodness knows what else, was caressing Kathy's forehead and even from outside the room I could feel him willing her to survive, to fight for her life, to live, to forgive him his many sins."

"I glanced at the medical man next to me, who shook his head, 'I'm amazed she's lasted this long'.

"His eyes roamed about the unit, watching different gauges and dials monitoring Kathy's progress, 'I'm from County Cork. Except for being a little rusty there's not much wrong with my Irish. But when we delivered the baby, Kathy spoke in a strange dialect. A sort of tinker-Gaelic from Connemara way. I only understood the odd word or two … 'Magda – Solders – Hanging'. She repeated it, like 'twas part of an ancestral history … a folk story, handed down the way travelling folk do. And then something that sounded like, 'Spanish fish-boy'. Sadly, very little of what she said made sense, I'm afraid.'

"The doctor had nodded towards James, 'Is that creature the father? Did that, keep her holding on to life, when in truth no life remained?' He shook his head, eyes fixed on the bedside scene, adding, 'The torment some women endure for love goes well beyond the principles of psychological knowledge. Sometimes I … ah! It appears to be ended.'

Matthew resumed the tale, "What must have been hours later, Joanne, James and myself stood over the infant's cot. The fisherman's eyes were sunken, black with pain. Giant tears silently dropped from the rim of his beard, falling, soundlessly onto the sleeping baby's fingers, without waking him. From somewhere deep inside him, James mumbled, 'Kathy spoke one word … Mayo. So that will be his name, Mayo.'

"Reaching out his massive arms he enfolded Joanne and me and we felt that his great sobbing would break our hearts. With his wet beard tucked into my coat he said, 'Matthew, I can't handle this. I just can't. Do what is necessary … I beg you, please. I'm - I'm bloody lost. Utterly lost. I'll be in touch.'

"He'd turned, stumbling away and in that ghostly hospital room the strong smell of his damp leather coat, beer, fish and tobacco, lingered. We heard later that he'd gone back to sea, driving his crew almost to destruction working in the foulest weather. There were rumours about sacking … jail … drunken madness and stories too crazy to contemplate.

It was to be nine months to the day when we next saw him …and my god but he was a changed man."

****

Chapter Fifteen

... James Francis.

Routinely, Station Sergeant Norman Banks began the nightshift by the book. Later, if the workload skidded slightly off-course, if his ulcer triggered indigestion or if certain young coppers bollocksed their reports, well, at least the watch had commenced according to Queen's regulations.

Sipping at a mug of cocoa, with a quick glance at the station clock, he started to write up the duty charge-book.

Milford Haven Police Station.
Duty Officer: Sergeant N. Banks.
Date: July 5th. 1966. Time of entry: 0030hrs.
Prisoners in cells: One: Frances. (James) Male. Age 36.
Occupation: Fisherman: No means of identity- but is known.
Charge: Drunk & disorderly.

There! That took care of official requirements. Now he could ease off creaking boots, resting tired feet until the first car reported back at around 0200hrs.

Walking to the small kitchen in stockinged feet the sergeant washed the empty mug before making a bootless inspection of the cells below ground. The dull glow from the 25watt ceiling light in cell number six showed a large figure stretched full length, on his back, snoring loudly. A battered leather coat covered most of his bulk.

One large toe poked through a ragged hole in a sock, on feet displayed in the ten-past-two position. The nail on the big-toe was discoloured, blue and yellow.

Shaking his head, Sergeant Banks walked gingerly towards the stairs leading up to his duty desk, mumbling, "Keep the bloody noise down, English."

As if in reply the snoring suddenly stopped. A deep-throated grunt, a clatter of exploding wind followed by another low grunt and then the steady beat of snoring resumed.

Two hours previously, Skipper Francis had been found lying in the middle of the High Street, adjacent to the Ferry Boat Inn, his arms stretched wide in the crucifix position. Blood, from a broken nose, trickled down over his grey beard.

The arresting officers patrol car had halted less than a yard from the prostrate figure. They'd lit a smoke, discussed Saturday's rugby and waited for the light drizzle to cease before getting from the car. The police driver smiled at the prone body, 'shall we run the bastard over, put him out of his misery? This is the third time this week.' Seeing the confused look on the other officer's face, he added, 'Only jokin', see.'

Checking that the smelly fisherman's wallet, along with any means of identification were missing, they'd delivered the unconscious lump, with some difficulty, to the station.

Shortly after 0200hrs, in need of a brew, the same two young constables returned to the nick. One was carrying a large cardboard box, which he carefully laid on the front desk.

Putting aside his book, Sergeant Banks reached out to open the box at the same instant the young policeman yelled out, 'Don't touch …'

Bootless, the Sergeant leapt back from the desk, a fluffy Jack Russell puppy firmly attached to his right thumb. Swinging in a tight panic-filled circle, holding the dog at full length, he screamed, 'what the …aagh' as the turn caused the frightening terrier to grip tighter. Completing a full 360 degree spin, Sergeant Banks was neither impressed nor unduly influenced by the young copper shouting, 'the little bugger's already bitten both of us, Sarge. Don't play games with the sod.'

At the commencement of the second turning circle, the puppy let go, causing Duty-Sergeant N. Banks to lose his balance. Grabbing wildly at the desk stool, he shot across the room, landing in a loud untidy heap in the far corner. As the winded man kicked out to dislodge legs and arms from the splintered stool, the bundle of canine temper leapt at and then held on to the police officer's big toe. "Get it off! For fuck's sake, get it off me."

Having donned his driving gloves, one of the policemen attempted to drag the wriggling animal from his Sergeant's foot, while the second man kneeled close to the fight, the box open, ready for a hopeful re-capture. It wasn't until the lure of the open box became more attractive than the odour of the Sergeant's toe, that the dog let go. In one flowing moment, the red-faced policeman flipped him into the cardboard container and secured the lid. "There! Gotcha, yer bugger."

Sergeant Norman sat nursing his bruised toe. There was a fresh plaster on his thumb. He still shook with anger. "I don't give a sod, see, that you found the little shit abandoned on the M4. If he'd been mine I'd have dropped it down a mineshaft." Shuddering, he added, "It looks and acts bloody mad. I might, even as we speak, be developing rabies." He gently rubbed his big toe, "apart from Fisherman Francis, we was 'aving a peaceful night, look-you!"

The smaller of the constables asked, "shall we contact the RSPCA, Sarge?"

"No way! Did you enter the mutt in your notebooks yet?"

"Not yet, Sarge…"

"Well, don't! Get back out there on patrol. Leave the little bastard to me. Come morning he'll have a new guardian. I'll teach drunken English mariners to pollute the streets of Milford, indeed I will."

As the two edged towards the door, the Sergeant called out, confusing their retreat. "Before you go, nip below and unload that mad thing into cell six. Then get shot of the damn box."

Life returned to the sleeping fisherman in sharp intermittent spasms. Blinding impulses arced across his nervous system, stabbing at brain cells that begged for relief. A lumpy weight on his chest convinced James he'd suffered rib and lung damage. He appeared to be breathing in and out at the same time. Something warm, like a wet tongue licked across his beard, mouth and up over his tender nose. Keeping his eyes closed, James reached out a trembling hand and the warm licking transferred to his big fingers. Forcing one eye open, the fisherman gazed into the deep brown inquisitive stare of the puppy's tilted head, only an inch from his chin, 'Hello, mister, do I know you?'

The puppy gave a whimper of comforting welcome and then resumed his licking. James Francis fell back into sleep.

When the duty night-sergeant opened the cell door, in company with his day relief, the dog turned, baring his teeth, growling.

"Right, Fisherman, get your arse out of here and take your wild animal with you. I trust you've got a licence for the bloody thing? Whatever … be assured, if you foul my patch again, I'll have the fuckin' pair of you put down, see!"

Milford's morning fish market was drawing to its close. Auctioneers had done their business. Wholesalers were smoking a quiet fag and having a gossip before hurrying off to phone-sell the morning's purchases. White-coated quay staff and porters bustled about, clattering boxes of ice covered cod, skate, sole and various species of pelagic fish towards waiting transport for onward destinations such as Liverpool, London, Paris and Madrid.

In a street behind the market, Skipper Francis sat in the Agent's outer office, angry and bewildered. The kindly receptionist poked her head through the sliding hatch. "Cup of tea, Skipper, perhaps a biscuit? Mr Jones won't keep you a moment, like"

Forcing his hand to stop shaking long enough to accept the tea, James nodded his thanks. Breaking a biscuit he slipped it into the deep pocket of his leather coat. Back at her desk, resuming her typing, through the open hatch the little lady glanced in amazement at the frantic movement inside the fisherman coat. Snapping, crunching sounds came from the pocket as James sipped at his tea, offering the poor woman a glassy eyed smile.

Mr Jones, without expression, passed the telephone to the dishevelled seafarer, "Your owner's office. Mr Turner, in Plymouth, Skipper."

"Percy? What's going on? Where's my bloody boat? Who's

taken her to sea, man?"

Mr Jones couldn't help but overhear the conversation from Plymouth, "Yes-yes! But you listen to me, Francis … I'm still the bloody owner, right? During the last six months you've landed more fish than any two of my other skippers, but at what cost?"

"I'll tell you at what cost, shall I? Wrecked gear, lost trawls, crews refusing to sail with you and that's just for starters. Bad weather damage to the ship, sailings delayed or cancelled 'cause you were pissed. Dammit, man, you're a Don-skipper … but you've become a liability I can't afford. At the end of the day I've got a company to run. There's no profit gained by you sitting on your backside in some bloody pub. In short, James Francis … you're sacked. Mr Jones will arrange any settlement."

There was a pause, then, "One more thing, maister, don't come on the Barbican looking for me in some drunken rage. If you do I'll set my fuckin' dogs on you." With that, the phone in Devon was slammed down.

James handed the receiver back to the agent. " Think I've upset Percy, Mr Jones."

Collecting a cheque from the agent, together with his kitbag, landed before the boat sailed, James strode towards the door. Before leaving, he turned and raised his battered cap,

"Thanks for the tea, Miss … and Mister says Ta for the biscuit."

She looked puzzled but pleased and watched the troubled man walk calmly towards the town … passing by the first public house.

***

Joanne said, "If you intend being out at 4am, I'll loan you an alarm clock."

The singer smiled her thanks, "I'm intrigued. You say that when he returned he was different?"

"Hardly recognizable. He looked like death. The once beautiful wild hair and beard were lank and grey. He smelt like a sewer and had lost a lot of weight. The only familiar landmark was the battered long coat. A total mess, he was. There was also a dog, a strange-looking Jack Russell puppy. It appeared to hate human beings. While James stood in the hall, the dog scrambled from his inside pocket, charging around growling and snapping at anything or anybody that moved."

Matthew took over the telling, "It was nine months after Kathy's death. Joanne looked after Mayo, albeit without the full blessing of the authorities. They wanted him placed in care but our solicitors fought against that one. Apart from the absent James we considered ourselves next-of-kin. We'd registered his birth, name and swore an affidavit that the father was one James Francis."

His voice lowered, "In a sound hardly above a whisper, James informed us that he was coming home to the cottage. He thanked us for attending to what should have been his responsibilities. It was his intention, he mumbled, to prove that in due course he'd be fit to look after his son."

Matthew grinned, "I saw Joanne stiffen. She almost hissed at him …'over my dead body, James,' adding, ' and get that stupid dog out of my home …now.'

"He'd faced Joanne for a long time, silently gauging her angry determination. Opening his coat, he called, 'Mister'. The puppy shot across the floor, leaping straight into the inside pocket in one flowing motion. 'I'll prove to you, Joanne. Right now, I ask only one favour … can I see him, for just a moment?'

"I'm sure it was on her lips to tell him to come back when he was clean …but she didn't. 'He's asleep, but you can peep in for a second. Come with me.'

"Standing over the cot, I'll never forget the poor man's face as he gazed at the sleeping child. Reaching down, he placed one finger, in slow motion, on the tiny pink cheek. The boy sighed in his sleep as the big man croaked a sound something like, 'Kathy'. The puppy suddenly scrambled out from the pocket wriggling between the bars of the cot before any of us could move. It lay beside Mayo, watching the slow breathing and then gently sniffed the boy's cheek. The fisherman scooped up the dog, transferring him back into his pocket, 'Time enough for that later, Mister.'

"Turning to Joanne, touching her shoulder, he whispered, 'Thank you.' Downstairs, at the door, he'd grasped my hand, crushing the bones. 'Won't let you down again, Matthew. Whatever it has cost you and Joanne …I'll repay. G'night!'

"For over a month he worked on, 'Receiver' almost around the clock. Single-handed, installed a new engine. Once or twice a week he'd come to the hotel, fresh and clean as a new pin, politely requesting permission to visit his son. Upstairs, he'd sit beside the cot, just looking, watching in wonder as the boy curled tiny fingers around his father's calloused fingers. Sometimes, taking him a cup of tea, I'd hear him chatting softly about Kathy, the old boat, or the sea. On a couple of occasions I'd take up a beer but later, after he'd gone, the beer would still be there, untouched. He began catching top-grade crabs and lobsters, asking me to deliver them to Plymouth market. Seems he wanted nothing to do with a past life on the Barbican. 'Take what commission you deem fair, Matthew. Whatever fish you require for the hotel … keep. No charge, of course.'

"At weekends, if the weather was fair, he'd come, asking if he could take Mayo for a walk. The first couple of times, Joanne was frantic, only calming down when she saw them coming up the drive again. He'd be in a Sunday suit, his bushy hair and beard now glowing white. While he collected the boy's pram, the dog waited outside on the steps, growling at anyone who passed. When the fisherman came down the wide steps they'd stride off, most times towards Cove village church where Kathy lay. He'd always return on the button, at the agreed time. By the time the boy was a year old they'd bonded. Father and son and a daft dog called, Mister."

Joanna began walking around the quiet lounge, puffing up cushions, tidying magazines and folding away yesterday's newspapers. "As the months rolled on, it became evident he was a reformed character. The drinking had gone … not that he lived like a celibate monk. There were times I'd cajole him into sitting for an art life class. He'd squat for hours, without noticeable movement … the grey/white beard and curls with the battered nose plus the salt-stained face, manna to budding artists."

She giggled, "Mind you, it took months to persuade him to

undress. Yet once he'd climbed that barrier, he warmed to the no-touch contact. James developed his own party piece that amused some students and embarrassed others. Sitting in the centre of the studio floor, nude except for a tiny hand-towel covering the private department, he appeared to drift into some lonely corner of his mind and yet, if an attractive student caught his eye, he could make the towel twitch, without batting an eyelid. I've seen them gulp, I've seen them blush and I've watched them sneak back from his cottage in the early hours as he set off to go fishing."

"Arranging Mayo's schooling was amusing, to say the least. We set off, the four of us, like some rural ménage a trois, completely confusing the headmaster at Cove infants. Matthew just sat there smiling, steadfastly refusing to explain, which only added to the poor chap's discomfort. Mayo didn't help either, kept referring to Matthew as 'Daddy-Matt and James as 'Dadda'. What the ordeal taught us was that it was time to arrange for the lad's father to officially adopt him. That wasn't easy. It took over twelve months banging on different doors but by the end of his first year in school, the name in his books, stamped into the labels of his blazer and raincoat was, Mayo Francis."

"Mostly he lived at the Quarry House. School holidays and some weekends he'd sleep at the cottage. In good weather, the fisherman took him to sea … he loved that. Mister, the dog, would call for him at strange times. Standing below the drive steps, barking once, waiting, his tiny head cocked to one side. If anyone other than the boy walked through the main door, he'd growl like something demented.

"They'd charge off into the woods, running, yelling, laughing and Mister barking. Gone for hours, they often returned covered in mud, wet to the middle, bramble scarred and breathlessly glowing.

Mister would be carrying a stone in his mouth, which he dropped at the driveway. Mayo would come on into the house, stopping at the door to turn and wave. The terrier would wait for the wave and then race off towards the cottage at breakneck speed. They shared the most magical relationship. When Mayo was down with childlike things like measles, chickenpox, or a gippy tummy, the dog would come to the lower step and lay quietly, as if knowing something was wrong."

Looking across to her husband, Joanne grinned, "Of course, he was soft. He'd talk to the daft thing. 'Sorry, Mister, Mayo's not well. Confined to his bed. You can visit if you behave.' As Matthew walked back the dog would growl but he'd follow him up to Mayo's bedroom. The fool would lay tucked over the boy's feet until somehow he knew it was time for James to return from sea …"

Maria Jo-Jo shook her head and glanced at her watch, "Oh god, I'm keeping you folks from your bed and I'm due on the quayside in a little over two hours."

Rising to her feet, she hugged and kissed them both, "Thanks, for the story. Goodnight." Heading towards the stairs, she added, "It will beat the hell out of me if Max makes it to sea in the morning. Sweet dreams."

****

Chapter Sixteen

... Boat Passage

Leaning over the protective rail on the quayside steps, Maria Jo-Jo looked downstream. A full-ball moon illuminated water, trees and shaded cliff-tops, casting a white glow that exaggerated the gorse bushes growing on the seaward rise of the silent creek.

The muffled putt-putt of the engine echoed through the still air moments before the boat came into sight around the southern bend. Misty trails, like broken strands of stretched elastic, lifted silently from the water, twisting and spiralling upwards, before vanishing.

When the blunt vessel appeared, bow wave grinning along the waterline, Maria Jo-Jo stamped her feet in excitement, fighting the urge to wave frantically.

She was dressed in skin-tight designer jeans, a blue sweater and a white, woolly hat, loaned by Matthew, pulled low over her ears. Joanne's contribution had been an oiled jacket, which while being a snug fit, kept out the damp.

After dressing, she'd tried the door to Max's room and finding it locked, walked barefoot down the curved stairs. Sitting in the porch outside the main door she slipped on her boots and walked towards the tiny quay. It was three minutes before 4am.

When Mayo flipped the engine into neutral, halfway through a tight circle approaching the steps, changing the pitch of the engine, the American singer descended the short flight of stone steps. As the rail of the boat touched the lower stone, accepting his hand, she stepped aboard, smiling, "Hi, What a beautiful morning, it's so still..."

In the shadows thrown off the quay wall she couldn't see his face clearly. Her hands wanted to reach out, to touch ...'Hang in there, girl. It's not yet real daylight and already your confused hormones are playin' games. Steady, lady!'

“I guess Max kinda’ missed the boat. He’d bolted his door. Likely against certain advances from one powerful lady artist.” Glancing at her watch, she added, “Well, Mr Fisherman, it’s three minutes after four, what you need me to do?”

He handed her a boathook, “Just shove-off the bow … that’s the pointed end.”

Maria Jo-Jo walked forward and pushed the bow away from the quay with the boathook. She saluted. “I’m with you, skipper.”

Slipping the engine into gear Mayo steered away from the steps. They’d moved less than a boat’s length when Max yelled from the quay, “Hold it, sailor. If I can rise at this god-forsaken hour, least you can do is wait a couple of minutes…”

Mayo reversed the boat back to the steps and Max launched himself, flapping like a broken windmill, landing hard on the boat’s rail. Maria Jo-Jo grabbed him, “Quit bitchin’, Max. Get your ass onboard. I didn’t knock … just in case you was otherwise engaged.”

Max stumbled awkwardly onto the after deck, one foot ending in a basket of smelly fish. “Don’t even go down that road, Song-lady.”

Stretching out a hand towards Mayo, he smiled, “Hi, Max Stone. You’ll be Mayo. No bull, but I’d rather be makin’ your acquaintance in office hours.”

Minutes later the crabber swung under the lower branches of the trees at the bend. Ahead, the moon rested its lower lip on the clifftop and began slipping from sight, changing shape, as if a giant natural eraser was at work. Within a few moments it was gone, pulling a dark curtain down across the water.

Flicking off the navigation lights, Mayo glanced at the dimly lit compass before dropping his cap over the glass bowl, effectively shutting out everything other than the dull reflection of sky against the greater substance of cliffs. Easing open the forward window, he leaned out as the craft closed towards the deeper shadows ahead.

Curved into a corner of the wheelhouse, Maria Jo-Jo peered ahead, her eyes fixed on the black mass appearing to rise hypnotically from the water, pulling them towards …

Half in, half out of the door at the rear of the wheelhouse, Max began to stutter, "Ain't this about t-time to engage something like a radar? H- how can you see what's up ahead, man?"

No one answered. And as the solid blackness worked its way higher up the outline of the foremast, enveloping it, Max exploded, "Jesus-H-Christ, mister, we all gonna' die. Where are the life-vests? Mother-of-God I gotta' …"

"Shut the fuck up, Max." Maria Jo-Jo whispered.

Entering a void deeper than night, the muffled acoustics of the cavern-like space changing the engine's pitch. The repeating echo invaded their heartbeats, vibrating with a rhythmic excitement that surged towards a cry for survival.

Unable to close her eyes, Maria Jo-Jo struggled to come to terms with what was happening. Her mouth and throat had become desert dry. She knew that both her hands gripped hard at the shelf of varnished timber beneath the window … the very same ledge that all those years ago her father might have gripped, on a similar voyage into morning. And, as if from another world she heard Mayo counting, " …five …six … turn …"

While part of her brain instinctively accepted and trusted the actions of the fisherman, her eyes bored into the total darkness, desperately seeking any change in its completeness. She became aware of a feeling of space, a different sound from the engine, as if they'd entered a larger cavern and in the background she could hear Max's faint, panic-filled whimper from somewhere in the stern of the boat.

For the twelve seconds or so that it took to transverse through 'Passage', Maria Jo-Jo prayed …'Please let it go on – on – on and on.' Floating on a wave of emotion that entered every muscle and joint, touching deep into each bone within her body, exploding nerve ends crackled, tearing her senses apart.

The feeling lingered, ages after the old vessel lifted on the belly of the ocean swell outside the creek. Trembling, the singer turned and looked back towards the land. Their exit point was invisible among the half-light painting the high grey-green cliffs. Her body felt deliciously drained. Perspiration seeped from every pore, stung her eyes, chilling her skin, chattering her teeth. "Oh sweet lord … when can we do that again, Mayo?"

Almost to herself she whispered, "In the time it took to come through, I felt the presence of my father."

Setting the autopilot to due south, before flicking the on-switch, Mayo looked over the heaving swell lifting the boat, breathing submerged energy towards the sleeping shore. "There's not a time through 'Passage' when I don't feel a guiding hand …"

A quiet New York voice from the transom mumbled, "Maria Jo-Jo, I've pissed my pants." And then, "I'd kill for some good coffee…"

The international singer, five million albums sold and counted, looked at the young fisherman. They both grinned. "Jesus, Max, you surely are the pits…"

Ten miles south, the crabber drifted alongside the first orange Dan-flag. Leaning over the rail, Mayo grabbed the lead rope and transferred it back along the deck to the spinning capstan.

When the first of the inkwell shaped pots trundled onto the wet deck, watching from the open wheelhouse window, Maria Jo-Jo and Max gasped at the amount of backs, legs and claws filling the willow framed enclosure.

With practiced ease, Mayo extracted large crustaceans from each pot, grabbing at a huge claw or placing the flat of his hand under the shell, pressing his thumb into the crab's abdomen before tossing it, without aim, into one of the plastic holding tanks.

The fisherman's arms moved with such speed that the two watchers had problems following the procedure. Max chuckled when Mayo tossed a crab that bounced on the rail, missed the tank and splashed back into the sea. He snorted as Mayo eased a couple of crabs aside with his boot, directing them towards the scuppers and freedom.

It took less than a minute to empty each pot, re-bait and launch, almost casually, over the after rail, while the whirling capstan dragged the next pot onto the rolling deck. After an hour, fifty pots had been recovered, cleared, baited and re-set. The plastic tank holding the large cock crabs was half full, with tightly packed hens filling about a third of the smaller tank.

Walking aft towards the wheelhouse, Mayo smiled at the singer, "In the corner there's a flask with some tea, please help yourself …yes, I'd love one. In a box, under the wheel, some sandwiches. Be my guest. Max, if you'd ease the engine ahead and steer about west, we'll move to the next string."

Warming to the request, Max tentatively pushed the throttle forward. Turning the wheel he brought the boat's stern into the glassy sun spraying light along the eastern horizon. "At the next string …hey, Maria Jo-Jo, I'm into the lingo, I'll give you a hand, I noticed you missed a couple back there. Some made it back to the ranch…"

Accepting a mug of tea from Maria Jo-Jo via the open window, Mayo smiled, "By all means, Max, glad of the help. The crabs tossed overboard back there were either dead or berried."

Gulping his tea, Max removed a sandwich from Maria Jo-Jo's hand, as she was about to take a bite. "Calories, lady." Munching, he enquired, "Dead? Berried? They're all gonna' end up in the boiler … so what's a little early deceased?"

Checking his watch, Mayo grinned, "West, Max, another ten minutes. A dead crab carries bacteria, poison. Hens carrying eggs, sometimes over a million, is 'berried.' It's madness destroying a future harvest, so we toss them back. Fishermen know it as commonsense while scientists stamp down a label marked, 'conservation of natural environment …' same difference.

As the sun climbed clear of the morning haze, the sea changed colour from grey/green to a deep blue. Mayo eased the boat northwards towards a tiny smudge that clouded the horizon. On the way back he explained the difference between the male and the female's apron. Max, leering from behind the wheel, commented that a female crab's underbelly was shaped like, 'Vegas pussy' … and the same colour. "We bow to your expertise on that subject, Max. About Vegas crabs, you must be the fountain of all knowledge," cracked, Maria Jo-Jo.

Three miles from the shore, with 'Receiver' beginning to lift on the ground swells, the fisherman outlined the act of securing the large claws with thick elastic bands to prevent fighting. Standing close, breathing in her fragrance, his fingers wanted to trace the curved nape of her neck and down over her beautiful back. When the boat dipped awkwardly in a trough between two waves, late bracing herself, she started to tumble. Grabbing the mast stay with one hand, Mayo gathered her around the waist, easing her close. Maria Jo-Jo held onto his arm with both hands, relaxing back into his grip. Max shouted from the wheelhouse, "More sandwiches and tea, wench."

"Pig!" She giggled, "but perhaps better we don't tell him …"

Entering the cave, hidden until the last moment by a large overlapping rock, Mayo eased the engine speed, allowing his passengers to observe the internal phenomenon, created most likely by some ice-age disturbance when the creek was a shaded gully filled with permafrost. The erosion of limestone structure, changing land and sea temperatures, probably expanded the ice, causing cracks to appear in the faulty layers.

Ten thousands years of southerly storms had worn away softer outer rock, forming an underground tunnel that penetrated inwards, creating a subterranean channel into a creek that most likely had been there since year one.

Inside the tunnel, with the boat barely making headway against the ebb, Maria Jo-Jo separated herself from the two men, walking to the forward end of the boat. Mayo's eyes followed the black singer's movements to the starboard rail where she held onto the mast stay with one hand, staring up at the pale limestone bridge towering above them. Easing the engine to almost tick-over, he guided the boat, almost soundlessly through the deep black water.

At the seaward entrance, 'Passage' was about fifty feet wide, increasing slightly as it approached the higher cavern halfway through. Rock along the tidal range was covered in brilliant green moss, worn glass-smooth by uncountable tides over unrecorded numbers of years. The pink shaded stone overhead rose in irregular formation, sometimes reaching sixty feet above sea level. The curving space compressed all sound to a dull whisper.

In the middle of the high central cavern, three small holes in the roof, directed sunlight, searching, pointing arrowlike onto the oily calm water.

As the strength of the tide eased, Mayo knocked the engine into neutral, steering towards the shafts of light. One after another, the diagonal stripes fell aft along the boat's deck, each finger slowly bisecting the American singer's head. Max had enough sense to remain absolutely silent and still.

With the cathedral-like dome astern, Mayo increased the engine revs, pointing the bow northeast, towards a narrowing turn that led back into the creek. If the manoeuvres required to traverse 'Passage' were laid down on a navigation chart, they would have resembled an inverted 'S' … but it was never so.

Entering the cave from sea, Maria Jo-Jo experienced a flicker of claustrophobic panic which evaporated almost immediately. Gliding deeper inside the womb-like space, her eyes marvelled at the change of colours. The limestone ridges became green in the dim light while the sea darkened to an almost inky black.

A strange experience, like a warm breeze eased over her whole body, causing her to walk away from the two men and stand alone at the mast. She could feel the unmistakable presence of her father's spirit. And as a ribbon of exquisite sunlight swept back along the timbers of the old boat, she lifted her head, breathing in the passing warmth of each beam.

Re-entering the sheltered creek was like suddenly breaking surface. Sheltered pea-green water, bright daylight, together with stretches of brilliant white sand along the eastern shore. On the western ridge splashes of yellow gorse grew in scattered clumps among protective peaks.

Pointing the boat towards the distant bend, Mayo increased the engine power before handing the wheel to Max. "Like to drive, Max? Just keep 'er in the middle. Deep water."

Excitedly, Max grabbed the wheel. "You bet, Cap'n. In the

middle … deep water … right!"

Walking forward, Mayo moved loaded fish-tanks over to the starboard side. Glancing back at the wheelhouse he could see Max, bolt upright, arms outstretched, hands firmly gripping the wooden spokes. On his face was an extended grin of satisfaction. 'Go, boat, go!'

Passing the beach where the schooner lay, halfway towards the boomerang-shaped bend, Max yelled from the wheelhouse window, "Hey, fisherman. That wreck … is where you live, right? Christ man, you're almost a pirate."

Preparing the for'deck for arrival, Mayo stayed clear of Maria Jo-Jo. She leaned over the rim of the whaleback, looking towards where they were headed, arms folded. He sensed she might be quietly weeping. Lifting a box containing four medium sized lobsters, he placed the dark blue shellfish under the shelter of the cuddy. "You okay?" he asked, softly.

She slowly nodded her head, not turning.

Mayo could make out the distant figure of Matthew waiting at the steps. Above, on the grassy verge, Matthew's small van was parked in readiness to deliver the morning's catch to Plymouth market. Moving close behind her, Mayo quietly asked, "You up to handing a rope to Matthew?"

Clearing her throat, half turning, taking the small rope from him, she said, "Y-yes… I'm fine, Mayo."

Walking aft, Mayo relieved Max at the wheel, "You did a grand job, Max. I'll do the bump alongside bit."

Tossing the rope Maria Jo-Jo handed him over a small bollard on the upper quay, the hotelier began transferring boxes from the boat's rail up the steps towards the van. Partway up, with the second box, he halted, "Ah, Max, nearly forgot. There was a 'phone call from a Mr Antony Zackadeus, from Phoenix, Arizona. Appears he'd like …his words, a meet. You, together with Miss Christmas, in Paris, lunch tomorrow."

Standing beside the wheelhouse, Max replied, "Hey, whaddya' know, Tony Zack … from Phoenix. Maria Jo-Jo, how does shopping and lunch in Paris, France, grab ya'?"

Maria Jo-Jo glared the full length of the boat. "How come that

Greek scum-bag knew this number? Ruby sure as hell wouldn't talk to him, neither would Frankie. It can only be you, sleeze-ball!"

Spreading his arms wide, Max exclaimed, "Hey, Lady! Business contacts. That's how the world works. Spend ten minutes in the john ... suddenly you're yesterday's sound. "

She wasn't listening. He'd betrayed her, invaded her privacy. Storming along the deck towards the steps she wanted only to be clear of him.

"...And don't you forget, song-lady, Greek scumbag-sleezeball, means ten million bucks record sales during the fiscal year. Plus, Tony Zackadeus controls the key to the Vegas deal and ..."

Attempting to match the singer's stride from the low rail to the first step, Max misjudged his reach, pushing the boat away from the quay wall by performing exaggerated splits. As the gap between boat and wall widened, Max's arms flapped in panic. Twisting, trying to retreat and advance in the same movement, he pitched, belly first into the creek.

His backside resurfaced first, quickly followed by a body turn that spun his head above water. Shooting creek water into the air, he yelled, "...can't swim!"

Leaning over the rail, Mayo pushed down on the wriggling head, holding it underwater for two seconds. The New York man's feet, performed a complicated shuffle, found bottom and pushed hard against fisherman's hand. Released, Max's bulk shot almost two feet out of the water and in mid air, Mayo grabbed his sweater, folding him neatly over the rail before transferring his grip to the seat of Max's pants. He hauled the limp body onboard, where it lay in a slushy heap, panting.

Five steps higher, Maria Jo-Jo stared down, anger and contempt filling her eyes. Matthew fought back a grin. On deck, bumping into and scattering crab pots, struggling to recover his breath, Max dragged his wallet from a back pocket. Checking that his plastic was intact, he pushed a fistful of soaked dollars towards Mayo.

From the steps, Maria Jo-Jo screamed, "Max ... what the fuck are you doin'? "

"... Saved my life ... Christ ... only right, " Max spluttered, spitting salt water, phlegm and partly digested pork sausage onto the deck.

Matthew transferred the last of the crabs into the van as Mayo helped Max onto the steps. Dripping wet, one shoe missing, he trudged up towards Maria Jo-Jo. "Okay-okay, So how was I to know the water was only tit deep?"

Disregarding him, she looked down at Mayo, "Tomorrow? What time?"

Moving along the deck, without looking up, Mayo pushed the bow clear before returning to the steering position. Engaging the engine, he leaned through the side window, "Five … on the button."

Maria Jo-Jo showered with a vigour that frightened her. Hot jets striking chestnut skin ricocheting as the water was rejected by her anger. There were times past when the singer used the warm undisturbed bathroom privacy to digest lyrics or melody of a new number. Today it was, 'Bastard – bastard – bastard.'

Switching the temperature control changed nothing. As ice cold water invaded her bones, she screamed in frustration. Shutting off the fierce shower she leaned against the damp tiles and sobbed.

Dried, powdered, standing in a descending cloud of misty Chanel talcum, clad only in pink silk panties, she stood before the full-length mirror and almost subconsciously began, 'lump-inspection'. Gently lifting the underside of her left breast she allowed a thumb to caress the white bird birthmark. Closing her eyes she drifted with the comfort of her own touch.

Tapping on Maria Jo-Jo's door, Max found her squatting cross-legged on the floor by the window, a duvet pulled over her head like a wigwam. "You comin' down to dinner, Song-lady? Seems it's the students last night. I might need protection from the big dike."

From somewhere under the padded cover she mumbled something crude and unflattering to his manhood.

"Listen, lady, about Paris. Some local people, Castle Air, will fly us to London. We collect some clothes from the apartment … Charles de Gaule by noon. From there we …"

Maria Jo-Jo's head popped from under the cover, "Max, you

don't listen. I-AM-NOT-GOING-TO-NO-PARIS …period."

"You go. Meet with Greek Tony or any other smut from the Vegas stable. But hear this Mr Stone, hear it well, sign NOTHING, agree NOTHING, in my name. I'm not ready! Not clear in my head. There's more to discover here."

Climbing to her feet, the duvet wrapped around her, she walked elegantly towards the bathroom. In her hand was the last letter written by her father. "And, Max, stay away …until I call. Got it? Now, shift your butt while I get dressed."

The evening meal was followed by Joanne's, 'Congratulations, thanks-for-coming speech to her art students. Maria Jo-Jo quietly strolled around the lounge, stopping at each production. To her untrained eye one or two paintings were outstanding, several good and some, well perhaps more heart than artistic. Making appreciative murmurs, she smiled at eyes seeking approval.

At Roy Milton's canvas she paused, walked on, hesitated and turned back. The picture captured the creek's calm beauty of first light. It caught the hazy splendour of changing shades of greens, blues and soft grey shadows. She'd journeyed through this scene… was it only hours ago?

The singer identified the ghostly shadows of the trees reaching down towards the slow moving water. Distant ripples, in varying degrees of acrylic colours, caused by something that had passed along the stream, appeared to trickle softly towards both sides of the sleepy shore. She'd seen this moment, yesterday, stepping from the Rolls.

With her eyes fixed to the painting, she whispered, "How much, Mr Milton?"

The tall man blushed, "It's not ready … I couldn't sell it unfinished. It requires more. Anyway, I've never sold …"

"Name your price?" She gave him her number one smile.

The artist shuffled his feet awkwardly, attempting to clear non-existent dirt from under his thumbnail by using the other. Next, he tugged at an ear, stammering, "I – I couldn't take your money, Miss Christmas. I don't paint to s-sell. The sta-standard isn't … sorry!" His face was now full red.

Maria Jo-Jo took another long look at the painting, nodding, as the results of the long day began to take hold. She touched his arm, "Whenever, Roy, I'd really love it, " walking on. 'Don't press the poor guy. If his picture ain't for sale … that's the end, girl.'

She joined Matthew and Joanne for coffee. "Coming back through 'Passage' this morning, my mind kinda' became numb. There's a spot inside like a cathedral, but mostly it's a tunnel, right? By the time we hit the creek I was pooped …emotionally drained."

Pressing back against a curved leather chair, sipping her coffee, she said, "Something puzzles me, Matthew. That big sailboat, where Mayo lives, he said my daddy was part responsible for her being there. How, in the name of the Grand Canyon did anyone get something that size in through the hole?"

****

Chapter Seventeen

... Schooner

The three-masted schooner, 'Madeline' was constructed at Galmpton, on the River Dart, upstream from Kingswear, in 1900. Measuring 86 feet from bowsprit to transom her beam was an inch or two under 20 feet. Fully loaded she could carry 90 tons of China Clay or 1,800 quintals of fish, deepening her mean draft to eleven feet.

During the schooner's early trading, departing from various South Coast ports with general cargo, she voyaged to Newfoundland, returning with dried cod for Viana de Castello, Cadiz or Oporto. In the First World War, requisitioned by the Admiralty, the vessel patrolled the Bristol Channel searching for enemy submarines. And after the conflict ended in 1918, returning to the coastal trade, she carried cargoes such as china clay from Par, coal from South Wales to Ireland or bricks from Torquay to Northern France.

In 1935 the vessel was purchased by a German consortium to carry potatos, cauliflower and onions between ports like Morlaix, St. Malo or Roscoff.

On the last day of August 1939, 'Madeline' departed from Roscoff's rocky harbour in Bretagne. On board were her Captain, four crew, twelve onion sellers with bicycles and a cargo of onions. Her destination was first Plymouth and then Weymouth.

Arriving in Millbay Docks on September 1st the onion sellers fanned out from the port peddling across the River Tamar as far west as Looe, in Cornwall, and out into the villages and market towns on Dartmoor.

Preparing to depart for Weymouth three weeks later, the schooner, her captain and crew plus the dozen onion sellers were arrested by the Devon police under a new act, accused of spying. They were charged, in camera, with photographing sensitive areas around Devonport Dockyard, logging the movements of merchant vessels loading at Cattedown and purchasing navigational charts of South Coast ports. Removed to Dartmoor Prison, without public trial, her crew would remain there for the duration of the war.

Following the crew's internment the Madeline was unceremoniously towed by a naval tug to a safe berth within the confines of the Dockyard. To safeguard against unlawful departure, the main mast and bowsprit were removed along with the rigging supporting the fore and mizzen, all of which were stowed ashore. The once proud schooner, her anchor cable drooping to a deepwater mooring-buoy near Torpoint, developed the air of something disfigured and lonely.

During May, '43, following a Combined Forces meeting in the offices of the King's Harbourmaster, a young American gunnery major stood at the protected window gazing down at the derelict hull of the schooner,Madeline. "Say, Commander, what's the drill on the wreck? "

Without looking up from his paperwork, the disinterested naval officer replied, "Well, chummy, one assumes it's the property of the crown. Waste of a perfectly good mooring, if you ask me!"

The American continued staring across the ebbing tide for a few moments, watching a slow moving frigate being connected to a tug, passing Drake's Island. In the Sound, two small day-haulers raced towards the western end of the main breakwater and a loaded tanker was embarking a harbour pilot just outside the eastern gap. With his back to the British officer, he quietly said, "In the trunk of my car are two cases of Scotch that say yonder boat would make a good target for practice for the Battle-school at the beach."

The Englishman didn't look up but he'd certainly stopped writing. Adjusting his uniform cap, the Major eased towards the door. "As a matter of fact, there's an extra case says towage to the sands would fix the deal … fine an' dandy!" He reached the door.

With his nose six inches above his notes the Commander muttered, "Ahem! Would Saturday be soon enough? In three days time there's a tug proceeding westwards."

That weekend, the British Admiralty salvage tug, Freebooter, departed from Plymouth Sound on passage to Belfast. Passing the Longroom Signal Station they were questioned regarding their tow. 'Hush-hush' came the flagged reply.

'Strange,' thought the young midshipman signaller from the shore, 'I'd swear that's the old French schooner she's towing. But why's she heading east? Belfast is west.' His mind moved on to the flighty Wren he's arranged to meet that evening …

That same evening, in foggy darkness, south of Prawl Point, Able-seaman William Ross (time served in Appledore schooners) leaned over the stern rail of the tug. Puffing at a battered pipe, he knocked out the ash and ... taking a knife from his pocket, in one swift movement cut the tow. Sauntering towards his bunk, William Ross mumbled, "Fuckin' yanks. 'Tis no way for a fine old craft to end 'er days. Bloody target practice indeed. Away ye go, me luvver."

An hour later, passing the Skerries buoy, within a mile of the Slapton Sands, the tug's boatswain reported to the master that the schooner had somehow mysteriously vanished. Without contacting the shore he turned his vessel and resumed his course in dense fog towards Lands End.

Two days later the ocean-going tugboat passed through Donaghdee Sound inside Copeland Island on the southern edge of Belfast Lough. On arrival in port her commanding officer did not report the loss of any tow to the authorities… because his sailing manifest stated he'd departed from Plymouth, pointed west. What reason would there be have deviated to Slapton Sands?

***

"What's the action today, Walter?"

"Well, Sarge, being Sunday, I'll take Annie tea and toast in bed. Give the ol'dear a lie-in. Day of rest, sort of thing."

Staring through the cottage window, dressed in dark serge trousers held in place by a wide leather belt, double-banked by webbing braces over a collarless shirt, he sipped a mug of tea

Jo-Jo had placed to hand.

The fisherman remarked, "Bloody-hell, soldier, the past few days you've become a dab hand with a teapot. Once you've mastered the art of dumplings, my Annie could be out of a job and that's a fact."

The coloured man watched the bulky figure he'd come to regard as his friend follow the flight of a white seabird heading downstream. "Walter, you're kinda' preoccupied, friend. Listen, if I'm an embarrassment ... just say the word and I'm outta here."

Not taking his eyes from the quay, the barrel-chested man groaned, "Don' be maize, Jo-Jo." He tapped the window, "Outside Passage, there's a fog bank, can feel it in mc water. But there's something beyond that ... I just can't put me finger on..."

He turned, his mind made up, "Tell 'ee what, ol' son, I'll take up mother's tea and toast and I'll wake bugger-lugs. Then we'll take a run out. I never did care much for puzzles."

Passing through Passage into bright sunlight, Jo-Jo was convinced that Walter had made a mistake. It seemed like a clear spring morning ...and then he noticed, about a mile south, the low wall of grey fog.

The fog lay like a displaced iceberg, stretching over the horizon, irregular, cold and ugly. Several wide-eyed gulls swam in different directions, as if afraid of the approaching shadow. As the boat encountered the first damp whispers, James delivered three mugs of tea into the wheelhouse. Taking his mug he sat aft on an upturned bucket, sulking, "Bugger ... Sundays is a right bugger!"

Jo-Jo observed Walter take a pocket watch from under his shirt. He checked the time, the compass point and the angle of the fast disappearing bleary sun. As the fog wrapped itself around the boat, the air temperature dropped and the engine hummed a lower beat.

Walter slowly eased the throttle back until the bow wave, lap-lapped across the silent waters. No one spoke. After five minutes or so, they couldn't see a boat's length ahead, astern or sideways. Walter kicked the engine out of gear and dropping a window, listened. He walked towards the bow, paused for a moment, head cocked to one side and then retraced his steps aft. In the stern he poked his son with his boot, "Can you hear anything?"

Not moving from his bucket, without looking up, James mumbled, "Sod-all, father …nothing."

Back in the wheelhouse, Walter eased the engine ahead, swinging the boat in a wide slow circle. After they'd crossed their own wake, he sent James forward and stopped the engine again. Leaning from the window, he asked, "Well?"

Slurping his tea the boy ambled back towards the wheelhouse, pointing to starboard, "Out there … 'tis well off, mind!" Then he went back and sat on the bucket. The old fisherman nodded.

Hugging a steaming mug, Sergeant Jo-Jo Christmas (Absent-without-leave from the United States Army) perched in the corner of the tiny steering space, convinced he was witnessing some strange West Country ritualistic witchcraft.

With the wet fog swishing over the barely moving boat, Walter dropped the other window and grunted towards son James. The youngster slouched along the deck, hands deep in his pockets and leaned against the mast. "What you want me to do?" Jo-Jo asked Walter.

"Go for'ard with the lad, " the older man said softly.

Standing behind the low whaleback, Jo-Jo noticed the boy's eyes were directed below the false horizon caused by the fog. About to ask what they were supposed to be looking for he held his breath as James raised a hand signalling to his father. Seeing the boy's arm pointed left, Walter pressed the engine forward and swung the wheel hard over to port. Almost before the engine reached full roar, he eased the lever back and then clicked it out of gear.

Peering down at the emerald glare of the sea, eyes burning, Jo-Jo suddenly caught sight of a frayed rope and before he could blink, something dark loomed above them. When the crabber gently bumped against a large wooden hull, in one movement James had tossed a line up over the high rail and leapt…

"Bloody strange," Walter muttered. "No name, papers, main mast gone … not a sign of life. What gives, I wonder?

She's Devon built but the hold stinks of old onions. Could be one of them onion-johnnies, use to trade Roscoff to Plymouth before the war. Right then! We'll need to cut the fore and mizzen mast away to get this lady in through Passage."

Three hours later the crabber emerged from Passage slowly tugging the trading schooner into the creek. Carried by the early flood, the fog had reached the coast, reducing visibility to less than a quarter of a mile. The journey through the tunnel had not been without adventure. The stern had become wedged on the first corner and required some full power and a lot of swearing before they entered the inner cavernous space. Checking for damage and finding only scratches they'd moved on. The stem had bumped along various parts of the northern exit dislodging a few lumps of limestone but aided by the tide the final narrow gorge was navigated without further hold-ups or bad language.

Chugging slowly northwards, Walter strapped 'Receiver' alongside the bigger hull and then called for consultation with his salvage team. "It's just after high water … we'll run 'er up the beach, 'ard like, and drag 'er anchors ashore into the woods."

At the large wheel on the derelict's after-deck, James stood grinning broadly from ear to ear. He yelled ahead to Walter, "Er steers like a beauty, father. Be us rich now?"

Winking at Jo-Jo, Walter shouted back, "Our fleet's increased 100% …course we'm rich. Now, let's get done. I can smell your mother's Sunday roast from 'ere."

During the last hours of the ebb, following one of the finest home-cooked meals he'd ever experienced, the American uncovered the army truck and off-loaded the 'dozer. He used the machine to push hard packed sand down the beach in line with the flat edge of the cliff. When the dam checked the next incoming tide he began to excavate a deep trench for the vessel's hull to settle into.

By high water on the Monday afternoon, they'd manoeuvred the schooner into a man-made channel cutting the creek at right angles. Both the bow anchors were dragged into the trees and buried with their cables beneath the white sand.

At the next low water the US digging machine, driven by Jo-Jo lodged heaps of boulders into place around the vessel's stern. The schooner now lay berthed in her own, specially excavated, protected dock.

At the Sergeant's request the fishermen left him alone on the beach while they put to sea through Passage to recover the weekend's catch.

When the stern of the crabber entered the exit hole, Jo-Jo set to work collecting evergreen branches from the copse. Later, driving the truck from deep within the woods to Walter's cottage, he gathered disused trawls, rusty beams, and pots of old tar. Then he returned to the beach.

'Borrowing' bundles of battle camouflage nets from the truck and utilising parts of the truck itself, he began to complete the illusion of an empty beach.

Late afternoon, returned from sea loaded with the weekend's harvest, Walter and son James passed within one hundred feet of the beached vessel … and they could hardly see her.

****

Chapter Eighteen

... Searching

The moment Receiver's bow came into sight the singer began waving. In the distance, Mayo raised a hand in acknowledgement. Sky-signs promised a beautiful day. The air sparkled with energy and beyond the creek, ahead of the rising sun, daylight hurried along a shadowed horizon.

Drifting alongside the steps, Mayo smiled, "Good morning. Is he late again?"

"Max? He's off to Paris-France to meet the Greek."

Stepping aboard, picking up a boathook, she pushed off. As the boat's engine engaged Maria Jo-Jo sat on the low rail, head in hands, shaking, tears ran down between her long fingers.

Before they'd made any real headway, Mayo killed the motor, allowing the boat to drift towards mid-stream. Moving to the hunched figure he sat, placing his arm gently around the heaving shoulders. "What's wrong? I'll take you back. Go shopping in Paris, Maria Jo-Jo. We can do this another day."

Taking a handkerchief from his jeans he began wiping the tears trickling down over the faint, almost indiscernible soft fuzz on her forearms. Peering through her fingers at his concerned eyes, less than a foot from her own, she reached out, encircling his neck with brown arms, smiling, "Sorry … I looked in on Max, making sure he was tuned to chopper-time, six. He was … there …"

She burst into deep laughter, resting her head on Mayo's shoulder, "… a tangle of legs, arms, heads, different private parts. I'm not sure who was doing what to who. Big-dike just lay there, no shame, squashing Max into the pillow, grinning, all British, 'Feel free to join the party, dear girl.'

From under a mountain of flesh Max stuttered, 'I- I promised these ladies a r-ride to London in the chopper … have a nice day, Maria Jo-Jo.' The little lady's head popped up asking what the hell was goin' on? A good question."

Conscious how close they were, her fingers entwined at the back of his neck, thumbs gently massaging the short hairs at the base of his skull. She knew that crazy though it might be, the next step, leading to wherever … was about to be taken. As the black singer's mouth moved forward alarm bells jangled, 'For the love of god, woman, you lost your cherry before this boy was born.' But as their lips touched, it didn't matter a damn.

A mile out at sea, a lone gull swooped across the crabber's wake, seeking breakfast. Maria Jo-Jo sat, bum against the whaleback, drinking from a large mug, arms resting on bent knees. A wispy breeze from the south chased ripples across the changing plateaux of long swells, disappearing in the troughs as the old crabber glided down blue-green ocean. When the craft lifted, Maria Jo-Jo could see the shape of the dead elm framed in line with the broken church higher up the meadow. The clarity of the shore's outline touched knee-hugging senses.

Boat, sea, sky … the young man standing just beyond her reach, displaced all thoughts of Max, contracts, Las Vegas … everything other than the sum total filling her present horizon.

Mayo's knifed flashed, tossing bait into a second basket. Without direct eye contact, he studied the American woman, more beautiful than a woman deserved to be, squatting against the for'ard bulkhead. The combination of Mexico's rarefied air mixed with Africa's fertile plains had created a genetic radiance echoing through generations of Maria Jo-Jo's ancestors. A woman, born from the warmth of the sun.

The young fisherman's mind scrambled to place that moment into some acceptable perspective. 'It was one kiss. One single share-my-laughter-kiss. Show business … they do it all the time. Besides, Americans are instinctive, friend or foe. Does this lady know, or care, about the ache in my … at best I'm vacation-English. Gathered to her magnificent chest in a moment of vulnerability searching for her father's story.'

Transferring the last of the bait to the second basket, his mind settled the argument. 'I'll take it! If that's all there is, with both hands I accept, whatever comfort is offered … '

Finishing her tea, looking astern, Maria Jo-Jo noticed the land was lost from view, even on the highest swells. 'If its only sex, I'll burn his needs. If I'm a joke in the hotel as his celeb-screw … so be it. Nights into the future this boy-man will recall my passion and, believe it … he will not consider it was remotely funny'

Rising to her feet, she moved towards the wheelhouse, 'Dear god, blind him to my age. Let him see me only as a woman. I'll live with the fact that it ain't love. Wanting my bones … for whatever reason, is love enough. Shit! I'm back into Rod McKuen's poetry.'

Disengaging the auto-pilot, Mayo reduced the revs before donning a wraparound apron for hauling. Passing each other on the slow-rolling deck, close enough to touch …they touched. Four fingers of her left hand traced the line of his cheek. Hesitating, Mayo smiled and flipping the capstan into low drive, he reached over the low rail to gather the first string of pots.

Three miles out, with smudges of land sprinkling the northern skyline, the fog overtook them. The first spiky wisps drifted across the stern, thickened and then began shutting out the sun, sky, horizon and the low distant shore. Maria Jo-Jo's first thought was how cold it had suddenly become.

Lifting a heavy coat from behind the wheelhouse door and draping it around her shoulders, Mayo said, "It's okay, the ol' boat knows the way home. You make some tea, I'll catch some lunch."

Dropping the speed to tick-over he fixed the auto-pilot onto a northerly course and checked his watch before switching the navigation lights on.

On the transom, clearing away a small scallop dredge Mayo tossed it overboard into the wake. When the dredge snagged on the seabed he returned to the wheelhouse, increasing the engine revs until the towing angle was to his satisfaction.

"How do we get back? What you fishing for? Do you know how old I am? " The three questions, tripping over each other, were spoken in quick gasps of hurried breaths between sips of tea.

"Getting home is easy … Scallops. Yes! I even know your birthday, from the albums. Numbers? Not important." Why are we speaking in whispers, he wondered?

"But …"

Feeling the grey damp pressing around the boat's hull she knew this wasn't time or place. In the claustrophobic environment of what was after all his natural element, she felt breathless, vulnerable.

Feeling the boat shudder, Mayo pulled the gears into neutral and carried the towline forward to the capstan drum. When the ground chains rattled over the transom rollers he secured the dredge. Leaning over he shook away seaweed, stones and sandy mud before heaving the boom onto the after deck, emptying a dozen large scallops, some black muscles and two small Lemon sole. Grinning at Maria Jo-Jo, standing crossed legged in the doorway, he said, "Lunch for a lovely lady."

"This lady accepts your kind offer, sir."

An hour later, slowing the engine, Mayo asked, "Do you notice any change?"

Wrapped in Mayo's coat, Matthew's unreturned woolly hat pulled low over her ears, the singer studied the green-grey water. "The swell's going one way but … hey! There's an undertow … outwards."

"Backwash …" Spinning the wheel dragged the compass to point east, he added, "At the rock face it will be calm … like so."

The sea flattened out as Mayo revved the engine, altering the boat's direction to north. He stopped the engine. As the vessel slowed, rolling slightly, he walked to mid-ships, bracing himself with one foot against the starboard rail. "Maria Jo-Jo …"

When she stood close, he nodded, "Land."

In the fog, within touching distance, she could make out the hazy shadow of rocks. Looking down she noticed kelp and tiny pyramid shaped limpets washed by the rise and fall of the swell. The close proximity of it made her jump back. Her higher vision felt rather than saw a dark mass reaching upwards beyond her range of visibility. If Mayo hadn't held her around the waist she would have run.

"It's fine. From here, piece of cake. That's Toe Point Rock. We're about a hundred yards south of Passage."

'Receiver' entered the gap in the limestone cliff without the cavern's sides or roof being visible. Once inside, the engine sound echoed. The fog magically evaporated. From overhead, mystical light sprayed the rocky chamber with an orange glow. With the boat drifting, Maria Jo-Jo walked slowly forward and held onto the mast. The craft slowed almost to a stop when Mayo cut the engine.

Breathing in great gulps she watched speckled ripples wash and whisper with the displacement of each captive swell. Each passing surge echoed through the inner chamber like a great …wh-h-oosh!

Seeing her tremble, the fisherman joined the singer at the mast and eased her back against his body. Resting her head against his shoulder, she said, "I kinda' said, 'hello', to my father."

***

The crabber curved the bend at the halfway mark in the creek, chugging towards the quay steps a quarter of a mile ahead. "Looks like we got company", Walter said. "Better nip below, Jo-Jo me ol' son. Stretch out in the cuddy till us see's what gives 'ere."

On the quayside Walter could make out a jeep, with MP painted on the side. Standing at the top of the steps, watching the boat's approach, were five men in American army uniforms. Three coloured men, armed with rifles, stood apart from two white officers, talked in whispers as the vessel drew alongside.

With a rope slung over his shoulder and a white handkerchief fluttering in his hand, James looked up at the Americans. "Ist diese Amerika, Kapitan?" He asked, without a smile breaking his young face.

The three enlisted men raised their rifles, noisily sliding a round into the breech. "Pack that in, you daft twerp. You'll get us shot." Walter yelled.

Glancing up, he addressed the plump officer wearing a major's insignia, "Sorry 'bout that, Colonel. The lad's seen too many Errol Flynn films.

Now, if you'm after lobsters, I'm afraid today's catch is spoken for, up at the big house. Rank gets first call, sort of thing. Still, I could let 'ee 'ave a couple of decent 'en crabs. 'ow does a couple tins of fruit and perhaps some gum for the boy sound as fair exchange?"

Major Willard Harris Jnr. walked slowly down the steps. "How in the name of sweet-fucks you're permitted to operate, is a great mystery, Limey. They do say there's a bit of paper, signed by general Bradley himself, givin' you 'freedom of access'. How you come by such power beats the shit out of me. However, we're here today seeking information on two different fronts. Firstly, we're trackin' a nigga' sergeant who killed an American officer, stole a truck and 'dozer and went AWOL."

Indicating the tall officer on the steps above him, he went on, "This is Major Brooks, Special Services. Top man. Next up, we're searching for US property gone missin' … namely a three-masted schooner. It would come as no surprise to me if the black-ass-sergeant didn't have a hand in that scam either. My question is, fisherman, have you seen either parties?"

James had secured the boat to the steps. "This Sergeant, is he a big coloured fella' with a whopper dick?"

"James!" Walter warned. "Take no notice, Colonel. We've never seen a man round these parts we'd call nigger. As for the schooner ... be there any rewards if us 'appens on 'er? "

Major Harris Jnr jumped onto the deck of the boat, drew his colt 45 and pointed it at Walter's nose. "Listen, you uppity British bastard, we're here in this godforsaken hog's-piss country to save your useless skins. Back home, we'd call scum like you, white-trash. I'm empowered by the Combined Chief-of-Staff to requisition any vessel to go search for the said missin' sailboat."

Slowly reaching up a large hand, Walter took hold of the pistol, shaking with the Major's rage. "Hang-about, mister. If you want to hire my boat for a couple days, fine. But you do need to ask politely … 'tis only manners. Also, you keep wavin' that cannon in my face, I'm likely to stick it so far up yer' bum, your 'at'll fall off."

Easing the Major's arm downward, Walter pressured the weapon back into the officer's holster. "There, that's better. Now, you and your troops be here tomorrow, dawn like, an' we'll go lookin' fer your lost schooner. Ten pounds a day … cash… plus fuel. 50 gallons of diesel, in jerry cans should take care of the first day. So, do you want these 'ens or what?"

James and his father watched the US officers stomp back up the steps. The three black soldiers, slinging their rifles, grinned down at the two fishermen before climbing into the jeep. As the jeep began moving away from the quay, James smirked, "Fifty gallons will keep us goin' for a week, father."

Walter began lifting boxes of crabs onto the quay. "When you listen to fools like the Major, me-boy, 'tis easy to believe the whole of America is built on wild exaggeration. Lets let Sergeant Jo-Jo out from the cuddy and get home to our dinner."

Next morning, at 0600 hours, sharp, the crabber, "Receiver" embarked US Majors Harris Jnr and Brooks from the creek quay. James shuffled up and down the steps carrying and stowing ten jerry cans full of diesel. Walter had greeted the officers on deck, "Ten quid, in advance, I think was the deal, gentlemen?"

Pocketing the cash, he added, "I'll let you have a receipt later. Now! If you want to agree a three-day charter, we could talk a small discount."

Major Willard Harris Jnr snarled, "Just get the fuck underway. Proceed to five miles south of Prawl Point. We'll box-search from there."

US Special Services Major Brooks, studying a nautical chart of the South Hams area, remained silent.

Approaching the invisible gap in the south ridge, both Americans showed concern. Passing the beach where the schooner lay camouflaged, their eyes concentrated, one hundred percent on seeking the exit route from the enclosed creek. Walter reckoned they wouldn't have noticed the schooner if Sergeant Jo-Jo had stood on deck waving the Stars and Stripes.

From a position five miles south of Prawl, Major Brooks laid out a charted box-pattern search grid. Walter was impressed. Shortly after noon, following a bacon sandwich, some K-ration, two apples and several candy bars, plus a mug of strong sweet tea, Willard spread his mark on the heaving swell, some fifteen miles southeast of Bolt tail. Several gannets diving in the boat's wake, fed, attracted by the recycled bacon sandwich and other goodies.

When the evening sun began to settle in full glory towards the western horizon, the officers called a halt and Walter turned the bow towards the smudge of land faintly visible on the northern horizon.

Nodding aft, towards Walter's smiling face, Major Harris Jnr grumbled, "Brooksie, we surely been screwed by these Limey shit-merchants. But that big jerk ... he ain't seen the last of Willard Harris Jnr...you can bet your best horse on it."

Just before entering the creek, in dimpsy light, James strung together a dozen mackerel they'd caught off-shore, handing them to Major Brooks. "We didn't catch no schooners, Boss, but these will make a good supper."

The tall American, who'd hardly spoken all day, smiled his thanks.

Once through Passage the two military men stood at the starboard rail, watching sand martins and kittiwakes pluck supper from the damp sand as the last of the ebb flowed out through the hidden channel.

"Take the wheel, boy." Walter called, "Father needs a pump ship."

Walking to where the two Americans stood on the starboard side, watching Willard light a cigar, the fisherman could see the stern of the schooner clearly visible in the man-made cutting in the gathering gloom. Walter quickly undid his buttons and began spraying urine onto and over the rail ... "Sorry, caught short."

Concerned about the direction and force of Walter's water, both Majors scrambled hurriedly across to the port side, seeking shelter in the lea of the wheelhouse. When they'd passed the schooner,

Walter shook the last drops over the side, refastened his flies and sauntered back to the wheel.

"Get the rope ready, me-boy. The jeep's already on the quay."

Moored at the quayside, Major Brooks passed the string of mackerel to the driver and before stepping ashore turned, smiling his thanks to James. Major Harris Jnr took one step onto the rail, paused and looked hard at Walter. "What kind of prick you take me for, Limey? You surely don't expect me to drive off into the sunset without searching this broken heap?"

"Be my guest, Colonel but don't take all night. Mother's got the pasties about ready for supper. "

Already halfway up the steps, Major Brooks halted, gazing in amazement at the scene unfolding below, slowly shaking his head. The jeep's driver, still holding the fish, leaned over the rail smoking an evil smelling cigar.

When Willard's head emerged from the tiny engine space beneath the wheelhouse, his face glowed pink. "It's blacker than a steer's gut down there … and smells like shit."

Marching forwards, kicking several boxes aside checking nothing was hidden, he opened the small hatch-door in the whaleback and crawled below, backwards. Up on the quay, the driver puffed cigar smoke into the air, a sheepish grin on his face. Major Brooks remained mid-steps and when Walter looked his way he shrugged his shoulders, embarrassed.

Pulling his bulky frame up from the cuddy, with his face deeply red, Willard breathed in short gasps. Coming abreast of the fisherman, he flipped open the holster, drawing his gun. "My name is Major Willard Harris Jnr, native-born son of Birmingham, State of Alabama, United States of America … God's own sweet country." Without pausing for breath, he rumbled on, "I'm proud. Army, from my brains to my balls." Nodding towards the cuddy, his squeaky voice gathering speed, "I tell you this fisherman, I can smell me a nigger five miles off in the desert night."

Cocking the Colt 45, he aimed the barrel at James' head. "You surely had a nigger down there, mister. Maybe's not today… but sometime. Now talk, or I blow the kid's fuckin' ears apart."

Up on the quay, the driver, blowing smoke rings, stopped in

mid-action and open-mouthed, stared down onto the deck space. Major Brooks descended two steps drew his gun and cleared his throat, causing Willard to fleetingly glance in his direction. Walter reached forward, gripped the revolver, lowering it in an arc away from his son.

The sound of a single shot echoed across the quiet creek like a cannon exploding. They all stared at Walter's left foot. An inch wide hole had opened up in the fisherman's boot, almost plum in the centre. Taking a step forward, Walter grabbed the astonished Major below both armpits.

Lifting him clear of the deck, he shook him until the gun dropped. Holding the struggling officer above his head, using the damaged foot, Walter kicked the Colt 45 across the deck into the scupper. He then tossed Major Harris Jnr like a limp doll, onto a heap of pots.

Scrambling over the tar-covered pots towards his gun, Willard screamed, "Shoot the bastard, Brooks, he ain't human."

Major Brooks raised his pistol, pointing it at his fellow officer, "Leave the weapon, Willard. We're guests in this man's county. I can't figure out why he not bleeding to death from that hole in his foot but you sure ain't gonna' try a second shot. So, get your fat ass onto the shore and we'll …"

At the top rail of the quayside steps the head and shoulders of Sergeant Jo-Jo Christmas suddenly appeared. "Leave these folks be, Major. I broke into this man's boat an' holed-up a couple of nights. They didn't know shit. I'm ready to surrender … but only to the Special Services guy, not you!"

Fisherman Walter and son James stood by the vehicle as Jo-Jo, handcuffed, was placed into the back. The two men glanced at each other, Sergeant Jo-Jo Christmas nodded to his friend and Walter nodded back.

Before clambering into the passenger seat, Major Willard Harris Jnr stood before Walter, muttering, "You have not seen the last of me, fisherman. Count the days … I'll surely be back for y'all".

When the grey/green jeep started up, James sprang to attention, saluting. Walter watched the motor gather speed, gears clattering, towards the beach road. "There goes a fine man, James."

"That's why I saluted, father."

Looking down at the gaping hole in Walter's boot, he added, "Mother's goin' to play hell about that boot. I think there's a plug in the store. With a lick of paint, she might never notice."

Glancing at the ragged opening, Walter mumbled, "Bloody fool Yank. I think the bullet split the grain from heel to toe. Bugger! Over the years I've grown fond of that block of teak."

***

Stretching her long legs from the boat's rail onto the steps, Maria Jo-Jo fed the bow rope through a steel ring and stepped back onboard. Having secured the line she watched Matthew's van arrive on the quay above.

As Mayo lifted the last full box onto the steps, she asked, "What now, fisherman?"

"Breakfast ... a shower and a couple of hours sleep, depending on the weather." Glancing downstream towards the wooded bend, he added, "There's rain coming, so the oil change can wait. Besides, I've sort off invited a lady to lunch."

The singer studied Matthew loading the final box into his van. "I'll check Max didn't blow the travel arrangements this morning, then I'd be happy to fix breakfast while you shower. Folks have killed for my scrambled eggs." Her voice dipped, "we can discuss the sleeping stuff if you survive my coffee."

Mayo smiled at her blushes. Coming slowly down the stone steps, Matthew said, "The helicopter got away just after seven. The tiny one, Miss Penny, well, she took fright. Her friend had to drag her yelling and kicking into the cockpit. Max phoned from London only twenty minutes ago, on his way to Heathrow. Said to tell you he'll call this evening from Paris- France."

Retracing his way back to the van, Matthew paused, "Oh! By the way, Maria Jo-Jo, there's a package for you in the office. Mr Milton, the quiet artist chap, left it with me before he departed. He mumbled something along the lines of ...'not for sale but she appeared taken so ...' Joanne says it's a splendid picture."

Climbing into the van he started the engine and before putting it into gear, rolled down the window, "Have a nice day. God! I must stop saying that. Its so bloody crass."

In the semi-darkness of the schooner's stairwell, Maria Jo-Jo hung Mayo's coat over the hook before easing off her boots. She noticed her hands were trembling. Overhead, on deck, she could hear Mayo cleaning the shellfish.

In the kitchen area of the main cabin, pouring some orange juice, she prepared eggs, mixed a finely chopped apple together with some sliced spring onions, sprinkled pepper and added a spoonful of tomato puree while waiting for the pan to heat.

When Mayo came below he was barefoot. Standing beside her at the hot plate, shoulders almost touching, he noticed they were just about the same height. "Whatever you're doing smells great. Mexican?"

"Close! You're kinda' short on tequila. Show me where you keep the bread, then take a shower, buddy. This will be table-ready in seven minutes … that's if I switched the coffee pot button on right."

Under the powerful water jets he considered shaving. 'No, that's presumptuous. But if you don't, she might feel … ah! come on, don't go through permutations of something so bloody unpredictable. There's a chance you'll end up with Mexican egg on your face … together with an unresolved erection.'

Soaping himself down, he realised that while the first part was being prepared in the galley, the other was involuntary forming its own conclusion, fired by the desire he felt for the beautiful singer.

***

In the years following school there'd been a mixture of encounters. A few platonic, some romantic and a few fumbled sexual exchanges in the summer heat. In the main, the girls were mostly on holiday from different parts of the country. Set free from parental restraints or protective control, the crisp Devon sea air fuelled teenage passions. In the meadow's waving grasses or in the shady woods, whispered promises of eternal faithfulness were made and then gently broken with each homeward bound departure.

There were a few 'specials.' Judith, Jewish. Fifteen years old had been extra special. Recovering from a serious illness, the tiny bone-thin girl with marble-white skin and dark brown eyes, had arrived one summer accompanied by her father, a gallery owner from St. John's Wood. They'd journeyed down by car from the capital for a two-week convalescent-cum-study-course.

Body language communications had begun in Joanne's art-class. Exchanged shy glances, followed by both looking quickly away. A smile and then later, further eye contact. After week one, they'd walked together through the shadowed trees along the creek. Coming back along the coastal path from the cliff-top towards the quay, they'd held hands. On her last night there were kisses … three. Judith promised to write and did, once a month. Mayo promised to answer but apart from a Christmas card, never did.

When Judith returned with her father the following year she was taller but thinner, her complexion ashen against her black hair. Because of hollow wheezing sounds from her chest, walking any distance became an embarrassment for her. Sneaking from the hotel, after her father had gone to bed, in white sand still warm from the sun, they'd made fumbled love. Judith clung to the young fisherman, panting, sobbing, pulling his hands to caress the gentle risings of her breasts.

One month later, she wrote informing Mayo that she and her father were returning to Israel's dry air. Medical recommendation aimed at assisting her recovery to good health. For six months there was no further contact. Then, on a cold easterly November day, an envelope arrived containing a tiny black card. It simply stated, 'Judith died.'

At the age of seventeen, working as crew on a private yacht in the warm Mediterranean, the yacht owner's under-aged daughter had tormented the frantic pattern of his hormones, exciting and yet frightening him with her knowledge and sexual demands. Each time he tried closing the door she threatened to disclose their illegal relationship to her Italian father who had offered both employment and trust to the youngster.

Crunch time arrived when the girl's stepmother, a beautiful French socialite, only ten years older than the daughter, suffering from an under-attentive husband, discovered what her teenage stepdaughter was enjoying in the crew's quarters and decided that she deserved some of the action too.

Unable to come to terms with the deception level required to pleasure both women, legally and morally out of bounds, Mayo deserted the super yacht in the port of Marseille on a cloudy Sunday morning, while the family were at mass. By Monday he'd joined a Greek tanker as Able Seaman and began trading to the Persian Gulf.

***

They sat at the small table enjoying Maria Jo-Jo's Californian eggs, toast and coffee. She'd searched in vain for matching knives, forks and a tablecloth even. Reluctantly she substituted kitchen roll for napkins, folded into funny shapes taught by Ruby, all those years ago on the road.

"Living solo, don't you miss people ... cities... crowds? Did you live here with your father? How's the coffee?"

The three questions rushed out almost in one breath, jumbled together. She felt like a nervous schoolgirl struggling to stabilize flustered emotions.

Munching the last of the toast and refilling both coffee mugs, Mayo answered, "No, to the first. People are fine but crowds I can live without. Last summer I almost bought another dog but ... I've been back in the creek for nearly four years. Converting this lady allows me to rent out the cottage. The coffee's excellent."

Looking across the table, his mind placed orderly facts in line.

'This is a worldly, sophisticated, beautiful international singing star. A magnificent woman ... and yet, perhaps because of this strange environment, her body language whispers that she's nervous, hesitant, unsure. Where the hell do we go from here?'

"There's plenty of hot water for a shower", he smiled, "if you'd like to freshen up. We don't run to Hilton dressing gowns but feel free to borrow a clean shirt". Mayo knew he was blushing. "I'll do the dishes."

The sound of hissing water from the shower in the adjoining cabin mingled with the first hard splashes of rain hitting the thick timbers of the deck overhead. Dark clouds changed the amount of light through the skylight, filtering the cabin space with mixtures of deep reds and blues. As the rain drummed harder, the sound from the shower room faded.

Quietly opening the bedroom door, in the half-light he could just make out her figure on his bed, chestnut coloured skin still glistening from the water.

Maria Jo-Jo, on her side, lay curved, facing away from the door, her crisp white head painting a halo on the shadowed pillow. When the door clicked, she'd twitched, her right hand reaching for her left shoulder, covering yet exaggerating the fullness of her breasts.

Standing close, Mayo ran his hand softly through her spiky, still damp hair. She purred at his touch.

He whispered, "So, you didn't find a shirt you liked?"

****

Chapter Nineteen

... Escape

The Sergeant woke in semi-darkness, his head throbbing. One eye closed, the lid badly swollen, ready to burst. He lay on a steel cot lined with rough boards. No mattress, blanket or pillow. The musty air reeked of urine and stale tobacco.

The only light seeped from a small crack in the base of what must be a door. From distant parts of the building, muffled sounds echoed through the same gap. A long high-pitched scream from somewhere was linked by low grunts and then the dull thump of a body blow, followed by sobbing.

For nearly a minute there was silence and then deep hysterical laughter.

Attempting to move his legs, excruciating stabbing pains caused Jo-Jo's arms to jerk. Breathing in shallow gasps he began checking for damage. Fingers first, touching and bending. Both hands felt stiff but not broken. The knuckles on his left hand were swollen and the thumb hurt. His lower stomach felt lumpy, spongy and bruised.

From his boxing days the sharp ache in his rib cage told him at least two were cracked. Reaching back to touch his kidneys, he screamed.

Taking short breaths he fumbled about discovering belt, boots and socks were missing. Reaching gently inside his pants his right hand found both penis and testicles were numb and swollen.

Trying to relax different bones, Jo-Jo willed the injured sections of his body, muscle by muscle, to ease towards recovery. In the confused semi-darkness, he struggled to recall what had happened and how long ago?

As the Beach-master's jeep had scurried up the narrow lane from the quayside, the sergeant remembered looking back just before they turned the first bend. The fisherman and James stood watching the departing motor. Walter's stance told the American soldier that the past seven days had cemented a friendship between the two men, opposite in colour, culture and continent that stretched beyond the insane conflict of war raging throughout the power-crazy world.

Another sudden flashback captured young James saluting as the jeep leaned into the lane's bend. The boy's gesture had warmed the surrendered soldier, while recalling, sadly, that he hadn't said 'G'bye and thanks' to Walter's wife Annie.

As the jeep gathered speed over the brow of the lumpy hill, Major Harris Jnr had leaned back towards the rear seats and smirked, "Before the Specials take you under their wing, you an' me, we're gonna' have us a little pow-wow, nigger boy."

Hustled from the jeep at the camp the prisoner had been dragged along a dark corridor of a low building and tumbled into a small rectangular room. The only furniture in the windowless cell was a bare iron cot at one end. The only light came from a single low-wattage bulb in the hallway.

The words of the Beach-master Major rumbled through his muddled mind, "Go grab some chow, Brooksie. Me an' this son-of-a-bitch ... we gonna' have a little southern interrogation ... in private."

Major Brooks had stared hard at the other officer. "Listen - this man's a prisoner but he's got rights. My people won't be here from Plymouth till morning but I sure as hell don't want to be truckin' a stiff back to base. There's far too many unanswered questions about Convoy T-4. I'm warning you, Willard ...."

"Trust me, Brooksie. I'm a southern gentleman." Jo-Jo could recall the Major's sneer.

More memory came tumbling back. Later, after Major Brooks returned saying he'd be back next morning, Major Harris Jnr had re-handcuffed Jo-Jo's hands behind his back and placed a wide strip of tape over his eyes and another over his mouth. The Sergeant sensed rather than heard the outside light being clicked off. Minutes later the door creaked. Jo-Jo felt at least two people had come into the cell. He smelt garlic. The first blow caught him high on the left ear, spinning him across the cot. Rolling onto the stone floor he sprang, lashing out a bare foot, aiming in the general direction of the garlic. The foot contacted soft tissue. He felt a nose break. Someone groaned and fell in a heap.

An object slammed into his ribs. Jo-Jo tried to scream but the only sound came from within. His ears popped as the next blow, a gloved fist, caught him just below the kidneys, skidding him along a tunnel of blinding lights that narrowed into merciful unconsciousness.

As if from a deep hole he heard the words, “Listen up, soldier, tomorrow, if you act the smart nigger … you’re dead meat.”

Another voice grunted, “When the Special-boys ask about diggin’ … you know nothin’. If you say one word leading the suckers to any field, you will surely take three long days to die…maybe more.”

Whatever else was said was lost to Sergeant Jo-Jo Christmas. He lay curled in a chasm of pain. Reaching towards Maria’s face, sliping towards a darker place, she gently called him back.

***

“I think you’ve killed me.”

Maria Jo-Jo’s whisper vibrated up into Mayo’s chest as her head rested on his stomach. Overhead, the falling rain had resumed, drumming its uncomplicated pattern on the wooden deck.

The singer could not remember, ever-ever, scrambling from a stranger’s bed without feeling physically revolted and ashamed, wanting only to be dressed and gone from the smell of overheated bodies.

Lying in his warmth, feather-light touching fingers rippled through the fibrous tissues in her vagina. Remembered poems about sex being beautiful, melodious …more. ‘Oh sweet fuck, this boy has plucked the moving strings of my being.’

Guiding his hand down over her breast, easing his fingers to the spot she never permitted anyone to touch, recoiling even from medical inspection of the pale pigmentation on mahogany skin, she traced his thumb across the stretched wings of the seabird …”can you feel that?” she murmured.

"It's a birthmark. We've made love for hours. When the light goes on, I couldn't take it if there was, well, distaste in your eyes."

That first touch, in the cabin's semi-darkness, he'd been amazed at how natural it felt. No frantic wildness or uncontrolled passion. And later, recovering, free from the restraint of being strangers, there'd been a holding-touching-searching type of calmness and also there'd been laughter.

Maria Jo-Jo had snuggled up to him, chuckling whispering apologies for screaming in his ear during her first explosive climax. "I never yelled like that in all my life … honest."

What she didn't have the courage to explain, not yet anyway, was that not only was it her first sexual scream, it was also her first real orgasm (not counting a couple of experimental battery-assisted occasions.)

Touching Maria Jo-Jo's birthmark had shocked him numb. He lay in the warm darkness holding the sleeping singer in his arms, her breath blowing soft against his throat. Looking down, the white bristles of her head glowed like an illuminated nightlight guarding a slumbering child. When she awoke he would have to tell her … show her.

Explain about the six year old being tucked up for the night, asking Momma Joanne about the white bird. Somehow he'd have to relate how Joanne had given the enquiring boy a cuddle while relating the history of his mother's ancestors. Tinkers. Shipwrecks. Soldiers. Travelling folk from Ireland's County Kerry.

His mark, Joanne had whispered, was a birthright, unique to him alone, proving that the spirits of ancient mariners watched over him in troubled times and stormy weather.

He'd told boys at school, gazing with envy, demanding closer inspection, different stories. The Devil's Brand, Cuckoo's spit, the mark of the lone Albatross and other childlike theories.

Judith had been the only other person he'd shown or permitted to touch but …perhaps best not to mention that.

As the rain began to ease, Mayo looked at the clock. It was ten minutes after seven. They'd lain for six hours in rain- induced darkness. He had tasted almost every part of her beautiful body. Had drawn her aroma deep into his lungs.

***

"Ah fuck! Willard, his head's covered." Major Brooks' voice echoed in the confined space of the cell. "He's been beaten. Fetch a medic … now! Do you hear me, man?"

"Calm yer ass, Brooksie. The nigger tried to escape last evening … after you'd gone. Caught his eye on the door, is all. I swear to you, this hombre is one sly cookie."

Major Harris Jnr. looked the Special Services officer in the eye, adding, "Sure, he's bruised some but he don't require medical attention … leastways, not yet. Not 'til he's made a statement to your department. Coffee?"

Snapping his fingers to a guard outside in the corridor, Willard, lowered his voice, "Now, here's what we gonna' do. We'll fix you a table, a chair and some coffee. You fire questions, write down every last place this black runner been over the past week … then we'll call in a little first-aid. Okay?"

Walking towards the door, Major Harris Jnr turned, "He shouldn't cause no problems, Major. After a good night's sleep, this fella'… well, he'll be more of a pussycat. Besides, Sergeant Christmas knows full well he ain't gonna' be shot by no German army … cause we aim to shoot him first." His chuckle was evil.

Major Brooks slipped off his jacket and hung it behind the chair.

"Before you leave, Willard, remove the prisoner's hood and 'cuffs. When the coffee comes, make sure there's plenty for two. Also, have one of your goons fetch warm water and a clean towel. And, another thing, keep your men away from this cell, I don't want to be disturbed. Do I make myself clear, Major?"

Holding the steaming mug with shaking hands, Jo-Jo sipped carefully. From his one good eye he studied the officer from Special Operations who'd bathed his battered face, moving cautiously around the puffed eyelid.

While Major Brooks was present, he was in no danger of further ill treatment but boxing experienced told him that internal damage had already been done to his body.

Before sitting at the small table the young officer had checked the corridor. Satisfied, he closed the door. Facing Jo-Jo, who sat on the cot, back braced against the painted wall, the Major drew a stack of papers and a pen from his briefcase. He began writing.

When he'd writen the date he looked up, "Sergeant, in your own time but, whatever you say, don't shit me. Neither of us got the time. I've little concept of what happened during the Exercise Tiger fuck-up. All I know is that Allied Command is screaming for explanations, hard facts and … a scapegoat. Sergeant Jo-Jo Christmas, at this moment in time, you're best picture in the frame".

"Right! Introductions. I'm Major Marty Brooks, Special Operations Department. My instructions come from no less than General Ike himself. To dig into and report what fucked-up on the beach."

"So, first, this is what we have. One: Over 600 US servicemen are killed in a single night-operation. An exercise supposed to be a dummy-rum, for chrissake. And, so far, nobody can figure … how come? Top generals and senior navy buttons are kickin' ass left, right and centre 'cause they ain't sure who's responsible … Krauts, the British or lord forbid, maybe we shot our own boats up the butt." He took a sip of coffee.

"Two: Twenty-four hours after the slaughter, all we got on file is that a young, apparently sane, Lieutenant blows his brains out for no reason. Three: A Negro Sergeant - you - from the same Lieutenant's company goes AWOL, stealin' a truck an' digger".

"The enlisted men in the same squad hear nothin' … say nothin' and would you believe this … know nothin' from beans."

He paused, drained his coffee and refilled both their mugs. Taking a sheet of paper he skimmed through the typed information.

Before being drafted by Uncle Sam, twenty four year old Marty Brooks had been an ambitious Assistant District Attorney in Boston. Marty wanted nothing more than to get this damned war closed down so that he might resume a career that promised satisfaction, mentally and financially.

"Right Sarge, question time. We'll do a run through. When I've sorted the correct tone of your answers, I'll draft a formal statement … okay?"

Jo-Jo nodded. Hauling himself slowly to his feet, he said, "Sure thing, Major. But first I gotta' take a pee. D'ya mind if I use the john?"

After some yelling down the hallway, two armed MP's arrived to escort the prisoner to the toilet. Moving with difficulty, Jo-Jo stumbled towards the door. Watching him, Major Brooks pushed back his chair, addressing the guards, "It's not that I don't trust you guys but I could use a leak myself."

In the damp toilet, Jo-Jo swallowed a hard groan pushing to empty his bladder. Glancing downwards he watched blobs of dark blood mix with his urine. The pain stabbing at the region of his kidneys almost keeled him over. Fumbling with buttons, the lower part of his abdomen bloated, he realised he was bleeding internally.

Back in the cell, Major Brooks sat at the table and poured more coffee. He watched Jo-Jo struggle to get back on the cot. Climbing to his feet he yelled along the hall, "MP, get another god-damn chair in here, NOW."

When the Sergeant was settled in a chair, the Major again checked the door. Studying the coloured man's face he said, "You're hurt bad, Sarge. You up to this?"

Nodding his head, Jo-Jo closed his eyes. "Let's get done, Major."

"Right. Day one, April 27th. '44. What was your duty call that day? He raised his pen ready to draft the soldier's reply.

Jo-Jo struggled with the words, "After briefing, we checked our equipment for next morning's attack." Pausing for breath he drank a little coffee, "Shore bombardment was due to kick-off at 0630 and stop at 0700 hours. Shortly after, T-4 LST's would bump the beach. We'd be waiting to off-load and secure. Hell, that was the plan. Most of us hit the sack early. Big day ahead an' all." He waited for the Major to stop writing.

"April 28th? The beginning. In your own time, Sergeant."

"It was kinda' dark when Lt. Brown woke me. Change of plan

…some foul up, he'd said. My squad was ordered to proceed from the sands. Lt. Brown riding point, two trucks, each carrying a 'dozer. "

He took a deeper breath that hurt bad. "No one seemed to know what the hell was goin' on. Map reading. Radio. We got lost a couple of times … Lt. Joe was jumpin' mad with Headquarters, that's a fact."

A racking pain tore at Jo-Jo's inside, making him want to be sick. "After … a couple hours on the road we arrived at a clearing, strange place in the woods. We dug three deep trenches, ten … "

The Major halted him, "What was the map references for the clearing, Jo-Jo?"

"Lieutenant Brown was holdin' the only map, sir. I just drove.

Right turn, left, right again … stuff like that. We sure didn't travel crow fashion. Musta' been goin' at least two hours before arrivin' at 'creepy meadow.'

"Go on. What happened next?"

Rubbing both hands along his knees, Jo-Jo concentrated on the series of events. "Yea, right! We dug the holes then sat around till the big trucks arrived … noon or close. Before you ask, Major, those trucks carried no marks or numbers. Black guys drivin', kept pretty much to themselves.

"Lt. Brown said we was buryin' unwanted war material but it sure smelt shit. By then we'd takin' a little drinkin' whisky, so it's a bit fuzzy." Jo-Jo paused. "I tell a lie there, Major … we'd sipped a whole load of Kentucky juice, that's a cert. I swear. Come sun-up we'd trouble findin' the open gate out from that field back onto the road. "

"Hang fire, Sergeant, I've got most of that. Okay! Next day, 29th."

Jo-Jo held his stomach, trying to gain comfort from his own arms. "That's a mite foggy, Major. My head was buzzin' from cookin' whisky drunk during the past 24 hours. Before chow I went to Lt. Brown's quarters. The poor guy lay in a pool of his own blood. Gun in his … it was a fuckin' mess, that's for sure, sir. "

"So, why run? How come you didn't get help? Why take the Lieutenant's weapon? Why …"

"Wait on, man … sir. The gun was still there when I hit out from the tent. Folded under the pillow, right hand. My mind clouded but there are things that stay fixed, no matter what …"

Major Brooks tossed aside his pen, which had dried, "That's no real answer, Sergeant," dipping into his briefcase, refilling the pen from an inkbottle. "Where'd you spend the next seven days? Before you answer, remember, you were seen in a bar at a Kingsbridge hotel."

Jo-Jo cupped the coffee mug tightly in his hands, sipping slowly, playing for time, waiting for the next wave of pain to wash on into a dull throb.

"I lifted the last quart of Bourbon from Lt. Joe's locker … then I took off. Don't recall much. Spent a couple of nights holed up in the woods. I broke into a fisherman's boat … he nearly caught me."

Major Brooks finished scribbling. Dropping his pen he stared hard and long across the table at the coloured soldier. Leaning forward, he lowered his voice, "You don't need me to tell you, Sergeant Christmas that you're in a heap of trouble … capital T."

"Major Harris, well, among other things he suffers from a certain lack of racial harmony. My department's aware that down the line there's a cover-up of global proportions. Malfunction in chain of command caused the death of hundreds of US servicemen, including the demise of Lt. Joseph Brown."

He glanced towards the closed door. "Incompetence from top-brass most likely resulted in a balls-up that rolled downhill from day one."

He began to pack his papers away. "At this moment in time, Sergeant Jo-Jo Christmas, the only sucker they got … is you."

Slamming shut his briefcase, he offered the coloured man a wry smile, "To me, what you did, was most likely stupid. But a German spy, no, I think not. Neither do I reckon you killed, Lt. Brown."

Climbing to his feet the young Major eyeballed the Sergeant.

"We both know you've not laid down one hundred percent of the story here. But I've enough details to make my report. There are still questions to raise in other areas."

Reopening his briefcase he removed several pages of notes.

"Here's what we do. While I take a walk, keeping Willard off your back, read these notes and if you agree, sign the bottom of each page. Six in total … plus two blank sheets. Write a letter home. I'll personally make sure it gets back to the States. You got maybe an hour."

Locking the case, he left paper and a pen on the table.

After Major Brooks left, Jo-Jo stared at the statement.

Reading slowly, he carefully signed each page. Sharp surges of hurt came in irregular jolts, twisting nerve ends at the base of his neck. Reaching for the blank sheets, with shaking fingers, he began to write.

Maria Darlin'
This damn war sure messed up some
durin' the past days. I guess that's why they sent us to this
gentle country, to practice ...makin' sure we got it right
before the final push across the water. Any day now, hon.
The Company Lieutenant, Joseph (Joe)
Brown, a good buddy, passed on last week. Just seemed to
declare war on his own mind. Lost the battle, surrendered
to his own gun.
I sure as hell miss you, Maria, honey. Lost
track of reasoning for a couple of days. Nothin' made
sense, no how. Then I was lucky enough to meet with some
fine folks from hereabouts. A giant fisherman became
a good friend, even though I was most likely the first
coloured guy he ever took home to meet his wife and son
Fisherman Walter guided me through a
special place called 'Passage'. Its beauty changed my
life. One day, honey you gotta' come see it for yourself.
Maybe we can show our daughter ...

A pink-faced military policeman from South Dakota opened the cell door. His eyes took in the prisoner lying face down in a pool of blood. Panicking, dropping his keys, he backed out, yelling, "Major Harris, sir, the Negro's dead ...oh my sweet lord!" Turning, he fled back into the hallway, still shouting.

Jo-Jo gingerly hauled himself upright, holding onto the table Special Services officer Brooks had used earlier that morning. Some moments before he'd pissed into a bucket, waited until footsteps sounded along the corridor before pouring the combination of urine and blood over the floor. He'd then lain down in the foul smelling liquid.

Gathering the guard's keys, Jo-Jo stumbled into a dimly lit passage, opened another door with the second key on the ring and was suddenly out in the cold night air. Slumped against the door, taking short quick breaths he locked the door behind him. From within the building the voice of Major Harris Jnr. screamed, "You stupid hog-brained bastard, you let the nigger outsmart you… he's gone. Call out the fuckin' guard. Move, move, you - you …"

****

Chapter Twenty

... the beach

Easing tired bones from the fireside chair, Walter damped down the embers, switched off the light and drew back the curtains. Gazing at the shadows over the silent quay he watched low clouds scampered across the moon. Searching beams pointing yellow towards the bend in the creek.

His eye caught a movement from the lane as an American jeep, without lights, slowly approached the quayside rails and stopped. The fisherman watched Jo-Jo struggle from the driver's seat and collapse, face down, across the bonnet of the vehicle.

Helping the injured American into the cottage, Walter eased him onto the couch, moving it closer to the fire. Adding logs to the sleeping embers he lifted a blanket from the chest in the corner and tucked it around the soldier. "You'm in a fair ol' mess, brother. Looks like you bin kicked from asshole to breakfast time."

He then made a pot of tea.

During the gentle ticking of the clock, with the glow from the hearth painting warm colours, they talked about different moments in their' lives, sometimes going back to the confused mystery of childhood. Things done, people met. Events long gone yet enclosed in compartments of the brain, secure from whatever troubles might invade the future.

Walter told the Sergeant about losing his foot in a trawling accident when he was about the American's age. Explained about his friendship with Albert George Mitchell ...

"Deep Sea Captain an' scholar. A lover of oceans. An east-coast master mariner who felt at home in Devon, just like he was born 'ere."

Croaking in short breathless whispers, Jo-Jo told how he'd met his beloved Maria. "She has the fire of old Mexico and, for some crazy reason she fell in love with me, a Harlem orphan."

He paused, waiting for the next pain to pass, "Any day now, we gonna' have a baby … a girl I reckon …she'll be the most beautiful creature ever walked God's sweet earth." He groaned, "Jesus, Walter, I hurt real bad, man."

Walter poked extra life into the fire, "I'll send the lad to the village for the doctor …"

In a whisper, more to himself, Jo-Jo said, "Too late. A sip more tea will do fine, Walter. Then, maybe I can lay some of my country's shame …tell the truth about Exercise Tiger an' poor Lt. Brown…" a sharp jolt twisted in his back, causing sweat to ooze from the black soldier's forehead.

"Pot's still warm, Sergeant. There's a bottle of Brandy somewhere …" Easing a pillow under Jo-Jo's head, Walter's large hand touched the cheek and found it sticky to his touch.

Chuckling, Jo-Jo's half-closed eyes followed the big man's movements towards the kitchen. "I'm not up to strong liquor, ol' friend …"

From the shadows of the other room, Walter replied, "The brandy's fer me …"

When the sky began stretching grey tones along the incoming tide, Walter watched the moon dip beyond dark shapes down at the bend. Sitting alongside the couch, holding a mug of tea mixed with cognac, he listened to his friend's breathing becoming slower, deeper, more laboured.

The army man had not spoken for several minutes. Apart from their breathing, the only sounds came from the occasional crackled spitting of the smouldering logs.

"It's a strange deal, Walter …" the words, barely audible, stirred the Devon man from his gaze through the window. "Here I am, dying in a country where I's got no history. Uncle Sam said, 'Go to Europe, Jo-Jo Christmas, kill this Hitler fella' who, by all accounts is beatin' the shit out of Jewish folks … gassin' old men, women and kids. Okay, I'm here, fair enough. But how come no one rode against General Custer for slaughtering North American Indians?"

He stopped, allowing the pain to have its way. "How come, I'm expected to lay down my life for France, Holland and Belgium?

Man, there's States back home, bigger than these countries strung together where they won't serve darkie boys a cup of mornin' coffee." The rage in his body gathered in pace, "Down south, some towns won't permit a coloured woman to sit up front on a public bus … Jesus, what do that say? Yet, Uncle Sam expects Negro soldiers to ride shotgun on a Sherman tank right down the main strasse in Berlin. It don't seem rightly fair, Walter."

Moving from his chair, Walter helped the Sergeant take a sip of tea. Placing the mug on the floor, he gently gathered the smaller man in his powerful arms, " Never reckoned life to be fair, Jo-Jo. Most times 'tis a sod. Five years back the only problems us 'ad was Cornish long-liners … now, the whole world's gone bloody maize"

The Sergeant squeezed his eyes as pain circled inside his stomach, stabbing upwards and outwards, poking at toe joints and fingers. Twitching nerve ends shuddered with electric shocks. "Walter, do me one favour, friend …"

Closing the New Yorker's eyes, Walter carried him to the quay, still wrapped in the blanket. The flood tide had reached its full range and stood, waiting to begin the quiet ebb. From the store he collected a spade, a tattered mizzen sail, some twine, a leather palm and needle and at the last moment an old apple box that had lain there in a corner, holding odd bits of the fisherman's life.

As the boat moved slowly away from the steps, the first faint lines of daybreak peeped above the higher cliffs to the south. "'Twill rain before noon, Jo-Jo Christmas ..."

Nearing Passage, Walter swung the wheel to starboard, turning the blunt bow into a narrow gully leading into a sandy cove, unseen from the main channel of the creek. Beaching Receiver on the first of the ebb, Walter carried a small kedge anchor ashore, jamming the flukes into a raised ledge. Returning to the boat he lugged the rest of the equipment onto the sand and walking to the base of the cliffs, he began digging.

By the time the first of the drizzle arrived, he'd dug enough. Spreading the red sail he returned to the boat and lifting the soldier's body, carried it to the hole. Laying his friend down he wrapped him neatly in the faded canvas. Remembering as a young deckhand on a barquentine, watching the ship's carpenter prepare a seaman's body for burial, when the last stitch in the canvas was complete, Walter felt with his left hand for Jo-Jo's soft nose and with one swift move passed the needle and twine through the dead man's nostrils.

Grey slates from the beach were laid in the bottom of the grave. The old apple box was broken down and placed over Jo-Jo's head. On the box Walter painted …

Sergeant Jo-Jo Christmas. US Army.
Died, seeking freedom for all men.
May 6th. 1944.

With the last grain of sand replaced the tiny beach looked as undisturbed as when they'd arrived in the early hours. Removing his battered cap, Walter stood for a moment. Lifting what remained of the cognac he drank until the bottle was empty. "Sleep warm, Jo-Jo Christmas."

He flung the empty bottle high against the cliffs and the amber glass shattered into hundreds of fragmented pieces scattering onto the fine sand.

Tossing the kedge into the boat, Walter lowered his shoulder against the stem. In the shallows at his feet he noticed a small slate shaped like a flag. Without knowing why, he lifted it from the foam and skimmed it out over the still water. The flat stone danced across the tide, skipping five times before spinning quietly below the surface. Bending his massive back against the bow planks, Walter heaved and when nothing moved he drew a deep breath, yelling to the sky. An old gull, perched on the cliff wandered to the edge and watched the crabber ease into deeper water.

***

Drifting in and out of sleep, Maria Jo-Jo listened to the sounds from the galley. A track from her first album floated softly through the bulkhead. Rising but not switching on the light, she fumbled in a drawer, finding and pulling on one of Mayo's shirts. Rolling the sleeves back, she fastened the lower buttons and slipped back into the bed, firming up the pillows.

In warm semi-darkness, the singer mimed the lyrics from the twenty-year old song …'the gentle flight above, carrying moments of my love …'

Smiling at the muffled combinations of cooking sounds and Mayo's baritone harmonizing, she drifted back into the pillow.

Light from the main cabin filtering into the sleeping cabin, woke her. Mayo stood close to the bed.

"Supper's almost ready. Before we eat, there's something I need to show you…"

Kissing sleep-puffed eyes, he eased her into a sitting position and switched on the main light before standing back a pace. He wore faded jeans, a towel draped over bare shoulders.

"You've shown me yours…"

When his towel dropped away she could see the white mark on his chest and ... suddenly she was wide-awake. The first thought rushing through her brain considered maybe he'd heard about the birthmark and had it copied by a tattoo artist. Yet, apart from certain negatives, which Max swore were destroyed, there were no photographs of the birthmark.

Inspecting Mayo's chest it was obvious the bird-mark was as genetic as her own. 'Christ! Oh no, it's not possible…we can't be related. My father surely didn't …'

They sat crossed-legged, facing each other, sipping red wine. Angled light streamed across the untidy bed from the main cabin. Maria Jo-Jo reached, drawing Mayo's fingertips to her breast and then she gently touched his.

"My therapist advised tracing ancestors. I invested big bucks. One genealogist reported my great-great grandma escaped from the Alamo. A crazy, one-eyed Indian woman from Baton Rouge, Louisiana, wanted to kiss it. When I refused she grabbed me, staring for a long time with her one good eye, mumbling about some ancient shipwreck. I don't know what dope she was usin' but it sure cost me plenty."

Mayo had filleted the sole, sliced the white scallop meat into fine strips and rolled them inside the sole. Placed in brown paper the fish was roasted until the paper crackled. Mixing the scallop corals with cooked mussels, he'd poached the mixture in white wine, tossed it in saffron rice, topped with sliced boiled eggs.

"This-is-fantastic. Come to LA. We'll open a fancy fish restaurant. I'll ... sorry - joke! " She lowered her head, mumbling, "No it wasn't." Lifting the wine glass she took a sip before handing the glass to Mayo ... "I'm done."

Reaching across the small table the singer gently touched the spot on his shirt where she knew the birthmark to be. "What did they ... your folks tell you?"

"Not much. When I was about ten, dad told me my mother had the same mark. I think it embarrassed him ... perhaps reminding him about lost years ..." He drank more wine.

"Kids at school made up different stories. I never paid much attention. Joanna said it was a mark of ancient West of Ireland travellers. She told me the sea would be my friend and seabirds would watch over me."

Clearing away the plates, Mayo said, "Shall we take a walk along the beach?"

They tracked, barefoot, through ripples edging the low-water line. Behind them the descending sun splashed the rock face with embers of sunset. Reaching the trees, circling towards the higher part of the beach, they stoped for a moment, looking back at the old schooner.

"When I was twelve, Matthew gave me a book about the Spanish Armada. The section I found most fascinating was about two ships wrecked on the southwest coast of Ireland. Over six hundred men were lost. A few survived. One was a boy who lived with a mountain farmer and his family. They named him Fish-boy. Apparently he had a special mark..."

Maria Jo-Jo took Mayo's hand, " Porno mags in the States would write our story as mother-fuckin' incest." She laughed, "Do you know, Mr Mayo Francis, I don't care ten cents worth about what historic roads led to ... this! " She gripped his fingers hard. "I love you. There! I never said that to another livin' man."

It was nearly dark. Mayo asked, "So, what now?"

She giggled, "Am I a sad-faced nympho for wanting to get you back in the sack? Don't answer that! First, let's skip some stones."

Running down the beach, she picked up a flat stone ….

****

Chapter Twenty-one

... Agreement

"Matthew? Max - Max Stone, from Paris-France. Buzz Maria Jo-Jo's room. Whadya mean, she ain't there? Christ, man it's nearly midnight. Okay-okay, maybe an hour back. European time is crap. Travel one hour and zip ...it's Greenwich plus, or is it minus? Where the fuck was I?"

Matthew waited.

Max charged on, "Matt, listen. Here's the bottom line. My flight gets into London Heathrow at noon, Thursday, right? The chopper people land me on your grass about two. Tell Black-lady, come Friday morning, we need to fax Vegas. This contract will zoom the bitch to multi-million dollar status..."

Matthew, still listening, smiled.

"What's that, Matthew? I didn't catch ... Say, Buddy, can I bring you something French?"

"How kind. Thank you, but no. I'll leave a note for Miss Christmas. Oh! By the way, I believe ..."

The 'phone gave a strange gargling noise, spluttered once and died.

"Your nightcap, darling." Joanne handed Matthew a generous measure of malt. "I take it that was Mr Stone?"

She stood by the window, watching puffy clouds play passing games with the full moon. "Do you think we should contact Maria Jo-Jo and Mayo?"

Matthew joined his wife at the window, placing an arm around her shoulders before tasting the whisky, "Whatever Max is using, purchased by the gram, I'm guess it's rich. Contracts, mega-bucks, Las Vegas, its another world out there, my love."

He observed changing shadows across the silent waters, "If the love-birds don't show by morning, I'll visit the schooner."

He kissed her ear, "Come on, we'll call it a day."

***

Through the skylight over the bed, Maria Jo-Jo gazed at strands of fluffy clouds speeding across the coloured glass. She listened to Mayo's steady breathing, knowing he was awake.

"I've even forgotten what …tomorrow's Thursday, right? Something inside wants me to tell you my secrets but I'm ashamed about some journeys I've taken."

Stroking his arm she whispered, "My Mom would have loved you. I want you to meet Ruby, Frankie, Hazelwood Boyde, his wife Lily and the twins. Show you the ranch … shit! I gave the ranch to Ruby and Frankie …we could visit."

Reaching for his hand, she eased his warm fingers down between her legs, whispering, "Something else, Mayo, I never-ever been so sore, excited, content … down there. No one ever made me cum before."

Mayo's fingers plucked a changing tune …

"Yesssssssss…please," she cooed.

When they woke it was completely dark. The moon had dipped past the rim of the creek. Mayo asked, quietly, "You awake?"

"Yes, time for sea, fisherman?"

"Not today. Spring tides. The current's too strong. When it gets light we'll go to Christmas Cove. I'll tell you things my father told me about Sergeant Jo-Jo."

Maria Jo-Jo snuggled against his back, licking his skin and mumbling into his shoulder. "Christmas Cove?"

"I questioned the name, years ago. Father explained the tide only reached it once a year … like Christmas. Sleep now."

***

Pictures painted in his memory began with being carried down to the boat on James' shoulders. Four years old, gripping tightly at the thick grey curls on his father's head … and they were both laughing. He remembered wild yelps from the big fisherman as they attempted to outpace Mister, the Jack Russell. Every few yards, energy renewed, Mister leapt, snapping at James' flapping trousers. "Down! ya silly bugger."

He recalled accepting their 'growing-up-together' situation as normal. Daddy-Matt was, well, Daddy-Matt. Just as James was Dadda. Joanne was Nanna. What should be different? Kids and teachers at school never questioned it. It was all part of village life.

Well into school years he'd slept most nights at the hotel. Joanne nursed him through teething problems, chickenpox, measles and mumps, cuddling the growing boy through bruised knees and cheering him on during sports days.

During the first two years of his education, Joanne drove Mayo up the winding hill three miles to the school gates in her battered Morris Minor. When he was seven, with Mister scurrying into bushes, chasing rabbits, squirrels and anything that moved, Mayo insisted on walking the lane to catch the school bus. The terrier would be waiting at the bus stop at the end of the day, escorting the boy home via several detours to the woods or the creek.

Mornings of summer holidays were spent at sea with his father, lifting pots, steering the boat, listening and learning to understand the different sounds from the breathing ocean. Afternoons, he'd run wild through the woods along the inner edge of the creek or clamber up and down the coastal paths on the outer cliffs. Each location produced a dream world of trackers, pirates, outlaws and spacemen. The common denominator of the equation being, 'stick-like-glue' four legged, Mister.

At twelve, he'd broken his nose. A warp parted, caused by pulling too hard on the crabbers' winch. He'd played outside left for the school team and scored a goal. With embarrassment he recalled daydreaming, allowing a cock-crab to draw blood on his chin. Both James and the dog hid in the wheelhouse, laughing as the lad scrambled around the deck trying to dislodge the angry crustacean. He was fourteen … it never happened again.

Mayo's first kissing session came during a school dance. In the girl's cloakroom a girl dared him to 'French'. They did it until tongues became swollen and teeth hurt. He'd run all the way home in the dark, crying, convinced he's made a woman pregnant.

The sexual journey took several confusing directions. In the flickering dimness of the Electric Cinema in Kingsbridge, sitting in the back row with a young London holidaymaker, Mayo had eased a hand under her tight sweater, struggling with clips and fasteners. She'd smacked his face, walking out, not because she wasn't prepared to encourage his advances but would have appreciated the opportunity to remove additional padding complimenting an undersized bust. He hadn't been worldly enough to follow her. Besides, it was a John Wayne Western, which he hadn't seen.

Before his sixteenth birthday, there'd been Judith. They'd fucked - he loved whispering the word to himself - in the warm summer grass. Six months later, beneath the hot sun of her native land, Judith had died.

On one of the first winter gales of '82 James put to sea on his own. At six o'clock he'd looked in on the boy and found him sweating from a fever caused by a saltwater boil on his neck, almost ready to burst. "Stay, Mister. Watch the boy."

The terrier had rushed from bed to door, following the fisherman down the narrow stairs, scampering, growling little yelps. "Quiet. Back to the bed. Don't wake 'im."

As James lifted his oilskin from behind the kitchen door, the dog leapt up at his chest, whimpering, licking his beard. "Ger-off, soft bugger …stay."

Mayo woke about noon. During sleep, the boil had exploded, spreading pus and blood across the pillow. In the middle of the sticky mess, resembling a small black clove, was the core. He pushed it with a finger. Scrambling from the warmth of the bed he found Mister sitting in the window staring down towards the creek. The terrier's back-hairs spiked along his spine, stood on end, his eyes watching every movement in the choppy waters. When Mayo touched him a low groan rumbled from deep in the dog's throat.

"Breakfast, Mister. The ol' man should be back soon."

Downstairs, when Mayo opened the cottage door, the dog dashed towards the twisting track dividing the creek from the open sea, following the same procedure on the rare occasions, for whatever reasons, the fisherman had gone to sea alone.

Each time Mayo had asked, "Why didn't you call me?"

There were several ready-made answers …"Called you once, 'Tis enough. Your brain needed the sleep. Clean forgot".

Or, "Sometimes, boy, there's a need to be out there on my own, 'twill 'appen to you, no doubt. No offence meant."

When Receiver hadn't returned by one o'clock, Mayo walked to the cliff edge on the seaward rim. Mister stood beside him, looking towards Passage, stiff, unmoving, silent. The wind had dropped. Visibility was so clear Mayo could make out a coaster, almost hull-down, ten miles to the southeast. Of his father's boat there was no sign.

The dog refused to leave. Mayo ran back to the hotel and Matthew phoned the coastguards. Twenty minutes later a Sea King helicopter skimmed low over the creek, heading south.

After an hour the 'copter was joined by the Salcombe lifeboat. They searched all day and found nothing.

When the sun slipped into the sea, Mayo lifted the terrier from where he'd stood the length of the day and carried him home. Throughout the night the dog lay at the door, making low groaning sounds. At first light, Matthew, who'd stayed at the cottage, opened the door and Mister was gone, racing towards his cliff-top lookout.

Mayo spent the day aboard the lifeboat. They searched, box-shapes, down tide from the outer Dan-floats and then steered to unlikely sections of the channel, just to double check. In late afternoon they returned to the pots and pulled the first string. They'd been emptied and rebaited.

The Cox'n called the boy into the tiny wheelhouse. "Almost time to go back for more fuel, Mayo. There's one place we ain't looked …inside Passage. Truth is, I'm not sure of the marks, something about a tree in line with a church. You want to show me?"

They discovered the abandoned craft drifting in the vast middle cavern, engine stopped, fuel tank empty. The fish hold contained fifty large cock crabs and five small lobsters. Of James there was no sign. The lifeboat searched deep water inside Passage, dragging grapnels along the gravel bottom. Two navy divers arrived from

Fort Boviesands at Plymouth, diving until their air was exhausted … nothing.

The next day the search extended along the coast as far down as Toe Rock. Hours after the sun surrendered to the western horizon, splitting sky and sea in a mass of burning gold, the search went on. Reluctantly, in fading light, they turned for home …empty.

Matthew and Joanne sat with Mayo into the early hours until Matthew sent his wife home to rest. The dog lay in the window, staring into the darkness, ears twitching, as outside, different night creatures disturbed the silence.

Mayo slumped in James' big chair - the same chair in which Walter had nursed the fire, all those years ago, thinking over things he'd wanted to tell his father and never got 'round to.

As grey shadows began changing the night, the boy woke Matthew, curled under a blanket on the couch, "Sorry, Daddy-Matt but I need to go look for him, at least one more time."

The low putt-putt of the boat's engine cut through the early mist like soft humming in a quiet church. Matthew made strong tea as Mayo guided the old boat towards Passage. The dog perched on the whaleback, his eyes flickering at the slightest movements on the shaded water. Approaching the hidden entrance, Mister suddenly scrambled to his feet, barking loudly, as a white seabird overtook the crabber, gliding silently into the dark hole ahead of them.

Outside, in the swell, the boat's scallop dredge tracked along the fine sandy bottom, first to the north where the tide might have dragged anything and then south. Mayo held one hand on the trailing warp, feeling the changing vibrations as it rumbled over a pebble ridge or a rock. They worked the whole day and found nothing, returning home the same way they'd come …

For two nights Matthew stayed at the cottage until Mayo begged to be left on his own. The dog took to living on the boat moored at the quay steps, watching from the bow. Every few hours he'd stretch, amble along the deck, pee against the wheelhouse and then hurry back to the stem. Mayo took food, but he hardly ate, just sipping at drops of water.

Seven days after James disappeared, the dog scratched at the cottage door, asking to be let in. During the following days he'd sit in the window and at night curl by the fire, staring into the flickering embers, shivering.

Mayo walked to the hotel, sharing a silent meal with Matthew and Joanne before strolling through the woods. Twice he went downstream to the schooner, leaning against the stumpy mast, looking back towards the bend. The terrier never strayed more than a few yards from the boy's footsteps.

Shortly before dawn on the tenth day Mister woke the boy, licking his nose and rushing downstairs to scratch the door.

Once outside, the dog shot along the cliff path so fast that in the dim light Mayo lost sight of him.

At a place known as Christmas Cove, he found the terrier standing in the shallow water, barking at something awash ten feet out in the tide. It took Mayo some time to drag the waterlogged body of his father from the shallow water. Mister yelped, leaping and tugging at the yellow oilskin coat until it tore.

There wasn't a mark on the fisherman's body. Like he'd come in from the rain, soaking wet, his beard and hair sparkling and gleaming. James' eyes were open, a faint smile almost making a lie of death. Mayo touched the eyes closed. "Stay, Mister. I'll fetch Daddy-Matt."

Coming down through the rough gorse track sheltering the tiny inlet, Matthew sensed shadowy figures sitting beneath the cliff. For a split nanosecond he saw his father, Captain Albert George, together with Walter and a small coloured man in uniform, watching over the soul of James Francis.

When they reached the body, Mister was sitting on the dead man's chest, head low, watching. He growled at Matthew's approach. "Okay, Mister … it's okay."

"We can't bury him here, Mayo … at least not right away. There are legal matters. Police, coroner's office, death certificates, lots of things to do."

"Here! Now! Today! Its what he would have wanted." It was a statement. Mayo wasn't arguing. It was clear intent and Matthew accepted it. The youngster walked close to the rocks where

Matthew had seen the ghosts and finding a jagged piece of sea-washed plank, began to dig into the clean sand. They took turns at the digging. When they'd reached the required depth, Matthew tossed the plank aside and scrambled from the hole, breathing in great gasps. "Mayo, this isn't right. Apart from breaking God knows how many laws, it's wrong to lay this man to rest without Joanne being present."

Mayo retrieved the piece of wood and jumped down into the pit. "Bring Joanne. I'll finish off here."

While Matthew was away, Mayo came to the remains of an apple box. He could just make out a few letters, 'Sergeant Christm … US army…194 '

Collecting flat slates from under the cliffs he prepared a level bottom in the grave, carefully covering traces of the apple box.

When it was done, Joanne quietly held the boy in her arms and they both sobbed. "I'll have a stone made. He'll sleep easy here, Mayo, watching you come and go."

The dog lived for five days. Taking to his bed by the cottage door, curled into a tight ball, head tucked in, quietly pining away. Mayo took him back to the beach, burying him close to where he'd laid his father to rest.

****

Chapter Twenty-Two

...Christmas Cove

Receiver's stem grounded in the shallow water. Tucked away in the southwest corner of the main creek, grey-blue limestone ridges on either side of the sandy inlet extended like the arms of a chair.

Tossing a small kedge ten feet up the beach, Mayo jumped into the ripples and offered Maria Jo-Jo his back. Abreast of the small anchor, riding piggyback fashion, she hugged him, playfully biting the soft skin at the base of his neck before easing herself from his shoulders.

Mayo pressed his foot on the kedge, increasing the grip. Maria Jo-Jo gazed around the enclosed space, studying the contours of the sheltered area. High cliffs scattered with gorse bushes shut out sight and sound from the surrounding shoreline. It was as if the hidden cove possessed uncharted boundaries of tranquillity. The singer didn't find it lonely, neither, she felt, was it a place to be feared.

Light-chasing shadows from the southern cliff caused Maria Jo-Jo to blink. And, in that single blink, she saw four hazy figures, three of them listening as a man in a uniform, talked … saw them smile and wave in her direction and, as the blink ended, vapourise.

Ten feet from the base of the towering rocks, partly buried, flukes uppermost, an old stock anchor, formed a cross. Perhaps to those who'd shared this particular spot down through the years.

"The anchor was Joanne's idea, more fitting than a stone, she reckoned. It came from the schooner. The stock's cemented in … only an earthquake would shift it. Matthew built a raft and on a big spring tide we floated 'er right up the beach. The rest was easy."

Running a hand over one of the flukes, he said, "See?"

She voiced the words chiselled on the first fluke, "James

Francis. (Fisherman.)" Crossing to the second fluke, sharply drawing in her breathe, she read slowly, "Sergeant Jo-Jo Christmas. (US soldier and my friend.)"

Dropping to her knees in the sand, forehead resting against the shank's gravity band, Maria Jo-Jo lifted her arms, stretching, fingers reaching each tip of the anchor … sobbing.

Reaching down, Mayo kissed the top of her head. "You'll need a moment. I'll be close."

Walking towards the lazy ripples washing into the cove, he turned. Her body leaned into the form of the anchor crucifix. For some moments he stood against the aging timbers of the boat, thinking back to his last visit to this secluded beach.

After burying Mister, he'd battened the schooner down, drained oil and water from the crabber and secured it safely alongside the large vessel.

"Daddy-Matt, I have to go. As much as I love you and Joanna, I need …I need to do something more with my life. Something not part and parcel of what I've known since I could walk."

Not only did Matthew understand the lad's turmoil but he made several 'phone calls and three days later Mayo was interviewed by Mr John Robin-Leech, managing director of Robin Cruisers, Southampton.

Within six months Mayo had become an active part of a team delivering custom-made luxury vessels to distinguished customers in different parts of Europe. One such delivery was a fast semi-planing cruiser, built for a retired Galway bookmaker.

Passing through Blaskets Sound, off the Dingle peninsula, on a bright August afternoon, Mayo studied the ghostly stone buildings dotting the deserted islands.

Silent ruins, scattered without pattern among emerald-coloured fields. Abandoned crofts, behind the protection of untidy dry-stone walls surrounding the Great Blasket Island. Even in sunlight the shadow from An Balscaod Mor's high peak spread a haunting shape, like a cloak drawn over the rugged coastline.

With his new craft zipping through the narrow tide-filled sound at twenty-five knots, the proud owner, Mr Patrick Kinsella, sat perched in a padded chair on the flying bridge, sipping a large Jamesons.

"Out there, English-boy-with-Irish-name, is our shame. Erin's black atrocities. Back there," he pointed astern, "is Inishvickillane and Inishnabro". He sipped more whisky,

"We're passin' Beginish Island just now. Out to the west is Inishtooskert." He went quiet, refilling his glass. "History books say that in 1588, two Spanish ships-of-war foundered there."

"Over six hundred seafarers perished …and not all from natural drowning, God rest their souls! "

In one gulp he finished his drink.

Checking the radar before resetting the new course on the autopilot, Mayo watched the silent islands drop slowly astern. The mystical coastline sent a shiver down his spine. He watched a white seabird drift effortlessly in the direction of Garraun Point … and he thought of home.

The boat's owner broke into his thoughts, "Your Skipper reckons we'll make Galway before dark, Mayo. Jesus, but sure the boys will take notice when Pat Kinsella arrives home with this beauty, so they will. We'll drink Murphy's dry…non-stop, so we will, English boy."

Nine months later, as Skipper/engineer, Mayo delivered an expensive motor yacht to an Italian shoe designer in Savona.

Impressed with the youngster's handling of the voyage, the owner, Carlo Dromas, persuaded Robin Cruisers Ltd to allow Mayo to remain as part of the guarantee cover. When the guarantee period ended, full employment was offered by the friendly businessman.

The sparkling clarity of Mediterranean life became slightly discoloured by the adolescent erotic demands of Carlo's fifteen-year old daughter, Martina. Mayo's confusion and indeed his guilt were further compounded by Martina's stepmother seeking inclusion in the teenager's nocturnal encounters.

Three weeks after his seventeenth birthday, guilt, shame and exhaustion made the young Devon seafarer jump from a position of luxury to the austere fo'cas'tle of a Greek tanker lying in Port-de-Bouce. On departure, the aging ship headed towards the Suez Canal and the uncomplicated waters of the Persian Gulf. Three months before Mayo's eighteenth birthday the tanker was arrested in Hong Kong for non-payment of port dues and he became a Distressed British Seaman.

A chance meeting with three Americans, taking time-off from Law-school to deliver a yacht from Kowloon back to the States offered opportunity to spend a month as cook/crew on a voyage across the Pacific Ocean to Santa Barbara, via Waki island and Hawaii.

After a sun-filled voyage that ended in, 'See you guys and thanks again,' a Greyhound bus journey from California took Mayo on a route across America that included Arizona, Colorado, Missouri, Kentucky and Virginia.

Although not holding a green card, in the coal-dusty harbour of Newport News, Virginia, the captain of an old tramp freighter engaged his services as 'deck-man'. Before sailing day he'd hitched a lift to Richmond, watching and listening to a black singer making a comeback after struggling against drugs and leukemia. On the wide stage, with a single spot hitting a piano, the music blew his mind. The singer's name was Maria Jo-Jo Christmas.

Casting off two harbour tugs in the foggy Chesapeake River on a damp December morning, the coal-scarred freighter stuttered southeast through both North and South Atlantic Oceans. They covered the six and a half thousand sea miles from Cape Charles, USA to Cape Town, South Africa, without once sighting land or any other floating object. The voyage took twenty-two days, stretching through latitudes from 40' north to nearly 40' south.

The onward voyage, Cape Town towards Perth, Western Australia, was crudely interrupted by shipwreck, in dense fog, on Cape Naturaliste. The experience of abandoning ship, being washed ashore, unsure of geographical position, stamped another signpost on the young man's road into life.

An extended walkabout across the Great Australian Bight led

Mayo through different employment. Meeting friendly, honest and some strange characters along the way tattooed an education into his young hungry mind. Later, a giant coastal barge offered sea-work from the port of Adelaide around to Brisbane.

Celebrating birthday number twenty-one passing Trinity Bay, inside nature's miracle, the Great Barrier Reef, he watched a lone white seabird glide silently across the long wake of the massive barge and not for the first time the gentle hills of Devon called him home … only this time, Mayo listened.

***

Walking slowly back up the beach towards the partly-buried anchor and Maria Jo-Jo, he watched her lowered beautiful head and hands, spread, touching both fluke tips, like a token of silent remembrance.

A few steps before he arrived, she lowered her arms, turned and sat with her back against the black shank. Mayo dropped beside her, taking hold of her hand. The singer's left hand reached into the fine sand, lifting and spilling silver grains between her outstretched legs.

The retreating tide leaned the crab-boat onto one bilge, slowly, like an obedient dog waiting for command. Whispering ripples below the keel lapped the wet sand like a steady pulse.

"Nowhere in this world is more beautiful." She smiled, squeezing his hand. "Christ, that was poetic. Thank you, lovely fisherman. You know, years ago in St. Peter's Square, Roma, a transcendental mystique appeared to draw all life towards one …one soul. And yet, looking back, compared to this gentle cove, the Vatican was like a bowling alley."

In the warmth of the climbing sun, they sat together, not speaking, just holding hands, watching the ebb tide bubble past the grounded boat, swirling on towards Passage. For one brief moment a chink of daylight split the inner darkness of the hollow, as, on the outside of the creek, the sun began a slow climb towards its zenith.

Reaching over, the black singer kissed him hard on the lips and then scrambled to her feet, shaking her head. Slipping off her shoes she began to circle the anchor, walking backwards, dragging her heel in the white sand. By the time she'd completed the circle the anchor was encapsulated in a rough sand-carved heart.

Mayo stood watching, shaking his head, smiling.

"I know … wind or tide will wash it away. No matter… they will know we marked it so." She laughed.

Suddenly, as if listening, the old boat bobbed upright in the tideway. Holding hands, Maria Jo-Jo and Mayo walked down the sand towards Receiver.

Approaching the quay steps, Maria Jo-Jo fell silent. Looking back down the creek, she sighed. "Max is back. It's make-up-my-mind time. Vegas town is magic … home to no one, yet folks spend mega-bucks, dreaming the impossible dream. A truly frightening phenomena. The mighty dollar is God."

As the old boat rubbed the lower step she moved forward, not wanting to see the wrong answer in his face. "Come to Vegas with me, Mayo."

Max's thunderous roar from the top rail shattered the moment.

"Where in the name of sweet-fucks you bin, Song-lady? We gotta' talk … contracts to sign … flights to arrange."

He gripped hard on the rail, red faced, confused by the scene below. "Move your ass back to the hotel so I can spell out the deal." He turned, white knuckled, looking down at the boat, "And another thing, ain't it a bit late in life to get maternal or horny?" Scowling at Mayo, he added, "or both?"

Before reaching for the lower step she held Mayo's face, kissing him on the lips, "Don't answer … don't say it won't work. Come to dinner tonight. His storm," nodding towards Max, "will rage for an hour … then zippo!"

Halfway up the steps, she turned, smiling, "If you don't show for dinner, I'll come looking for you, fisherman."

***

After a shower and a change of clothes, Maria Jo-Jo sat in the lounge window seat, sipping coffee, only half-listening as Max ranted.

"Dedication, loyalty, ambition, millions of bucks, plus, " he lowered his voice, "grave concerns of speculative, 'family' investors in the Vegas hotel industry! I've worn my butt flat on this contract! You … okay, we, move into super-tax. The basics are simple …are you ready, lady? A three year contract at FIVE million per annum."

He sat back waiting for the sum to sink in and receiving no feedback, charged on, "Rehearsals start next month. Only six shows a week for three months … then, one month's break … free! "

Maria Jo-Jo still didn't respond. Long graceful fingers circled the cup raised to her lips. Chestnut coloured eyes looked down towards the bend just visible in the distance, where the descending sun had begun to lengthen the shadows of the tall trees.

Max yelled, "Lady! You're not hearing me. This is opportunity numero-uno! At your age …hey! No insult intended … this chance points in one direction. Maybe one last grasp at the big pot?" Taking a pen from his pocket he scribbled figures. "With contracted albums, a TV Christmas Special, we're talkin' 20 million gross, in the first year. Twenty million, pure green magic notes."

Maria Jo-Jo lowered her cup, "Hold it there, Max. Recap. Item one - three months doing seventy-two shows … then one month, free? No, I spend it recording a new album, right? After another three months slog, I go on the road to promote the album, right? During the final twelve weeks of the year, in the desert dust, I work mornings and Sundays filming a Christmas Special … am I right, here? And, it rolls on, Max. In the name of sanity, when do I ever see the light of day …watch a sunrise even? In that first year I become a dried up twisted crow … right, Max?"

Reaching for her hands, Max gently stretched the long fingers, "Maria Jo-Jo, Baby, your voice belongs to … When you were ill, the business skipped a beat. Melody became a forgotten word. After two years they wrote you off. But you fought back … showed the bastards that Maria Jo-Jo Christmas is a great talent."

He squeezed her hand, "I for one, wasn't sure you could make it back up the hill but, Ladybird, applause breathes life into you.

You require that special buzz when the spot hits, settin' you apart from the rest of us mortals."

He gave her his best Max Stone, New Yorker, grin, "Besides, how would I support five, or is it six, ex-wives in the manner ... without a slice of the action? Don't do this to me, Maria Jo-Jo. Don't do it to yourself...."

His smile faded, his voice dropping, "Think on. The 'family' consortium who set this deal have invested millions in a project centred around the Maria Jo-Jo Show. If we walk, it's lights out time. We'd never work major, ever again. You'd be lucky to book YMCA's. And, once the TV and radio companies black you ... the records would dry. Believe me, Honey, they're unforgivin' bandits out there. It's a rat race. Only the rats are permitted to win. There'd be nowhere, but nowhere, for you to go ..."

Looking him full in the eyes, long years of tangled association exchanging meanings ranging from contempt, mistrust, loneliness, friendship and compassion even. "I could stay here, Max. My Daddy's buried here." Her voice trailed away, "...and there's Mayo!"

Max banged his whisky glass on the small table between them, "Woman, are you crazy? Sure, okay, I rode with time-out to discover about your poppa. And, no surprise, when my back's turned you get your rocks off with the local stud. Lord knows, but you've had little enough physical entertainment in the carnal department over the years ... but to stay here? For Christ's sake, Maria Jo-Jo, why? "

Lifting the amber liquid, he drank deeply. "Listen to Max, Lady. You can buy ten Mayo's in Vegas ...change them each weekend. Don't you get it, we're about to be up there super-rich? You can order sex, room service. Man, I can even work it as tax-deductible..."

"You don't understand, Max ...You have no conception of what I feel about this ...boy."

"Bet your sweet ass I know what you're feeling ..." His glass was empty and he looked around for a refill.

"Right, Lady, if this fisherman is necessary to scratch the itch, so be it! Fly the bum to the States, first class, if that's what it takes.

I'll lay odds its over, three months tops. Shit … there's crabs a plenty for the catchin' in Vegas." He smiled at his own joke.

"Mayo is coming to dinner tonight. Don't talk ultimatums, contracts or Vegas. This is personal … do you hear me, Max?"

****

Chapter Twenty-Three

... Lobsters

Walter observed the Major leaning over the quayside rail soon after turning the bend. Approaching the steps, the bow carved a tight circle in the calm water. From the quay, Willard spat a ragged cigar butt ahead of the slowing boat.

Leaping ashore, James slipped a rope through a steel ring and scrambling back, passed the American officer, who began walking calmly down the steps.

The Major paused about six steps above the boat, drew a pearl-handled Colt 45 from a low-slung leg holster. As if by a pre-arranged signal, three coloured soldiers appeared over the top rail, pointing carbines towards the man and boy on the boat's deck.

"You got it all wrong, Major. Lobsters be best killed with boiling water, improves the taste, like. Beats a bullet up the bum any day. Now, sir, what can I sell you?" Walter eased closer to his son, making signals to the youngster to watch movement and mouth.

"Smart-ass limey bastard. I've come about the nigger."

James lifted a box of small wriggling lobsters, placing it over a crate of prime blue shellfish, destined for a large Services Hotel in Plymouth. "Hey! Mr Yank, I heard John Wayne say that, in the pictures, last week. Or was it, 'I've come fer ma boy'?"

A deep flush rose from Willard's neck and his eyes popped. Up on the rails two of the gum-chewing soldiers tried not to smile, while the third man looked around, wondering what the hell was going on.

The red-faced Major waved his weapon from the older fisherman to the boy and then back again. "Cut the bullshit, fish-man. We found the jeep, back of your cottage ... a mess of blood inside 'er. Now, on a personal basis I don't give a one-dollar-fuck if you killed him ... trespassin' or such. But it surely points like you stole the vehicle. That motor's Uncle Sam's property. Itemised equipment of war. Stealing such property is aggression against the United States of America. The penalty is death by firing squad."

Willard was in full flight, enjoying the power. "It surely lies in my remit to line you bastards against yonder wall and fill you full of lead … yessiree!"

"I - I heard that one in …."

"James. " Warned Walter. "The Major ain't buying today, son."

Slowly reaching across the gap between boat and steps, Walter gripped the officer's ankles, one in each hand, pulled cleanly, and then let go. The Major's mouth opened as he sat down heavily on the stone before bouncing onto the deck of the boat, landing bolt upright in Walter's arms. "Welcome aboard, Major."

Struggling free from the big fisherman's grasp, Willard glared up at the three soldiers aloft. "Stand ready, you good-fer-nothin' niggers. I'll search the boat. If one of these pricks makes a move, take 'em out, got it?"

Watching the American shuffle aft, James opened his mouth, getting as far as, "I seen …" when a look from his father cut the words.

From the small wheelhouse the Major charged towards the bow. Throwing back the cuddy door he turned, clambering down the angled ladder, backwards, reappearing about a minute later, even redder and puffing hard. Dragging great breaths, he snarled at Walter, "Okay, he ain't there now! But I smell nigger. Maybe I'll come back with the Special Investigation boys. They'll make you Limeys sing a different shanty …yessir!"

Struggling from the boat's low rail onto the steps, Willard re-holstered his pistol and began ambling up the steps.

"Even if us knew what 'appened to Sergeant Jo-Jo, we wouldn't tell 'ee … you fat bugger!" James yelled.

Walter blinked, praying that the American would keep walking and, with a sticky grin on his face, he did just that … for three more steps and then he stopped, smiling as he turned, re-drawing his pistol, before starting down the steps again. Jumping ungainly back onto the deck, he pointed the gun, at arms length, at Walter's head.

"I don't recall specifically namin' names, Englishman. Now, do I get the full story or are you an' the kid dead meat?"

In one flowing movement, James reached into the stowage box and tossed a one-clawed lobster at the Major. As it curved through the air the officer instinctively fired at and missed the shellfish.

Walter caught the dark-blue crustacean with his left hand, tugged open the American's belt with his right and stuffed the lobster down the Major's trousers. Grabbing Willard in a great bear hug, Walter breathed into his ear, "We call that beauty a Nelson … one claw, you understand. The single claw's a crusher and any second now, you're about to discover why!"

Trying to wrestle free from Walter's powerful grip, thc continuous force on the serviceman's body numbed hands and fingers, making it impossible to raise his gun. His attempt to head-butt only reached the padded bulk of the fisherman's shoulder.

Screaming up at the black soldiers staring with glazed eyes at the encounter on the deck, Willard yelled, "Shoot the kid … shoot 'em both … get me free, you yellow bastards. Aaaaaah! Mother of God, it's got my balls…pleeeeese."

His voice lifted several octaves. His head tossing back as an extended deep-throated moan echoed along the waters of the creek.

On the quay the three men exchanged frightened glances. The tallest man mumbled, "Major-sir, we sure didn't join dis war to shoot no children."

The second, chewing faster on his gum, echoed, "Guess you better call this one, even … Sir."

The third infantryman slowly raised his rifle, "Well I's gonna' shoot the mother-fucker … that's fer sure."

Tightening his grip on the American, who began passing out from the pain, Walter said, "If you fire at my son, soldier, I'll break the officer's back."

"Your boy? Shit man, I's a mind to shoot the fuckin' Major."

Quietly, Walter said, "Why don't you lay your guns aside and we'll see if we can save this man's testicles."

He eased the pressure on Major Harris, who groaning, slipped into unconsciousness. The three black soldiers propped their weapons against the quay rail and descended the steps towards the boat.

Lying Willard on the deck, Walter spoke to James, "Fetch the bolt-cutters, see what we can salvage here."

With his trousers and underpants at half-mast, Major Willard Harris Jnr looked a sorry sight. A sadder sight was the one-clawed lobster stretched along the man's plump thigh. Shaped like a boxing glove, it gripped both the American's testicles, which were squashed flat and had turned an ugly shade of purple. The Major's penis lay parallel to the body of the shellfish and was almost the same shade of blue.

Holding the lobster's head, Walter snipped the body from the main claw. "There …better leave it at that. Get him back to base hospital, pretty smart. If I removed the claw he might bleed to death before you reach camp."

The taller soldier collected a stretcher from the jeep and together they edged the bulky figure up the steps. Just before the quay the Major regained some consciousness and began moaning under the army blanket.

Helping to load the injured officer into the rear of the jeep, Walter said, "Major, if you're a family man, I hope you already got children, 'cause, me ol' 'ansome, I reckon your fathering days are over."

Addressing the shorter soldier, he said, "When the medic takes a look, tell him to snip just there …" pointing to a mark behind the inner edges of the rounded nodules, "'Tis my guess the Major can say cheerio to what was once a fair set of balls."

To the soldier holding the discarded lobster body, Walter grinned, "If you intend eatin' that, mister, you need to get her in the pot pretty quick. Dead, they can poison…"

The soldier offered a crooked grin, "Eat? No sir! Mr Fisherman. I's gonna' make a whole mess of dollars showin' this ball-crusher back at the beach." Climbing into the jeep, he called, "See ya' man. Yo!"

***

Maria Jo-Jo smiled towards Mayo. "I'm going to climb into some walkin' boots, then maybe we can wander up the green trail towards the church."

The meal was over. Max, extra attentive, had not mentioned Vegas, contracts or future agendas once. "After that excellent dinner and good wine, I'm not sure I could make it past the lobby."

"Don't give it a second thought, 'cause you ain't invited, Mr Stone, honey. Mayo and I got things to discuss, private like."

She rose from the table, kissed Mayo's head and moved towards the hallway. Max and Mayo watched her go.

Max poured wine into his glass and leaned across to refill the fisherman's glass. Mayo placed a palm over his glass. "Not for me, thanks, Max."

"Listen, son. She wants you in Vegas. Don't take this wrong but what Songbird wants, most times she buttons. She can surely afford you. " He let the words sink in. "I like you … you're a fine person but, let me spell out the small print in this deal." He glanced over his shoulder, making sure she wasn't headed back.

"International stardom, out there in electric city, is a culmination of hard work, dedication, talent and ass-kissin.' During the past fifteen years there's been mountains of butt-action. Not only by yours truly … but also by Maria Jo-Jo Christmas … yes, sir."

Max sipped the wine, checking once more that the singer wasn't in sight before blundering on, "Let me lay down the high cards in the pack, Mayo. A banker's draft, one hundred thousand sterling, made out in your name ... provided you don't show at the airport. Do you read me?"

He waited, looking directly at Mayo. "First week into rehearsal … she'll have forgotten your name. Believe me, I've seen it all before."

"So, what have you seen before, Max?" Maria Jo-Jo enquired from behind him.

"Rip-off artists …" Max blustered. "I'm explaining to Mayo about scum operators in show business. This young man's no concept of the invisible power a single 'phone call can produce."

Gulping the last of his wine, Max stood up. "Enjoy your walk. Remember, Lady," checking his watch, "It's noon in Vegas. By four, desert time, we need to be talking money."

Steering Mayo towards the main door, she replied, "Yes-yes-yes, Max. But, when we get back, I call Ruby in London first.

Goodnight, Mr Stone!"

Maria Jo-Jo and Mayo stood with their backs against the ivy-covered south wall of the old church. Lower down the meadow the big elm stretched spidery branches, casting shadows over waving corn. The sun, just below the western horizon, left trails of speckled haze over the swells breathing silently towards the shore.

Above their heads a black-backed gull paraded wobbly offspring along the narrow granite parapet, shepherding the grey chicks back to the protection of a matted nest. Sensing that the humans caused no threat to her young, she took off, beating westwards, seeking supper.

Hugging Mayo's arm, her cheek against his shoulder, Maria Jo-Jo gazed at coloured patterns along the horizon. "From this spot, I watched you fade into Passage. It took forever to …God, was it only five days back?"

She felt the fading light ease the tension drumming away behind her eyes. "It's easy to understand how you feel about this place." The next few words were almost inaudible, "I … will you come to Vegas with me?"

For a moment he remained silent. Turning slightly, he kissed her temple. "It wouldn't work, Maria Jo-Jo. I'd be way out of my depth in your techni-coloured city."

He kissed her again. "Neither can you stay. Go to Vegas … Sing. Its what the pain's about. Nothing will change between us." Feeling her shudder, he added, "Come, its time to make that call."

Inside the church gates, to the right of the half-circled archway, overlooking the twinkling lights from the distant hotel, Mayo showed her a gravestone. Carved on the weathered stone were the names of his grandparents, Walter and Annie Francis.

Reaching out her hand, the singer touched the ageless granite. "For the kindness and friendship you gave to my poppa …thank you, Mr and Mrs Francis." …

"Stay. Kick Max in the nuts. You got one life, girl. Pass on Vegas. Hell, lady, don't do it fer' the money. If'n you need it

…the ranch is yours.” Ruby’s voice softened. “Let’s all go home, honey. Sit a while in the garden shade. Frankie can read to us. We’ll watch the twins flower into beautiful women…”

She waited, as Maria Jo-Jo quietly cried.

“Okay … if the hunger’s still there, do it! Show those Mafioso bastards you’s the greatest voice ever to grace their fuckin’ neon desert.”

Down the phone line, Maria Jo-Jo could hear her friend was weeping. “Frankie an’ me, we’re at the airport tomorrow evening. If you show, fine. If not, that’s okay too. The little Sicilian and yours truly will vacation … whatever! We don’t need space, one bedroom is all … know what I’m sayin’ here? Last word, Maria Jo-Jo, take the road where your heart leads.”

In the spacious lounge of the Quarry House Hotel, Cove, in South Devon, the wooden hands of the hundred year-old clock read eleven thirty. Thirty minutes short of a new day.

In a mogul style penthouse office, Hollywood, Southern California, digital numbers on a stainless steel timepiece totalled twelve. Thirty minutes short of the lunch break.

“Mr Faricombo? Hi! Max, Max Stone. How ya doin’?” Max was yelling, talking fast in an attempt to eliminate the half-second lag caused by the satellite link. “How’s your beautiful lady? Listen, I met with Tony, in Paris-France … two days back. We kicked over contract deals between my singer and the syndicate … sorry, what was that?”

The time pause and the controlled voice on the American end caused Max to hesitate. “Sure-sure, I –well, appreciate the dollar expenditure of this venture, Mr Faricombo. Managing the hottest song-lady in the trade, I’m together with the need to secure intent. Tony and me, we shook on the deal …”

He glanced across to Maria Jo-Jo and raised his eyes, blushing. “Let me lay down our agenda, Mr Faricombo. Right now we’re in Europe. The Albert Hall concerts were a smash. Tomorrow, we’re booked London/L.A, direct. Concorde! What d’ya say to a ten o’clock meet, your office, day followin’ tomorrow? We can clear the paperwork and the lady starts rehearsals in … ten days?

Pardon me? I kinda' missed that … sure, she's right here."

Covering the mouthpiece, Max looked scared, "He wants to speak to you!" He paused, the 'phone still covered, his face pale, hands slightly shaking. As she took the 'phone he whispered, "Don't fuck with this guy, lady."

"Hello, Joseph. It's been a long time. How's the plumbing?"

Max groaned, reached for his glass, drunk deep and closed his eyes, tight.

"No, I didn't go to Paris. I stayed in England, searching for my father's grave. He died here, during the build-up to World War Two, in '43. It kinda' seemed important to lay certain things to rest." She listened for a moment and then chuckled, "There's more to life than music or money, remember, Joseph?"

Max groaned again, louder. Taking another drink. He was close to real tears.

Maria Jo-Jo listened intently to the quiet voice from distant California, sometimes nodding agreement with the conversation unheard by the others in the room. At one stage she murmured, "Hmm-hmm, accepted."

Later, with eyes closed, she said firmly, "Joseph, you know that's not possible … I need a life!"

Cradling the 'phone she looked across to where Mayo stood and winked. "Yes. My word! I'll be there … day after tomorrow. We'll eat some pie and work out the details, before Max and the suits put pen to contract. What was that?" She listened and then laughed, "Sure the hair grew back but white. Bye, Joseph, have a sensible lunch."

Max had turned grey. "What the fuck gives, Maria Jo-Jo? That guy is Joe B Fericombo, Family! Number one Don. It took a full year for his secretary to return my calls. Six months arranging preliminary discussions. Jesus! Even then I was beggin' …on my goddamn knees", he halted, dragging in great breaths, "So! How come, lady, you call this Sicilian icon, Joseph?" He finished off his whisky in one gulp.

The black singer eased across the room and stood beside Mayo at the window. Outside, the sheltered valley cast shadows over the silky waters of the creek. Touching the fisherman's fingers lightly with her own, she quietly said, “Let’s go.”

Standing at the quayside, watching night patterns flick light tones across the dark water, she told Mayo the story. Told him about meeting Mr Joseph B. Fericombo at St David’s hospital, in Sacramento. Both in the first week of chemotherapy, both scared shitless, convinced that life was ending.

She squeezed Mayo’s hand, “They have a garden room. A quiet place, where folk waitin’ for chemo-treatment come to terms with their soul …or just scream in private.”

“Over the following weeks, we’d meet and talk. He was there because of a growth eating away his stomach. A multi-millionaire, two network TV stations, a major film company and President of top Vegas hotels … yet he knew full well that all his stock couldn’t buy him an extra year of life.”

“Sometimes, we joked. He reckoned a bald black dame might look sexy. Even offered me a part in ‘Alien 3’. There were times, bad days, we’d just sit quiet, maybe hold hands, you know, comfort like. For a man who spent desk-time, looking down on Californian smog, he was well informed. Knew most of the tracks on my early albums, even the arrangers. He remembered numbers I’d sung at a Benefit out in Pasadena, four years back.”

“During the last week of our treatment, he came face-on with Frankie. They’d stared at each other for a long moment, turned away and then back. Seems their parents came from Licate on the south coast of Sicily. Mucho’ tears and hugs.”

“When we said our goodbyes from St David’s, it was closing a chapter on a friendship. The last piece of advice the man offered was …’Dump Mr Max Stone, Maria Jo-Jo, the guy’s a sad Yiddish non-event.”

“I never told Max about knowing Joseph, it was kinda’ private.

Max is crazy but he’s like, well, family. You learn to accept the weakness. We’ll fly to L.A. Max will talk dollars. I’ll talk time. Maybe we’ll do business with the desert Emperors but if this deal comes to pass … it will be on my terms. Now, let’s get your old boat started.”

Walking down the steps they climbed onto Receiver’s deck. As Mayo started the engine, a distant church clock from the village higher up the valley chimed midnight. Sweeping away from the quay wall, the crabber chugged slowly beneath the umbrella of trees, heading towards the boomerang-shaped curve halfway down the night-calm creek.

The black American singer, pressed between the small steering wheel and the warmth of the young Devon fisherman, hummed a tune as yet un-penned. Her hands covered his as he guided the boat towards the darkened hull of the old schooner. Securing the crabber alongside, Mayo switched off the engine and helped Maria Jo-Jo up onto the schooner's deck.

In the dim light, a sea breeze drifted across the transom as she reached for him. "Mayo, fame and dollars don't mean shit, unless they're shared. Givin' Ruby and Frankie the ranch did as much for me as it did for them. Come with me to the States. You can buy a boat to fish from Santa Cruz, Monterey or Santa Barbara, even. It's only an hours' fly-time from Vegas … we could be together weekends. We could …" She clung to him, crying softly, knowing that he wouldn't come.

Holding her close, until the sobbing ceased to an occasional sigh, his silence transmitted answers to her brain that her heart found unacceptable. Freeing herself, she took his hand, leading him towards the curved doors over the companionway.

They made love slowly, breathing deep on senses and tastes. She climbed onto him, drawing her knees tight against his chest, lowering her sex onto his. From the precise moment of penetration, Maria Jo-Jo began to weep and climax in unison. Orgasmic pulses, beginning at fingertip nerve ends reached to the very tips of her toes in less than a single breath. Tiny electric shocks invaded brain chambers, surging through arteries and channels of the heart, pumping raw emotion into the fountain of her womb.

When she awoke, it was still dark. Through the skylight above the bed, stars peppered the coloured glass with a dull glow.

She reached out, every bone and muscle aching, her skin coated in a sheen of perspiration that had dried like a film … and he wasn't there.

Standing on deck, Mayo sipped a mug of tea, watching high clouds drifting slightly south of west. The faintest tinge of pinkie-grey etched the lower edges of the rolling nimbus. In less than an hour, dawn would begin.

Drinking the last of the tea, he went forward to the big fridge to prepare the day's bait. Lowering the loaded basket into the smaller craft a lightning flash split the sky somewhere beyond the Eddystone lighthouse. Without thinking, he counted the seconds between flash and thunder … fourteen, fifteen. There'd be heavy rain and a fresh breeze before the sun started its steady climb from the eastern horizon.

"There's a little blow coming and some rain. Stay here, I'll be a couple of hours …" In the semi-darkness, sitting on the edge of the bed, he offered her a drink from the same mug he'd used on deck. "When I get back we'll go to …."

"No! I'm with you, fisherman." She sipped the tea and placed it aside, scrambling from the bed. Light from a faraway flash of lightning skipped through the skylight and exposed the white birthmark on her left breast. He leaned down and kissed it.

Two hours later, Receiver drifted alongside the first Dan-float marking the inner string, nine miles south of Bolt tail. Guiding the drop-rope around the whirling capstan, Mayo glanced south, studying the dark squalls gathering along the skyline. There'd be time, just, to re-bait the string before the blow hit them.

As the first rain splattered against the wheelhouse window, Mayo tossed the last baited pot over the side. Clearing the scurrying shellfish into the storage containers, he grinned at Maria Jo-Jo before checking his watch and signalling her to turn the boat around.

Shutting the wheelhouse door, Mayo flicked cold raindrops from his hair across the back of her neck before easing her giggling body back against his. Reaching around her he adjusted the autopilot heading to north before clicking it on lock. "There, that will take us home. Now, another mug of tea?"

Positioned in the corner of the wheelhouse, sharing one mug, they watched the sturdy crabber lift higher with each passing wave. On the crest of a large swell the old boat wobbled in negative equilibrium before sliding back into the deep trough,as the increasing rain reduced visibility to less than a few hundred yards.

Pulling Matthew's woolly hat over her ears, Maria Jo-Jo thought about the time Ruby had dragged her onto a white-water ride at Disney World.'I'd vowed never again and here I am, doing it for real. It's crazy. I'm not strapped in, have no concept of when or how it will end and yet not one nerve in my body wants it to be ended.'

As the boat lumbered up the back-end of a cresting wave, Mayo glanced at his watch and then ahead, searching for the coast. In the swirling rain he could just make out the darker grey of shoreline before they tumbled down into the silence of another trough. When the next surge lifted them through frothing foam, he switched the autopilot to manual and dropped the window. "The next half-mile will get a little 'interesting', Vegas lady."

On the top of the next breaker, Maria Jo-Jo could make out white surf beating against grey cliffs. The rain had scurried on, coursing northwards, leaving an untidy curtain of precipitation trailing into the distant high land. She recognized the Mariner's church and lower down the meadow, the spreading branches of the dead elm tree.

Turning to Mayo, she said, "It reminds me of a poem by Robert frost … something about,

The shattered waters made a misty din,
Great waves looked over others coming in,
And thought of doing something to the shore …'

"I can't remember …" her voice trailed off.

Easing the engine speed to control the boat's frantic progress towards the shore, the fisherman spun the wheel, keeping the course as steady as possible. "Under the seat there's a lifejacket. It might give you some comfort during the next few minutes."

She smiled, resting her arms across the open window, "You're all the comfort I need. Anyways, I'm not much of a swimmer."

Gunning the engine revs to climb the next swell, then easing back as they surfed down the leading edge, Mayo laughed, "Dad taught me, before I could walk. Tossed me into the creek and when I got into trouble, threw the dog in after me. Hold on, this next wave's a bit special."

Maria Jo-Jo glanced astern as the boat lifted before rushing at reckless speed down into the deep valley of green water. On the peak she could see mountains of ocean crashing into grey rocks … less than two hundred feet ahead.

Mayo, pulling the window shut made her jump. Turning she watched him study the following sea as it tumbled over itself before exploding green and white, towards them. His left hand eased the throttle while his right hand struggled to control the boat's direction. Catching her concerned expression, he smiled, "Just a couple more, Maria Jo-Jo, and then it's all down hill."

As he spoke the heavy hull was kicked sideways, ancient timbers groaning as tons of shattered spray crested over the wheelhouse, filling every square inch of the windows.

When the sea passed, the foredeck spluttered, struggling to clear the salt water pushing the limits of buoyancy. And then it was free, lifting upwards, drawing breath as the water cascaded from open scuppers.

As the crabber shook, Mayo spun the wheel to port and pushed forward on the throttle. Sixty feet from the shore a swirling backwash separated stone from sea. Ahead, he could make out the spray-curtained entrance to Passage.

"Here we go, Maria Jo-Jo Christmas … hold on."

Once inside the outer cave the wind noise reduced to a muffled whisper. In the middle cavern a single arrow of light from overhead pinpointed the crabber's journey northwest. Emerging from the shadows into the creek's sunlight, Mayo directed the salt-drenched craft towards the hidden cove. The blow was over.

"For a time there, fisherman, I wasn't sure … I found myself watching a struggle between storm and boat. You had a look in your eyes, a determination." She reached over, kissing him, "I wouldn't have missed that experience for a great bundle of gold discs …"

At Christmas Cove they paid their respects. Holding hands. Praying silent prayers. Before leaving the buried anchor, Maria Jo-Jo touched the flukes, “Sleep warm, Poppa … I’ll be back.”

Mooring at the quay, the singer pulled a rope through a ring, securing the bare end around the bow bollard. Walking slowly along the deck her trailing fingers touched capstan, deck-pump, empty fish-boxes and the salt-crusted windows. Standing together, abreast of the weed-covered granite steps, Mayo could see her eyes were full.

****

Chapter Twenty-Four

... six months have gone by

"Ladies and gentlemen ..."

Without being over-powering, the voice was informative, warm with respect. "The Management of 'Ala Bianco' Hotel, Las Vegas, proudly presents, celebrating her one hundredth performance ... Miss Maria Jo-Jo Christmas."

Three and a half thousand people, in the night-coloured auditorium, seated at four hundred and fifty candlelit tables, gasped as a pencilled beam picked out the lone figure in the centre of a darkened stage.

The lighting engineer toned the soft filter of the spot, focusing on the performer's bowed head, drawing attention to the brilliant white hair, spiked and sparkling against the midnight blue backdrop.

A ripple of applause beginning from the rear of the theatre, trickled down and outwards, slowly increasing until the vast space echoed with thunderous clapping, foot-stamping and shrill whistles of enthusiastic appreciation.

Maria Jo-Jo, eyes directed at the tips of her shoes, counted slowly, 'five - six - seven', before lifting her head and smiling a 'Thank-you' to the unseen audience, hidden in the darkness. Accompanied only by the piano, she began the song, "If I could choose ..."

For the first few bars there was a hushed silence. A collective holding of breath from the audience as the crystal voice gathered strength, climbing with the haunting melody, balancing music and words that filled ears and minds with wonder.

Almost without the audience being aware it was happening, the curtains glided back to include the full orchestra, section by section intermixing with the opening number's second line, "...it would be a quiet time."

Palmed, out of sight in her right hand, she held a discuss shaped piece of polished pitch pine. It measured just over an inch across, almost half an inch thick. Encapsulated on one side of the aged timber was the face of a twenty-five cents American quarter. Embedded on the reverse side was the King's head of an English one-shilling coin.

During Maria Jo-Jo's six-day stay in South Devon, unknown to her, Mayo had hacked both coins from the schooner's mizzen stump, polishing and oiling the pale wood until the darker grains appeared to be laminated. On that last morning, nearly seven months ago, at the top of the quay steps, he'd kissed her lightly on the nose and quietly folded the disc into her hand. "Nevada is only distance, Maria Jo-Jo … nothing important."

Walking down the steps, starting the engine and heading the boat downstream, she knew he wouldn't look back. While she watched the crabber make its way towards the bend, Matthew arrived and began loading the day's catch into the van. "Good-morning, Maria Jo-Jo."

She neither heard nor answered. As the boat disappeared from view, leaving only the wake, she'd looked down at the circled coins he'd placed in her hand.

As he'd left the quay, acknowledging that if he turned, just once, to look at her, he'd be lost to an indecently exotic electric-oasis, tucked away in the lower corner of the America … neon-light years away from the sounds and smells of the sea.

He'd waited until the boat curved around the middle bend, waited until the schooner's hull was in full view, waited until he knew that she couldn't possibly see him … and then the tears began.

Six weeks after driving away from the quiet Devonshire creek, in an explosive mind-blowing opening at the new multi-million dollar Las Vegas hotel, Maria Jo-Jo had commenced her first desert show … and now, it was number one hundred.

After the opening song, she signalled for the house-light to be raised and smiled acknowledgment to distinguished politicians, invited celebrities, business associates, friends and warm strangers.

At one of the Premier tables she watched Streisand, on her feet, yelling and clapping in energetic appreciation.

At the next table the newly elected Governor of Nevada scrambled up, flashing structured teeth at the TV cameras, shouting towards the stage, "Go, Maria Jo-Jo, go girl." Before sitting down again, he posed in the spotlight directed at his table, waving to 'his people'.

Maria Jo-Jo caught sight of Max, with wife number seven, a tiny beautiful Jewish lady, wearing something extravagantly expensive by a Japanese designer whose name the singer couldn't remember. Max looked great in a brilliant white tuxedo, more West Coast than New York. The pony tail had gone, the thinning hair shaved, achieving a Bruce Willis look …who, by a strange coincidence was seated two tables away with Demi Moore.

Ruby and Frankie were seated next to Hazelwood and Lily Boyde. Completing their party, the twins, ten years old but already sophisticated young ladies dressed in 'hot-outfits', sat entranced. The girls had been on their feet, ahead of the rapturous audience, whistling and screaming.

Between Hazelwood and Ruby there was an empty seat. The invitation had been sent, reservations made but deep in her heart she knew he wouldn't be there.

As the house lights dimmed, she'd walked over to the Musical Director, whispered a word and returned to the mike.

"The next number is for two special ladies. Great friends of mine … my God-children in fact, who, by rights should be fast asleep but heck, it's that kinda' occasion. Beth and Joanne … this is for you."

Her unaccompanied voice began, "Mornin' Smile And Then Some…"

After three months in the Nevada desert, performing two spots each night at nine and midnight, the show had broken all previous Vegas box-office records. Every third Sunday she did a Benefit for Cancer Care, Aids or Save The Children, at venues such as the Hollywood Bowl. Her 'free' time was spent in a downtown, ultramodern recording studio in Los Angeles working on a new album. Fifteen new songs, rehearsed, re-mixed, re-arranged and laid-down on a Master disc.

Sixteen frantic days of screaming, swearing, tears and temper and a little soul searching that would produce, according to the market men, a smash that would soar to number one on the international charts.

"Mayo? Did I wake you? Listen, honey, I'm in Paris-France two Fridays from now. It appears French fans flipped over the last album. It's a charity concert, Africa's Children or something. A couple of songs on Saturday night and fly back to the States, late Sunday. " She lowered her voice, giggling, excited at the thought of seeing him again, "How would you like to spend 24 hours shacked up with a seriously hungry hot black singer?"

From across the ocean, Mayo joked, "You mean Whitney Houston will be there?"

Walking from Charles De Gaulle Airport into the cool evening breeze, Mayo requested the cab driver, "Grand Hotel Inter-Continental, s'il vous plait."

Smiling at the elegant young receptionist inside the splendour of the hotel's foyer, the fisherman inquired, "Can you direct me to Miss Maria Jo-Jo Christmas' suite, please?"

As the girl moved her lips to reply, a pinstriped under-manager, working at a computer screen, almost without moving his lips, retorted, "There is no one of that name staying here ... sir."

And, taking a quick glance at Mayo, sneered, "Journalist?"

Ignoring the questioner, Mayo increased his smile to the receptionist, "Would you kindly buzz the lady's suite and say that ..."

In a flurry of fast French passing between the aggressive pinstripe and the blushing receptionist, the only words that Mayo understood were, "dormir ... instructions clair ... incognito ... journalist, non ... Francis."

Dropping his passport onto the dark oak desk, Mayo quietly said, "My name is Francis. Fisherman. English."

In the opulence of the penthouse suite, overlooking the winding river, they'd clung to each other, loving with a gentleness that gradually dispersed the frustration of the one hundred and eight days, six hours separation.

As the late August sun dipped behind tall buildings to the west of the ancient city, they lay in a spacious Jacuzzi, watching unpredictable traffic patterns cast white/yellow/red traces between darkened boulevards.

Sitting behind her, Mayo's hands cupped foamy warm water over her birthmark. After room service had cleared their meal, they dragged the king-size duvet across to the low picture window and propped up with giant pillows, watched the clustered illuminations below in the silent metropolis.

Later, they'd wept, laughed, talked about Cove, Matthew and Joanne and made love as night sounds hummed from ten floors below. Maria Jo-Jo told him about the wonders of the desert, omitting to mention the exhaustive work schedule, the tiredness and the gradual destruction of her body clock. Falling towards sleep, holding him close, she breathed the ocean from his body.

Two hours after midnight, waking, she lay in the cool darkness watching Mayo at the window as he gazed at the un-orderly lights criss-crossing different sections of the streets below. "Can't you sleep?"

He'd laughed, "No. I can't hear the sea. Let's walk along the river."

They'd wandered, holding hands, under curving old bridges fording the ageless river. Strolling along narrow cobbled streets close to the water, the couple watched cargo barges, some deeply laden, some empty, chugging upstream and down, gone, voyaging into the darkness.

With the sky beginning to turn nightshades towards dawn they'd sat in an all-night cafe, sipping hot chocolate, observing the city cleaners begin their daily tasks. Back at the hotel the lift whizzed them almost silently upwards to the lofted sanctuary.

A limousine took her to rehearsals after noon. She'd asked Mayo not to accompany her. "Let tonight be special."

Before it was time for the concert, with other tourists they'd stood, quietly absorbing Michaelangelo's 'Two Slaves' and they'd wept again. In the capital's National Museum of Modern Art, Maria Jo-Jo had added to the comments book, 'Great but incomplete … it lacks an original Milton.'

In a tiny antique shop, tucked away in a side street off the Boulevard Saint-Germain, the singer purchased a gold African ring carved in the shape of a fish. The Afro-French proprietor, with a thousand year old face, swore on the honour of his mother that the ring had been commissioned for the Master of a British slave trader. Inside the gold band, barely visible was engraved, 'Cobh. 1590.'

Later, after the concert, she'd knelt, naked, on the crumpled duvet and slipped the gold ring onto Mayo's finger. "I is your slave now, Massa Fisherman."

In the early hours she awoke with a pulsing headache, discovering her nose was bleeding. Easing herself from his arms she'd cleaned herself up in the bathroom, took a strong painkiller and fell asleep again.

From his seat in the seventh row Mayo had listened as the singer's voice soared, blending with the orchestra into almost perfection. When she'd announced the first number, 'Take My Love' the people in the vast hall had scrambled to their feet, applauding wildly. Halfway through the second song, 'Paris Dreamers', as she reached the top notes, the arena had erupted causing the Musical Director to miss a beat. Maria Jo-Jo blew the man a kiss and they both smiled.

When the stage lights dimmed almost to darkness, a single spot picked out only her head as she'd eased into, 'Morning Journey'

There wasn't a dry eye among the thousands listening.

Although Mayo felt her words and music were directed towards him, he was aware that this was 'her' world. Up there, held in the spotlight, drawing the captive audience under her spell … fisherman and singer were separated by different planets.

Before the car arrived to take them to the airport on Sunday evening, Maria Jo-Jo outlined her agenda. "September-October-November, Vegas show-time. The last two weeks in November, rehearse and video the Christmas Special. Thanksgiving, I'm with

Ruby, Frankie and the Boyde tribe out at the ranch. First two weeks in December the L.A. studio is booked for work on the album. I'll go back during week three to polish some tracks."

She knew her words were tumbling out, trying to diminish the building pain of parting. "Listen, fisherman and believe …five days before Christmas, my black ass is on a plane to England."

They'd said their goodbyes in the VIP lounge. He'd watched her plane lumber into the sky, speeding the singer west across the Atlantic Ocean. Collecting his bag he'd headed for the departure gate, her final words echoing in his mind …"I have become a gentle soul, seasoned by the passing hours we spent together."

During the month of September, Maria Jo-Jo settled back into the Vegas routine, performing twice nightly, Monday to Saturday. Most mornings at about 3am, she'd take a shower, grab a snack and crawl into bed, sleeping through till noon. There were many nosebleeds.

On three Sundays during the month, after the last show, she'd nap for two hours before catching the 'before dawn' flight to San Francisco. Frankie would meet the plane and Ruby would have eggs and juice prepared by they time they'd reached the ranch.

Most times they'd just sit quietly on the porch, munching breakfast, catching up on gossip, or watching the sun paint changing colours beyond the meadow leading to the river.

In October, Ruby voiced concern after discovering Maria Jo-Jo wiping blood from her nose. "You lookin' beat, girl. How many nosebleeds you bin havin'? Maybe I'll come to the desert … make sure you gettin' plenty sleep an' stuff."

"Ruby, don't fuss woman. I'm fine. I get all the sleep I need. The desert's bone dry and the air conditioning at the hotel has a mind of its own. Hey! Look at thc time. I'll give Mayo a call."

She didn't mention a word to Ruby or Mayo about the three-times-week, at least, nosebleeds or that nothing eased the growing tiredness crowding her thinking, even after eight hours solid sleep. What she did agree to was for her friend to come to Vegas during November, to help with rehearsals for the Christmas TV Special.

A week before Thanksgiving, Maria Jo-Jo was awarded a

'Golden Globe' for the Vegas show. The media, in the shape of national journalists, columnists from 'Variety', 'Stage' and other show-business publications, together with TV stations, descended mob-heavy, scrambling for exclusive interviews.

Max was working overtime as at least twenty-six Talk Shows requested his singer to appear on network television.

"What you wear in bed, Maria Jo-Jo?"

"Is there a man in your life?"

"Is it true you're going to star in a Hollywood musical based on Ella's life?"

The questions rolled on, getting crazier with the asking.

When December came, Ruby insisted on staying, using the pretext of assisting with recording the next album. After Monday's late show, after only three hours sleep, they caught the seven o'clock shuttle to L.A. Arriving at the studio by ten, the session lasted through until after six. Maria Jo-Jo then did an interview for the Johnny Banks Happy Hour Show and following a room service dinner, they crashed out, close to midnight.

Towards the middle of the second week's recording, Ruby exploded. "You can't keep this up, lady! You gettin' rich … but you gonna' be dead-rich. Shit girl, you losin' weight as I look. This schedule's a killer. We didn't work this pace back on the road … well, okay-okay, maybe we did but we was twenty years younger…"

Too drained to argue, Maria Jo-Jo headed for the bedroom, slammed the door and turned the key. Hearing the key click, Ruby charged across the room and hammered her fists against the polished timber. "Don't you dare lock me out, black-mother-bitch! Open this fuckin' door or I'm out of this crazy hole."

She lunged, banging her forehead against the thick door. There was silence. Then, in a tired voice she whispered, "Maria Jo-Jo, I surely hurt my head…"

When the key clicked, one hand holding her bruised temple, Ruby marched into the large bedroom. Maria Jo-Jo, retreating towards the window, turned. The two friends gazed at each other and quietly began to chuckle. Ruby gathered the singer to her great bosom and began rocking her. "Baby-baby, listen to Ruby. This is what we gonna' do. Tomorrow mornin' we fly to Sacramento. I'll phone the doctor-man at St. Davids. They can do tests …ease your mind, girl."

"The studio can take a down-day. Now! You fix a hot tub while I fix the appointment, cancel tomorrow's session and by the time your butt is dry, I'll have your Mayo on the phone, ready to sweet-talk. One last thing, honey, don't bullshit me. I been collectin' your laundry, I know how much you bin bleedin'."

Two days later, in the calm consulting rooms of the cancer specialist at St. David's, Maria Jo-Jo paced the floor, gripping hard on the embedded coins. Dr Sam gently explained that, sadly, conclusive tests showed that the leukemia had returned. It was back with a cruel vengeance that would outpace any effective treatment that St. David's … or anyplace in the world could offer.

"How long?" Maria Jo-Jo had whispered.

With enduring honesty, his eyes holding hers, "A year … perhaps two."

"How will I function? Will I get real sick? Suffer?"

"No. You'll hardly notice the changes, maybe a little tiredness. First, we'll take blood, in slow stages, over the next few months, clean it and place it back into your system …"

His voice drifted across the room through walls and windows, slipping beneath the gap under the door, anywhere but registering in her brain. And yet, his kind simplicity tapped into her reasoning, eventually touching home with, "That'll hold the progression for a while."

Watching her face and knowing she expected the full prognosis, he went on, "When the time comes, later, there might be some discomfort but we'll prescribe something that will allow you almost full contact with the world." Reaching across the desk, he touched her clenched fist, "Go home, Maria Jo-Jo. Do what you want with your life."

When she came from the consulting room, Ruby read the message. She took her friend's hand as they walked in silence back to the car. Before starting the engine, Ruby asked, "What now, lady? Can I tell Frankie … something? What about Max? Vegas? Will you go to England for the holiday?" The engine purred into life, "Tell me to shut-the-fuck-up, Maria Jo-Jo."

Reaching across, the black singer rested her fingers on Ruby's knuckles gripping the steering wheel. She smiled, "Drive to the ranch. After a sleep I'll …."

As the car began to move she quietly added, "Yes, tell Frankie but, not everything. When the time's right I'll give him the full story. Tomorrow, I'll speak to Max and the Vegas people."

"What about …."

Easing the passenger seat into recline, Maria Jo-Jo Christmas, closed her eyes, "Ruby! Shut-the-fuck-up… just drive."

Twenty-four hours later, on the wide porch, they watched the sun's descent change the colours of the distant mountains. Frankie carried fresh coffee from inside, just as Max's rage clicked in. "Are you stupid, woman? Contracts - recording dates - TV specials - for Christ's sake, Hollywood's knocking."

He took a deep breath, lowering his voice, "Wife number seven is talkin' big D."

Placing the tray, loaded with coffee and doughnuts on the table, Frankie rubbed his hands on his shirt and with a short left uppercut, lifted Max clean into the air. Max appeared to travel in slow motion and horizontal, landing at the base of the porch steps in a crumpled heap.

"What … what the fuck was that about?" Max rubbed his jaw. "You wop bastard, you cracked my crown. You're insane…"

"Correct in one, asshole. You got smacked because not once did you inquire about the lady's health. Now, how d'ya want your coffee?"

A day later, in the penthouse Boardroom, overlooking the Nevada desert, Maria Jo-Jo addressed the President, Vice-President and other associated members. "It's over, gentlemen. I'm out. As from this moment."

With the exception of the President, the top executives, blowing cigar smoke in every which-way direction, muttered, snorted, rattled coffee cups and some banged their fists on the vast extended table. Joseph B. Fericombe said nothing.

From various sides came, "We hold your goddamn signature,

bitch." "Four years, with options … bottom line."

"We'll sue you broke…." "Walk and you'll never work in this man's town…" and on and on, getting deeper and more crude.

Mr Joseph B. Fericombe, President and chief stockholder in the multi-million dollar 'Ala Bianco' had not spoken a single word throughout the collective verbal abuse delivered by his angry executives. He'd gazed the full length of the table, his eyes locked onto the face of the black singer. As the others, slowly, one by one, looked in his direction, he quietly rose to his feet.

The room became silent, watching, as Joseph B. opened a wall safe and withdrew a small package before walking back to his chair. Placing the bunch of papers down, he calmly lit a large Cuban cigar and puffed smoke towards the ceiling. Not once, after rejoining the other Board members had his deep eyes wavered from Maria Jo-Jo's stare. The men gathered around the table waited in smug anticipation for their President to deliver his ruling.

For at least sixty seconds, through the smoke-filled atmosphere, Joseph B. studied the papers. Those seated on his right held their breath, while the men on his left fixed their eyes on the singer.

Almost without moving his head, Joseph B. looked at Maria Jo-Jo and nodded. Without averting her eyes, Maria Jo-Jo silently returned his nod.

Reaching for the 'phone, still watching the singer, he pressed a button and spoke, "Julia, have my jet placed at the immediate disposal of Miss Christmas. Thank you, Julia."

Replacing the receiver he lifted the papers and tore them in half, tossing them into the wastebasket. Smiling, he said, "May your God walk with you, dear lady." And rising, began to walk from the room, "Gentlemen, this meeting is closed."

****

Chapter Twenty-Five

... Goodbye

"Hi folks. This is Station KLXI, California. Dan Moore. This week the music industry offered the latest - they do say, final - collection of songs by Maria Jo-Jo Christmas. Come on, do we really believe that? "

The radio voice eased out over the night airways with a touch of scepticism. "Don't get me wrong, night-people. I've been a fan of this lady from way back when. Word is that a recurring health problem caused the singer to quit her sell-out Vegas show. Now! Is this true or are we selling albums here?"

"But that thought remained for the twelve seconds it took for the first track to reach my soul." His voice lifted, " SELL the car. Hold-up a bank. Pass, on next month's payment on the house. DO IT! Go buy Maria Jo-Jo's new album. IT will surely become a standard. Enough! Here's the first track from, 'Passage' ..."

***

"It's ten days, girl. Tomorrow is December 19. Two days from here, you're booked for England, for Christmas ... Peace on earth, goodwill to all men. Does that include boy-fisherman, who you say you luv? You ain't spoke to him since Sacremento. What the hell you playin' at, lady?" Ruby's voice echoed down through the green valley.

They had driven out from the ranch, parking the 4wheel-drive in a lay-off on the side of the timbered hill overlooking a hollow dropping away towards the river. It was a favourite 'thinking spot' for both of them. The ranch's low stable buildings were just visible between aging pines clustered along the ridge. Below, the slow moving stream twisted, curving through a long meadow with pony tracks. A mile towards the furthest bend, the water circled past the gable-end of the Boyde house, coursing on, splitting Hazelwood's paddock, before passing through an avenue of greenhouses, glistening in the late afternoon sun.

On the crown of the southern horizon, only a speck on the invisible road, an orange coloured school bus moved in dusty silence before disappearing into a hidden dip.

"I've tried, Christ, I've tried. Picked up the phone, buttoned his number but, crashed-out before it rang. What do I say? 'Hi, Mayo, sorry, can't come this Christmas … my blood needs changing to stop me dying. What's that? Oh sure … the works - treating, cleaning, replacin' the whole tank … and for what?"

As the tears began, scrambling from the station wagon, she dropped to the grass and kicked at the big tyre, "Fuck – fuck and double fuck."

Ruby quietly said, "You start simple. Askin' how's the fishin' business? Or maybe, How you doin', lover? Then you ask if maybe he'd like to visit California?"

"Shit, woman, I scream for him to be here, to hold me, help me make this … He'd come, sure! But do I have the right to expect that kinda' love?"

Opening her arms, taking in the whole valley, trees, sky and winding river, she murmured, "This ain't his world."

Reaching through the open window at the driver's side, Ruby took the singer's hand and placed it against her own cheek. "As I see it, girl, you're his world, no matter what place he lays down to sleep. Besides, you gotta' tell him. The boy gotta'a right to know."

She placed Maria Jo-Jo's fingers inside her mouth, gently nibbling, "Cause if you can't do it ... sure as God's my sister, I will. Now! Let's head home. Frankie's doin' a pasta special for supper."

After only five tones, Maria Jo-Jo heard Matthew's recorded voice, "So sorry, we don't appear to be here right now. Please give your name, number and we'll get back to you, ASAP. Oh! If this is Maria Jo-Jo please leave a message, I'll make sure it's passed on. By the way, Merry Christmas … whoever's calling." Faintly, she heard, "There! I think that will do, Joanne."

"Did you call the man?"

"Yes. It was hooked to the hotel's answer service."

Maria Jo-Jo sipped her morning juice. "I left a message."

She didn't look at Ruby. "Said I'd picked up a virus and couldn't fly over for the holidays. Said … Jesus-H-Christ, don't give me the evil eye woman. When the blood-thing is done, I'll feel stronger. I'll go then … So, there!"

Ruby remained silent. Slamming down her empty glass, Maria Jo-Jo snapped, "Frankie, will drive me to the hospital today."

"Is dat' you, Fisherman-Mayo? My name is Ruby. We ain't met, although sometimes I feel your picture's tattooed on my brain. I'm instructed to button my lip but … listen for a moment."

When Maria Jo-Jo and Frankie returned from the hospital, the singer looked exhausted. "Any word? Did Mayo phone?"

Ruby, sitting on the porch, reading a detective story, didn't look up. "Nope! He surely did not call." Turning a page she added, "Supper will be twenty minutes."

"Not for me … I'm beat. Early night. Thanks for today, Frankie." She didn't look at Ruby.

Frankie's eyes followed Maria Jo-Jo as she walked inside before speaking. "She had a bad day at the hospital. Why you being so bitchy, woman?"

Not looking up from the book, Ruby mumbled, "Don't ask, man … just don't ask, is all."

Shuffling towards the inner door, Frankie shook his head, "Perhaps someday, someone will explain what the hell's goin' on. I need a drink."

Lifting her reading glasses, the large black lady smiled sweetly at the little man, "Make mine a double, lover."

***

Maria Jo-Jo sat in the swing-seat on the west porch. During the late afternoon she'd been reading, cat-napping, sipping occasionally at a glass of juice. From the kitchen, preparing dinner, she could just hear Frankie's bad impression of an early Dean Martin Neapolitan love song, with breaks for tasting and sipping.

Ruby moving about the wide porch, nervously fussing, jumped

when the 'phone rang …

"No one! Crap call. Some hombre sellin' time shares in Texas."

Pouring herself some juice from a jug close to Maria Jo-Jo, she gabbled, "Hazelwood, Lily and the twins will arrive about five … I told you that, right?"

Glancing nervously at her watch, she snapped, "Are you gonna' change, lady? What about the Mexican dress? It's Christmas-fuckin'- Eve."

Looking in the dressing-room mirror, the beautiful Mexican dress painted the full picture. Maria Jo-Jo could see her mother gazing out from the glass. 'God! I must have lost twenty pounds in the past month.' Easing her hands under full breasts, she smiled, 'Well, at least my titties are still firm.'

Staring at her reflection, she whispered, "I'm so tired, Momma. The hospital visits for blood-change drains me. One more and then, leastways, that part's over."

She was delighted at the thought of seeing Hazelwood, Lily and the twins … watching the excited glow on the girls' faces as they opened their' presents. The two youngsters, speeding towards teenage years, eased for a time the burning pain of the malignant leucocytes. These lovely folk, soon to gather for a festive meal, were, 'family.' Max was family …well, perhaps 'family-in-law'. The thought created a grin.

Yes! She'd make a special effort. Later, during the early hours, when the pain made it impossible to sleep, she could return to the cool solitude of the porch, carrying her deepest thoughts, eastward over sleeping States, on across the Atlantic Ocean.

Leaning against a timber post on the porch, Maria Jo-Jo watched the dust from the Boyd's motor, a mile away, drifting silently in and out of the evening shadows as it hurried towards the gateway leading to the ranch. When it changed direction, slowing to enter the driveway, she could make out Hazelwood behind the wheel, with Lily sitting beside him. Both girls leaned from the rear windows, waving and calling as they journeyed the last quarter mile to the front steps.

As the station wagon drew to a dusty halt, forty feet from where Maria Jo-Jo waited, Hazelwood and Lily remained seated. Beth leapt from the rear passenger door, bounding towards the five steps below the porch, her innocent face glowing with anticipated pleasure. Dressed in a black suit trimmed in silver, with a hem cut about five years above her knees, she chuckled, "Merry Christmas, Maria Jo-Jo … we, we've brought an extra present."

Rushing back to the vehicle she pulled open the rear door. Joanne, wearing a similar suit but silver with black trim, made a ladylike descent and turned to watch him alight.

Both girls grabbed Mayo's hands, pulling him forward. At the bottom step, looking towards the singer, Beth whispered, "If you ain't happy, Maria Jo-Jo … we can surely take him home with us."

Without any need to cast her eyes beyond the immediate circumference of her vision, Maria Jo-Jo Christmas acknowledged that gathered around were all those she held closest to her pounding heart.

In the massive doorway leading into the house, Frankie, dressed in cookie-whites, complete with a floppy chef's hat, held a tray of drinks. Glancing towards Ruby, his eyes asked, 'What the hell gives here?' Out loud, he said, "Grab some drinks, people, I'll set another place at the table."

Turning to shuffle inside, he glanced at Mayo … "Welcome to California, young fella."

Quickly wiping away a tear, Ruby moved to collect Frankie's tray. Passing Maria Jo-Jo, she side-mouthed, "Hold fast, lady. I called him, sure, but I didn't write the full script."

A few feet from the lower step, organic farmer, Hazelwood Boyde stood, almost on the same spot he'd stood all those years ago, one arm looped over the shoulder of his wife, Lily. They watched their daughters school-girlish interactions. Harmless adoration normally reserved for flavour of the month's Rock band.

Joanne, tightly holding Mayo's left hand, addressed her famous godmother, "We surrender this man to you, Maria Jo-Jo but, heck, well … you know, woman to woman stuff."

Watching her face smiling down at him, Mayo could clearly see something was wrong. She'd lost weight. The glossy chestnut glow in her eyes, so obvious in Paris, was no longer there. No doubt the crazy hours under Vegas spotlights had taken their toll, as had TV work, recording sessions and album promotions.

Ruby's call had been a little evasive. The tone of her voice, travelling six thousand miles, told him she wasn't explaining the full extent of the problems.

Taking a deep breath, Maria Jo-Jo knew that this wonderful moment would be cherished. From his confused expression, he clearly didn't know the full story. She would tell him … but not today. There would surely be time … Please!

****

Chapter Twenty-Six

... Another Beginning

The waiting was nearly over.

Spiralling mist in the upstream shadows gave the crabber's bow-wave a sparkling crest. Without looking in the direction of Christman Cove, Mayo steered the old boat towards the darkness of Passage.

The three men and the scruffy dog had watched in silence as wash from the passing craft lapped Walter's boots. James, taking two steps from the dying fire halted ... knowing.

The American soldier, smiling, touched the buried anchor.

The dog's gaze followed the disappearing stern into the darkness, before scampering towards the water, barking.

High on the southern ridge, the lone gull stamped its feet, before squatting in the tufted grass.

Once in the central cavern, Mayo eased the engine, allowing the boat to stem the incoming tide. Unseen, the outside ocean appeared to draw giant lingering sobs through the solid rock.

Spinning the wheel, he pointed the bow towards a splinter of light directed from a hole in the rock above and when the light beam touched the whaleback he cut the engine.

The single arrow of light drifted along the deck, falling onto a small urn sitting amidships.

It was an April dawn, one year, four months and thirteen days beyond that Californian Christmas. Outside Passage, the restless sea spread underwater echoes vibrating through the high chamber, growing ever louder.

Coming from the darkness, back into the creek's glassy water, not yet fully lit by daylight, Mayo turned the bow towards Christmas cove and when the stem grounded, he killed the engine.

Not bothering with the kedge, he jumped into the shallows and walked up the beach towards the standing anchor. Behind him the old boat leaned over, resting on one bilge.

Around the anchor, patterns in the drying sand, cast hydrographic marks. The fisherman dropped to his knees and began scooping the sand with his bare hands. A foot below the surface the sand became compacted. Getting to his feet, Mayo went to the cliff face, selected a sharp flat slate and resumed digging. At a depth of two feet, still on his knees, breathing deeply, he tossed the slate aside.

Walking back to the boat, he collected the urn.

From different parts of broken shade, four sets of eyes watched him ... in total silence. Carefully, slowly, he poured the urn's contents into the hole and lowering his arm pressed his palm into the ashes.

His falling tears made tiny indents, turning the sand to the same chestnut brown of Maria Jo-Jo's eyes. Taking the small disc from his pocket he laid the pine embedded coins on the mark made by his palm.

Placing the flat slate carefully over the ashes, Mayo began scooping the damp sand back into the hole. When it was done he smoothed the fine sand, "Sleep warm, Maria Jo-Jo. I will hear your music."

Lifting the china urn he tossed it hard and high towards the cliff and watched it sail through the air, spinning and turning, almost in slow motion.

The urn was joined in its flight by an empty cognac bottle and together they flashed in the first shafts of sunlight before smashing into the dark rock, scattering fragmented pieces in different directions over the lonely cove.

Three feet behind Mayo, Walter stood beside son James. Mister, lay close at heel in the sand, watching, his tiny head cocked to one side.

The American Sergeant had slowly dropped to his knees, holding the anchor.

Walking down the beach, placing a shoulder against the blunt bow, which, on the flooding tide now stood upright, Mayo pushed. The old boat didn't budge. James quietly walked boots-deep into the tide, leaned his bulk against the planks and heaved ... the boat remained fast aground.

Walter, standing at the lapping water, offered, "Jump aboard an' give 'er a good kick astern, boy."

Clambering up onto the deck, Mayo pushed the engine button, kicking it into life and then jerked it into reverse gear. The crabber wobbled twice but held fast. Walking into the shallow water, Walter pressed his great shoulders against the opposite bow from James. Together they both groaned, "One-two, steady, heave..."

With the propeller gripping deeper water, slowly, juddering over the sand, the hull backed off. Swinging Reciever around in a graceful arc, Mayo took one last look back at the cove.

It was silent.

Empty, except for the sunken anchor, standing like a cross ... and high up on the southern ridge, one lone seabird, watching.

As the old boat moved towards the hidden opening, the bird took flight, drifting down from the cliff, briefly touching the crown of the anchor before silently gliding in the boat's wake towards Passage.

****** **The End** ******